Praise for *The Or*

"As in the first novel, the authors are skilled at blending horror, fantasy, science-fiction and crime story elements, ensuring the unsettling atmosphere developed in the previous book permeates this narrative throughout. As the various plot strands relating to Sarah's death, a missing baby, Noble et al's investigation, and the mystery of the Orbriallis Institute draw together, the novel's pace quickens, building to a revelatory and satisfying climax...this is a thoroughly entertaining novel. Fans of Part One will find plenty to enthrall them here."

— *Blue Ink Review*

"With fictional foundations in supernatural suspense and sci-fi horror, the novel's carefully crafted premise makes it easy to get hooked. The themes floating beneath the narrative are also timely and thought-provoking – ethical responsibilities within scientific research, privacy, and parental authority, alternative treatments for mental illness, and irrational reactions to things deemed either strange or unknown."

— *Self Publishing Review*

"I read the first book, and this is just as gripping and eerie. It's a story that will keep you hooked, reading until the very last page as your mind begs for the answers to the mysteries in this book and the unanswered ones from the first part. It is action-packed all the way, with plenty of spooky twists and turns to keep you invested. If you like eerie supernatural/horror stories with plenty of twists and mystery, this is the book for you. Another fantastic offering from two clearly talented authors and incredibly enjoyable."

—*Anne Marie-Reynolds, Reader's Favorite* (five stars)

"Part One of the Lost Grove series merely tantalized with its mystical elements and unsolved crime, but this ethereal second act fully embraces all things supernatural. Whether time travel or witchy incantations, the possibilities seem limitless within this small town. Still, the authors keep the story tethered to reality by staying within their own defined lines and allowing readers to feel included in the suspense and unraveling mystery. Thrills and chills swirl into a freaky collage of depravity and camaraderie in the nail-biting mystery, The Orbriallis Institute. "

— *Indies Today* (five stars)

"Charlotte Zang and Alex J. Knudsen's *The Orbriallis Institute* was a fascinating and intricate read. It moved quickly with all the turns and twists, and I never knew what would come next. I was in suspense and kept on the edge of my seat during this page-turner. I was too scared to put the book down for even a minute for fear of missing something. The characters were authentic and relatable. This well-written story includes murder, betrayal, mystery, and obsession, and a number of the subplots come together seamlessly. The ending was superb, and it exceeded my expectations by far."

— *Alma Boucher, Reader's Favorite* (five stars)

"The authors manage to maintain the intense tension and eerie atmosphere created in the first book…There's much to enjoy about this conclusion. Wrapping up the enticing layers introduced in book one takes us in a lot of satisfying directions. Zang and Knudsen have done an excellent job bringing this mystery to a close. What a memorable plot and cast they're leaving behind! I know I won't be alone in thinking about this series months from now, daydreaming about the shady city and which mysteries were left behind beyond the established lore."

— *Independent Book Review*

"Author team Charlotte Zang and Alex J. Knudsen have crafted another chilling novel to perfectly complement the first half of their superb thriller tale. The constant sense of dread and the meticulous unraveling of secrets amongst the ensemble cast kept me on edge. I would certainly recommend *The Orbriallis Institute* as a captivating and thought-provoking read that fans of the first book will adore"

— *K.C. Finn, Reader's Favorite* (five stars)

"Blending horror, fantasy, science fiction, and crime, the authors maintain the eerie tone of their previous work while driving the plot forward at a gripping pace. Their vivid descriptions create an immersive atmosphere, and their focus on character development and internal conflicts adds significant depth to the story. The inclusion of supernatural elements, such as visions, adds another layer of complexity, illustrating how human experience often intertwines with the inexplicable, challenging our understanding of reality."

— *The Prairies Book Review*

Praise for *Lost Grove: Part One*

"Zang and Knudsen infuse the investigation with intrigue by crafting diverse characters with idiosyncrasies, secrets, and mysterious pasts... it's the many tantalizing portents, clues, and seeming impossibility that makes Lost Grove shine. Balancing the central story and a myriad of characters with finesse, the authors expertly set the stage for a gripping conclusion" — *Book Life* (editor's pick)

"Thriller, mystery, and gothic horror combine in Charlotte Zang and Alex Knudsen's LOST GROVE: Part One. It is a page-turning novel about a missing-person investigation in a small coastal town that offers depth, surprise, eeriness, and great characters."

— *IndieReader*

"Satisfyingly structured, carefully paced, and packed with surprises, Lost Grove is an intriguing mystery that impeccably blends horror elements such as vampirism, telepathy and changelings, into its modern-day crime narrative. Far from gimmicky, these unnatural features add immeasurably to the story's mood, with the eerie locality of Lost Grove serving as a supernaturally charged backdrop for the investigation...In lesser hands, these tangential character arcs and plot threads might have crippled the novel's pace. However, the authors do an exemplary job of weaving these various threads into the main narrative." — *BlueInk Review*

"Marked by supernatural intrigue, the mystery novel Lost Grove reveals a town's misgivings and secrets...In Charlotte Zang and Alex Knudsen's gripping novel Lost Grove, a young woman's death reveals a web of mysteries in her small town." — *Clarion*

"A dark dream for fans of contemporary horror...the sinister storyline laced with vicious cults, mental illness, amateur sleuthing, and divine

forces makes for a multilayered and gripping read that will satisfy readers of both psychological thrillers and horror fiction."
— *Self Publishing Review* (four stars)

"Lost Grove is what would have happened if the TV show Twin Peaks (1990) had taken a more supernatural path...Because of the unraveling threads, this book can get addictive quickly. The city's lore will grip any reader's attention, and there is so much alluring strangeness going on...A paranormal mystery well worth reading, Lost Grove (Part 1) will have you questioning constantly why this creepy town is the way it is."
— *Independent Book Review*

"It is a testament to the authors' ability to craft a story that is as haunting as it is enthralling. This book is highly recommended for readers seeking a narrative that seamlessly blends mystery, thriller, and horror with a dash of the supernatural, creating a unique and memorable experience."
— *Literary Titan*

Also by Charlotte Zang

See all of Charlotte's books and where to get them on her website at:
https://www.charlottezang.com/

Lost Grove
[Part One](#)

[Blooding](#)

[Consuming Beauty](#)

Lysander O'Connor
[Satan's in Your Kitchen](#)

Also by Alex J. Knudsen

See all of Alex's books and where to get them on his website at
https://www.alexjknudsen.com

Lost Grove
[Part One](#)

[The Nawie](#)

The Orbriallis Institute
Lost Grove Part Two

Charlotte Zang and Alex Knudsen

This novel is a work of fiction. All of the names, characters, organizations, places and events portrayed in this novel are either products of the author's imagination or are used fictitiously. Any resemblance to real or actual events, locales, or persons, living or dead, is entirely coincidental.

Copyright © 2023 Charlotte Zang & Alex Knudsen

All rights reserved. No part of this publication may be reproduced, stored or transmitted in any form or by any means, electronic, mechanical, photocopying, recording, scanning, or otherwise without written permission from the publisher. It is illegal to copy this book, post it to a website, or distribute it by any other means without permission.

Printed in the United States of America
First Printing, 2024

ISBN 979-8-9897962-4-3 (paperback)
ISBN 979-8-9897962-3-6(e-book)

To the witchy women, weaving spells of love and light into the world.
-CZ

To Mr. Smarjesse, my high school English teacher, who was a crucial influence on me, always supporting and pushing me to go after my artistic career goals.
- AK

Prologue
The Green Man

The sun had set on Lost Grove, and the streets were deserted as the night's chill wrapped around the town. The nearly full moon threw long shadows over the quaint homes, illuminated windows marking the occupants' evening routines inside. In one particular home, a gingerbread-style structure with white shutters and a bright red door, the Horne family was settling in for the night. The mother was downstairs feeding her youngest, but most of the food ended up on his chin and clothes instead of in his mouth. Weary and regretful, she tried to cling to sanity. The father had retreated to his office for some respite from parenting duties.

Upstairs, the eldest daughter stepped into her room, phone in hand. Blue light glowed on her face, and golden lamps illuminated a cozy atmosphere. Smiling, she tucked the device between her shoulder and ear as she chatted with a friend. Her hands worked to draw the curtains partially closed, unaware of the eyes watching her or the gleeful squeak released when she stepped into view.

"There now, at last." He released a contented sigh. His stomach flipped end over end, ecstatic at the sight of her. "I know this isn't the one I'm meant to be watching, but I needed to check. I wanted to check, I had to. I had to. 'No, you don't have to do anything, Raymond.' That's what he always says. 'You want to, but you don't need to, you don't have to,' but sometimes I think I do. That's why I had to stop here first, to check on her. I have to, that's what he doesn't understand. I'm not doing anything. I'm just looking, making sure. 'Making sure of what?' That's what he would say. I say, making sure she's happy, that she's still happy, even after what I did, what I had to do because you made me. See, then, I had to because you said, 'Raymond, you have to do this,' then I did it. She looks happy," he whispered to himself, his breath hitching in his throat.

Raymond LaRange crouched on a rooftop peak in the shadow of an elm, its gnarled branches casting spindly shadows over his face and body. Raymond had been a fixture here for years, and he knew how to blend into the trees like they were a part of him. He was so quiet that even the rustle of leaves underfoot didn't betray him—but he didn't need to make a sound to watch—a ghost haunting the backyards of Lost Grove.

From this vantage point on the neighbor's roof, he could see straight into Antoinetta Horne's bedroom—the cozy space she'd made her own with silk sheets and wispy curtains that billowed gently in the breeze on hot summer nights. Many nights, he'd watched her, but on those summer nights when she would lie on her bed playing with her phone or computer, he grew jealous of the breeze that got to caress her skin.

Raymond spent countless hours on the Millers' roof, wishing to be the breeze or the friend she was laughing with. He knew this roof as he knew the forest paths, his feet traversing across the shingles like a dance. He spent more time on this roof than any other roof in town, though he knew he shouldn't. Dr. Owens had forbade him. But what Dr. Owens didn't know wouldn't kill him, and Raymond knew how to keep a secret, even one of his own.

He wasn't afraid of being heard by the Millers, he had "special talents" that could help with that. But Raymond liked testing the boundaries of safety, performing stunts to see how far he could push the Millers. Even when he danced a jig, or that one frigid winter he pretended to be Santa Claus, the Millers were never roused to suspicion.

Did they not care about the potential danger on their roof? Were they hard of hearing or even deaf, like the wife of the man who owned the drugstore?

"You don't tell, so I won't tell. Just like her. She knows I took him. You tried to tell everyone, but they wouldn't listen, Antoinetta. Poor Antoinetta. But you're okay now. Are you? No, no, no. You laugh, you smile, you pretend. All the time. But you still look out the window. Sometimes, you look right at me, but you don't see me. Not anymore. Because you're looking for him, not me. You want to see him; you want me to bring him back to you, but I won't. You'll never see him again."

He watched her tap her phone and toss it to the bed. Her hands moved to the hem of her shirt, and she raised her arms as she walked behind a curtain. Raymond shimmied down toward the gutters, his feet clinging to the shingles, closer to the elm, closer to her window. The frigid night air snaked around his body and ruffled his clothing as he descended closer and closer to the elm outside her window. His heart raced faster with every inch, sending shivers down his spine, blood to his loins, and raising goosebumps on his covered flesh. Another fleeting glimpse of her passing toward her closet. Her slim, pale body protected by nothing but a thin tank top.

He leapt to the tree and crouched in the crook of the elm. He leaned into the trunk, its rough bark digging into his cheek. The clock in their family room chimed a tune, alerting him to the hour.

"It's time to go now. I'm not supposed to be here. I have orders. I've been given my orders. 'Do not fail me, Raymond.' Fail, fail, when? Never. Under mother maybe, but not you. I have to go now, Antoinetta. Tonight, I visit someone else close to you. I've seen you together, with both of them, your friends. You have friends. You're happy. Don't worry, though. I won't take her tonight. 'Not tonight, Raymond. There's a special time, and it's very important, the time. Just look, just study, prepare yourself.' Okay, I'm going."

Raymond moved quickly back across the Millers' roof, hands and feet in a blur as he crab-walked backward up the steep incline like a giant spider. At the peak, he tucked into a tight ball and spun himself across the apex before careening down the other side. He clung to the chimney and leaned over, his ear pressed against its sooty opening, listening intently for any sign of life from within.

"Did you hear me, Randy and Verna?"

Raymond carefully wrapped his arms around the edge of the chimney, feeling the sharp and cold brick between his fingers. He pulled himself over and descended slowly into the Millers' yard below. His boots made no sound as they touched down on the moist grass, and he beelined for the back door, sneaking a peek at Randy and Verna in their kitchen washing dishes side by side.

Raymond suddenly took off like a silver bullet, his feet pounding the ground in a frenzied rhythm. He jumped the Millers' fence with ease and sprinted across the Gradys' yard, dodging flowerbeds and scurrying past their slumbering Labrador retriever. Then on through the Harrisons', then the Matlocks', then Mrs. Gorman's, then the Alexander-Walkers', swiftly across McKinley Avenue, around the corner of Grant Avenue, onto Lincoln, then Crowley Avenue, taking an abrupt right through Rich and Allison Godfrey's front yard, along the property line butting up against Vince and Linda Hollinger's land.

Raymond picked up speed as he pounded past the edge of their house, then sprang into the air, and curled his arms around a thick, horizontal branch of the giant cedar tree in their backyard. He swung his body up and over and rotated gracefully before settling on the limb. He weaved through the branches like a gymnast until he was perched just across from the window of the second story of the house behind the Hollingers'.

"The light's on, but you're not there," he whispered.

Raymond scanned the other windows facing the Hollingers' backyard. A dull, flickering light from the living room was the only other sign of occupancy.

"Good, good, you stay there, both of you. But not you. Where are you? Your light is on and waiting for you to step into it. I wait, that's what I do. I wait and wait and wait and wait and—oh!"

A shadow danced across the far wall of the bedroom, across two large bookcases filled with books and trinkets. Every few seconds, a thin, fleeting shadow skittered across the room as if it were trying to decide whether or not it wanted to stay.

"And you'd like to play, wouldn't you? I know you would. Come out from behind those shadows and play with me. Dance with me. Let me guide you with my eyes."

Then she came into view as if summoned by his delicately whispered words, crossing her room in nothing but a bath towel and her damp, golden hair caressing her shoulders.

"Oh…oh…oh…I see. Oh dear, you did come to play, didn't you?"

Digging into her dresser, she pulled out—

"Little shorts…socks…a shirt, and oh…yes, grab those tiny underwear. So soft, so clean, just like you."

As if solely to taunt him, she walked back across her room and out of view. Only the flickering of her shadow played across the back wall as she took her time dawdling with her clothes.

"Get back out here, young miss. I won't play with shadows; no, I will not. That is a rule I shall not break. No shadows. Now get—"

She walked back into view draped in an oversized, well-worn T-shirt of her father's, her feet tucked into a pair of fuzzy slippers. Making her way to the corner of the room, she slumped into the chair at her desk and pulled open the lid of her laptop. Its bright light illuminated her delicate features.

"Why, hello, Zoe Andalusian."

That's the Guy

Nate Abbott sidled up next to his best friend, Noble Andalusian, leaning against the wall that declared Lost Grove Senior High "Home of the Wildcats." They both wore their school track sweatshirts, their hands tucked in the pouches, shoulders shrugged up against the biting October wind.

"Damn, it's cold," Nate complained. The strong winds tousled his medium-blonde hair, and he followed Noble's initiative, pulling the hood of his sweatshirt up over his head. It wasn't that it didn't get brisk on the coast in Northern California, but the cold spell after the storm last week was downright glacial.

"Fucking frigid," Noble agreed, though his eyes were on the door to the junior high. His longer dark-brown locks fluttered out from under the hood of his sweatshirt.

"I don't get it," Nate said. "Why would someone leave a personal message? Why not call 911?"

"What?" Noble was distracted. Usually, his younger sister, Zoe, was one of the first ones out of school. She was late by ordinary standards, and he wondered what was keeping her.

"Sarah Grahams. Why would someone leave an anonymous note on Chief Richards' doorstep? Or wherever they left it." Nate raised his brows in question, pressing Noble to voice his thoughts on the topic of the recently discovered body of a local woman, Sarah Elizabeth Grahams, on Mourner's Beach just four days prior. She had been a senior when they were freshmen. They'd seen her around town, at school events, and now she was dead by mysterious circumstances. This morning, the chief of police, Bill Richards, and the sergeant, Seth Wolfe, had called the students into the auditorium to assuage any fears and give the students and teachers a brief overview of the case. But Nate knew what they'd really been after: information.

Nate was hoping Noble would say he didn't know why anyone would leave a note so that he could expound upon the many theories running through his mind. He wanted to discuss the case with someone. Nate was an avid true crime fan looking to attend the academy and get a degree in criminal law enforcement. He wanted to be a detective or, better yet, an FBI agent. Because stuff like this rarely happened in Lost Grove, as morbid as it was, he was champing at the bit to unravel the mystery of Sarah's death.

Noble had thought about it. A lot. Since his friend Anya Bury put the idea in his head this afternoon when they met in the library, he couldn't help but wonder if Mary Germaine, the town's rumored vampire, was the anonymous tipper. But there was also the pressing, sickening possibility his father, Peter, had left the note. His father had skipped town after a similar event years ago. Another young woman had been found dead from suspicious circumstances with links to his father. Now Sarah Elizabeth was found, washed ashore the same as the previous girl, and Peter had left that very morning. Noble had discovered that his father also had links to Sarah, likely working with her at the local Devil's Cradle National Park over the summers when she was a camp counselor for her church's day camp.

"I don't know…I haven't thought about it," he said instead, not keen to discuss his thoughts with anyone at the moment.

"Right, so here's what I'm thinking," Nate started with hungry enthusiasm. "One, the person has to know Chief Richards, right? They'd have to know where he lives, which means they're local."

Noble cringed, catching himself in time to stop it from being blatantly obvious. He looked away to the doors, to the ground at his feet, anywhere but at his friend.

"Two, there'd have to be a reason they didn't want to deal with the police. An anonymous note? Come on, that's the oldest trick in the book. It means they did it!"

A lump now formed in Noble's throat. His gaze drifted back to the doors of the junior high. Where was Zoe? And where were Anya and

Nettie? They were supposed to find out if Nettie could identify the man, Raymond LaRange, as the same man she called the Green Man. He doubted there could actually be a connection. No, that wasn't entirely true. Wasn't it oddly random that Nettie's ill brother, George, would randomly mutter words that sounded like the nickname of a man who sexually abused two girls decades ago, Papa LaRange. Furthermore, that man would then go on to be treated at the renowned Orbriallis Institute here in town, the very same institute where George was being treated for his late-onset autism. Though, if Nettie was to be believed, he wasn't autistic but a fake child. A not-child, as Mary called them.

"I'm not sure it means that. People freak out when they see dead things, let alone the dead body of someone they—"

"Exactly. That goes to my third point," Nate interrupted. "They must have known who she was. They had to have known."

Noble's brow furrowed, his glance darting to his CSI-loving friend. The problem with everything Nate was saying? Noble had been thinking the same things. There were too many coincidences surrounding his father. The news of the anonymous note left at the home of Lost Grove's chief of police made Noble's palms sweat. His mom said his father had gone up to Alaska for the crab season. But was that true? Did she know something she wasn't letting on? "Why would they have to know her?"

"Noble," Nate sighed, "any other person would have dialed 911. They'd get the dispatch center, not our local PD. Whoever did this wanted Chief Richards to know. This person wanted our police officers to find her, to handle it. They live here, and they know Sarah. It all gels. It's some top-tier serial killer shit."

Noble scowled. "Are you suggesting there's a serial killer living in Lost Grove?" He turned his eyes back on the junior high to see Zoe skipping out, her large Doc Martens and oversized corduroy jacket making her look even younger than she was. She cradled a shoebox in her hands, golden-blonde hair streaming behind her, and the smile on her face radiated into Noble's heart, spreading a smile of his own.

"Could be. I'd be willing to…fuck," Nate growled as Zoe approached, knowing he had to table this line of thought.

Zoe came to a sudden stop before her brother and let out a quiet squeal. "Guess what's in here?"

Noble shook his head, feeling her excitement. The little sister he so hoped he could protect from the rumors and foul words the townspeople were spreading about their dad was about the only thing that could throw his growing concerns aside. "What?"

"A baby owl!" Zoe's pitch rose, but she tried to keep it a whisper in consideration of the bird.

"What?" Noble said with a smirk that spoke of mock disbelief and the authority of an older brother.

"Really? Let me see," Nate asked, leaning over.

Zoe lifted the lid off the shoebox and let Nate and Noble peek inside. Noble leaned down from his six-foot-three-inch height. Nate bent at the waist from his lower five eleven. The little ball of fluffy feathers tucked itself into a corner, enormous eyes blinking. "I already texted Mom. She says she knows what to do with it, so I'm bringing it home."

"Jesus," Noble said under his breath. Like mother, like daughter. They were always saving animals and bringing them home for rehabilitation.

"Holy shit, it really is an owl," Nate said.

"This one's been out of the nest for a while," Zoe said. "I hope we can keep it alive. Probably blew out from the storm on Wednesday night last week. Poor thing."

Noble stood back up. "Okay, well—"

"So let's go! I've got to get her home to Mom."

"Just…go to the car. Here," Noble said, handing her the keys. "I have to talk to Anya about something."

"Okay, but don't take too long," Zoe instructed, swiping the keys and hurrying off to the car.

"What do you have to talk to Anya about?" Nate asked, grinning ear to ear, recalling that he'd seen them holding hands. Not to mention they'd met for ice cream last Saturday.

"Class project," Noble said, an excuse but not too far off. It had been a project, trying to make sense of a jumble of incoherent words, though it most definitely had not been for school. He didn't want to get into the details of Nettie's little brother speaking. Nate was of the mind that Nettie Horne was one of those people who was born a little kooky, would always be kooky.

"A *project*, he says," Nate jeered. "More like Project Take Your Pants—"

"Nate? Can we go?" Cheshire Abbott, Nate's younger sister, appeared out of nowhere, sprinting up to them with her head down, hands clutching the straps of her backpack. "Like, now."

"Yeah, jeez, chill." Nate stood from where he'd been resting against the school sign. Cheshire took off like a cheetah for her older brother's car. "I swear, I do not know what is up with that girl. One day, she's sweet. The next…she bit my head off this morning for pouring orange juice too loud. Orange juice!"

"She's going through the same hormonal shit we all did." Noble laughed as his friend walked away.

"Well, it's a hormone monster 'cause she is a fucking roller coaster," he yelled. "I'll see you back here for practice."

"Yep," Noble called to his friend.

"Hey," Anya said, coming up behind Noble with Nettie.

Noble turned, unable to keep from smiling. Anya's aquamarine eyes caught the sunlight, and it felt like he'd been swallowed into the Caribbean. She was pulling on her hand-knit stocking cap, shoving her long orange-to-blonde ombre hair underneath. She was becoming the second person who could always bring a smile to his face. "Hey," he answered, looking from Anya to Nettie and back again.

Anya raised her brows and spun toward her friend. "Should we step over here?"

"What is this about?" Nettie asked, looking suspiciously between her classmates. Her thin legs were protected from the chill by tights and a flimsy looking floral skirt that hung just above her knees. Noble thought she'd be frozen in about three minutes. When she shrugged deeper into her pea coat, he guessed it might be more like two.

"Um…" Anya let her words trail away, already heading away from the front of the school and parking lot.

Noble followed, motioning to his sister he'd be one minute. Nothing was going to come of this. He didn't actually believe the man, Raymond LaRange, was running loose in Lost Grove, masquerading as the Green Man.

"Okay, what the heck?" Nettie asked when they'd walked a suitable distance away from the other students.

Anya stopped and spun around, but she couldn't think how to start this conversation.

"What?" Nettie pushed, her smile cautious, eyes darting from Anya to Noble.

"I don't know. This seems kinda stupid now," Anya said toward Noble.

An awkward laugh escaped his lips. "Um, I don't see what harm—"

"What seems stupid?" Nettie asked. Her mouth curled in an uncertain smile.

Anya took a deep breath. She had let her mind run rampant since Noble showed her the articles. At first, she thought the idea of Raymond LaRange being released by the Orbriallis crazy, the thought of him escaping even sillier. But then she realized how long ago he'd been admitted. What if he actually progressed, and the doctors thought it was safe to let him out? "I just think the chances that—"

"Jesus, just tell me!" Nettie demanded with laughter.

After a moment of silence, each of them looking at one another, Anya finally said, "We think maybe we found a solution to what your brother said at therapy last week."

Nettie's lips parted, her eyes widening a little. She cast a gaze up at Noble and back to Anya. "You told him?" she whispered, as if Noble couldn't hear. She wasn't thrilled Anya had brought this up to someone else. The whole town thought she was a little crazy, thinking her brother was taken by a creepy man who looked like the pied piper with things that looked like children trailing after him. They all believed the doctors when they said that George Horne was autistic, even her parents. They didn't believe the thing living with them right now was even a real child, was her brother.

"He was the one who came up with the answer. Or what might be the answer," Anya responded. Then, noticing her friend's panic, she squeezed Nettie's arm. "It's fine, I promise."

"I…yeah, okay." Nettie offered Noble a tight smile. "I didn't know you'd told anyone."

"Well, it was kind of an accident," Noble jumped in.

"He found me in the library during study hall and asked what all my scribbles were about. So, I told him about Not-George speaking and how we thought it could be something."

"Yeah, I mean…" Nettie jumped in. She didn't want to deal with the repercussions of Noble spreading the news that she thought her disabled brother was trying to communicate with her. She'd spent years getting over the fallout from her younger days when the kids teased her for an overactive imagination and said she was too old to believe in things like the boogeyman anymore. The last thing Nettie wanted was this new development to break open old wounds. "I'm just trying to help my parents, you know? They want to… They hold on to every little thing it—he—does. So, I'm trying to give them hope, or, rather, I'm trying to—I mean, if he is trying to communicate, right?"

"Sure, yeah," Noble agreed, nodding. "But, um, for starters, I'm not going to tell anyone about this. Anya made me promise. And I'm promising you now that I won't."

"Okay." Nettie felt better hearing that, especially that Anya made him promise, but did he only promise because he didn't want to associate with the silly notion?

"I just thought I'd help." Solving this riddle, or at least attempting to, had been a pleasant distraction for Noble. It was a puzzle he might resolve while the mystery surrounding his dad gathered more and more strings for him to follow. "We found something. I think it's definitely a long shot, so maybe it is stupid. We just—"

"Well, now you have to tell me." Nettie looked at Anya. "It can't be that stupid if you guys got to this point."

Anya looked at Noble. Maybe her hesitation was because, deep down, she feared what would happen if it was true.

Noble wasn't sure what Anya was trying to communicate to him. She looked nervous. "We can wait and show her later if—"

"Seriously?" Nettie asked. Her mouth hung slightly open, brows raised. "Come on, guys. If it's goofy, that's fine. I'm starting to think I made too much of this, anyway. But I want to know what you both thought. Is it super ridiculous? Like the name of some Swedish candy or something?"

Anya wrinkled her nose.

Noble drew breath in through his teeth.

"Guys! What might it—he—have said?"

A shiver ran along Noble's spine at hearing that "it" again, raising the hairs on the back of his neck. He didn't know how to bridge the connection between Nettie's weird brother and Mary's not-children, which she also referred to as "its."

Anya finally conceded. "Noble may have found a name."

"A name?" Nettie's pulse increased. The trepidation caused sweat to prickle at her scalp. It was the same when she was little. When she knew she'd look out the window and see the Green Man slinking out of the woods.

"Yeah." Noble elongated the word.

"It's something we were trying to make fit and—" Anya began.

"What was the name?" Nettie asked Noble.

Noble wanted to protest, but what the hell? He reached into his backpack and removed his tablet, clicked it on, and found the tab with the photo of Raymond LaRange. He turned the tablet so Nettie could see. "This guy, Raymond LaRange."

Nettie's eyes skimmed the print before settling on a grainy black-and-white image. From the base of her skull down her spine and along her arms, goosebumps appeared all over her body. Her heart rate increased as her stomach flipped over with a surge of nausea and childhood anxiety. It was like she was standing at her window, watching him creep out of the forest behind their house. There he was now, on a computer screen, younger, but it was him—the same beady eyes, the hook of an Adam's apple, the hint of a sneaky smile. That was him, the man from George's windowsill. The man who'd placed a finger on the side of his nose and winked at her. The queasy feeling in her stomach traveled up into the back of her throat.

Nettie pulled backward, away from the tablet.

Noble was keenly aware of the shift in the atmosphere. He sensed Anya moving toward Nettie in an act of concern and comfort, but he felt unable to move.

"That's him," Nettie croaked, covering her mouth.

Anya gaped a moment, hands midair as she approached Nettie to console her. "Nettie, I…" Finally, her hands landed on her friend as Nettie continued backward.

Noble stared at them, confounded. She was saying this man who had been tried for the molestation of two little girls over thirty years ago in Utah was wandering around her house when she was a child. His head snapped toward his car, to his eleven-year-old sister he'd left alone. The car was empty. Still holding the tablet, his hand dropped. His feet involuntarily moved toward his vehicle, eyes darting around the parking lot in search of Zoe. He was three steps away from the girls when he caught sight of his sister, clutching the shoebox with the little owl, keys dangling from her fingers, waiting just a few feet from them.

"What are you doing?" he demanded, approaching her.

"I came to see how long you were—"

"I told you to wait in the car," he reprimanded.

Zoe opened her mouth.

"Didn't I tell you to wait in the car?"

"Yeah, but you were taking so long."

"Jesus," he fumed, grabbing a hold of her shoulder and looking around to the depleted parking lot. "You've got to listen to me when I tell you to do things."

"It's not that big of a deal. Why are you yelling at me?"

"I'm not yelling," he yelled.

"You are," she whimpered. Her large eyes grew wet with the threat of tears.

Noble pulled her into a hug. "No, I'm sorry. I didn't mean to yell at you."

"Well, why are you?"

"I just thought…I thought for a minute." *Someone had taken you,* he didn't voice.

"What?" she asked, pulling away from him. "You're smooshing the box."

"Nothing." Noble looked back over his shoulder at Anya and Nettie. Nettie had her arms folded tight across her chest, while Anya rubbed her hands up and down the other girl's arms, looking like she was telling her to take deep breaths. Nettie shook her head as Noble turned back to his sister.

"Is she okay? Why were you talking about that guy again?" Zoe asked.

"What guy?"

"That LaRange guy. You were talking about him on Saturday with Anya when we got ice cream."

"Did you go through my iPad?"

"No." Zoe wrinkled her nose. "I overheard you just now say it."

"…And I want to know. Noble?" Nettie had approached from behind. "Who is this guy? What was the article about?"

Noble turned to find Nettie looking peaked, neck flush and splotchy. Anya was just behind her, shrugging. "The—"

"The man you just showed me, Raymond LaRange. What was he in the paper for?" Nettie's attention moved briefly down to Zoe at Noble's side and back up.

"I'm not sure you want to know the details."

"Okay," she said, shifting her bag around so she could open it. "I'll just look him up myself."

"The article is about a court case," Noble said, stopping her.

"A case for what?" Nettie's voice had gone hoarse.

Anya stepped forward. "It's not good, Net." She leaned in close to Nettie's ear for a conspiratorial whisper, wanting to keep the awfulness away from Zoe.

Zoe leaned closer to see if she could hear what Anya was whispering. Noble gently pushed her back and shook his head. He turned back to see Nettie standing still, arms limp at her sides. She took a moment, swallowing hard before she raised her eyes to meet his, then Anya's, somehow looking even more pale than before.

"And then what happened? He went to jail?" Nettie could barely verbalize her questions.

Owl talons scratching on cardboard drew Noble's attention down to the box his sister was holding. She leaned down and cooed soothingly, trying to settle the baby bird.

"Noble?" Anya prompted. "Sorry, it's just, I didn't really read all the articles."

"No, yeah. Um, so, the case was… No, he didn't go to jail. His IQ was below seventy, which apparently made him unfit. There was a lot of legal stuff there. And they apparently believed that he didn't know he'd done anything wrong. At least that's what they argued. They said he couldn't tell the difference between wrong and right. See, he thought…" Noble paused, glancing in his sister's direction at his side. "He thought they were playing a game. Like they were playing house, if you…get what I'm…" He hoped that was enough to get the point across. In his testimony, Raymond made some comment that what he'd done was what Mommy and Daddy were supposed to do.

Nettie began shaking her head while she rubbed the palm of her left hand on her thigh. "So?" she gagged on the word.

Noble let out a sigh.

"We could do this later," Anya suggested, taking hold of Nettie's hand.

"No. I want to know. You made a connection. What is it?" Nettie asked, her voice rising, agitation setting in.

"They sentenced him to psychiatric care, and then they transferred him from someplace in Ohio to the Orbriallis Institute," Noble said and grimaced.

Nettie's mouth fell open. It was true. She hadn't imagined anything. "Oh my god."

"Right. So…"

Nettie slowly shook her head, trying to gather her composure. She snarled, her chest heaving up and down. "When?"

"The case was in 1992," Noble answered. He didn't see a point in stalling with the information, though he tried to deliver it softly.

"1992?" Nettie blurted. "They let him out?"

Noble shrugged. "Nothing I could find suggests he left or got released. I can't find anything about his sentence, like how long it was or anything."

"But he is out," Nettie whimpered. "He's out, and he's wandering around the streets of this town."

Anya wrapped her arm around Nettie.

Nettie ran her hands over her face, trying to breathe.

A small tug on his sleeve drew Noble's attention. He leaned down, Zoe cupping her hand over her mouth to whisper, "Is she okay?"

Noble nodded, standing back to full height. In the library, he hadn't absorbed what Anya had explained. Nettie saw the man who took George. The problem was, George was still there. He wasn't a missing child. He was just different. The chemicals and synapses in his brain didn't fire as they would in an average person. That was all, wasn't it? But now, here she was, backing away from a photo on his tablet screen, her face turned ashen and green, hyperventilating.

"Nettie, you need to breathe," Anya instructed, her voice drawing Noble back to the conversation.

"Wait." Noble tried to contain his pressing need to ask questions. He leaned in close, voice hushed. "You actually did see someone take your brother?"

Nettie was staring ahead at nothing, her eyes petrified open. "I saw him every night. He'd sit on the windowsill and call George to come and play with him and those other little things," she explained. She'd been telling the same story for years, and no one listened to her.

Noble felt his body go cold. The way she emphasized "things" was the same way Mary had done last Thursday, with vehemence and disgust. "But you told your parents this, and they didn't—"

Nettie urgently whispered, "I told my parents a hundred fucking times before they eventually asked Chief Richards to come around. But he couldn't find anyone. I used to wonder if he was invisible to adults. I thought maybe I'd made him all up, so many times…" Nettie trailed off, again looking into the distance. Her body shook.

"Okay, we need to get you home," Anya said.

"Do you want a ride?" Noble suggested.

"We have our bikes—"

"Let me just drive you guys to her place. Then we can come back for the bikes," Noble suggested. He steered his sister toward the car, while Anya coaxed Nettie. She ushered her into the back seat, Zoe climbing into the front with worried, wide eyes.

"Noble?"

"It's okay, Zo. Nettie's just had a shock," Noble assured his sister. He started the car and pulled out of the parking lot.

"He's real, and nobody sees him. No one but me," Nettie lamented from the back seat.

Anya was nodding, rubbing her friend's hands between her own.

"What do I do?" Nettie asked plaintively.

Noble's eyes darted to the back seat via the rearview mirror.

Nettie swiveled her attention to him. "What do I do with this, Noble?"

Noble looked back to the road, unsure just what in the hell he had gotten himself into. First Mary, now Nettie. "I don't know."

"We're going to figure something out," Anya stated, drawing a sideways glance from Nettie. Anya smiled and nodded affirmatively. "Yeah?"

Nettie swiped at her nose with the back of her hand.

"We're going to figure it out," Anya said once more. "Now, take a deep breath."

Nettie took in a long breath through pursed lips and then let it out slowly, following Anya's instruction.

"Okay, this is shocking. You're in shock right now, Nettie. Your body is dealing with the trauma and adrenaline rushing through your system. It's science, okay, and it's normal," Anya continued.

Nettie let out a strange cough-laugh. "Leave it to you to explain my meltdown scientifically. Jesus."

In the front seat, Noble tried to stifle a giggle, which prompted Anya to laugh, and then Nettie broke out into strained giggles until the whole car filled with awkward laughter. Zoe looked at them like they'd lost their minds.

"Shit, is it this house?" Noble asked, forcing his foot onto the brakes.

"No, the gingerbread home with the red door, up ahead," Anya instructed.

Nettie let out a long sigh, brushing tears from her eyes and cheeks. She couldn't have identified what she was feeling. Elation? Anger? Fear? Trepidation? Relief? Perhaps she was feeling all of it. She had this information, concrete information of a name. She could put a name to the Green Man, but did she want that? Would it help anyone? "I don't know what to do."

"We don't need to do anything right now. You need to process this. It's a lot of information for you to…you know…" Anya trailed off, trying to think of the right word.

Nettie turned to look at her as the car came to a stop. "Process?" She offered.

"Yes, process." Anya laughed. "Let's go upstairs. You and I can talk about it. We can talk about everything."

Noble turned in his seat as Nettie got out of the car. He promptly unbuckled and jumped out. "I can pick you up after practice. Grab your bike and hers and come get you, if you want?"

"I…yeah. I'll text you if something else comes up, but yeah. That sounds good." Anya smiled at him.

"I'm sorry," he called after her and Nettie as they moved up the stairs to the house.

"It's not your fault, Noble," Anya called back. Her smile melted some of Noble's regret for having dug so hard to uncover this information.

If this was what finding the truth looked like, was it worth it to know what skeletons his father was hiding in his closet?

Off the Record, On the Record

It was a brisk, quiet night as Seth Wolfe, sergeant for the Lost Grove police, made his way home from the station. Then again, most nights were quiet in Lost Grove, even on Fridays and Saturdays. It didn't matter that it was only just before nine p.m., the townspeople were in for the night. The music of a night in Lost Grove was a vehicle driving down Main Street at sparse intervals or a dog barking in the distance. Since that morning on the beach when he experienced a horrifying bout of déjà vu, Seth swore he could hear the waves hitting the shore on his walks home, even though the ocean was over two miles away. Maybe he did. Maybe he always had.

Today felt like it had gone on forever. The morning started with a bombshell. Sarah Elizabeth had never gone back to college at Baylor after the winter break when she was last seen by her friends, her pastor, and reportedly her parents. The only problem was that her parents claimed to have dropped her off at the airport to fly back to Texas, followed by Sarah apparently changing her phone number, ghosting them, and everyone else in her life, for over two and a half years. Finding out that she never returned to Baylor was the first break in the case, one that gave Seth and Chief Bill Richards the ammunition they needed to force Richard and Bess Grahams to come clean about what really happened with their daughter: that they brought her to the Orbriallis Institute, the world renowned research facility auspiciously located in the small town of Lost Grove, to treat her insomnia and visions.

The Grahamses claimed she was there until just shy of a year ago when she was released, per Sarah's request, and placed in a women's safe house where she could start to work herself back into society. They claimed not to have seen or spoken to her since and had no clue she was pregnant. With the flood of lies that had already spilled out of both Bess's and Richard's mouths, Seth found this claim hard to swallow. He rushed directly to the Institute while Bill took the Grahamses into the station to get their account on record.

Seth didn't expect to see anyone since it was already six p.m., but he got her doctor's contact information and left an urgent message. He planned to call again tomorrow morning, and if there was no response by noon, he planned on making himself known. With their prime suspect, Peter Andalusian, reportedly on a fishing vessel off the coast of Alaska, the Orbriallis Institute was the key to solving the mysterious death of Sarah Elizabeth Grahams.

Seth approached Main Street. He had been staying in the tiny one-room apartment above his father's drug store for the four months since returning home after vacating his position as lead homicide detective with the San Francisco Police Department. He was hesitant to commit to a permanent residence here in Lost Grove. Not a day had gone by that he didn't second-guess his decision to come home. He told himself it was because of his dad's severe stroke, but he could have easily afforded to pay for someone to help his mother care for him. Deep down, he knew he needed to step away after the haunting investigation at Dolores Park one month prior to leaving the big city.

Turning the corner on Main Street, Seth spotted someone quietly pacing in front of his door. Were they waiting for him, or was it just a local meandering the sidewalk? Streetlights fashioned after the original vintage lampposts dotted the street, but this person, a woman, was lurking in the shadows. Could it be Story Palmer, the town librarian whom he'd grown close to while gathering information for the Sarah Elizabeth investigation? They last spoke over wine and tea (he was still on duty) at the Lost Grove Victorian Inn, where Seth asked her about the boy, or man, she believed Sarah was dating. Story was the only person in town who believed it was even a possibility that Sarah had a boyfriend, and despite not knowing who that person was, it was a vital clue that could help him and Sheriff Bill Richards solve the enigmatic case.

Seth closed the distance, and the woman looked up at him. "Hi, Seth."

"Mary Germaine?" Seth asked rhetorically of his old schoolmate, her face unmistakable despite not having seen or spoken to her in over twenty years. The same narrow eyes. Long, dark eyelashes and thick eyebrows that almost looked fake. Her dark-blonde hair was even styled the same, which meant no style to speak of, just long mildly wavy hair falling past her shoulders. "Wow, it's good to see you."

Mary smiled humbly. "Yeah, you too."

"I thought I had spotted you running a few early mornings when I was out patrolling, but wasn't positive."

"That was me. I like to run early. And late."

Seth nodded, trying to ascertain what Mary Germaine was doing here. "What, um…" Seth looked across the street and back down the side of the road for anything that was still open. He knew there wasn't. Even the town pub was "officially" closed Monday through Wednesday, despite locals often being in there most nights.

"I'm here to see you."

Seth looked back at her. "Oh."

"That's why I'm standing in front of the door to your apartment."

"Right." Seth nodded at what now seemed painfully obvious. "How did you know where I live?"

Mary rolled her eyes. "Everyone knows where everyone lives. And I've seen you up in the window."

Seth's eyes narrowed.

"On my runs." Mary answered Seth's questioning glance. "I wasn't trying to look. I just noticed." She pointed up toward his window.

"Yeah, I guess it's right there overlooking Main Street." Seth chuckled, trying to allay her uneasiness. "So, what can I do for you? I mean, are you here to report something? Sorry, I shouldn't assume. It's just that no one outside of my parents has—"

"Yes." Mary quickly checked her surroundings. "It's about Sarah Elizabeth."

"Oh," Seth said, his interest piqued, also thankful for her cutting him off. He felt like he was putting his foot in his mouth. He motioned over his shoulder with his thumb. "Did you want to go back to the station with me? We can—"

"No," Mary said forcefully, quickly looking again to see if anyone had appeared on the street. "Story said I can trust you. I only want to talk to you."

The faintest of grins shifted the corner of Seth's mouth upward.

It made complete sense that Story and Mary would have found each other and become friends. Mary always stood out in school as being "different," so much her own person that the rest of the students seemed plain. Unfortunately, she was teased and taunted for this, something Seth couldn't stand for if he was present. Especially because Mary was so demure and quiet, never standing up for herself. Story was an adult, but she stood out the same way, though she was unabashed in her demeanor. He imagined she couldn't care less if someone looked at her oddly. He got the sense there were even times when Story welcomed the curious glares.

"Okay, that's not a problem," Seth said. "I do have a private office we could—"

"Can we just…" Mary motioned with her head to Seth's apartment. "I don't want to be at the station."

"Of course." Seth took out his keys and unlocked the deadbolt. He stepped in and flipped on the light switch, the dim bulb high above illuminating the sea-foam green walls. The stairwell was steep and narrow, the wooden steps so shallow Seth had to walk on his tiptoes up and shuffle sideways down. He held open the door for her to follow, glancing to see if anyone had come outside. People were already talking about Story and him. The last thing he needed was to be seen leading Mary up to his apartment late at night.

"How is your father?" Mary asked.

Seth reached the top landing and turned to smile at Mary. She was staring at her fidgeting hands. "He's doing well, thanks," he said as he quickly unlocked his door, pushing it open. "More so mentally than physically. Come on in."

Mary looked up to see Seth standing halfway inside his apartment, extending his arm out. "I'm sorry," she said and followed him inside.

"It's okay." Seth placed his keys on a hook and removed his jacket. "He's fighting through the rehab. It's going to be a long road, but he's got the right mindset."

"That's good," Mary said as she moved into the apartment, surveying the quaint, open space. She had always wondered what the rooms above the stores on Main Street looked like, what they were used for. The walls were the same cream color as the outside of the drugstore, the ceilings much higher than she imagined. The window frames looked original and well kept, a dark varnished redwood, Mary guessed. She appreciated the soft, warm lighting. Whether it was like this before Seth moved back home, she wasn't sure, but it created a comforting environment.

Seth threw his jacket over the nearest of two chairs placed around the small wooden table of the eat-in kitchen. "I know it's not much," Seth admitted as he shut the door. His sparse furnishings consisted of a full-size bed, nightstand, and armchair. The amenities were a small kitchenette and a claustrophobic bathroom. "That's actually my bed from high school."

Mary looked back at him and smiled. "I still sleep in mine as well."

Seth laughed. "Well, good, that makes me feel a little better."

"Didn't you bring anything with you from San Francisco?"

Seth shook his head as he walked to the kitchen area. "Just my clothes, a few books, and—"

"What's his name?"

Seth spun around to see that Mary was bent over, looking under his bed. "Oh." Seth squatted down. "That's Reggie. He came with me as well."

The black-and-brown cat was staring at Mary, seemingly unperturbed by her presence. "Why Reggie?"

Seth raised his eyebrows. "He just seemed like a Reggie to me. I've never known a Reggie. Didn't name him after a character in a book or movie or anything. How did you know he was male?"

Mary stood back up straight and shrugged. "He just seemed like a male," she said, opting not to tell Seth that she could smell it. Just another specialty that came with her bizarre ailment, which also included a desire to put strange things in her mouth, eat raw meat, and consume blood.

Seth pushed himself back up. "Would you like some water? Or orange juice? That's about all I have, I'm afraid."

Mary examined the marble kitchen counter and floating shelves with glasses on them. Everything appeared rather spotless. "Water would be fine. Thanks."

Seth grabbed two glasses and filled them with water from his Brita pitcher on the counter. "Here you go," he said, handing her the glass. "How is your mother?" he asked, recalling that her father had passed away their junior year from colon cancer.

Mary's eyes fell to the glass she held to her chest. "She died. Five years ago. From breast cancer."

Seth winced. "Mary, I'm so sorry."

Mary looked back up and saw genuine sympathy in his eyes. She smiled, happy for Story that Seth was back in Lost Grove. Mary had a crush on Seth in her late teenage years, back when she could still consider having a crush on someone. She hoped he and Story would find happiness together. "How did you know it was me when you saw me running?"

Seth smiled. "You look just how I remember you. It's almost like you haven't aged while I was gone."

Mary's cheeks warmed. "You look older."

Seth lifted his eyebrows. "Oh. Well, working as a detective for years—"

"Better," she clarified. "You look older, but more like a man. Still tall, same black hair. But more handsome and developed. And the scruff is nice."

"Ah, thanks for clearing that up," Seth said with a laugh. He desperately hoped Mary actually had information on the case and wasn't here for something else entirely.

Mary looked down, grimacing. She should have kept her mouth shut. She didn't want him to get the wrong impression. Not that she didn't find him attractive, and in a different life, she would—

"Are you living in the same house?" Seth asked and took a sip of his water.

Mary looked back up and nodded, thankful he had changed the subject. "I inherited it." *And a rather sizable sum of money,* she didn't voice.

"Well, that's something, at least. So, what do you do for work? I haven't seen you in any of the shops here or up in Eureka."

Mary sneered at the thought of having to work at a store, having to deal with people. "I sell art on Etsy."

"Really?" Seth asked, his eyes wide.

"Yep."

"Wow, that's great. That's just…I'm not surprised at all, actually."

"Why? What do you mean?"

Seth grinned. "Art class with Mrs. Young. I thought your drawings were by far the coolest in class. You were one of maybe two kids who had any talent whatsoever, and your stuff was the most interesting. By far."

Mary's eyes opened wide. She didn't think anyone noticed anything about her in school besides dressing differently and constantly chewing on things.

"I'm sure that I told you so back then," Seth said.

Mary shrugged.

"There was that one with the really weird creature. I think it had five or six legs and…doesn't matter. What do you sell on Etsy? Drawings? Paintings?"

Mary was in a state of shock that he remembered that painting. If he only knew what it really was. "Um, mainly mixed textile collages. Some really tiny," Mary said, holding her pointer finger and thumb apart, measuring about three inches, "and some so big I have to ship them in crates."

Seth shook his head. "That's just amazing. I could use some around here to—"

"I know who Sarah Elizabeth's boyfriend was." Mary couldn't handle it any longer. She needed Seth to know why she had really come.

Seth froze, his hand stuck motioning to the bare wall opposite the two windows facing Main Street.

"Tommy Wilder. He's the janitor at the high school."

Seth's eyelids fluttered. He was surprised tears didn't fall down his cheeks. "Wow, okay, that was not what I was…um, here, do you want to come sit down over here?" Seth asked as he strode toward his paltry excuse for a dining room table and swept the case files for the Kelly Fulson case off the top into his hands. He had been repeatedly going through the files of the local girl who was found dead seven years prior in an eerily similar state to Sarah Elizabeth, both having been pregnant at the time of their deaths.

Mary obliged, walking over to sit as Seth sprinted past her and threw some folders on his bed.

Seth raced back, pulled his notepad and pen from his jacket pocket, and plopped down across from Mary. "You said Tommy Wilder?"

"Yes," Mary confirmed and finally took a sip from her glass of water.

"And the janitor?" Seth looked up, his face scrunched like he had bitten into a lime.

Mary nodded. "Not like you think. He's young. Older than her, but still very young. I think he's probably twenty-five now."

Seth sighed and jotted down the information.

"Not like our janitor back in the day. Ronald?"

Seth looked up. "Roland, I think."

"Anyhow, Tommy is a handsome enough kid."

"And he's still here in town?"

Mary nodded.

"Do you happen to know where he lives?"

Mary held out her hand for Seth's pen and notepad.

Seth reticently slid them over to her.

Mary scribbled down Tommy's address and handed them back.

Seth looked at the address, wondering how or why on earth Mary knew it. He looked up at her. "And how sure are you about this?"

"The address?"

"No. Well, yes, how sure are you—"

"One hundred percent."

Seth nodded. "Okay. But I was more meaning—how sure are you about Sarah and Tommy?"

Mary set her glass down on the table. "I saw them kissing, holding each other. Many times."

Seth slowly shook his head and leaned back in his seat. "How in the hell did no one else in town seem to know about this or even think it was a possibility that she had a boyfriend? Her best friends, her teachers, her parents. I don't get it."

Mary smirked. "You'd be surprised what you can get away with if you're careful. And they were very careful."

"But how? And how did you see them and no one else?"

"Like I said, I go out very early and very late to run. Or just to walk. It calms me."

Seth held his hand out, palm up, fiddling with the pen. "And?"

Mary shrugged. "And I saw them sometimes at the playground of the elementary school, or on the side of the high school where the river runs through, late at night. Places where they could easily duck out of view. Even saw them a couple of early mornings. It all seemed very innocent."

"How late or early are you talking?"

"Mmm...after midnight. Maybe even as late as two or three a.m. Morning, around four thirty a.m., no later than five."

Seth slowly jotted down the information as he thought back to the layout of the Grahamses' home. Sarah would have walked by her parents' bedroom, and he couldn't imagine one of them wouldn't have heard the deadbolt turning, the latch clicking, or the door shutting. "Her window?" he muttered to himself.

"Yes."

"Hm?" Seth looked up.

Mary was taking another sip of water. She swallowed and set the glass down. "I followed her home one night. She went in through her window."

"What?"

"Well, them. He walked her home."

"Why?"

Mary brought her wandering gaze to Seth's eyes. "I believe he wanted to make sure she got home safely."

Seth shook his head. "No, Mary, you? Why did you follow her home?"

"Same reason."

Seth sat back and took a deep breath. What else did Mary do at night? Did she know the secrets of the entire town? He glanced down at the table, and his breath caught in his chest. His eyes shot up. "Mary?" he said, reticent, almost disappointed.

She looked back at Seth, biting her lip.

"Um. Did you leave the note for—"

"Yes."

Seth stared at her in bewilderment.

"Am I in trouble?" Mary asked, wincing.

Seth's mouth hung open, unsure how to respond. "Uh, you're certainly not in any legal trouble. I just don't—"

"It was so early in the morning. I didn't want to talk to some switchboard operator. I just wanted to let Bill know."

"Right…"

Mary looked down. "It's hard for me to talk to people. It always has been. Being here right now…"

Seth swallowed, feeling a swell of empathy for her. "It's okay."

Mary glanced up to see if he was serious or just saying that to get her to tell him more. "Are you sure?"

Seth grinned and tapped his pen on his pad. "I mean, I wish you would have called or come in, but you did let us know…in your own way, I suppose. And I can understand how scary it must have been to see a dead body."

"Oh, her body didn't scare me."

Seth raised his eyebrows.

"I fear people. I don't want their attention and questions and funny looks."

Seth nodded. "I understand," he said and set down his pen. "I really do. And I'm sorry for the way people treated you in school. There was no reason for it."

Mary's eyes welled up. "You stood up for me. More than once."

"I had a strong upbringing. My parents are both—"

Mary shook her head. "No. You. You're a good person. Just because you're brought up a…certain way doesn't mean you turn out well. Or make hard decisions that others…" Mary looked back down, not wanting Seth to see any tears.

Seth wished he was in a more appropriate setting to give her a hug. "Well, thank you for saying that, Mary. And thanks for coming to see me. I know that can't have been easy."

Mary nodded and casually tried to wipe the tears from her eyes.

"Look, if I showed you the crime scene photos we took that morning, would you be willing to look at them and tell me if you notice anything different from what you saw?"

Mary shrugged. "Sure."

Seth smiled. "That's great. Would you also be willing to come into the station to give me an official statement so we can—"

Mary looked up. "Will my name be on record?"

"Um, yeah, there's really no way around that."

Mary crossed her arms and considered. Just imagining all the other officers staring at her, wanting information, filled her with anxiety. "Can't you just come to my house to do it?"

Seth pursed his lips. He had never been asked this before and probably wouldn't have even considered it in San Francisco. But this was Lost Grove. And this was Mary Germaine. "Sure, yeah, that would be fine. I can do that."

Mary nodded. "Okay. I'm going to go now." She stood and looked at Seth. "Can I go?"

Seth held his arms out. "You came to me, Mary. And you didn't have to." He stood up and walked over to his door. "I am…I can't even tell you how thankful I am that you did. Seriously."

Mary joined Seth at the door. "Okay."

"I was certain Sarah Elizabeth had to have a boyfriend, but not a single person could corroborate it. Well, except for Story, whose intuition told her she did."

Mary giggled. "She's my friend."

Seth laughed as he opened the door, but then a swell of sadness came over him. How many more friends did Mary have, if any? "That's great," he said as he stepped back. "I'm sure she's a great friend. She's pretty—"

"She is," Mary said with a smirk.

"No, I was going to say she was—"

"Bye, Seth," Mary said as she stepped out the door. She turned back with one foot still on the top step. "It was nice to see you again."

"You too, Mary." Seth waved, shut the door, and collapsed back into it, his heart racing. What on earth had just happened? Two massive mysteries solved in fifteen minutes. The note, clearly not from the perpetrator, much less a serial killer, was now a huge thing off the board. And the boyfriend? A young janitor. Not a pastor, not Peter Andalusian, or anything salacious, putting aside the fact that she was likely underage when they started dating. Mary mentioned kissing and holding, nothing more. So was this Tommy Wilder really the father of the missing infant? And why was Seth leaning up against the door, contemplating instead of doing?

"Bill," he answered himself and leapt toward his jacket to grab his phone. He unlocked the screen, tapped on Bill's name, and waited for him to answer.

"Hey, Seth, what's the word?"

"Bill, we've got a huge breakthrough."

"I just saw you an hour ago. What happened?"

Seth paced as he relayed everything Mary had confessed to him.

"Jesus," Bill exclaimed.

"What do you know about this kid? Or young man, I should say."

"Not much more than what you said. He's the janitor at the high school and worked at the Market for a spell beforehand. Don't see him around town much nowadays."

"Obviously we need to add Tommy's name to our list of suspects, right at the top next to Peter Andalusian."

"No question. Guess we better go see Tommy first thing—"

"I'm going there now, Bill."

"Well, I was just about to sit down with Linda for a late dinner. Can we—"

"You can meet me later," Seth said as he put on his jacket. "I'm not waiting."

"Okay, I'll try to make it quick, then. Give Sasha a call at the station. She can pull up the address for you. I think he lives a few miles down the Wildcat, just past—"

"I already have it. Mary gave it to me." Seth grabbed his keys and opened the door.

"I see. Is there anything she doesn't know about this town?"

Seth shut and locked the door. "I would have to guess, no."

"My word," Bill sighed. "Call me if you wrap up before I get there."

"Will do." Seth hung up and raced down the stairs.

A Box of Secrets

The Bury farm sat on the eastern outskirts of town, past the cemetery, past the Willow Creek Trailhead of Devil's Cradle State Park, down a single-lane road barely big enough for the tractors and milk trucks that used it most. Noble steered onto the road, bumping along the potholes and dips in the decaying pavement, with Anya in the passenger seat.

"She's gonna be okay, right?" Noble asked.

Anya nodded. "She's gonna be okay. I just don't know what to say now. I said we'd figure out what to do, but what the hell is that gonna entail, you know?"

Noble had been considering that since the moment he dropped them off earlier. Was there a connection between Mary's not-children and the one Nettie thought was now living in her home as her brother? What would they do now that they had this information? Nettie said something about her parents calling a police officer about a man creeping around their house back when it happened. "Hey, what about the police officer from back then? What was he, or she, called around for exactly?"

Anya took in a breath. "Well, Nettie told me it was Chief Richards who was the one who came over. I think, for a moment, her parents considered that there was a man, a lurker or something, wandering around. I mean, Nettie kept talking about it and talking about it, so at least they had a moment of suspicion. But then Chief Richards came around and found nothing. Said they'd keep their eyes out for anyone they didn't know. We talked about that. Could we bring this information to him?"

"Uh…" Noble choked out.

Anya laughed. "I know. Go to him with what? This is what I mean," she said with a sigh.

"But does she feel better knowing this guy is real?" Noble asked, his face contorting in pain at the thought.

"I can't tell. I think so," Anya said. She turned to look out the window as they bumped down the road. "Hey, um, how much do you believe in the forbidden woods around here?"

"How much do I believe in them?" Noble couldn't fight off the sight of Mary, crouched down near the woods, blood coming from her mouth. She explained to him what happened, but that didn't null the horror of the image. "I guess I don't enjoy testing long-held traditions."

Her brow wrinkled. "What do you mean?"

"Stan's of the mind that if her people kept away, we should keep away," Noble explained. His other best friend, Constance, known to all her dearest friends as Stan, was from the local Indigenous tribe, and they believed people should not trifle with certain parts of the woods around Lost Grove and surrounding areas. They weren't haunted in the general sense of the word. To them, the woods contained monsters of folklore, strange beasts and creatures, and, yes, even a few ghosts. They didn't go into those parts of the woods without good cause. Mostly, they kept clear of them altogether.

"Oh, right, sure. She probably has an amazing story about them, huh?"

Noble tipped his head back and forth. "She does."

Anya nodded twice, thinking about what to say. "I should get her to tell me one day."

"Why did you ask about them?"

Anya's throat closed over words she *wanted* to say, and instead she came up with words that, for today, she *could* say. "It might be part of this whole thing, is all."

"How so? Is this it?" he asked, pointing to a large, white Victorian farmhouse.

"Yeah, that's it," Anya replied. "Well, he came from behind her house. The Green Man. Raymond," she explained.

"I'm confused," Noble said, pulling into the gravel driveway and up to the house.

"Nettie always said he came from behind her house. Behind her house is a part of the woods that everyone thinks is cursed."

Noble put the car in park. "She can't have meant he lived behind her house, can she?"

Anya shrugged, pulling her bag from the floor of the car.

Noble followed her out, heading for the back to grab her bike. He lifted the trunk door, pulled out the bike, and set it on the ground. His mind was reeling. All thoughts pointed toward Mary. She had to know more information that could help them, help Nettie. "I, uh…I might know someone who can help."

Anya squinted, brow wrinkling. "What? Who?"

"Uh, a person?" Noble offered with a smile.

Anya returned the smile and furrowed her brow deeper. "Okay," she said. She took a hold of the handlebars, her fingers brushing his. "You can't or won't tell me who?"

Noble bit on his lower lip.

"You don't have to," Anya said, pushing the bike toward the garage. Their old Pyrenees Shepherd mix came trotting out of the dark to greet them. "Hey, Bear," she said in greeting.

Noble followed. "It's just that…she's shy. Damn, that's a big dog."

Bear gave Noble a sniff and accepted the pats from both teens.

"So you'll go talk to her and see if she can help?" Anya asked. Bear followed them, bumping into Noble for more attention.

"I can, we can." He rubbed the dog's head as they walked.

"If you think she won't talk because of me—"

"No, she'd be fine with it. I don't want to scare her, is all."

Anya let her bike fall against the wall of the garage, wondering who Noble was referring to. She reached for the handle to pull the garage door down. Noble brushed past her to grab it himself, dropping it quietly to the ground. She caught the smell of his sweat from practice, like salt and sand. He had the most peculiar of smells. "What, in particular, do you think she can help with?"

Noble stared down into her blue-green eyes. "I think she knows a lot more about what Not-George is. Or what Nettie thinks he is."

Anya raised her eyebrows. "Okay. That sounds interesting and mysterious. You officially have my attention."

"We can talk to her tomorrow. After school."

Anya smiled and finally pulled her eyes away from his, heading toward her back door. "Sounds good."

Her back door opened. Her father, Ethan, pushed open the screen and looked out at them. Their cattle dog, Birdie, took off like a bolt across the driveway to jump around Bear like the playful pup she was. "Hey, kiddo," he greeted his daughter.

"Hey, Dad. You remember Noble." Anya pointed over her shoulder, mounting the steps into the home.

Noble jogged up the steps, extending his hand to the man who matched his height at six-foot-one but appeared to have thirty extra pounds of muscle on him. "Nice to see you," he said.

"You too. You're Peter's son?" Ethan shook the young man's hand.

"Yeah," Noble responded, wondering if Anya's father would say anything more, mention anything about the fight he got into on Saturday with his daughter present.

Ethan gave him a nod and a fatherly squeeze on the shoulder as he headed down the stairs. He felt bad for the kid and had an urge to console him, to tell him not to listen to what people said, especially drunks like Jeffrey Tacet. But then he thought he'd try to play it cool and not mention the complete debacle of this past Saturday. "Your mom needs some help feeding those kittens if you wouldn't mind," he said to his daughter and left them alone on the steps, heading out to the shop.

"We don't know where the mother cat ran off to, so now we have thirteen kittens we have to feed around the clock." Anya shuffled her bag higher up her shoulder.

"That's fun," Noble commented. His mother and Anya's mother would get along well.

"It can be. They're incredibly cute. You can come see them if you want."

Noble shook his head. "I have to pick Zoe up from ballet."

"Right," Anya nodded.

"So, see you tomorrow?" Noble asked, backing down the steps.

"Yep! See ya tomorrow." Anya smiled, watching him head back to his car.

Noble smiled and waved as he left, turning back onto the road and heading into town to pick up his sister. The idea of sitting in his house, imagining all the scenarios that could place his dad on that beach last Thursday morning, writing a note on purple paper, and leaving it on the chief of police's doorstep made his stomach clench with anxiety.

Noble showered and finished some homework after bringing Zoe home from ballet. To keep his mind away from the damning thoughts of his father, he switched over to a fresh search page on his computer and typed in "reporting a missing child." The results were all the same—hotlines, tip lines, helplines—but nothing that he could really use. What about child services? What was there to report? That the "real" George was actually still missing and that the "thing" called George living in the Horne home was a not-child? Yeah, that would go over well.

He sighed as he grabbed his phone. He needed some help, and the only person he knew with the creepy knowledge he was looking for was going to ask more questions than he could answer. Noble would deal with the repercussions later.

"Good sir," Nate answered on the fourth ring.

"Hey," Noble replied, setting his phone on speaker and placing it on his desk.

"Oh, okay. What's up?" Nate immediately picked up the tone from his friend and dropped their usual witty faux-British banter.

"This is weird, and I can't give you all the details, but do you know anything about missing kids?" Noble laid out the question.

On the other end of the phone, Nate hit speaker and tossed his phone onto his bed. "Missing kids, like…what? In what regard?"

"Here in Lost Grove," Noble interrupted.

Nate blew a raspberry. "Shit, yeah. You don't remember? That summer was bullshit."

Noble briefly recalled what he was talking about, memory jogged.

"Everything we did, you had Zoe with you. Unless she was with your mom up at the ranch," Nate continued, his voice slightly muffled.

"Yeah, I remember. Okay, give me the specifics."

Nate grabbed the phone, bringing it with him as he set off for the kitchen. "Four years ago. Lucas Rotunda. Taken from his bedroom in the middle of the night."

Noble's skin crawled. Nettie said the Green Man came out at night and was trying to steal her brother.

"How old was he?" Noble asked.

"He was four," Nate continued. "His dad went to wake him in the morning and found an empty bed. He thought the kid had already gotten up, was hiding or playing or some shit. So, after checking all the usual places, he starts to panic, wakes the wife, and says he can't find Lucas. They search the house, and she notices the window isn't fully closed. They rush outside, check the yard, the playhouse. No Lucas."

"They called the police?"

"Next thing they did," Nate said. He opened his fridge, pulled out some juice, and poured it into a glass, slowly and carefully, in case Cheshire was near. "Search party goes out. They alert the whole town to keep an eye out for Lucas. Police ask if there are any enemies, anyone who'd want to hurt Lucas. Nothing turns up."

"Enemies? He was four."

Nate sighed. "Not Lucas, you idiot, his parents."

"Oh, right. Did they?"

Nate shook his head. Not that Noble could see it. "Not that they admitted. But who knows?"

"Where did they live?" Noble asked, wondering if the kid could have wandered into the woods and gotten lost, or worse, if they lived near the cursed woods Anya was just asking about.

"Um," Nate said, taking down a few gulps of juice. "5th Street."

"5th?"

"Yeah, in town," Nate explained. He downed the rest of his juice.

Noble pondered the connection, if there was one. "They never found him?"

"Not yet. Doubt they will at this point."

"Did they have any suspects?" Noble asked.

Nate thought over the facts of the case that were available to the public or had become local chatter. "Nah, they had no one. Nothing. It was like he was sucked up into a spaceship."

"Huh." Noble's brow wrinkled in thought.

"Maybe you could ask Clemency. She's all into ghosts and aliens and shit."

Noble chuckled, thinking about the eccentric barista and co-owner of the Main Street Cafe.

"Okay, and now, this is where you tell me why you're asking about this," Nate demanded.

Noble's brow loosened, his lips twisted into a smile. "I can't."

"Bullshit," Nate argued.

"I can't, bro."

Nate snorted. "Let me deduce…"

"Oh, Christ." Noble sagged into the back of his desk chair.

"You've been spending a lot of time with Anya. Not to say I blame you, but she isn't typically in your close-friend group. So, clearly, there's something brewing there. Then, today, you said you had to talk to Anya, but I noticed Nettie was a part of that conversation as well. Oh yeah, if you thought I didn't see, you're gravely mistaken, my friend."

"I'd expect nothing less," Noble mocked.

"Missing kids? Well, he's not missing, but his crazy older sister thinks he is. You're talking about George Horne, and I kind of want to know why. Because that answer eludes me." Nate flopped onto his living room couch.

"I can't tell you."

"Come on. I won't say anything," Nate said.

"I promised I wouldn't. I can ask and see if it's okay for you to know—"

"But it is something to do with Nettie and her brother."

Noble said nothing.

"It is," Nate said with confidence. "You should ask. Because if you're trying to solve something and leaving *me* out of it? Huge mistake. I know how these things work. I'm your best asset! Which is obviously why you called me."

Noble laughed. "Yeah, okay. I'll ask." He clicked on the pop-up of texts from Anya to find a series of photos of the kittens.

Nate swung his feet off the couch and sat up, resting his elbows on his knees. "But seriously. I could help. I know a lot about this kind of thing."

"I know," Noble exaggerated.

"I'll start doing some preliminary research. Get the ball rolling."

Knuckles wrapped on Noble's door.

"Honey, you busy?" his mother, Jolie, asked from beyond the door.

"No," he responded, turning his chair.

"Hi, Mrs. Andalusian!" Nate called over the line.

"Hi, Nate," Jolie replied.

"Okay, I've got to go," Noble said.

"Yep, see ya," Nate replied and ended the call.

Jolie busied herself with folding some of her son's clothes that were draped over the door handle. "Zo and I are going to town. We need a syringe with a bigger opening for Merryweather."

"Merryweather?"

"Pretty sure it's a female, the owl."

"Ah, and Zo named her Merryweather."

Jolie smiled. "And I should pick up some meat to grind up for her. Probably need some mice, too. We'll get that tomorrow, I suppose."

Noble grimaced.

"I'm gonna pick up pizza. Want the usual toppings?" Jolie asked, moving close to her son and kissing him atop his head.

"Sounds good."

She smiled down at him. "Okay."

"Okay." He swiveled back toward his desk with a million thoughts.

He sat at the desk, listening to his mother and sister chatter, keys being gathered, coats going on, the door closing. He still sat there as the car started and listened to it pull away until he could no longer hear the engine. And still, he sat. Noble pulled up the text conversation with his father, the last text from his dad asking him how the fight on Saturday started.

Dad: Your mom wants me to talk to you about it, so let's hear it. What happened?

Noble had responded: Some drunks came out of the bar, said some creepy shit to my friend, coming on to her, and had a few things to say about you as well. So I hit him.

There had been no reply since.

Like a spastic reflex, he jolted from his chair and headed to his sister's room. Neither of them told the other to stay out of their stuff, but he was still confident she'd be heartbroken if she found him snooping through her things instead of simply asking. The only problem there was he didn't want to have to explain his suspicions. Not to her, never to her.

His sister's room was filled with knickknacks, books, patchwork quilts, lace, and plants. The desk was a maelstrom of papers and notebooks, none full. He flipped through them quickly because he would never want to stumble across her personal thoughts. He opened her refurbished school desk from the early twentieth century, and his heart jammed into his throat. One notebook had pale purple paper. It was lined paper. *Had the cops mentioned if the paper was lined? What color purple had they said? Lilac? Lavender?*

Noble tore out one sheet as neatly as possible and folded it, jamming it into his pocket. A feeling akin to anger bubbled inside. He left his sister's room and headed for their parents' bedroom. Pausing in the doorway, he considered what he was about to do but pressed on. His father's dresser stood beside the window on his side of the bed. It was tall and thin, nothing remarkable. The first drawer held socks and boxers. Noble looked through them and felt along the back of the drawer for any hidden compartments or loose pieces.

He proceeded through the whole dresser, feeling like a burglar, then moved to the jewelry box on top. It was polished cherry and contained a few pieces of jewelry—a watch that no longer worked, a couple of rings Peter used to wear when Noble was younger. There was a gold chain necklace, nothing complex or fancy. Underneath the top compartment was a locket on top of a small envelope. Noble hesitated and then pulled out the locket, opening the latch. Inside was an old picture of a man in uniform, possibly from World War I, but Noble wasn't knowledgeable on historical army attire. He knew his grandpa had served, as had his father, but this seemed even older than that. Still, it could have been a family heirloom that his dad held on to, to give to Zoe someday. Before placing the locket back, Noble grabbed the manila envelope. He pressed the edges together and noticed the distinguishable green of money. He carefully pulled it out and unfolded it to find seven hundred-dollar bills. That wasn't precisely suspect, but it was strange. Why would he have a secret stash of money, of any amount? Putting everything back as it was, he moved to the closet.

Noble and his dad were the same height, so if there was anything he might want to keep from his daughter or his wife, he'd stash it high. On a shelf above the hanging clothes, he moved aside old comforters, sweaters, and two shoeboxes filled with formal shoes he'd never seen his mother or father wear. There was nothing.

As one last effort, Noble swiped his hand behind the top of the closet door, a ledge the width of a book, and felt his fingertips brush against the corner of a box, hearing the subtle shift of it on wood. He rose on his tiptoes and extended his arm up just high enough to grab it and pull it down. It was cheap wood, easily breakable, with an equally cheap gold-colored clasp. With a flick of his thumb, the lid flipped open. Noble fumbled the box, awkwardly dropping it on the bed.

"Fuck," he whispered.

Inside was a liquid-black handgun, an equally shiny magazine of bullets, an old cell phone, and a roll of more cash. Noble looked toward the bedroom door, swiping a hand under his nose. He almost expected his dad to be standing there, a look of disappointment on his face. What the fuck had he just stumbled upon? He closed his eyes, beyond morally conflicted at this point.

"Just fucking look at what else is in there," he encouraged himself.

Noble looked back and dared to place the gun on the bed and picked up the thick roll of money. Temptation urged him to unroll it, but he didn't know if he could get it back into such a pristine, tight roll again. He surmised if it was all hundred-dollar bills, it could be close to a couple grand he was holding. He placed the money back and picked up the flip phone. The battery and chip, uninstalled, sat in the box. Noble put it all together, fumbling with shaking hands, and turned it on. There were no saved numbers, and the call log was empty. He didn't know where to go to see if there was a way to recover those things, not on a phone this old. He dismantled it and pulled out yet another envelope before putting it back. It contained pages from a book and a handwritten letter. It was a usual letter about the kids, the weather, and a broken car Peter was trying to fix. Noble couldn't recall his dad ever fixing up a Trans-Am. After looking at it twice, he realized his father had addressed the letter to Paddy, his local drunk friend. Why write a letter and not send it? Why was there no address on the envelope, just "Paddy"?

The last thing in the box was a business card. The edges folded and torn. There was a smudge of dirt on one side. If there had been any information on it at one time, it had worn off with age. A handwritten number in a blue ballpoint pen was on the other side.

Noble felt like he couldn't breathe, couldn't move, couldn't think. He clenched his eyes shut and concentrated, taking breaths like he would for long-distance training. Between Mary, Nettie, Raymond LaRange, the not-kids, and now this, Noble thought he was going to be the first kid to have a heart attack before the age of twenty. And if he wasn't the first, he was certainly the next.

"Agh," Noble grunted as his finger snapped on the edge of the card. His phone was out of his pocket and in his hand before he could think. He pressed the numbers and almost hit the call button.

"No, wait." Noble tossed his phone aside and put the flip phone back together. Again, he typed in the numbers. His thumb hovered over the call button until, finally, beads of sweat now covering his forehead, he pressed it.

There was silence and then ringing. It rang to the point Noble was going to hang up, but just as he was pulling it away from his ear, he heard the click. Then a breath. A voice came across the line, "What the hell are you playing at? You left h—"

Noble hung up and took that phone apart so quickly he thought he must have broken a world record.

"Fuck! Fuck, fuck, fuck," he released. "What the fuck?"

Noble felt like he was in the middle of a Jason Bourne film. Guns, money, secret phones, strange letters. Someone answered the goddamn call. What the hell was going on? Someone had this number programmed into their phone. Someone expecting a call from his father.

Tommy Wilder, Janitor and Boyfriend

Seth slowed his Bronco to a crawl, peering through the dusty windshield to read the street sign partially obscured by a sagging branch from an overhanging tree: Taylor Lane. He veered right, into the small trailer park a mile and a half from the main stretch of town. He'd driven past the road several times but hadn't needed to check on any of the residents until now. His tires crunched against the gravel as he pulled onto a large dirt patch at a safe distance from the first trailer and turned off the engine. His mind had been racing through a dizzying amount of potential scenarios on the short ride over, preparing himself for whatever he was about to face. Seth's priority was to find out if Tommy Wilder was even home. It had only been two days since news about Sarah's death became public. If Tommy had anything to do with it, he may have fled.

Seth pulled his police-issued firearm from his holster and checked the cartridge and the safety. Though he was required to carry the weapon, there had yet to be an occasion for him to even consider placing his hand on it since returning to Lost Grove. In San Francisco, his hand was always ready. Tommy Wilder was a legitimate suspect and potentially the father of the missing child, so Seth would treat the young man as potentially dangerous. On the other hand, the chances of a high school janitor knowing how to perform a symphysiotomy or a pubiotomy, the horrific medieval operations performed on Sarah Elizabeth in a believed attempt to save the child, were slim to none. He placed the gun back in his holster, hoping this wasn't going to be the first time he was given cause to reach for it.

The moonlight cast deep shadows across the lot, revealing six trailers scattered around him. Three homes had lights outside their doors, illuminating a faint layout for him to follow. He grabbed his flashlight and moved toward the first trailer, directing its beam onto the address plate beside the door—2164. Looking for 2178, he moved on. At the next set of trailers, Seth spotted a faint glow from a fire to his right. He kept the beam from his flashlight trained on the ground as he approached.

A man with grey hair who looked like he belonged on a public access fishing program was sitting in a teak chair in front of a small fire in a brick pit, holding a bottle of beer. The trailer behind him looked as if it had just been placed on the lot. With a small wood porch and a fresh coat of paint, it seemed that this man took care of it. He looked up at Seth, not remotely startled by his presence.

"This the Wilder residence?" Seth asked.

The man shook his head and jutted his thumb over his right shoulder. "Last house on the left," he said in a dark, affected tone and snickered.

"Thanks." Seth was familiar with the movie, the snicker not lost on him. He turned and saw a woman peering out a window in the trailer on the other side of the road. He gave a friendly wave, and the curtains closed.

Seth strode along the sidewalk, his pace quickening as he passed two more homes before coming to a halt in front of the last unit on the left. The front light was off, and the wood stairs leading up to the front door were covered in a film of lichen and rot. Soft orange light spilled out the windows, lightly diffused by faded JC Penny catalog gingham-and-lace curtains circa 1991. Having called Officer Sasha Kingsley on his way over, he learned Tommy lived with his younger brother and mother, who clearly hadn't bothered to update her interior decor.

Seth clicked off his flashlight and approached the door. His stomach churned with anticipation. He knocked on the metal screen door, the number 2178 marked to its right side.

Seth heard a woman's loud voice before the front door opened and the front light switched on. A tall figure stood in the doorway. With his body backlit, Seth was unable to make out a face but could tell he wasn't holding onto a weapon of any kind. He quickly clicked on his flashlight and pointed it at the person's face. A young man with dark curly hair raised a hand in front of his eyes.

"Who is it, Tommy?" a shrill voice bellowed from inside.

"Chill, Mom!" Tommy yelled back and then opened the screen door to step out. "Hey, can I help you?"

Seth dropped the light to the ground. "Tommy Wilder?"

Tommy dropped his hand to his side and raised his eyebrows, still partially squinting from the effect of the light. "Yeah."

"I'm Sergeant Seth Wolfe with the Lost Grove Police Department. I need to ask you some questions."

Tommy swallowed. "Okay," he said with some hesitation.

"Who is it, Tommy?" a young boy asked as he hopped up to the screen door. "Is that the—"

"A friend." Tommy stopped him. "Can you grab my jacket, Clint?"

The young boy nodded and jaunted off.

Tommy looked at Seth. "Sorry, do you mind if we step away from here to talk?"

Seth shook his head. "Not at all." His first impressions were that the young man posed no immediate threat, unless *jacket* was a code word for *gun*.

Clint reappeared and opened the screen door to hand Tommy a red-and-black corduroy jacket. "Here it is."

Tommy grabbed it and jostled the boy's hair. "Thanks, kiddo. Get back inside and close the door. It's cold out."

"Okay."

"Who the hell is it?" the woman's voice echoed from inside.

Clint closed the door as he said, "A friend of Tommy's."

"Little brother?" Seth asked as he backed away from the abode, heading back toward the trailer camp entrance. He kept his eyes on Tommy's hands, keenly aware there were many places he could be concealing a weapon. The young man had put on his jacket and now shoved his hands in the pockets of his pants to keep them warm.

Tommy stepped in line with Seth. "Yeah, Clint's nine. The pleasant voice from inside is our mom. Just the three of us."

Seth nodded, smiling in a polite, police officer fashion. "No father in the picture?"

"Nope. Clint's dad bailed before he was even born. At least mine stuck around for a couple years before leaving."

"Know where he's at?"

"Think my dad's still in Sarasota, Florida. Haven't talked to him for a couple years."

"Sorry to hear that."

"Yeah," Tommy sighed.

"We can just talk up here," Seth said, pointing to his Bronco. They walked in silence past the trailers until they arrived at his vehicle. Seth turned to face Tommy and leaned back against the front fender, wondering if he would leave here alone or with the boy. "Do you know why I'm here?"

Standing still in front of Seth, Tommy glanced down toward the ground and shrugged.

Seth felt mild relief. The boy's body language was as good as an outright admission that he knew why he was there. "Were you dating Sarah Elizabeth?"

Tommy slowly nodded. He looked up, his eyes glistening. "Yeah."

"When did that start?"

Tommy wiped a tear from his eye with the back of his hand and sniffled. "Start of her senior year."

"Is that when you started working at the high school?"

"No. I had been working there for two years beforehand."

Seth would typically jot down notes but wanted to maintain the friendly intimacy of the conversation. "So, pretty quickly after you graduated."

"About six months or so after. I worked at the Valley Market throughout high school. I had always planned on going to college. But"—Tommy nodded over his shoulder—"I couldn't leave Clint here alone. So…"

Seth felt a pang in his heart for the boy but kept it in check. He'd had years of feeling that same pang, hearing all the terrible stories of suspects or victims throughout his years at the SFPD, and he knew how to temper it, knew how you'd only survive so long on the job if you couldn't learn to let that feeling go. "That's admirable of you to put that off."

"Didn't really have any choice. Our mom doesn't work that much. When she gets her shit together and cuts out the drinking, she'll get a job at a fast-food joint in Eureka, but it never lasts very long."

"So, how did you and Sarah start dating?" Seth asked, getting back on track.

Tommy took a deep breath through his nose, staring into the past. He grabbed the bridge of his nose and dropped his head, sniffling.

Seth was withholding judgment on whether the boy was crying from loss or guilt. *Could be both,* he reminded himself.

"I just can't believe she's dead," Tommy whimpered.

"I am sorry, Tommy. But I need your help here. We still have a lot of missing pieces, and I think you may have some of them."

Tommy nodded and wiped the tears from his cheeks with both his palms. "Sorry. I just…I haven't seen her for so long, and I…I always hoped she'd come back."

Seth watched every muscle move in the boy's face and studied the tenor in his voice to gauge how much Tommy actually knew.

Tommy looked up and let out a heavy sigh. "Sorry, what was the question?"

"I asked how the two of you met and started dating."

Tommy nodded. "Right. Um, I guess I met her the same as a lot of the other students there, just nodding or saying hi in the halls. There aren't that many students, so you get to know them all pretty quick."

"Still about 150, I would guess?" Seth asked.

Tommy's eyes narrowed. "Yeah, last year's class was 162, I think. Did you…"

"Class of '99."

"Oh…I guess you made it out of here, then."

Seth nodded. He'd made it out for a while. Now he was back, and he wasn't sure for how long. "Back to you and Sarah."

"Yeah. Um, she was just a nice girl. Like, not just cordial and saying hi. She actually talked to me, asked how I was doing, how my weekend was, things like that. And we just eventually became friends."

"And how did things progress from there?"

Tommy shrugged. "I guess it was after school let out. She would stick around and study a lot. And it was when no one else was really around that we started getting to know each other more. And…" Tommy paused, smiling. "I was washing down the chalkboard in Mr. Landry's room one day, and I caught her out of the corner of my eye, standing just inside the doorway. Kind of startled me. She had her backpack on. I figured she was just saying bye, but she walked up to me and said, 'I like you, Tommy.'" Tears welled up again.

Seth felt a rush of nostalgia, that innocent excitement of first love. He recalled how Jaime Goodacre had come up to him after one of his baseball games to tell him how talented she thought he was and that he looked good in his uniform, sending his heart racing.

"And I said, 'I like you, too,' thinking she just meant it like friends," Tommy said. "But she shook her head and grabbed my hand and said,

'No, I like you, Tommy.' I thought I was going to have a heart attack." He recalled it fondly until the end, when he was reminded she was gone. Then he broke down, turning away for a moment to regain his composure.

"So, why did you keep your relationship secret?" Seth asked once Tommy seemed to have collected himself.

Tommy raised his eyebrows. "Have you met her parents?"

Seth nodded. "I have, and I can understand that. But it wasn't because she was technically underage?"

Tommy sneered. "What? No, that wasn't even a thing. We kissed once before she turned eighteen in November. And even then, nothing ever happened that would have been…you know."

"Okay. I'm not judging. I was eighteen when my girlfriend was seventeen our senior year. I'm just trying to understand why and how no one knew about the two of you. Not even her best friends."

"Like I said, she definitely didn't want her parents to know, and if one person knew, even Brigette or Jeremy, there was always a chance something could slip. Then the whole damn town would know. You must remember what it's like here."

Seth sighed. "I do. And I've been reminded of it ever since I came back."

"And that wasn't the only thing she kept from her parents," Tommy tossed out.

Seth stood up and decided it was time to take out his notepad and pen. "Do you mind?" Seth asked, holding them out.

"I don't give a fuck what they find out. And I sure don't care what they think."

Seth held in his surprise at the first bit of vitriol the boy displayed. "Okay, good."

Tommy's sneer quickly faded into a smile. "Once she turned eighteen, Sarah went in for treatment at the Orbriallis Institute."

Seth's pen almost fell from his hand. He glanced up at Tommy. "What for?"

"She had terrible insomnia. She said she always had, as long as she could remember. She wanted to get better. It had been getting worse during her senior year. It was really affecting her."

Sarah's insomnia aligned with everything they had already found out. He wondered if Tommy knew about her visions. "And why didn't she want her parents to know about that?"

"Oh, they knew about her insomnia. Her vivid dreams. Her…

visions," Tommy hesitantly said.

Seth nodded. *Well, that answers that question.* "Okay…"

"She wasn't crazy," Tommy defended her.

Seth held up his hands. "I don't think that at all. I'm just trying to understand why she sought treatment in secret if her parents knew about her condition."

Tommy shook his head. "Because they made everything about themselves. They pressured her constantly about her grades, her studying. And then when she got straight As, Sarah said they would celebrate like they were the ones who did it, like their parenting was the reason she was so smart. It wasn't. Sarah loved studying. She loved learning about new things. She didn't need them pushing her. And when Sarah first told her parents about one of her visions, they freaked. She was young, but she knew she couldn't share them again. And it's not like you think. I'm not sure if she would be half-asleep or what. It didn't matter. I believed she saw things."

"Like what?" Seth jumped in.

Tommy stared at Seth, wondering how much he should say. "She saw people, or places, that she didn't know, but she had this understanding that she would know them, at some point. It was always at night when Sarah was lying in bed, unable to sleep. She said she had the sensation that she knew the people in the visions intimately, but often she didn't recognize them. If she had the chance to explain it to you, I'm sure it would make more sense."

"Okay, is there anything more specific you can recall?" Seth asked, highly intrigued by where this might go.

Tommy pursed his lips. "Look, she told me this stuff in confidence. And even though… Can you just not write this stuff down or put it in any report?"

Seth closed his notepad and dropped his hands. "Of course. I can't imagine the details about her visions are pertinent to my case," he said, not fully believing it.

"So, like I said, Sarah had visions of people or places come into her mind so clearly that she said she felt like she was there. Like, a dream, but not actually in a dream. She felt it. Like, have you heard about the boy, Gino, she found at Devil's Cradle?"

"Yes, briefly," Seth answered.

"Okay, so that one was weird. I'm messing this all up, but she typically had the visions while sleeping or trying to sleep. But this one came over her all of a sudden, in the middle of the day, while they were looking for him. She was in the bathroom, washing up before heading back out to keep searching, when she got it. What she told me was she didn't just see what he was seeing, through Gino's eyes, she felt it—the way the breeze suddenly picked up, the smell of pine sap. She could feel the fear, the cold trail of tears running down his cheeks as if they were her cheeks, and then she saw a ranger—his name was Paul Bowditch—approaching Gino and the look of shock on Paul's face when he saw the kid running toward him. She felt the way his legs moved, the way his heart kicked in his chest, and the way he began sobbing when he saw the ranger and knew he was safe. Most importantly, she recognized where Gino was."

Seth felt cold sweat percolate on his forehead. The connections between him and Sarah Elizabeth, which had been endlessly swirling in the back of his mind, felt like they were crashing down on top of him. The sensations Tommy described her having were identical to the ones Seth had when he time-traveled to her death scene over twenty years before he walked it again in reality. He gripped his notepad and pen tightly.

"When she left the bathroom, the only ranger there was Paul Bowditch. She told him that she knew where Gino was. And when they got there, she watched the same scene play out. The point is, they weren't just fleeting images. She felt what they felt, saw what they saw. Sometimes, she was an outsider too, watching them. Seeing a scene play out before her like she was a ghost, a fly on the wall who couldn't stop what she was seeing even if she really wanted to. There were a couple that really got to her. One was a recurring vision she had of this man. Sarah said it felt like she knew him from when he was younger or something like that. She felt empathy for him, like she could understand him, or maybe it was more like they had something in common. But the visions themselves scared her. She always felt empty and cold when she saw him. And when she, I don't know…like, snapped out of it, she would be freezing cold, even covered in blankets."

Seth suddenly felt dizzy, a complete lack of control of his body. Then he felt his lower back hit the fender of his truck.

"Hey, man, are you okay?"

Realizing his vision had clouded, Seth blinked multiple times and saw Tommy standing closer. Was the boy holding him? Seth looked down to see Tommy's hand on the side of his arm. He shook his head. "Yes, sorry. I just…I haven't got much sleep since we found…"

"I haven't either." Tommy took a step back, rubbed his hands together, and then blew into them. "Anyhow, the other one, the first one she said she really connected with, was of this girl about her age. I think this was when Sarah was about twelve or thirteen. At first, she thought she was seeing herself. It was like she couldn't tell the things that made them different. But then the girl spoke in a voice that wasn't hers, and that's when she knew it was someone else, someone she, again, thought she knew. The girl just said, 'I'm sorry,' and that was it. But something about it traumatized her. She wouldn't really tell me fully about that one. It scared her too much."

Seth focused on his feet touching solid ground, consciously locking his knees so they wouldn't buckle. If Sarah's experiences were any indication of what he could expect, his own vision, his own experience of time travel, would likely not be the last.

"And the one she first told her parents had something to do with a man telling her stuff about a baby. They tried to tell her it was an angel or a servant from God speaking to her. Sarah had crazy faith, but she swore that wasn't the deal. But her parents insisted it was a message from God. After that, they kept pestering her, asking if she had any more visions involving a child."

"A child?" Seth barely found the words to mutter.

"Yeah, they went on and on about it. They were obsessed. That's when Sarah stopped telling them about any of her visions. Just so they would back off. And that's why she didn't tell them about going to Orbriallis. She didn't want them to start pestering her again."

Seth found enough self-control to bring his notepad back up and jot down notes of what he was being told, even though his insides were trembling. He looked up and locked eyes with the boy. "So, how long did the two of you date? Throughout her time in college?"

Tommy slowly shook his head. "No, man, I haven't seen or talked to her since that first winter break she came back home from Baylor."

Seth held his gaze. The boy was telling the truth. It was a mad irony that Tommy knew Sarah Elizabeth was seeking her own treatment at the Orbriallis yet didn't know that her parents brought her there less than a year later. She had been so close to him this entire time. He was certain Tommy's heart would shatter when he found out. "What was she like during that time?"

Tommy sighed and looked down at the ground. "She was really disconnected. From me, I mean. I don't know, maybe everybody. But things were just different. She was really fidgety and seemed nervous. I kept begging her to talk to me, but she was closed up. She was never like that before. She would tell me everything. That's how we were so connected. It was never anything sexual. I mean, it hadn't gotten there yet, but that didn't matter. We were in love. Or I thought we were."

Seth would be sure to come back and check on Tommy Wilder. He sensed that depression could kick in hard after the shock wore off, and that level of darkness could spur some bad choices. Maybe that was what Tommy's mother was doing, seeking a cure for her depression or all the wrongs that had happened in her life. Tommy seemed like a kid who deserved more, though Seth once again shut those thoughts off. He was finding it harder to do here in Lost Grove, knowing he'd see these people around town. "So, what happened? Did she break things off?"

Tommy shook his head, still looking down. "No. It wasn't anything like that. I mean, she said she loved me. We kissed and held each other, but she was just distant. You know, before she went off to college, and even in the early months of her being there, she always said she was going to become a doctor and that she was going to come back and get me and Clint out of here. I never knew why she wanted to be with a guy like me, but I believe she meant it."

"Hey," Seth tersely said, "look at me."

Tommy looked up sheepishly.

"I can't imagine a reason why she wouldn't want to be with a guy who sacrificed his own life and his own future to stick around and care for his younger brother. It's the same reason I'm back here now, to take care of my father. She clearly trusted you. And from what I've gathered, Sarah seemed awfully particular about who she let get close to her."

Tommy swallowed hard and nodded. "Thanks."

Seth tapped his notepad against his leg, internally battling whether or not to tell Tommy that Sarah was pregnant and there might be a child out there still alive. The boy said things hadn't become sexual, and Seth believed him, as much as he could until they found the child and could run a DNA test. Still, he was here, and Tommy had been nothing if not forthcoming.

"What?" Tommy asked.

"I'm just curious. I'm trying to understand everything I can about who Sarah was, how she behaved, and what led to her death. You mentioned things hadn't progressed to being sexual between the two of you. I know she was quite religious, but you were clearly in love with one another. Was it just a religious decision or…"

Tommy took in a heavy breath. "To be honest, I think it was more me than her."

Seth furrowed his brow. "Meaning?"

"It's not that the urges weren't there, believe me. We talked about it. She told me she had never had a boyfriend before. She had once kissed a boy at a birthday party, but it was more of a dare. I had a pretty serious girlfriend for a couple years in high school. Sarah didn't care that I wasn't a virgin. I really believe that. But I cared. I didn't want her to regret doing anything too soon. I told her I wanted to wait until she was one hundred percent."

"And she wasn't?" Seth asked, fiercely debating if and how he should tell Tommy about the pregnancy. It would be public knowledge by tomorrow or Wednesday at the latest.

Tommy was slowly nodding. "She was. And I was. I guess I just wanted to be strong or something, to show her how much I respected that decision. I don't know."

"That's a commendable decision, Tommy."

Tommy tilted his head back. "I guess. I still wanted to. We both did."

Seth closed his eyes and silently sighed before opening them back up. *Fuck!* He wanted to be there for the boy when he found out, but the fact remained, the baby was not public knowledge yet. He couldn't risk it. Seth would talk to Bill about the timing of the press announcement and see if he could meet Tommy just beforehand.

"Look, I think I've got all I need for now," Seth said. "Would you be willing to come to the station tomorrow to give a formal statement?"

"Of course. I'll do anything I can to help. I want to help."

"I assume you have a cell phone?"

Tommy huffed. "Yeah."

Seth opened his notepad and clicked on his pen. "Could you–"

"Sure," Tommy said and told him his phone number.

Seth pocketed his notepad and pen and then extended his hand. "Thank you. I'll call you with a time, but make yourself available all day."

"I already called in sick today and wasn't planning on going back to work tomorrow."

Tommy shook Seth's hand. He gave a final nod, turned, and headed back to his trailer.

Seth sank into the cracked leather seat of his Bronco and drew in a long, shuddering breath. The dashboard light cast an eerie green glow inside the cab. He ran his trembling hands through his hair and gripped the steering wheel tight to steady them as he attempted to process the information he'd just acquired. He thought about Sarah Elizabeth, her disappearance, her death, and the strange twist of fate that seemed to link them. He thought about the Orbriallis Institute, and looking into his rearview mirror, he could just see the spire tower of that esteemed institute towering over the redwoods. Shadows passed over the moon, and the tower appeared to fade into the forest. His stomach twisted into a knot of dread as he reached for his keys and turned the ignition.

Inside the Walls

Seth parked his dusty Bronco in front of the imposing Orbriallis Institute, a mix of old and new architecture that loomed over the small, rural town of Lost Grove. The original High Victorian Gothic hospital, fortified with the addition of a steel-and-glass tower built in 1984, was a light-reflecting beacon amid the dark boughs of cedars and pines. It was a monolithic presence, as out of place as a log cabin in the middle of Manhattan. As a child growing up in Lost Grove, Seth had never questioned the strange disparity between the town's quaint surroundings and the massive medical facility. To him and his friends, it was simply where some of the best doctors and scientists from around the world came to work. But as an adult, he couldn't help but wonder why such a prestigious institution would choose to be located in such a remote area. How many employees actually lived in Lost Grove or nearby Eureka? And why not set up shop in a bustling city like San Francisco or Seattle instead? These thoughts swirled in Seth's mind as he stepped out of the Bronco and gazed up at the daunting building before him.

He tabled the questions, slammed the door, and made his way through the parking lot toward the entrance. As he approached, he noticed an underground parking structure, but it was reserved for employees only. Seth pushed open one of the four tall glass doors and entered a grand foyer that seemed more fitting for a city hall than a remote research facility. The marble floors gleamed beneath his feet as he looked up to see skylights and discreet lighting fixtures illuminating the thirty-foot ceiling. To his right, there was a plush sitting area reminiscent of an Art

Deco lounge. On his left, a large cafeteria with a geometric dome ceiling and tinted blue glass gave off a futuristic aura.

Seth shook his head to clear his awe and confidently approached the reception desk, which also acted as security.

"Hello, Officer, what can I help you with?" asked the young man behind the counter with slick, dark hair.

Seth glanced at his name tag. "Yes, Taylor, I'm Sergeant Seth Wolfe with the Lost Grove Police Department. I'm here to see Dr. Jane Bajorek. I left a message last night and again early this morning."

"Okay, thank you. Let me look into this," Taylor said as he typed away on his keyboard.

Seth glanced over at the security guard sitting to the left of Taylor, a burly, redheaded man with a thick mustache.

The man, sensing Seth's eyes upon him, looked up from his monitor. "Hey, fella, how ya doin'?"

It was about the thickest Irish accent Seth had ever heard. He smiled and nodded, noticing the man's name tag read "Seamus." Seth wondered how this man arrived at the Orbriallis. He seemed as out of place as the building itself.

"Did anyone return your call, Sergeant?" Taylor asked. "I'm not seeing anything on the books."

Seth shook his head. "I'm afraid not."

"Ah, I see. Well, I can schedule something—"

"I'm not here as a patient or a prospective client, Taylor," Seth cut him off. "I'm investigating the criminal death of one of Dr. Bajorek's patients."

Taylor brought a hand to his chest. "Oh, my. Nothing that happened here, is it?"

"I can't divulge details of the case, but it's urgent that I speak with her now."

"Let me see what I can do," Taylor said, picking up the phone and dialing a number.

Seth looked back over at Seamus, feeling the man's eyes burrowing into his skull. The guard had turned in his chair to face him and was looking at Seth with an unflinching glare. "Murder then, is it?"

Seth couldn't help but notice the size of the guard's fist and forearm resting on the desk and prayed he never had to break up a brawl with him like the one between the drunk Jeffrey Tacet and Noble Andalusian. "Still under investigation," he said as firmly as he could and looked back to Taylor, who had just hung up the phone.

"Dr. Bajorek is currently with a patient, but the head nurse will see you."

"Fine," Seth said, knowing he wouldn't get any further with the young man.

"Seamus," Taylor said, turning to the guard, "would you please take the sergeant up to the seventeenth floor?"

Seamus slapped the desk. "Let's go, then."

Seth walked into the elevator, followed by the guard, who had to be at least six-foot-five, a few inches taller than him, and at least sixty pounds heavier, all muscle from the looks of it. Seamus scanned his security badge on the card reader, tapped the button for the seventeenth floor, and stepped back shoulder to shoulder with Seth. "Criminal death, huh? Funny way a puttin' it."

"Unlawful?" Seth offered.

The guard chuckled. "Whatever ya like, pal."

Seth looked up at the floor display, the numbers slowly ascending. "How did you end up here at the Orbriallis?"

"What, you don't think I'm from Lost Grove?"

Seth cocked an eye at the guard.

Seamus laughed. "Ah, I'm just playin' with ya. From Ennis, small town in the south of Ireland."

"Haven't heard of it. I've, unfortunately, never been there."

"Came over here with me dearfiúr, my sister," he clarified with a grin. "She's the smart one in our family, a scientist. Our great-uncle gave her an opportunity to come work for him, and I tagged along."

Seth looked up at the physically intimidating yet cheerful man, his brow furrowed. "Do you mean your great-uncle runs Orbriallis?"

Seamus nodded. "Aye. The big man around here."

"Who—" The chime of the seventeenth floor interrupted Seth. The doors opened to reveal a woman in a business suit who appeared to be in her mid-to-late forties, Seth gauged. She had a dark complexion, an angular face, and dark-brown hair clipped behind her head, and she radiated authority.

"Sergeant Wolfe, I'm Cassandra Wellington, the head nurse of the psychiatric department," she said in a thick British accent as she placed a hand in front of the elevator door so it didn't shut. "Please, follow me."

Seth stepped out, looked back at Seamus, and nodded.

"Good luck with your case, pal." The guard saluted as the doors shut.

Seth turned to follow the head nurse down the hall along the scarlet-red carpet. The walls were stone blue, and glass sconces lit the hallway. The ceiling was shockingly high, roughly ten to twelve feet. He spotted security cameras on both sides, aimed down at the doors.

"We're on the psychiatric department's administrative floor, " Cassandra said over her shoulder. "Floors eighteen through twenty-four are where we house the patients."

Seth's head jutted back. "Seven floors just for psychiatric patients?"

"We are at the forefront of psychiatric care in the United States, arguably the world."

"I'll admit, I don't know near enough about the Orbriallis, but I always thought this was more of a research facility."

Cassandra turned a corner and continued down the hallway. "You need patients for research, Sergeant. The advances we make in psychiatric care coincide with helping and curing patients, some of which are the most severe cases on record."

"The more you know," Seth muttered.

Cassandra glanced over her shoulder. "I'm sorry?"

"Nothing. Just an old commercial."

Cassandra stopped in front of an office and extended her arm. "We can talk in my office."

Seth nodded and stepped into a small room with dark shelving, charcoal carpet, and no windows, giving the room a glum vibe. "Look, I appreciate you seeing me, but I really need to speak with Dr. Bajorek."

Cassandra shut the door and made her way to her desk. "I'm afraid the doctor is completely booked today. Her openings are few and far between. Have a seat," she said as she sat down in her leather chair.

Seth pulled out his notepad and pen as he sat down across from her. Again, he noticed a security camera up in the corner. Were they in every room? Seth cleared his throat. "I'm sure you were told, but this is a highly urgent matter dealing with the suspicious death of one of her patients."

"Yes, I heard. But that doesn't change Dr. Bajorek's schedule. I'm sure she will accommodate your request at her earliest opening. In the meantime, how can I help you?"

Seth had no shortage of history dealing with the challenges of scheduling time with doctors, lawyers, and political leaders in San Francisco. He had hoped in Lost Grove he wouldn't have those issues. Sadly, it was proving the opposite. "Do you remember a young woman named Sarah Elizabeth Grahams?"

"Of course I remember Sarah Elizabeth. She was a special girl. We were all saddened to hear of her passing."

Seth didn't sense any heartache in her voice. "Can you verify the span of time she was treated here?"

Cassandra looked up, drumming her fingers on the desk. "Oh, I would say we admitted her a little over two and a half years ago, in early 2021. And she left here earlier this year, in January, I believe," she said and looked back at Seth.

Seth looked up from his notepad. "You say she left. Does that mean you released her or that she was—"

"We cleared her to leave. She had progressed very well and was ready to get back to her life."

Seth tapped his pen on his pad. "Right. And do you know where she went from here?"

"I know we went to great lengths to place her in a safe home for women. It's not common for us to arrange things of this nature, but it was at her request. Her parents agreed."

"Can you give me the location of this home?"

"The specifics of the location and contact would be with Dr. Bajorek."

Seth narrowed his eyes. "So, you never spoke to anyone there?"

"Sarah Elizabeth wasn't my patient. As head nurse, I'm aware of and help to oversee all patients in our care, but any sensitive information and documentation remains with their doctors."

"Right. And this is why I really need to speak with her doctor."

Cassandra let out a light sigh through her nose. "And I've already told you—"

"Was Sarah Elizabeth pregnant while she was here?"

"What?" Cassandra snapped. "You can't be serious. She was here under our care for over two years. There would have been no way—"

Seth held up his hand. "Don't say there was no way for her to get pregnant. There are over three-thousand employees here, the majority of them male."

"That is rather tawdry, Sergeant. I think you must watch too much television. Things like that—"

"Happen all the time, unfortunately. And worse."

"Well, not here, they don't. And I don't appreciate—"

A sharp knock at the door interrupted them.

Seth turned around to see the door open, and a tall woman with shoulder-length black hair stepped in wearing a lab coat.

"Sergeant Wolfe, hello, I'm Dr. Jane Bajorek. I'm sorry to keep you waiting," she said, stepping forward and extending her hand.

"Hello." Seth stood up, pocketed his notepad and pen, and shook the doctor's hand. He sensed the slightest hint of an accent but couldn't place it.

"Cassandra"—Jane looked past Seth—"please move my next two appointments." She looked back at Seth. "I know this is an urgent matter, and I want to do whatever I can to help. I was very close with Sarah and am devastated by this news."

"Yes, I am sorry. She seemed to be beloved by everyone who knew her. Thank you for making the time. It is rather urgent, so I appreciate it," Seth said with a humble smile.

"Let's go to my office."

"What can you tell me about the visions she was having?" Seth asked, as much for the case at this point as for himself. He was sitting in a plush, blue armchair across from Dr. Bajorek on a matching couch. A pot of hot tea rested on the polished oak table between them. Warm light filled the office, sunshine coming through sheer crimson curtains over the windows behind her desk.

"In what regard?" the doctor asked before sipping her tea.

Seth tapped his pen on his notepad, trying to better formulate his question. "I mean, was there a certain theme to them? Were they dark, apocalyptic, biblical or spiritual, personal, family oriented…"

"I wouldn't say they were necessarily dark in nature, though many of them did frighten her, mainly because she couldn't understand them. She encountered people she felt she had a profound connection with but had never met. They were personal, intimate even. She believed the encounters were as real as you and I sitting together right now. She felt the experiences were vital, life and death even."

Seth leaned forward. "Life and death?"

"Mm." Dr. Bajorek finished taking another sip of tea and set the cup and saucer on the table. "She felt the people she came into contact with were in grave danger. On the rare occasion, this took the literal form of someone standing on the edge of a cliff or being swept out to sea by an undercurrent. There was one experience she had when she opened her eyes—this is how she described her visions starting—and saw someone being pushed or held out a window, up high like we are here," she said, pointing to her windows, "but couldn't move, couldn't find her voice. It was brief, and she didn't see what ultimately happened but felt a tremendous amount of guilt afterward. She wept uncontrollably."

Listening to the descriptions of Sarah Elizabeth's visions and her emotional reactions had Seth short of breath. His chest swelled with anxiety. He reached for his cup of tea and didn't notice that his hand was shaking until he tried to grab the handle.

"Are you alright?" the doctor asked.

Seth finally looped his finger through the minuscule handle and looked up at Dr. Bajorek as he raised the cup. The concern in her voice and the look of empathy in her large brown eyes brought on a flush of gratitude tinged with sadness that he couldn't explain. He cleared his throat. "I'm fine," he lied and stopped himself from saying he could empathize with Sarah Elizabeth. "You keep referring to Sarah's visions as experiences. I'm curious as to why."

Dr. Bajorek held Seth's eyes, trying to discern his palpable emotional reaction. "Because that's what they were for her. The term *vision* does not fully encompass what Sarah Elizabeth went through during these episodes. This was not just imagery in her mind or something equivalent to a dream. They were fully lived experiences that induced increased heart rate and blood pressure and brain wave readings beyond that of a heightened physical and emotional experience observed on fully cognizant patients. And this is nothing to say about her emotional response to them. The clarity of her memory of these experiences was phenomenal."

Seth swallowed his third gulp of tea, the warm herbal concoction easing the tightness in his chest. "So, would it be safe to say that you believed she was having these experiences?"

Dr. Bajorek briefly furrowed her brow. "Beyond believing, we have concrete medical proof."

Seth nodded. "I guess, I mean to say, did you believe she was...seeing the future?"

"Do you know what makes the Orbriallis Institute so special, Sergeant? What brings researchers and scientists here from all over the world?"

Seth set his tea down and picked up his pen, his hand still mildly trembling. "I, um...I guess I don't, I'm afraid to admit."

"Why does that cause you embarrassment?"

Seth tilted his head to the side. "I grew up here. I left when I was eighteen and just recently came back. But I feel like I should know more. And details in this case have been coming in so quickly, I haven't had the proper opportunity to research as much as I would have liked."

Dr. Bajorek looked to her left and nodded toward a collection of framed diplomas and photos on the wall. "Those two beautiful women there are my parents."

Seth stood up and took a step toward the wall for a closer look. Dr. Bajorek was standing between two stunning women who looked like sisters. They shared the same black hair as the doctor, albeit with wisps of grey. Her mothers both had elevated cheekbones, full lips, and enormous oval-shaped brown eyes. Their exotic look spoke to foreign heritage and likely birth. Seth returned to his seat and nodded at the doctor. "They are indeed very beautiful. They look like sisters."

"They are," Dr. Bajorek confirmed, her eyes still on the photo. "Half-sisters, but sisters nonetheless."

"Oh…did they adopt you?"

"No, no. It's a complicated story, but my father passed away before I was born," she said, her voice faltering.

"I'm sorry."

Tears welled in the doctor's eyes, and a single tear rolled down her cheek before she wiped it away. "Yes. I would have…would do anything to have met him. I know him, though. My mother was engaged to him." She pointed to the photo. "The one on the right, Marcelina, loved him more deeply than I've ever seen or experienced in my life. His name was Jack. They named me after his mother, who passed away when he was a young man."

Seth felt like he was in the middle of a dual therapy session, not a murder investigation. He couldn't help feeling a deep sadness looking at the doctor as she gazed upon her parents, remembering a father she never knew.

Dr. Bajorek finally looked back at Seth. "I'm sorry, Sergeant."

"No." Seth shook his head. "Please, don't be."

"I don't speak much about him, but you seem a very…open man. Understanding, empathetic."

Seth had no response to this other than to offer a half smile.

"This all goes back to why the Orbriallis is so special and your question of if I believe Sarah Elizabeth saw the future."

Seth nodded. "Right, yes."

"When I was thirteen years old, I didn't get the same talk other girls my age did about sex. My parents sat me down to explain that they were both possessed."

Seth narrowed his eyes as his mouth fell open. "Um, as in…demonic possession?" Seth asked, raising an eyebrow.

Dr. Bajorek shook her head. "No, not really. They believed the spirits of family members possessed them."

"I see."

The doctor grinned. "I can understand your hesitancy. I felt the same way at first. It was something they alluded to throughout my childhood but didn't make clear until that day. We were all born in Poland, though we've been in the United States since I was five. They taught me of many superstitions and traditions growing up, so it wasn't as shocking as it might have been to someone with a different heritage or upbringing. Initially, I didn't understand, and couldn't comprehend, what they were claiming. As I made my way through high school, I came to believe they were deluded, psychologically troubled. But I loved them both dearly and desperately wanted to help them."

"And this is how you decided you wanted to become a doctor?" Seth asked, now wholly invested in her story.

The doctor nodded. "Yes. So I focused all my efforts and studies on psychology, searching for reason, explanation, signs to look for in every possible mental illness. But nothing made sense. Nothing lined up. Then, during my first year at med school, I experienced something. For the first time in my presence, I witnessed the possession take over my mother, Marcelina. If Apolonia, my other mother, wasn't there, I have no earthly idea what I would have done. She was uncontrollable, ravenous. Or, rather, I should say her twin sister, Ania, who died during childbirth, was ravenous. That's who had taken over my mother's body."

Seth was transfixed by this story.

"Her eyes had changed, not physically, of course, but there was no doubt they were not the eyes of my mother. Her entire body language was altered, her gestures raw and unhinged. And she spoke only in Polish. Not that our family couldn't speak our native language fluently, it was just abundantly clear that Ania could not understand a word of English. I'll leave the story there, but suffice to say, my perception had drastically changed. My new aim was to understand possession at a scientific level.

And my goal was to find a medical and/or psychological treatment or cure so my parents would never need to go through this again, to carry this burden that no one, or rather very few, could understand."

Seth was on the edge of his chair at this point. "And the Orbriallis…"

"That's right," Dr. Bajorek said. "I continued my education at the University of Minnesota and received my doctorate degree in psychology, the whole time studying anything I could find on possession and scouring the world for any place where medical research on such a repudiated affliction would be allowed."

"I mean, we heard rumors as kids about things that happened at the Orbriallis, but I never believed that any of them were true," Seth admitted.

Dr. Bajorek let out a soft laugh. "We're aware of many of the rumors around the community, and most of them are not true. Most. But this is what makes the Orbriallis so special—our willingness to explore anything, to fund research that no one else will in hopes of discovering and proving things beyond the currently accepted beliefs, to find cures to diseases and ailments that are believed to be impossible. So, you ask me if I believe Sarah Elizabeth saw the future?"

Chills rippled down Seth's spine as his own experience—there was that word—came into focus and plausibility. "I assume the answer is yes."

Dr. Bajorek nodded. "Sarah was a very, very special girl. I cared for her a great deal…"

Seth could see the doctor getting worked up again, her chest slightly jutting out in what appeared to be a defiant pose.

"She had such profound empathy, not only for those she encountered during her visions, but for everyone else around her. She wanted to help people who suffered like she had. I saw the same drive in her that I possessed at her age. Pardon the pun."

Seth smiled.

"Sarah would have done great things, helped so many people. I desperately want you to find who's responsible for her death, Sergeant Wolfe. Whoever it was, and however it was done, they deserve to be punished for taking away such a special human being."

Seth tapped his pen on his notepad. There was something about the way she spoke her last sentence that raised alarms. Did she know more than she was saying? Did she suspect something or someone she didn't want to vocalize? He'd follow up with her when the time came. "I wholeheartedly agree, Dr. Bajorek. And trust me, I will do everything in my power to make sure that happens."

"I want to be as transparent with you as I possibly can. I want you to understand her, truly understand and believe what she was capable of, in hopes that it will aid your investigation."

Seth nodded. Her words seemed so carefully chosen, he was certain now there was something she felt she could not divulge, and he would have to find the time and place to encourage her to speak on it. "I am extremely grateful for your insight and your openness, Doctor. And not only about Sarah."

Dr. Bajorek nodded.

"I know I've already taken up so much of your time, but could I trouble you with just a few more questions? Should be quick."

"Absolutely."

Seth glanced down at his notepad to ensure he wouldn't forget anything after the surprising turn in their conversation. He looked back up at the doctor. "I've been told Sarah Elizabeth was discharged to a women's shelter about a year ago. Can you verify this?" The first smile Seth had seen cross the doctor's face slowly melted away.

"Yes."

Seth waited a moment to see if she was going to elaborate on that. She did not. "Okay, do you have the information on where this house is, when she went there, and who the contact is?"

"Yes, I have that information and will write it down for you. I would be very interested to know what they tell you."

Seth laid his pen down flat on his notepad, holding the doctor's cryptic gaze. "Is there something you want to tell me, Doctor?"

Dr. Bajorek brushed lint off her slacks. "There are, of course, certain things I cannot say, Sergeant, because of confidentiality agreements and ongoing medical and scientific research. But something clearly went wrong, somewhere, and I lost someone I viewed as a surrogate daughter because of it. So, please, just keep me in the loop with anything you're permitted to tell me."

"I will. And if you change your mind"—Seth pulled his card from his breast pocket—"call me literally at any time. I promise you, it will remain confidential."

Dr. Bajorek took the card. "Thank you," she said and made her way to her desk.

"Of course." Seth closed his notepad and placed it and his pen inside his inner jacket pocket. He stood and waited for the doctor to finish writing the information regarding the women's shelter. Seth looked toward the door and spotted yet another security camera above it. "What the fuck?" he mumbled. Is this why she was being so tight-lipped?

"Here you are," Dr. Bajorek said as she walked over and handed Seth a paper.

Seth grabbed it and looked down, noticing it was a prescription card with the name, phone number, and address of the shelter on it. He smiled. "Last question I have. Did you know Sarah Elizabeth was pregnant?"

Dr. Bajorek looked down at Seth's card and sighed through her nostrils. She looked up, closed her eyes for a moment, and then said, "No."

If Seth had ever heard a no mean yes more than that in his career, he couldn't recall when. If there were this many cameras at the Orbriallis, he had to assume audio was also being recorded. Earlier in his career with the SFPD, Seth had responded to a domestic dispute call. The woman who answered the door, Kara Oliver, was visibly shaken, her cheek swollen, but insisted she panicked on her 911 call and that everything was fine, despite her eyes begging for help. He followed up with Kara two days later after her husband was at work and got the real story of ongoing abuse. He convinced Kara to let him take her to a friend's house. Thankfully, Kara found the strength not to return home and started a new life. Seth would find the right time soon to get the real story from the doctor. "Very well. Thank you, Dr. Bajorek."

She shook his hand before walking him to the door. Before opening it, she turned and looked Seth in the eyes, holding his gaze. She sensed a story there. She was certain it was what tripped him up earlier. Her mothers would be able to tell, would have seen it instantly. "Sergeant?"

"Yes?" Seth asked hesitantly.

"I helped my parents. I helped Sarah Elizabeth. If you're in need of help or need someone to talk to, I'm here. I promise you, I will believe anything you have to tell me."

An amalgam of emotions coursed through Seth's body—shock, fear, gratitude, hope. He nodded as goosebumps sprouted across his flesh. "I appreciate that."

Are You Home, Mary Germaine?

"Stay inside and wait for me to come back," Noble instructed his sister as she got out of the passenger seat. He was tired, a bit on edge, and his brain wasn't operating on all cylinders. He'd spent hours last night trying to find a position comfortable enough to lull him to sleep, his mind a rampage of speculations, fears. When he finally fell asleep, he was met by nightmares. One was a particularly chaotic dream that felt dystopian where time, locations, and the "story" jumped all over the place. Those details were insignificant. The haunting part of the dream was that his dad was in it, dealing with shady characters, and eventually morphed into the Green Man. Noble had no desire to dig into the psychology of that nightmare, but it certainly represented everything playing havoc with his mind the past few days.

Zoe rolled her eyes. "I heard you the first twenty times."

"Yeah, well, I mean it," he said out the rolled-down window. "I'll come inside and get you when we're done. I don't want to see you pacing around outside."

"Okay." Zoe smiled, clutching the book she needed to return to Ms. Palmer to her chest. She galloped up the steps and used her whole body to open the massive wood door into Lost Grove's public library.

Noble ensured she was inside, and the door closed before he signaled back into small-town traffic. The fact that Raymond LaRange was the Green Man who had kidnapped Nettie's brother George (a detail Noble struggled to believe) was now a constant source of stress over Zoe's safety. Besides worrying about his sister's obedience, he had his coach breathing down his neck as the competition approached, his mom asking him every two minutes if something was wrong, and now the task of going to see Mary Germaine with two fellow students in tow.

"You're a good brother," Nettie said from the back seat.

He looked into the rearview mirror to see Nettie staring out the window, but Anya was smiling at him.

"Are we going to my house first or something?" Nettie asked when they turned down her street.

"Nah," Noble said. "She just lives on the same street as you."

Nettie furrowed her brow, already on edge after Anya told her Noble had someone they could talk to about the not-children. Who else in town would admit they existed, and why did Noble know the person?

Noble pulled over to the side of the road, put the car in Park, and turned off the engine.

Nettie looked from one side of the street to the other, trying to figure out who they were going to see. They were two blocks from her house, and she didn't know everyone on the street. Anya opened the door to get out; Nettie hesitantly followed suit.

Noble stepped onto the pavement, feeling queasy and light-headed. He leaned on the car and started his breathing practices reserved for cross-country meets. What on earth was he thinking, bringing these two to talk to Mary Germaine? How would Mary react to the intrusion? Everyone in town knew she kept to herself, and here he was showing up on her doorstep, unannounced, to ask questions about the not-children. He shut the door and stepped up on the sidewalk.

"You good?" Anya asked, coming to stand next to him.

"Yeah," he said, offering her a smile, unsure that he was. He headed past the picket fence to the wrought iron gate encasing Mary's front yard.

"Are you serious?" Nettie asked, coming to a stop behind him and Anya.

Noble opened the gate. "Do you want to know or not?"

"Oh." Anya looked from Nettie over to Noble. "Is this Mary Germaine's house?"

Noble raised his eyebrows and nodded, holding open the gate. "Let's go."

Anya grabbed Nettie's hand. "Come on, Net, she's harmless. And if she really does know stuff, you won't be alone. *We* won't be alone."

Nettie swallowed and allowed Anya to pull her in through the gate. "Okay. She weirds me out, though."

"Don't say that," Anya admonished her friend. She knew what people thought and said about her mother and never liked that sort of talk.

Noble shut the gate. "She's actually easy to talk to once you open up to her. Just make sure to be polite. She doesn't know we're coming," he said, walking past them toward the front door.

"What?" Anya and Nettie voiced simultaneously.

Inside the house, Mary was working on a new mixed-media collage when she heard a car pull over, the engine turning off, and then three doors open and shut. High-pitched girls' voices asked a question as footsteps came up her stairs. Mary turned from her easel, the paintbrush in her hand held but forgotten. Someone tapped on her front door—not a knock, but someone's open palm softly slapping the wood. Mary sat on her swiveling stool and took several shallow breaths before she stood, placed the brush in the glass of paint water, and made her way out of her studio room, down the hall, and toward the front door. She saw the top of a head through the upper windows in her door and watched the dark brown hair ruffle in the breeze, trying to place who it could be. Seth's hair was shorter, so it couldn't be him coming to see her unannounced with the crime scene photos he'd mentioned last night.

"I can't believe you didn't tell her," Nettie stated, arms folded across her chest.

"Is she even home?" Anya asked.

"It's not like I have her number." Noble shrugged.

"And how do you know she will even answer?" Nettie asked.

At the door, Mary paused, looked down at herself, wondering if she was dressed appropriately. Other than Story, she couldn't recall the last time someone came knocking at her door. She picked up her mail at the post office, so even the mailman didn't come by. She looked back up and grabbed hold of the knob, twisted it, and opened it to a trio of teenagers. One of them was Noble Andalusian. Her eyes widened. She thought the hair was familiar but didn't expect to be seeing Noble so soon, or ever again for that matter. After their chat last week in front of her house, Noble told her that he believed her about the not-child and they were "okay," but she was left feeling dispirited.

He smiled. "Hi, Mary."

Her throat felt dry and prickly with all of them standing there looking at her. "Hello," she sputtered.

Anxiety trickled through her so intensely it felt physical. Her arms jerked, moving as if she was about to fall face forward and needed to catch herself. She took in a breath, the wind carrying with it the subtle scent of teenage masculinity, feminine perfume, and salty air. The salt drew saliva to her mouth and, with it, an instant desire to slam the door in their faces. Her stomach clenched as her affliction—what doctors had once diagnosed as pica—reared its ugly head. Mary grabbed hold of both the door and its frame to keep her hands from reaching out and grabbing one of the pebbles she collected just outside her door. They sat in a concrete flower urn, all flat and smooth.

"Um, I was wondering if we could talk to you about that not-kid. And maybe other not-kids?"

Mary blinked. Why would he bring that up? Why would he bring his friends with him to talk about it? The two girls looked as nervous as she felt. Noble looked…exhausted.

All three teenagers waited for her to say something, but Mary seemed struck speechless.

Noble pursed his lips. Perhaps she was confused, wondering why he'd want to bring up the subject when it had been swept under the rug last week. He tried another tactic. "Have you ever met Nettie Horne?" he asked, rotating his torso to indicate Nettie's presence.

"Not formally," Mary responded with some difficulty. *Use words. Speak!* she reminded herself.

"Oh, well, this is Nettie," he said.

"Hi." Mary offered a quick smile at the teenage girl.

Nettie, still with her arms crossed, lifted a few fingers as a wave.

"And this is Anya," Noble introduced.

"Hello!" Anya greeted her pleasantly.

Mary nodded. "Yes, I know Anya."

Anya's mouth opened and closed, her brow cinched tight. Why Mary Germaine responded with such alacrity to knowing her was a mystery.

"Her mother. I know Anya's mother," Mary abruptly corrected, seeing the girl's confusion.

"Right, nice," Noble said. He shifted from foot to foot. Mary was staring at them as if they were spirits returned from the nearby graveyard. Beside Anya, Nettie stood with her arms crossed and lips pursed in a tight line. Not a word had escaped her mouth thus far. The awkwardness was palpable, and he couldn't shake off the feeling that this encounter would end in disappointment. "So, I was thinking—"

"Do you know the Green Man?" Nettie blurted at last.

Mary's eyes snapped into focus, her full attention laid on Nettie.

Put aback by the piercing glare, Nettie took a step backward, teetering on the edge of the bottom stair.

Mary looked back at Noble, her mouth forming a question.

"*Do* you know about the Green Man?" he asked with a shrug.

"Why?" Mary asked the moment after Noble finished asking his question. "Why would you ask about him?"

Nettie's mouth fell open. "You *do* know."

Mary's eyes darted to Nettie, then back to Noble. "Why are you here? I thought we cleared this up."

"This isn't about that. Well, not directly about that. Remember, you asked me if I really hadn't seen the children you said aren't children, and I hesitated? And you said, 'You know someone,' like you caught it in my eye that I knew someone who knew about the not-children? Well, you guessed right, and Nettie is that someone. Her brother—"

"Not my brother," Nettie interrupted.

Noble sighed. "Well, the kid living in their house—"

"I know," Mary interrupted this time.

Noble hesitated. "You know what?"

"It's not really her brother," Mary said.

"Oh my God," Nettie muttered as her eyes welled with tears. "You know?"

The overwhelming urge that they shouldn't have this conversation in earshot of nosy townspeople overcame her fear of visitors. "Come inside," Mary urged, waving them in, eyes darting around the neighborhood. What were these teenagers doing coming to her house unannounced, asking questions about that hideous man?

Anya was the first to obey. She stepped past Mary and, trying to keep the conversation alive, said, "Thank you for asking us in. It smells so nice in here! Like lemon and—"

"Lavender," Mary finished for her. "They're the only scents that don't make me hungry."

Anya nodded with raised brows, finding the comment interesting. Nettie followed her inside in a catatonic state. The past two days had been a real treat in the department of sick and twisted information. How had this happened so quickly? Was it the modern age she had to thank or the simple utterance of a few slurred words from Not-George?

Mary tugged carefully at Noble's jacket, jolting his feet into moving. "Come in, come in." All inside, Mary shut the door and ushered them into a cozy, clean living room.

"Thanks for seeing us," Noble said. "And sorry for not—"

"Why would you want to know anything about that man or those children-things?" Mary asked while they all decided if they should sit and where.

Anya set the example again, gently instructing Nettie to sit next to her on a sofa that looked like it was preserved from the 1950s.

Noble noticed Nettie had gone into that "staring off into space" mentality, probably coping with this new bombshell of knowledge. He looked at Mary and nodded, unsure why.

Mary narrowed her eyes at the boy. Was he high?

"So, Nettie saw the Green Man take her brother," Anya stated, drawing everyone's attention. "I mean to say, she saw him try, many times, but then she'd chase him away."

"Chase him away?" Mary asked in a whisper.

"But then one night, when she was sick, her parents left the window open. You see, Nettie always made sure the window was locked, but that night, she had passed out before her parents tucked George in and cracked it open. And this is when the Green Man came in and stole her brother, replacing him with one of the not-children things. Basically."

Mary's heart ached seeing the pain the story brought to Nettie's face. "I'm sorry."

"Um, yeah, sorry," Noble added and then looked at Mary again, nodding.

Mary wasn't sure who she was more concerned for, this poor girl who had her brother stolen or Noble. She looked back at the girls, wringing her hands as she paced from one foot to the next in her living room. "I'm sorry. I don't have company over. I don't really know what—"

"It's a very nice house," Anya offered, smiling.

Mary looked around the living room. "Thank you."

"I don't understand," Nettie whispered. "If you know he's real, why haven't you said anything?"

Mary shrugged. "Like what?"

"That he took my brother, for one," Nettie said, voice raised.

Mary flinched.

"Okay, let's take it one step at a time," Noble reassured Mary, hovering his hand behind her shoulders. The other held out for Nettie to pause a moment. What he really wanted to do was lie down on the couch and take a nap.

"That's not how he works," Mary offered, moving to sit on the chair opposite the small couch where the teenage girls were perched. She promptly stood again. "He has an ability to make himself not be seen."

Anya cocked her head to the side. "Like he's invisible?"

"Up here," Mary replied, tapping her temple. "That's *if* he's seen, which I don't think happens very often. He's very good at sneaking around. I'm sorry. I didn't know you'd seen him."

Nettie opened her mouth to protest, but Noble cut in. "No, why would you know that?"

"The whole town knows it," Nettie grumbled.

"Okay, I do know that," Mary recanted.

"And you've said nothing!"

"What would I have said?" Mary asked, eyes wide, hands held out.

"That you've seen him, too!" Nettie shrieked as she tried to stand, but Anya pulled her back down. "That you've seen him and that there are things that look like children, but aren't, who run around with him at night. Say something. Say anything! You're an adult. No one believes me. They'd believe you!"

Mary softened. "No, Nettie, they wouldn't. People don't listen to me. They all think I'm strange. I think you all know that."

Nettie looked down at the ground.

"And, sadly, there's no proof."

"Sorry," Nettie mumbled, feeling guilty for yelling at this woman everyone made comments and judgments about, including herself.

Noble could feel the depressing tension in the air. He took a step forward and lifted his finger like he had an astute observation. "What about the kid from the woods?"

Anya looked at him. "Huh?"

Mary shot him a hesitant look. "What about it?"

"Couldn't we show them…" Noble trailed off, knowing all the answers to his questions would be no. Could we show it to them? Ask the authorities to send it out for testing? And explain all that, how?

"What happened in the woods?" Anya asked.

"Nothing," Mary said.

Noble caught the glare in Mary's eyes and looked back at Anya. "Nothing. I was thinking of something Nate told me. You know how he is."

Anya's face twisted. "Are you sure you're okay?"

"Me?" Noble asked. "I'm…I'm great. Didn't sleep a whole lot, but doing well."

Anya frowned.

Noble's eyes lit up, and he turned to Mary. "We know his real name. What do you think about that?"

Mary turned to him, eyes wide. She was having trouble keeping her thoughts in this conversation, especially when anything came out of Noble's mouth. He seemed rather scatterbrained, and she was of the impression he was normally rather focused and astute. The presence of these young people in her house was making her palms sweat, not to mention the overbearing urge to stick something in her mouth, to bite down hard until her teeth creaked.

"The Green Man's real name," Anya helped clarify.

Noble pointed at her. "That's right," he said and turned back to Mary. "It's Raymond LaRange. He was brought up on charges of molesting two underage girls. They committed him to psychiatric care and then transferred him from Ohio to the Orbriallis in 1993."

"The Orbriallis Institute?" Mary asked redundantly.

Noble closed his eyes and nodded.

Nettie finally looked up from the ground. "Do you know… Do you think I could find my real brother with them?"

Mary shook her head. "I don't know. I wish I did."

"How can nobody have noticed him or these…things?" Anya asked.

"He's good at hiding," Mary said, sitting again, fingers clasped tightly around one another. "I've only seen him out along the gulch road, mostly. I shouldn't say only. I've seen him in town twice. He comes out at night—late, late night. He's around but not visible. Come to think of it, I rarely see him in the summer. The days are too long. It's the winter he truly loves."

"Lucas was taken in the summer," Noble blurted before he could stop himself.

"Who?" Anya asked, voicing the question Nettie was also about to ask.

Mary nodded. "Yes, Lucas was taken in the summer, right from his bed."

"Who's Lucas?" Nettie asked.

"About four years ago, four-year-old Lucas Griffiths went missing.

No leads, no reason, just gone," Noble explained.

"Oh, yeah. I kind of remember that," Anya said. "How did you remem— Wait, let me guess. Nate?"

"You told Nate?" Nettie asked, aghast.

"No!" Noble waved his hands out like he was a baseball umpire signaling a player was safe at home. "I said I'd have to ask you guys first. But he knows all about this stuff, so he seemed the best person to ask."

Mary looked from Noble to Nettie, trying to make sense of who and what they were talking about.

"He's oddly obsessed," Anya offered as a comment.

"With missing children?" Mary asked.

"No. True crime," Anya said. "Mary…can I call you Mary?"

"Of course," Mary said.

"That is her name," Noble added.

"Do you know where they come from?" she asked, ignoring her sleep-deprived friend.

Mary gazed at the expectant eyes in her living room. "They come out of the cave system. But I don't think that's where they come *from*."

Noble shivered, recalling a horror movie with a race of sub-humans living in caves. Could that be what they meant by saying the children weren't human? Meaning they were some kind of a mutated race of humans because of horrible living conditions?

"What do you mean? If they live in the caves, isn't that…"

Mary shook her head. "I think they *stay* in the caves, but that isn't where they came from originally. I don't think that's where they came from originally."

"But you don't know?" Nettie asked.

"No," Mary said. "That's just where I've seen them."

"The caves," Noble muttered.

Anya looked at Nettie and smiled, patting her hand.

Mary couldn't take the uncomfortable silence. "I'm sorry I can't be of more help." She moved to the door, feeling caged with all these people in her house, pressing her for answers. Her gums hurt where her teeth threatened to elongate. A tremor crept into her hands with the smell of all their teenage hormones clouding her home.

Noble took the hint. "Thank you. We know a little more now, which is great."

Nettie stood from the couch, sweeping across the room and out the door without so much as a word.

Anya sighed. "Thank you, Mary," she said, smiling, and departed.

Noble paused in the door, offering a smile. "Sorry to just come by here like this. I didn't really know how to get a hold of you."

Mary offered him a pained smile. "It's fine."

"It was helpful, though. And don't feel bad. You're right. What would you say to anyone, you know?"

Mary nodded, closing the door on his heels. She pressed her cheek to the cold wood of the door and then flew through the house to her kitchen, opened her fridge, tore through the plastic packaging of raw meat, and indulged in her cravings.

Noble got in the car, finding the girls sitting in silence.

"She didn't tell us a single thing we didn't already know," Nettie griped.

Anya was in the front seat, and she turned around. "She knows them, Nettie. Isn't that enough? What do you expect her to do?"

"She's been letting me go around saying this crap and never once—"

"She told you why. Mary's an outsider too, Nettie," Noble interjected, starting the car. "Look, even if it was me, right? Even if it was me who was like, 'Yeah, I've seen weird not-children and the Green Man,' do you really think it would change anything? Your brother isn't missing."

"He is," Nettie growled.

Noble put the car in gear. "You know what I mean," he said, turning the car around and taking them back down the street toward Nettie's house. "Do you want me to drop you off at home, or are you guys going—"

"You can drop me," Nettie said.

Seconds later, they were in front of the Horne house. Nettie climbed out, pulling her bag with her.

"Do you want me to come in?" Anya asked.

Nettie shook her head and walked toward her home.

Anya sighed. "I feel so bad for her."

"Yeah, she must be pretty messed up with all this."

"If we figure out anything else, maybe we should keep it from her, unless it's something concrete, you know?"

Noble nodded. "Good idea. Are you okay if I pick up Zoe first and then drive you home?" Noble asked.

"Of course," Anya said. For a moment, she was silent as they maneuvered the small-town streets, but she felt pressed to speak. "Don't you and Stan go spelunking and stuff? At the state park?"

"Yeah, we do."

"So, there are cave systems around here?"

Noble nodded, pulled a U-turn, and parked the car in front of the library, turning it off.

"What if we looked?" Anya suggested with a shrug and a lopsided smile.

"Are you kidding? Behind her house? For a psycho serial child molester?"

"Are there maps of the area? Maybe we could confirm a cave system is back there, and then we wouldn't have to look."

Noble nodded. "Yeah, okay. Okay, let me ask Stan if she knows or has some maps of the area. Jesus, I can't believe what this has turned out to be."

"Neither can I," Anya agreed, sitting back into the passenger seat and letting her head fall into the headrest.

"I'll be right back," Noble said, getting out of the car, tripping over his own feet, almost falling to the ground.

"Noble, be careful," Anya called after him. The turn of events in the mystery of George Horne's pseudo-disappearance played in her mind like a movie. All conjecture, her imagination ran wild. Noble had been gone for only a few moments before Anya's imaginings got the best of her. She was overcome with a tingling sensation, like she was being watched.

The Littlest Witch

Comfort. That's what the library offered. It came in the form of books, thousands of them, all enveloping and softening the sounds inside the walls, leaving the essence of peace. They offered escape, warmth, stories, and more information than you could possibly squeeze into your brain in a lifetime. Books littered her bedroom, on her shelves, on the floor, under her bed, a virtual landfill of literary gold. She enjoyed the organized chaos of it, and her mom understood that. She still had to make her bed and keep her clothes on hangers or in drawers, but the books stayed put. Most of her weekly allowance went toward books in the thrift shop or the local bookstore if she really wanted something new and exciting. But mostly, she checked out books from the library. Zoe loved the library.

Ms. Palmer, Story, as she insisted on being called, had shifted the library-going experience even more since she took over. Now the place whispered. The books actually seemed to speak, imploring you to read them. The smells were richer and far more pleasant, not at all like the musty perfume the old librarian, Mrs. Flority, used to wear, which found its way to the farthest corners of the library. Story was always finding new recommendations or offering Zoe advice like, "I think if you walk through the reference section, turn left after the Ms, and go straight until you knock into a shelf, a surprise may find you."

Sure enough, her wisdom always proved useful just at the moment Zoe needed it. But it wasn't always like that. Story was very considerate not to bother Zoe when she just wanted to peruse the shelves or sit with a book in her lap in the middle of an aisle and get lost. Having read the novel *Practical Magic* by Alice Hoffman, Zoe didn't wonder if the book had been trying to tell her something about the woman who owned the hedges she'd found it in or if the woman, Story Palmer, had left the book there specifically for Zoe.

Zoe took careful steps into the library today, knowing she had a special book to return and not one that belonged to the library. On the first page, written in well-practiced cursive, read the phrase, "This book belongs to Story Palmer." As much as she wanted to keep the book, read it a hundred times, devour all the notes a younger Story had made in the margins, she knew it was only right to return it, especially since there were recipes and what Zoe could only gather were spells written in sharp pencil throughout the pages. She took a deep breath and approached the main desk.

The gloomy teenager, Becky, was shifting things about. "Returns can go in there," she said to Zoe, without making eye contact.

"Is Ms. Palmer here?" Zoe asked, still clutching the book to her chest.

Becky looked up from her work, peering over the desk. "She's putting books back. Somewhere."

"'Kay, thanks!" Zoe said, turning promptly and rushing off to find Story. She headed into the depths of the library, turned at the reference section, walked past the glass room with all the computers and the sole microfiche machine, turned again at the end of that row, and headed into the far-left corner of the library. Just as she rounded the corner to see Story standing on tiptoe, pushing a book into place, Ms. Palmer greeted her.

"Hello, Ms. Andalusian. I see you've found my book."

Zoe stopped at the end of the row, her body tingling with a thrill she didn't understand. All her mind kept thinking back on was how people described the feeling right before lightning struck.

Story lowered to the ground, and it dawned on Zoe that her feet looked angled as if she were standing on her toes, but her toes hadn't been on the carpeted floor. They'd been hanging just an inch off the ground.

The young girl gawped.

"Is your brother with you?" Story asked, settling one more book on the shelf before turning to Zoe with an open smile.

Zoe shook her head. "He's with his friends. They're going to see Mary."

Story raised one brow and asked. "Mary Germaine?"

"I think so," Zoe responded.

"Curious," Story whispered. She let the interesting tidbit go for now and focused on her pet project. "How did you like the book?"

Zoe's face blossomed with delight, and she felt herself rising onto the balls of her feet. "Oh, I like it a lot!" she replied, in her excited, soft, library voice.

"You know, that book came out when I was six," Story explained, walking toward Zoe. "Of course, I didn't find it until I was ten. I borrowed a copy from our town library. Funny, I always thought Alice Hoffman had to be a witch, though I've never had that confirmed. This book," she said, pointing to it as Zoe held it in her hands, "is the truest depiction of witches in a work of fiction I've ever read."

"But," Zoe began, stopping herself. Her small brow wrinkled with concern and confusion.

Story waited. The young girl needed to find assurance in her gut feelings and listen to what her third eye was telling her. She was confident Zoe had these kinds of feelings all her life, but no one was around to show her how to listen to them. Or rather, no one was around to tell her she should and that those inklings were far more than a sixth sense.

"But they're not real…" Zoe trailed off, not sure if she was stating or asking.

Story's laugh was light and lilting. She took gentle hold of the young girl's shoulder and ushered her toward a table. "You don't honestly believe that, do you, Ms. Andalusian?"

Zoe wiggled into a chair while Story took a seat opposite her, hands clasped together on the tabletop. The silver rings on Story's fingers glittered in the warm, dim light. "Well, I mean." Zoe giggled and then drew her eyebrows together, sternly. "You *are* a witch, then?"

Story nodded.

"Like Sally and Gillian?"

"In a way, very much like them. In another, completely different." Story lifted her brow. "Zoe?"

"Yes?" Zoe leaned forward.

"Did you see my notes in the margins?"

Zoe nodded. "So many notes, they almost cluttered the words of… the…book…" Zoe felt warmth rushing in her belly as she watched the light dance in the eyes of the woman sitting across from her. Zoe should not have seen those words, not if she was normal. She thought she knew it when she was reading it, but she was certain of it now. The notes in the margins were too many to actually fit. They had covered the writing itself. But when Zoe wanted to read the story, the printed letters popped out on the page. When she wanted to see the faded notes, they bled onto the page, growing darker and darker.

"It's my first grimoire. Do you know what that is?"

"Umm…" Zoe shrugged.

"It's a book of instructions—magical instructions."

Zoe's eyes lit up.

"I loved the book so much, it only made sense to write the very first of my incantations, my castings, my spells on the pages I loved so dear. Of course, no ordinary person can see them."

Zoe released a strangled, high-pitched noise from her throat.

"If I had to guess," Story started, leaning forward across the table and drumming her fingernails on the top, "it's your father with the bloodline."

"My dad's a witch?" Zoe fumbled out the very first question to pop into her mind.

"Yes." Story laughed again. "He just doesn't know it. He doesn't use it—well?" Story tilted her head. "He may, now and again, but not be conscious of it. Your brother, too. But it's you, Zoe, who has the… Are you familiar with the phrase 'je ne sais quoi'?"

Zoe felt she had heard it but wasn't going to lie. "I think so?"

"It's a phrase for a quality that cannot be described in words. You have that amongst your family. You have the je ne sais quoi."

Zoe wrinkled her nose. "Do I want the je ne sais quoi?" she asked, only slightly butchering the words.

"Oh goodness, yes," Story enthused. "But, in the end, it's your choice."

Zoe thought for a moment, looking at the table, the book. Her fingers carefully tapped the worn cover. "My choice to do what?"

"It's your choice whether you want to learn to use the power you have," Story said, gentle and kind.

Zoe brightened, her feet kicking the air. "You'd teach me?"

Story's smile bloomed. "I'd teach you."

"Do I have to get my mother's permission?"

Story nearly fell over laughing. "No. No witch needs permission to be what she is. You're free to tell her, of course."

"I don't think she'd believe me."

"Oh, she will. In time she will," Story reassured her.

Zoe was quiet for a moment. "I'm not sure I'll tell her to start. Maybe later, when I know how to do things. Oh! Can you light a candle by blowing on it, like the Owens sisters?" the young girl asked eagerly.

"Mm-hmm," Story answered. "Or just by looking. It takes concentration, but eventually it's like snapping your fingers. It's all in the look."

"Can you fly?"

Story laughed, sitting back and crossing one leg over the other. "No. We can hover."

"Not even on a broomstick?"

"It saddens me to say it, but no." Story sighed. "I know, believe me. You'd think the broomstick would be real, with all the depictions. I wish it were!"

"Can you make potions for people to go away?"

Story offered Zoe a kind smile. "We can do many things. But, and this is very important, you may never abuse your abilities to do something that will hurt another person. We should only use witchcraft for good, or else it will circle back around on you and bite you in the butt. Of that, you can be sure."

"Nothing bad," Zoe reiterated, like she was taking notes in class.

"And it harm none, so mote it be," Story said. "A turn of phrase to live by."

Zoe whispered the phrase to herself many times. She seemed to notice she was still clutching at the book. "Oh, you should have your book back," she said, pushing it across the table.

Story stopped her. "No. I want you to keep it. Study it. Practice if you wish."

Zoe's eyes flew wide. "Just like that?" She sank into her chair, recognizing how loud she'd just been.

"It's in you, Zoe. You have no need to fear what you can do. The ground rules are all here, in this book," Story said, tapping the well-worn copy of *Practical Magic*. "Alright, here's something simple to start with." Story reached into her pockets and pulled out a string of yellow-and-blue cord. She held it up to Zoe and pulled it through her fingers as she spoke. "Cord magic, or knot magic, is an ancient magic indeed, but it is a tried-and-true way all young witches practice intention. It helps us focus our powers into a singular spell," she explained, taking one end of the string before continuing. "Now, cord magic is all about trapping your desire in a series of knots. It's all about focus. So let's say you have a big test coming up. This blue-and-yellow cord? I'd recommend these for wisdom, patience, intelligence, and memory. Focus all your intentions on knowing the answers, on remembering all that you've studied.

"You start with a nine-inch string or a nine-inch rope. The pattern goes like this:

By knot of one, the spell's begun
By knot of two, it cometh true
By knot of three, so mote it be
By knot of four, this power I store
By knot of five, the spell's alive
By knot of six, this spell I fix
By knot of seven, events I'll leaven
By knot of eight, it will be fate
By knot of nine, what's done is mine

Or, you can say, what's done is thine, if you're making it for someone else." As she said the instructions, she showed where each knot should go on the string. "So, would you like to give it a try?"

"Yes," Zoe enthused, grasping the string Story held out for her. "I have a big test coming up, too, in math."

"I know," Story said with a wink.

Zoe's mouth dropped open and then turned into a grin.

"Now, your brother is on his way back to get you, and I'd like to ask you something."

Zoe put the string and the book into her bag. "Okay."

Story leaned onto the table, arms crossed, conspiratorial. "What does your brother have to discuss with Mary Germaine?"

Zoe shrugged. "I don't know. He's had some to-do with Anya about Nettie's little brother. Something about a man who did something that got him arrested, but he doesn't like me listening in because it's bad."

"Ah." Story nodded, sitting back. This was a strange situation indeed. Nettie Horne's brother, Mary Germaine, Noble Andalusian, and a strange man arrested for doing something bad. Story puzzled over the connections between all the players in this peculiar circle of acquaintances. "Well, you must listen to your older brother. He has good sense, and he's protecting you."

"I've only overheard a little." Zoe shrugged. "And I wasn't trying to."

Story smiled and pushed back from the desk, standing up. She waved for Zoe to follow. "Best to leave adult things to adults."

Zoe nodded emphatically. "I'd rather it stay that way."

Story laughed. "No smarter words have been spoken," she said, turning them into the library foyer just as Noble opened the library doors. "Good evening, Mr. Andalusian," Story greeted the teenage boy.

"Good evening," he responded. "You good?" he asked his sister.

Zoe sneered at him, half playfully. "Yes."

"Ah, wait," Story said. She moved to the desk and grabbed a set of books. "Here are the books you wanted." Story handed the books to Zoe, both books on witchcraft.

"Thanks," she said, eyes gleaming.

"Thank you," Noble said, ushering his sister toward the door. "Do you have a project in school?" he asked as they headed outside.

Zoe giggled as the door closed, but Story's concern wedged deep in her rib cage. The young man had a growing sense of unease about him, and she wanted to know if it had anything to do with what he'd seen Mary do that morning on the forest trail.

Dr. Owens

"Geiger and his wife, Ilsa, had trouble conceiving. Did you know that?" Dr. Neil Owens sank into the plush, burgundy, leather chair positioned behind his grand ebony desk, looking dapper in his tailored suit, golden tan, and perfectly styled dark-brown hair, greying at the temples. The floor-to-ceiling windows behind him cast a cool, blue glow over the room, giving it a futuristic ambience. However, the elegant Art Deco furnishings and warm lighting added a touch of vintage charm to balance out the modernity. Across from him sat a thin, pinched-faced man with an ill-fitting suit. *Would it be too much to pay a little extra and have the damn thing fitted to your weak shoulders and slim waistline?* Neil thought.

Despite being in his mid-seventies, Dr. Neil Owens moved with the vigor and grace of a man in his fifties. He was believed to have immigrated from Ireland as a teenager, earned a PhD, and started working at the Orbriallis in 1968. Some of the older residents of Lost Grove claimed he was only in his early twenties when he was hired by Geiger. In the 1970s, Dr. Owens was an active member of the community, but over time, he retreated further into the walls of the Institute, eventually building himself a luxurious penthouse atop the building. Some townsfolk still claimed to catch glimpses of him around town, which was akin to spotting a mythical creature like a mermaid or giant owl (both actual rumors in Lost Grove). In reality, Dr. Owens hadn't left the Orbriallis in over twenty-five years.

"I have heard the stories." Dr. Arnold Foy, who was interviewing for a promotion to chief of operations in the medical research lab, leaned back in his chair, trying not to show that the eccentric and intensely private head of the Orbriallis Institute intimidated him. Arnold had a good idea that the position was practically his, but this conversation with Dr. Neil Owens was taking an unexpected, almost completely tangential turn.

Neil flinched with a pained smile. "The stories?"

"Yeah, the stories about Geiger and Ilsa. Everyone tells them," Arnold said, realizing he should have kept his mouth shut.

"Hmm," Neil hummed. "This isn't a story. They had difficulties for years and believed they may never have a child. But then, a miracle—Ilsa became pregnant and was able to carry the child to term. Sadly, it was to be a tainted miracle because their baby was born with horrible, debilitating deformities. And why? Why was such a blessed couple burdened with a little girl who looked like a monster?" Neil let the question hang. This fool in front of him would likely try to answer.

"Sir?"

"That is what Geiger wanted to know. He wanted to understand why it happened, how it happened, and more importantly, what he could do to remedy it." Neil's voice rose as he accented each point by jabbing his finger into his desk. "He built our reputation in medical research on his own back. It started with fertility, yes. But did he stop there?"

"No, sir," Dr. Foy stuttered.

Neil shook his head with a cocksure grin. "No, he did not. And Geiger, never a selfish man, brought in scientists and doctors renowned in their field of IVF, gynecologists. He saw an opportunity to help the world, to end a bit of suffering."

Dr. Foy cleared his throat, fiddling with his hands in his lap and adjusting his crossed legs. "He was a great man who established this outstanding facility."

"And do you hope to do more?" Neil asked.

"Of course, yes. I've spearheaded the ocular nerve research, and I have to admit, it's exciting, the progress we have made."

Dr. Owens sat forward in his chair, spreading his hands wide across his desk. Dr. Foy lacked the fevered excitement he was hoping to see. Could a man this bland and untidy ever be someone he could trust with the more progressive research and experiments their esteemed institute conducted?

"Yes, I am thrilled with the results of that as well," Neil commented, wanting to throw his Serendibite paperweight at the man to spark some vigor. It wasn't that Dr. Arnold Foy lacked intelligence. He was a very good research doctor. It was the little things, the sheer boredom of the man, Neil hated—the way Arnold trimmed his fingernails or his dry hands with flecks of dust from the sterile latex gloves he constantly wore.

Dr. Foy swallowed what felt like a lump of coal down his throat. Dr. Owens's glare was so severe, Arnold felt like crying.

"You've been working with the geneticists on that, haven't you?" Neil said more than asked because he knew every detail of all the research taking place in his facility.

"Yes," Dr. Foy replied. He had prepared for days on end to answer hundreds of potential questions, thinking he had even a faint clue how this interview would go. Now he wondered if Dr. Owens would even ask him a single question about the position he had been dreaming about.

Dr. Owens pushed back from his desk and stood, straightening out his custom-fit jacket. "Bringing geneticists into the mix was my idea. It was 1968, and Geiger had taken the fertility research as far as he could. That's what he thought." Neil turned to the windows, closed his eyes, and took in a deep breath. He felt sick that this air coming into his lungs was being shared with the pitiful, unhygienic man. "But I took the idea further. Do you see what I'm getting at here?" he asked, turning back to Dr. Foy.

Arnold offered his superior a smile, his eyelids fluttering a few times as he adjusted his position in the leather chair on the opposite side of the desk. Sweat began to percolate on his forehead and back. "I see how far we've come because of that brilliant—"

"No, no, no, Arnold!" Dr. Owens sliced his hands through the air as he made his way to the credenza housing an elegant bar setup. He uncorked a glass decanter of cognac and poured two glasses as he continued. "Stories you mentioned earlier. This entire facility was born from stories—stronger yet, a reason, a vital reason. Of the hundreds of doctors we have working here, most, I'm tempted to say all, have a reason they strove to be the finest, the most specialized in their field. The best. They want to give their little brother sight. They want to give all the little brothers and sisters out there the ability to see, either again or for the first time." Neil turned and offered Dr. Foy a glass.

Arnold shook his head. "I better not. I still have—"

"They can't wait to see how a small implant behind the ear"—Neil paused and set the extra glass down hard on the bar top, sneering before turning back with a grin—"will light up a child's face when the implant is activated and the child can hear for the first time. Maybe more rewarding because their own child never had that opportunity. Or their niece or nephew. They want to cure a form of possession, *genuine possession*, that, in our modern era, has long been misdiagnosed as schizophrenia."

Dr. Foy furrowed his brow. "Did you mean that the other way around?"

Neil wanted to hurl his vintage rocks glass at the skull of this close-minded buffoon. If he didn't get this man out of here soon, Neil wasn't sure he could control his impulses. "No, Arnold, I didn't. I do not misspeak. Ever. Let's continue instead onto something your mind can comprehend. They want to make sure that no parent has to suffer the loss of a child to hereditary disease or bear the weight that comes with raising and caring for a child who cannot function in normal society. I've heard hundreds of stories, thousands even, from the doctors, nurses, and scientists that we employ here, but I have not heard yours. What is your reason, Arnold? Where is the passion? What drives this pursuit to make your mark here at the Orbriallis?"

Arnold shifted once more in his chair. "I've always been intrigued by the possibility of—"

A knock on the door, followed by the scuffle of a toddler's entrance, interrupted Arnold's reply. Soft footsteps of heeled shoes followed. Arnold turned to observe an older woman who wore a scarf around her head, and most of her face, enter the office behind a young child.

"I'm sorry to intrude," the woman said in a voice that was soft and deep.

Arnold looked over at Dr. Owens, unsure how to react to the situation.

Neil gulped down his cognac and set the glass down. "No bother. Arnold here was going to have a good hard think about what I've asked him and perhaps come back more prepared." Dr. Owens glanced down at Arnold, his grin spreading wider.

Dr. Foy, physically shaking at this point, stood promptly, buttoning up his ill-fitting suit coat. He gave a firm nod to Dr. Owens, opting against a handshake, and offered the woman a pleasant smile before seeing himself out.

"Why is he here?" Neil seethed, motioning to the child now frolicking around his immaculate and richly decorated office with a toy airplane he was zooming through the air.

"I keep trying to tell you about his dreams. He's had another after his nap," the woman explained.

"Not this again, Lina. They are just dreams."

"No, I don't believe they are. He said he saw a pillar surrounded by trees and a woman on the waves of the ocean he could see out his window. Then the pillar fell, and he was falling with it."

Neil looked over at the child, a small shudder of horror barely contained. The young boy, Thomas Jeremiah, had just turned two, and already he was speaking fluid sentences, capable of executing precise dexterity exercises, and running around like a child of four or five. He also had a peculiarly formed head, mismatched and misshapen eyes, and unusually long fingers. The birthmark on the child's neck and chest, a maroon red glob, marked him as the malignant aberration he was. "Children as well as adults dream of falling."

"That is not what this is, Neil, please. I do believe he has potential to—"

The desk phone buzzed to life, a loud blare that broke the quiet of the office. Neil stepped over to his desk and hit a button. "Yes?"

"Dr. Owens?" a gruff voice, heavy with an Irish accent, asked through the speaker.

Neil's eyes fluttered. "Who else would it be, Seamus?"

Seamus chuckled. "Ah, right you are. Sorry to bother, but your man is here."

"Christ, about time in all this mess. Send him up. What is he even doing coming through the front doors?"

"No, not that man. The bloke, Richard. He's here making all kinds of…" The voice on the speaker trailed off as another voice came on in the background, calling Neil's name, saying it was urgent.

Neil picked up the phone. "Stop him from ranting, and bring him up here now," he ordered and slammed the phone down.

Lina flinched.

The boy stopped running around the office and looked at Dr. Owens. "What is the matter? It seems you are deeply disturbed, Neil."

Chills crept throughout Neil's body. He pointed at the boy. "Not another word out of you, Thomas."

The boy covered his mouth.

Dr. Owens spun around. "This idiot is making more of a mess… Lina, I don't have time for this right now. Take the boy, please, and go. I have to deal with Richard Grahams."

"Very well." Lina nodded and held out her hand. The child scurried over, taking it and following her back out of the office.

Neil repeatedly pounded the desk with his clenched fist. "Goddammit!" He gripped the edges of the desk and emitted a deep growl before releasing it and running his fingers through his hair, which had become dislodged from its clean, slicked-back mold. Neil closed his eyes and let out a long exhale through pursed lips as he reached inside his suit coat and pulled out a small gold bottle with a nozzle and a pump on top. He inserted it into his nostrils, one at a time, squeezed the pump, and inhaled deeply. Neil then unscrewed the nozzle, revealing a smaller one underneath. He tilted his head back, brought the bottle up, and released one drop of liquid in each eye.

Neil moaned in an almost sexual release. His face and shoulders slowly relaxed as he pocketed the bottle. He straightened out his jacket and started to pace casually around his office with his hands clasped behind his back.

A knock on the door was followed by Seamus pushing it open to allow Richard to walk through, who immediately fell into a frantic pace. "I'm done. We're done. It's all…fucked."

Dr. Owens raised his eyebrows, having never heard the man curse in the twenty-five years he'd known him. "Richard, what did I say about coming here?"

"You good here?" Seamus asked.

Neil smiled at his great-nephew. "Yes, but if you could just wait outside the door. This shouldn't take long."

Seamus nodded and shut the door.

"I know what you said," Richard said, still marching back and forth, "but you haven't had the police breathing down your neck for the past four days. It was just a matter of time before they found out she never went back to college."

"We knew this would happen, Richard."

"But they know everything, Neil!" Richard stopped and turned to Dr. Owens. "They know she was pregnant. They know what happened to her…my baby girl, oh God, my baby girl." Richard dropped to his knees and started crying.

Neil's eyes fluttered as he looked up at the ceiling and groaned. He walked over to his credenza, grabbed the glass of cognac he had poured for the inept and ill-prepared Dr. Foy, and made his way to Richard, kneeling down next to him. "Here, drink this. You clearly need it."

Richard dropped his hands from his face and looked at the glass. "Hard alcohol? We only drink red—"

"Oh, shut up, and drink this. It's from a $4,000 bottle of cognac, for Christ's sake." Neil shoved the glass into Richard's hands before standing back up. "And get up off the floor. Have a little self-respect," he muttered, standing over Richard.

Richard pushed up from his knee and wiped the tears from his cheeks. He sniffed the cognac, took a cautious sip, and swallowed. He then licked his lips and took a larger swig. "Mm."

"Now, tell me exactly what you told them. And please tell me when you say, 'they know everything' that means everything they could possibly find out on their own and you haven't completely lost your mind."

Richard shook his head. "No. I just told them what you told us to say. But he knows there's more. He knows we're lying. He knows I didn't tell him everything, I just know it."

"I thought you said Chief Richards wouldn't be a problem. And what is all of this 'I,' 'I,' 'I'? Where the hell was Bess in all of this?"

"She screamed at them and then locked herself in the bathroom. They came to our home. And it's not Richards. It's Seth Wolfe who is the problem."

"I'm supposed to know who that is?"

Richard shook his head. "He's from here. I went to high school with him. He'd been gone for, I don't know, twenty years and just recently came back to take care of his father. I guess he had a stroke and—"

"Richard!" Dr. Owens shouted. "I don't give a shit about whoever this man's father is. Just tell me why he's a problem."

"Sorry," Richard said and took another swig of the cognac. "This is superb. Um, he's a sergeant here now, but he was a big shot homicide detective in San Francisco for...a bunch of years. And he's...really intimidating."

Neil's nostrils flared. "And you, what, caved under the pressure?"

"Bess just left me out there, cornered by these guys. And I only told them what you told me—"

"You didn't think to tell me that a legitimate homicide detective was going to be leading the investigation, not our Podunk sheriff, whose biggest issues are someone's cows getting loose?"

"I had no clue what Seth Wolfe had done with his life after he left here," Richard pleaded. "I didn't even know he was back until I was in an interrogation room with him. And it's not my fault that my daughter's body ended up on the damn beach! You said you were going—"

"Enough!" Dr. Owens bellowed. "That is another issue entirely that I am dealing with. You"—Neil pointed at Richard as he approached him—"You and Bess both need to disappear."

"Huh?" Richard's face contorted.

"You need to step away from this situation. You've already done enough damage. I can't have you cracking under pressure again and revealing things you should not breath a word of."

"I…"

Neil put a hand on Richard's shoulder and leaned in closer. "I'm going to have someone come by your house. They will tell you everything you need to do. We'll take care of all the planning."

"What do you mean, planning?" Richard asked.

"Well, you can't stay here in town. Neither of you can. Bess locked herself in the bathroom? Abandoned you to deal with the police? And I thought she was the strong one."

Richard looked down. "She still won't talk to me."

"Exactly my point. The situation has gone from bad to toxic. You need to take a vacation, from the stress of everything. We'll book you at a nice, fancy resort, and you stay away until we have this all under control."

Richard raised his eyes. "We can't just leave in the middle of the investigation. Can we?"

"You can, and you will," Neil said and patted Richard on the back, walking toward the door.

"But can't they charge us with—"

Dr. Owens looked over his shoulder. "Oh, I'm sure they will. But those charges will pale in comparison to what they could charge you with if either of you slips up worse than you already have."

Richard stepped over to Dr. Owens's desk and set down the almost empty glass of cognac.

Neil opened the door and motioned for Seamus to come in. He leaned into his great-nephew as he stepped in and whispered, "Follow him home. Stay outside to make sure they don't go anywhere until Renner shows up."

Seamus looked down and cocked an eye. "And what if they do leave?" he asked.

"You just make sure they don't." Neil patted him on the chest and turned back to Richard. "Okay, off you go. Chop, chop," he said, clapping his hands.

Richard shuffled toward the two men and looked at Dr. Owens. "What about her body? They were going to release it—"

Neil placed a hand on Richard's lower back. "I said we would take care of everything, and I mean everything. We'll make the arrangements for the funeral and have her properly taken care of. Now, Seamus will walk you out."

Richard looked up at the hulking man and swallowed heavily. "Okay."

"Do try to patch up things with Bess. You've already lost enough."

Seamus put his hand on Richard's upper back and led him out the door. Richard turned back to Neil. "Dr. Owens, when can we see her?"

Neil smiled, tight-lipped. "Soon. Very soon," he said and shut the door.

Dr. Owens walked over to his desk and sighed. "On my desk?" He removed the glass of cognac and brought it over to the credenza. He returned to his desk and pulled a pager from the drawer, along with a piece of paper. Looking from one to the other, Neil typed in the code Renner had provided to him.

Looking at Ghosts

What does one do when everything they've ever believed true to the rules and laws of the universe gets upended? Just last week, Seth woke up to the usual routine of mundane tasks and a predictable life. Seth was simply an ex-homicide detective living back home, taking care of his ailing father while doing routine patrol duty for the Lost Grove Police Department. But then came a life-altering experience that shed light—too much fucking light—on a caving accident when he was seventeen. He'd become trapped and was struggling for air, which caused an out-of-body experience, transporting him to Mourner's Beach where he saw the lifeless body of a young woman.

So last Thursday, when he was called to the scene of a homicide, he stepped onto Mourner's Beach knowing every experience he was about to have. Every detail was the same as when he'd been trapped in that cave over twenty years ago. The constant in both experiences was the woman—a young woman who had strange visions of the future—whose mysterious death he was investigating. And now, he found himself falling for a woman who claimed to be a witch, getting his daily coffee from a woman who saw ghosts and alien spaceships, and met a renowned doctor whose parents were possessed by otherworldly entities. Everything he thought he knew about logic and humanity was being challenged by these experiences, and it all seemed connected to Sarah's death. The most unsettling part? He believed every bit of it. But none of it was helping him solve this case.

Seth gripped the steering wheel tightly as he drove down Highway

17 toward Mourner's Beach. The clock on his dashboard read 10:03 p.m., and a gentle drizzle began to decorate his windshield. What did a good detective do when he hit brick wall after brick wall on an all-important case? He went back to the scene of the crime, having met more dead ends at Grady-Angel House, the women's safe house that Sarah purportedly stayed at after leaving the Orbriallis Institute.

The shift manager at Grady-Angel, Rosalie Daniels, had confirmed Sarah's stay from January of this year until two weeks ago, when she'd left on her own recognizance. Inexplicably, Mrs. Daniels claimed she had no clue Sarah was pregnant, despite the fact she was at the end of her last term. She said Sarah had put on some weight during her stay there, but "she just looked healthy." Being a safe house, there was no surveillance footage from inside the house that would have visually confirmed Sarah's presence. And even if there was, Seth would have needed a court order to obtain said footage, a point Mrs. Daniels knew well, informing him of such when he inquired about the security camera outside the entrance.

Seth left Grady-Angel, his mind a jumble of frustration, confusion, and exhaustion. He'd dialed Bill's number as he drove home, relaying only the essentials of his visit—no time for details in his current state of mind. A new press release was being prepared, announcing that Sarah Elizabeth was pregnant and her child was missing—a fact that weighed heavily on Seth's conscience. Had they waited too long to go public with this information? Would the baby still be alive? Seth would never forgive himself if the child had died in the time elapsed in this investigation. Morbid thoughts swirled in his head like a hurricane. But there was no time to dwell on them now—he had work to do.

He wasn't about to take that chance with Peter Andalusian. Tired of waiting for his wife, Jolie, to reach him, Seth called Sasha, tasking her with tracking down Peter Andalusian through the Coast Guard. He wanted concrete proof that Peter was actually on the fishing vessel he'd registered to be on. Seth instructed Sasha to say that he was a person of interest in a murder investigation and that it was imperative that they speak with him immediately. If he was on the fishing vessel, great—the Coast Guard would bring him back to shore. If not, they would issue a national alert for his whereabouts, and Seth would pay another visit to the Andalusian residence. The clock was ticking, and Seth refused to waste more time in finding the missing child.

He needed something to jar his thoughts. But did Seth actually think returning to the spot where Sarah Elizabeth's body was found would provide any new information for this case? Or was Seth returning there to satiate his own need to confront the event that had left him shaken? The truth was the two reasons weren't mutually exclusive. After hearing in-depth analysis of Sarah's visions and what they meant, not to mention the intimate details about Dr. Bajorek's mothers being possessed by dead relatives, and that they were being medically treated for it, Seth left the doctor's office accepting the one truth that had been staring him in the face since he relived his time-traveling experience—he was a part of Sarah's story, linked to her death before she was even born.

If Seth could understand more about his experience, how or why he traveled through time, then maybe that would help shed light on a case that was perplexing and more bizarre than any in his entire career.

Seth pulled his Bronco over to the side of the road—the same spot he parked last Thursday morning. A dirt inlet framed by a small cliff overlooked the ocean. He gripped the door handle, pushed open the door, and paused with one foot on the ground. He was about to take off his utility belt, but his instincts were telling him to keep his gun on him. Who or what did he think he would encounter, alone on a beach at night, that would necessitate a gun? Seth questioned if it was fear, not instinct, setting off that tingle in his gut. But he never reached for his firearm out of fear in his life.

Taking his first stride onto the dune leading to the beach, he couldn't deny he was almost hoping he would relive the same divinatory experience for the third time—to fall into the dreamlike state, floating on air, hearing, smelling, feeling clues that led to Sarah Elizabeth's body being placed near the immense piece of driftwood. Yet, as he ascended the peak of the dune, all he felt was the frigid ocean breeze smack him in the face. The shattering of waves hitting land filled his eardrums.

Seth shoved his hands in his pockets, gripping the lucky acorn Story had given him last Thursday morning with purpose. "Come on, Story, bring me some luck with this thing." He surveyed the panorama of the beach, allowing his eyes and senses to soak in every shadowed shape, every moonlit reflection. What had he missed? There was something that morning, a missing link, the first puzzle piece to connect with the rest. What had Mary seen that dark morning before the rising sunlight cut across the surface of the Pacific Ocean? He needed to see her tomorrow and show her the crime scene photos.

Seth squinted into the darkness, scanning the turbulent waters. The air was crisp and cool, with a faint smell of salt water drifting in from the ocean. Seth began his trek toward the piece of driftwood that would forever be linked to Sarah Elizabeth.

"Do you know I'm here?" he asked without a shred of self-judgment. He wanted to hear her, see her in his mind. A sign, something to push the case forward to bring her justice, a justice he knew in his heart she would feel, wherever she was.

Seth brought the acorn, housed in his clenched fist, to his mouth and blew on it. "I won't miss it this time. I'm ready. For anything."

With each step, Seth could feel the sand giving way beneath his boots, a sensation similar to sinking in quicksand. He clicked on his flashlight, shined it on the ground, and saw his own footprints leading back. The thought of losing this crucial piece of evidence made his heart sink even further. Despite the strong winds whipping across the beach, he couldn't believe that they would have erased footprints this deep. Sarah's body had only been there for a short time before they arrived. And according to Wes' initial photos of the scene, there were no footprints around her body. Something didn't add up.

Seth turned back around, switched off his flashlight, and relied on the moonlight to guide him as he made his way forward. As a detective, Seth knew that finding physical evidence at this point was unlikely. He needed to rely on his senses, his memory, his instincts, and maybe some cosmic help. Seth closed his eyes and took a deep breath, focusing on the surroundings, trying to piece together why someone brought Sarah Elizabeth's body to this particular beach and leave her unclothed.

The stretch of sandy beach was not lacking in hiding spots for a body. The majestic ocean to his left was an easy choice for someone looking to dispose of evidence. So why here? Why near the driftwood? And why strip her naked? Seth knew these details were important and could hold the key to solving the case. Someone was sending a message, and it was up to him to decipher it.

Slowing his pace, Seth opened his eyes and batted his eyelids to clear away the fog just as a blood-curdling shriek almost lifted Seth's soul from his body. His heart and body froze in a moment of sheer terror before his instincts thrust him into a galvanized sprint in the scream's direction.

Seth lifted his flashlight with one hand, pulling his baton from his belt with the other. "Lost Grove Police! Stay where you are! Do not move!"

He swept the light beam back and forth across the beach until he spotted a figure in black crouched down on the ground about thirty yards away.

"Stay down, and put your hands up in the air! Now!" Seth slowed to a brisk walk, taking long strides toward the person crouched in the sand, their hands in the air. As he approached, Seth could see that the hands were trembling. The person was trembling all over, in fact. He pulled the baton back, his grip firm, ready to strike, just as the person lifted their head, squinting from the light. "Story?"

Seth dropped the baton and slowed as he neared her, shock sending chills throughout his body. *What the fuck is she doing here?* "What on earth are you doing here?" he asked, taking in the tears streaming down her face and the alarming pallor of her skin. He had an urge to pull her into his arms, comfort her, and wipe away her tears, but his professional brain just managed to address this as a possible assault.

Story held a hand in front of her eyes. "I'm...I..." she stuttered.

"Did someone attack you?" Seth whipped the light in a full 360 around them and then brought it back on Story, held just low enough to illuminate her face but not blind her.

"No...I...I need a minute." She moved awkwardly from the blanket she was kneeling on to the driftwood behind her and settled her backside onto it, dropping her hands to her knees.

Seth scanned the sand, noticing a mirror, a candle that had sputtered out, and a small trail of oddly white smoke hanging like a will-o'-the-wisp in the air, unmoved by the breeze shifting across the beach. He swallowed, eyes locked on the smoke, trying to make scientific sense of what he was seeing. He'd already crossed the bridge of logic days ago. "What is this?" he asked, turning back to Story.

Her shoulders heaved with the silent shedding of tears as she brought her hands to her face, wiping them away.

Seth walked over to her and squatted down to get a look at her face. "Look, I really need you to explain to me what you're doing here and what all of this is about," he said, motioning to the paraphernalia behind him.

"All that pain, and still, all she wanted was to know if it was alive," she whispered.

The hairs on Seth's arms stood on end. "What?"

"She was in so much pain, and all she cared about was making sure the..." Story trailed off, her hand circling in the air as if she had lost the ability to form words.

"Making sure the—what?" Seth almost asked her who she was talking about, but the answer was obvious from the few words muttered.

She finally sat upright, still leaning on the massive driftwood for support. "I'm sorry. This must be confusing for you."

"Confusing? That would be one way to put it. You nearly gave me a heart attack. What the hell were you screaming about? Why are you here?" Seth pointed his flashlight back at the items in the sand. "What is this? A-a-a…ritual?"

Story snorted.

Seth pointed the light back on her, again noticing the terrifying paleness of her skin, her lips, as if she'd lost a lot of blood. He reached out, lifting her chin up so he could look into her eyes, see if she had all her faculties. He touched her skin as an officer assessing the scene, but her soft, warm flesh gave him a distinct set of shivers. Her pupils dilated and contracted as expected. He let go of her chin, immediately missing the contact, and let out an exasperated sigh. "What the fuck, Story?"

"I'm sorry. I'm sorry. Let me explain."

"Please," he urged.

"I was practicing mirror work."

"Mirror work?"

"Scrying. Seeing into the Otherworld. Spirit talking." Story took a deep breath to steady herself. "I was talking, well, no. I was communicating with Sarah Elizabeth."

Seth swallowed, and his spontaneous decision to come here tonight came into poetic light, the precise light for which he was searching.

Story wiped at her tear-stained cheeks. "She was in so much pain," she said.

Seth looked from her eyes to the driftwood and out toward the sea. "What are you saying? Are you saying you…conjured her with all this?" he asked, sweeping his hand to the ground and looking back at her.

Story looked up and met his eyes. "There was another living being attached to Sarah."

Seth's mouth gently parted. "Another—"

"A baby." Story watched the emotions sort themselves through Seth's eyes. Disbelief, a sense of fear. For a moment they danced around her, taking her in as if there was some physical sign to denote what she was. Then realization came, of what she'd said. Realization that she had just discovered a piece of information she shouldn't know, and at last, it resolved into the eyes of the detective he'd spent so many years of his life being.

Seth stayed focused on Story. Ask him in another life, a life where he was still a detective working cases in the San Francisco Police Department, where the worst things he saw were acts committed by humans upon other humans, and he would have found Story's knowledge suspicious. He'd have brought her in for questioning. He wouldn't have believed a word she was saying. But that was another life, one that seemed to be a distant past—an unlived alternate course. Whatever Story was, or whatever powers or skills she possessed, revealed a truth about Sarah Elizabeth that she had no other way of knowing.

Seth squatted down to lean against the driftwood next to Story. The flashlight hung between his legs. She sniffled beside him, and he could feel her eyes on him. He could even feel the hesitation sitting on her shoulders like a bird of prey. "Is it…you said you felt the baby? Does that mean it is also…gone?" Seth asked.

Story shifted to sit beside him. "I couldn't tell."

He stared at her bare feet poking out from under the layers of her long dress. He wanted to massage them, to ease whatever pain she experienced doing…whatever it was she was doing. "So, what, um, you mentioned something about mirror work?"

Story couldn't help but smile. She initially planned on easing Seth into her world, what she did, bit by bit, not wanting to scare him away. But whether she liked it or not, the bandage was now torn off. She looked up and into his eyes. He wasn't scowling at her or wincing in anticipation of her outrageous answer. His mind was open. Story turned her body to face him and pulled her knees to her chest, wrapping her arms around them. "Mirror work is like scrying. It's a—"

"Scrying?" Seth asked.

"Yes. It's like fortune telling or trying to see into the future. The hope is to see something, hear something, a sign or an image that you can interpret. If you're lucky, it's something obvious that doesn't need to be read into."

Seth looked over at the mirror, noting the large feather next to the candle. "And the candle, the feather…?"

"Is all part of it, yes."

Seth narrowed his eyes, realizing just now in this moment, leaning up against the driftwood, that they were sitting directly over Sarah Elizabeth's final resting place. The hair on his arms and neck rose. Part of him wanted to spring up and away. But this was what he came here for in the first place, wasn't it? He was exactly where he was meant to be. He looked back at Story. "Did you…how did you know where her body was?"

Story smiled. "Mary told me."

"Of course." Seth sighed. "So, being here, where we found her body, is that part of mirror work?"

"It's not necessary, but in this situation, it's the most conducive to a hopeful outcome—more potent. I wanted to…" Story paused, her eyes dropping to the ground as images, feelings of what she went through, coursed back through her body.

"Are you okay?"

Story gripped her legs tighter and spoke into her knees. "I was hoping to connect to any residual energy Sarah had left behind. I wanted to speak with her, or listen to her, to see if she would answer any of my questions. Or show me a sign or a symbol. But what happened…it was nothing I've ever experienced. Nothing I've even heard of. I didn't even start asking my question before Sarah appeared over my shoulder in the mirror. Her face was…I could hardly fully gasp before I was… She pulled me into her world. Her…her experience. What she went through. She didn't just show me a sign or whisper an answer into the night. She pulled me inside her body so I could experience what she went through, her last moments on earth." Story hardly got out the last word before she started crying.

Seth's heart kicked against his chest. What Sarah had gone through, the intolerable pain she must have felt, the barbarism performed on her body, a symphysiotomy, in which the cartilage between the pubis and hip bone was severed, in addition to a pubiotomy, where the pubic bone was sawed through. Story was suggesting, claiming, she had just experienced it all. Seth wrapped his arm around Story and pulled her into his chest.

"It was… I was there. I could feel everything," she said through tears. "She just wanted to see her baby. To hold it. But she never even…"

"I know. Unfortunately, I know." Seth let her work through her tears as he tried to sort through what this meant. He came to Mourner's Beach tonight to reconnect with Sarah Elizabeth, to understand their connection, to find a missing piece to the puzzle. Yet, somehow, inexplicably, Story Palmer had her own experience, beating him to the punch. What Story was telling him, going into someone else's body, traveling back in time, it was like there was now a triangle connecting all three of them. *And if Story was there and saw through Sarah's eyes…*

Seth gently pulled away from her, keeping his hand on her back as she sat up and wiped her eyes. "Story, I hate to ask you this, but if you were there, inside Sarah Elizabeth's body, did you see who else was there? Who was trying to…?"

Story shook her head. "No. It was so quick. It didn't feel that way, but it was. I just saw…her. She was looking down at her body, her legs were up, and then…there was so much blood. I'm sorry," she said and looked up at him with her red eyes.

Seth shook his head. "No, don't be sorry. I just…"

They sat in a comfortable silence before Story gathered her senses enough to ask the obvious question. "Why are you here? I mean, I'm glad you are, but why did you come here tonight?"

Seth lifted his eyebrows and let out a long exhale. "I guess I came for the same reason you did. I just didn't know how to do it. But you did. I don't have any control over…"

"What?" Story asked, seeing his eyes becoming introspective, his head dropping. "Is this what's been with you? What you've been carrying?" Story had sensed a deep, internal conflict inside Seth from the moment he questioned her about Sarah Elizabeth. She commented on it last Friday when they met for wine and tea, but he wasn't ready to open up then.

Seth ran his hand through his hair. His heart rate ratcheted up again. "Yep," he said, elongating the e. Why even bother keeping it in any longer? It was the perfect, bizarre moment to let it out, to explain to someone, the only person who would believe it.

Story shifted her body to face Seth head-on and crossed her legs. She placed her hand just below his knee and gave it a gentle squeeze.

"I don't even know where to begin. There's two periods in my life that are…the same."

"Tell me the story. From the beginning."

Seth reached in his pocket, pulled out the acorn, held it up in the air. "I've kept this with me since you gave it to me last week."

Story smiled.

"It was odd. I didn't know you. Not really. But I found myself gripping it, twirling it around in my fingers at important moments during the case and whenever I thought about what happened to me. It calmed me, helped keep my focus," he said, gripping it once more, and then turned his gaze just past her to the ocean. "I had two best friends growing up here. Steve Wistie and Hart Garner. We knew each other in grade school, but we became tight the summer before junior high when we joined the summer baseball league together. Anyway, we did pretty much everything together from that point on, up through our last summer before we all left for different colleges in different states. We were outside all the time—biking, hiking, playing frisbee at the beach, flashlight tag in the woods at night, camping, taking road trips as soon as we got our licenses."

Story beamed, hearing parts of Seth's childhood, watching his eyes relive it. Her heart and mind were sending messages through the ether to her sisters, Asterin and Mable, who were waiting to hear all about this link that had drawn Story to Lost Grove in the first place. They'd be happy to know a genuine connection was finally happening.

"I guess I would say that I was the risk taker of the group," Seth said. "I mean, we were all adventurous, but I was always the first one to go climbing the tallest tree or wade out into the ocean, diving under the waves. There was this famous Norwegian explorer, Roald Amundsen, a polar explorer, taking ships and crews to the South Pole and then the North Pole. I thought, *Wow, can you imagine?* Being the first person on record to step foot on new land? I was attracted to all sorts of adventurers growing up, but I really gravitated toward him. He went out like a hero—he died in a failed aerial rescue mission. I thought, man, what could I do to make a mark like that? I had a slew of ideas of what I might be when I grew up—a firefighter, a storm chaser, a geologist, a whitewater rafting guide. I had never even rafted once in my life, but my stupid, fearless mind thought, *Shit, how hard can it be?*"

Story let out a light chuckle.

Seth continued. "It was the summer before our senior year, and we wanted to do something awesome, something leaps and bounds above anything we had done up to that point. We weren't sure what the summer before college would bring, when we would each have to leave, so this was our farewell tour. There were plenty of rumors growing up in Lost Grove about weird creatures in the woods—out-of-town campers who would disappear without a trace—but the one that intrigued us most was the rumor about an underground cave system, only accessible through the mountains. We had, of course, dipped our toes in this trek numerous times, but we never made it past the immense hurdles of steep drop-offs we couldn't even see the bottom of with a flashlight. Crevices so tight it was a coin toss of whether you would get stuck and never be able to get out, and cave entrances so high up we needed gear we didn't own. Not to mention the knowledge of how to use it. So, that's what we did that summer. We pooled our money together, bought all the gear, and checked out books from the library about climbing. By late July, we thought we could have climbed Everest. So stupid."

Story was lost in Seth's eyes, the wide eyes of a boy reliving his past through a man's body.

"So, in we went. We knew the route we wanted to go. There was one path that would take you to a dead end, where you either had to go down, go up, or turn around and go home. We were brave, but considering we couldn't see how far down the drop was, we opted with the smarter choice—to scale the cave walls to the tunnel entrance. We did surprisingly well, considering this was essentially a test run, having never put the equipment to use before. After we got up, we went on a long trek. To where? We weren't sure, but there were crazy rumors about gold left by diggers who died and never came back for it, treasures of various kinds, and one about a path that led to a secret society, a door to a place not accessible by land. We didn't find any of that by the time we came upon our first, our only, roadblock.

"It was one of those tight crevices we had seen on ground level, but this one, I knew I could get through. Steve was a little heavier and wider, so he was out. Hart could have made it but said, 'No way.' Me? I was Roald Amundsen. If he could be the first person, or at least first on record, to set foot on both Poles, then what was a little crevice? I got through alright, but it wasn't long before I got lost. I had to crawl on my hands and knees and eventually lost my internal compass. We were smart enough to bring walkie-talkies, but I couldn't even reach mine by the time I found myself wedged between two walls, trying to reach a crack I saw with light from outside shining through.

"The crack wasn't wide enough. I started to lose my breath. There wasn't enough oxygen making its way in, and I was fading. Before I passed out, I thought, *Roald Amundsen lived to be fifty-five, and here I am dying at seventeen.* And it was then that I had…what I thought at the time was a really fucked up dream or the afterlife. It was an experience of walking along Mourner's Beach, so slowly, almost floating is what it felt like. In the distance, I saw a coroner's van, yellow police tape, and a body—the nude body of a woman, deceased on this beach, in this very spot. This driftwood…" he said, reaching back and knocking on the wood.

Story straightened, goosebumps sprouting all over her body.

"And just as I reached the body, Bill woke me up. He was a young officer at that time. He apparently used a pickaxe to break through the small crevice I was reaching for and pulled me out just before I was probably taking my last breath. I didn't know what that experience was then, but I knew, without any doubt, I was going to be a police officer."

Story's eyes were wide, the icy breeze from the ocean making itself known.

Seth looked back at Story. "The experience lingered with me for a while but eventually disappeared from my consciousness. That was until last Thursday when I lived that exact same event, step for step, the same van, the same tape blowing in the wind, and the same…Sarah Elizabeth, lying dead on the beach."

Story blinked her eyes. "You time traveled."

Seth nodded. "Apparently so. I came back here tonight to…I'm not sure. Maybe to relive it again? To see if I could remember something previously forgotten, if something else came to me, or…happened to me. I even tried to speak to her. Turns out you were, too."

Story twirled a ring on her index finger. "Did this experience, this time travel, ever happen again?"

Seth shook his head, surprised, though he knew he shouldn't be, that Story was accepting his story at face value. "No. Just that one experience."

"Did you ever *try* to do it again?"

Seth huffed. "I didn't even know it was a thing to try again. I had chalked it up to a vivid dream or some sort of oxygen-deprived hallucination. It wasn't until last week that it all came to light what it was, what I had seen."

Story looked down, her eyes darting back and forth, and then looked back up at Seth. "Was that the morning I gave you the acorn?"

"It was."

"I knew there was a reason. It was so spur of the moment, but I could feel the energy coming off you. It was fear, desperation, confusion."

Seth sighed through his nose. "Yeah, I would say that was accurate."

"And to think, we'd both be here on the same night, trying to do the same thing. Did anything…before I screamed, did anything happen?"

"I didn't really have that much time before I heard you," Seth admitted.

"I'm sorry."

"Don't be. Clearly, this was all meant to happen the way it did. God, I can't believe I'm even talking like this." Seth dropped his head back between his shoulders.

Story gave Seth's leg another squeeze. "And here I was, thinking how hard it was going to be for you to believe what happened to me."

Seth laughed. "If this was a week ago, I'm not sure what I would have done."

"But it's not," Story said and smiled.

"No, it is not. But I'm also not really sure what to do now."

Story leaned in closer to him. "I could help."

Seth narrowed his eyes. "What do you mean?"

"You wanted to reach Sarah again."

"Mirror work?" Seth blurted. "After what you just went through?"

"It wouldn't be the same. That was my experience. That's what she wanted to show me. You're connected to her, Seth. And there are other ways."

Seth shook his head. "I think I've had enough for today. It's been…a long, long day."

Story dragged her hand from Seth's leg. "If you change your mind…"

Seth looked at her and thought that day would probably come, sooner rather than later, if he didn't get any further on the case. "Did you drive?"

"I told you. I walk."

"Right." Seth pushed himself up to his feet and reached his hand down to her. "Come on. I'll give you a ride back."

Story grabbed his hand and let him pull her up, firm but gentle. "Thanks."

There's Only So Much a Heart Can Take

Seth entered the Lost Grove Police Department just before dawn, holding a large cup of coffee. The first thing he saw was Sasha Kingsley, his brightest officer, hovering over the shoulder of his most junior officer, Joe Casey, looking at his cell phone. The contrast between the two was remarkable. Sasha, dark tattoo-covered skin with a muscular physique, stood a solid eight inches taller than Joe, scrawny and ivory-skinned with a mop of sandy-blonde hair. Yet the biggest difference between the two, something that made their older sister/younger brother relationship often entertaining, was that Sasha was bold, sarcastic, aggressive, and fiercely intelligent, whereas Joe was timid and soft-spoken, if not also eager to learn and showed great commitment.

"Holy shit. That's crazy," Sasha said and then looked up. "Morning, Seth."

Joe glanced up. "Oh, hey, Seth. How's your—"

"You get a hold of the Coast Guard yet, Sasha?" Seth asked.

Sasha could see the dark circles under Seth's eyes as he approached them, and his tone and expression didn't give off the vibe he was in the mood for frivolity. "Yep, first thing. I told them exactly what you said, and they took it seriously. I told them we needed an answer today, not later. They said it wouldn't be an issue, and if, for whatever reason, they couldn't reach their radio, they'd send a helicopter out to track down the vessel and board it."

Seth nodded with approval. "Good. I have two urgent meetings this morning, but—"

"I'll call you the moment I hear."

"Thanks," Seth said and took a sip of his coffee, knowing it would be the first of many today. "Joe, what have you got for me?"

Joe jogged over to his desk and grabbed a small stack of papers. "Background checks and financial records on the Grahams. Backgrounds are clean. I didn't see anything suspicious in their finances, but you'll probably want to look."

Seth stepped over and grabbed them. "You get anything on Peter Andalusian?"

"Just a bunch of hurdles I'm trying to get through. His background check hasn't come through yet. He banks through a military credit union, which sent me a load of forms to fill out. Bill said getting anything useful from the government about his time in the military would be highly unlikely. Not sure why."

"He was in Special Ops. Guessing it would all be confidential. Anything else?"

Joe looked over at Sasha, who shook her head. "Well, there is something that happened early this morning. It has nothing to do with the Sarah Elizabeth case, but I thought you'd want to know."

"He doesn't need to hear about that right now, Joe," Sasha said.

Joe shrugged. "I can tell you later. Just thought—"

"Go ahead and tell me. Just make it quick. I've got to talk to Bill and then get over to the high school before classes start."

"Right." Joe nodded. "So, I got a call from Ricardo Esteves at five this morning reporting scratching at his window in the middle of the night. He said it was piercing, like a garden cultivator or a hand rake—whatever they're called—or like lion or bear claws or something."

"A lion?" Seth asked, bewildered.

"That's what he said. And after seeing the window in question, it's easy to see where he's coming from."

"Window in question?" Sasha mocked.

Joe shot her a look and then pulled his phone back out. "Here. Check it out." He scrolled to a picture of the window and showed Seth.

"Jesus," Seth remarked, taking in the massive claw marks on the window.

"Ricardo said he was too afraid to go outside to check, so that's when I went over."

"So brave," Sasha said under her breath.

"And this is so crazy. Look at this." Joe slid past the window photos and stopped on one with what appeared to be two huge rocks. "Do you know what those are?"

"Just tell me."

Joe nodded. "Sorry. They're owl pellets."

"Owl pellets?" Seth asked, zooming in on the photo.

"Yeah, didn't you have to dissect them in school?"

"So gross," Sasha voiced behind them.

"I did," Seth answered. "But these look massive. How big were they?"

Joe smiled. "I placed my foot next to one for reference," he said, swiping the photos until he found the right one.

Seth frowned. "What in the world?" he murmured.

This was the last thing Seth needed. There was enough strange shit going on in his life. He didn't need giant owls mixed into the equation.

"That's why I wanted to show you," Joe said and scowled at Sasha, who, in turn, gave him the finger. Joe looked back at Seth. "So, I cut them open, and there was a possum inside one. Like a full possum. Check it out."

Seth held out his hand, stopping Joe. "I don't need to see it. I'd like to finish my coffee without feeling sick to my stomach."

"Right. Sorry."

"Did you send them to the lab?"

"Dropped them off on my way back."

Seth nodded and looked from Joe to Sasha. "Thanks, guys. Sasha, I'll be waiting for your call."

Sasha gave him a thumbs-up.

Seth walked into Bill's office, shut the door, and set his coffee and the papers on his desk.

Bill grabbed them and put on his reading glasses. "Did Joe tell you about the owl?"

Seth shook his head. "Yes, and I don't want to talk about it. I've got too much on my mind this morning to deal with that."

Bill looked up from the papers. "You in a bad mood?"

"Yes, I'm in a bad fucking mood. We found out who left the note on your door, identified Sarah's mysterious boyfriend, got her parents to finally confess to all the shit they were holding back, though I'm still convinced they're not telling us everything, and we're still no closer to solving this case. There's some weird shit going on at the Orbriallis Institute. I have to go tell the boy who was in love with Sarah Elizabeth, who's already devastated from her death, that she had a child and it's probably not his. And I swear, if I find out Peter Andalusian is not on that boat, I'm going to lose my mind."

Bill leaned back in his chair. "We don't know the child isn't his."

"There are few things in this case that I'm positive about, but one of them is that Tommy Wilder is not the father of that baby. Not that we are any closer to finding out just where in the hell this missing baby is so we can run a DNA test to attest to that." Seth tossed his hand in the air and started pacing.

"What did you mean there's weird shit going on at the Orbriallis? You told me they confirmed she was there and gave you the information about the safe house she was staying in."

Seth ran a hand through his hair. "I know. But the whole place has a strange vibe that I can't explain. You should have seen the size of this security guard. He had to have been six-six and 250 pounds of solid muscle. Not the type of security guard you'd imagine at a medical research facility. More like someone guarding a military compound."

Bill stood up and adjusted his belt. "Not sure that counts as being weird. Plus, they've got a lot of psychiatric patients there that could pose a threat."

"Then why wasn't he up on that ward? And their head nurse had no emotional reaction to Sarah being dead, much less wanting to help."

"Okay," Bill drawled.

"But it was Sarah's doctor. There wasn't anything strange about her. In fact, she was extremely open and helpful." Seth stopped pacing and stared up at the board. Part of him wanted to tell Bill about Dr. Bajorek's mothers, but he had the feeling that she'd shared that with him privately. "We talked for quite a while, but as soon as I got to the topic of the safe house, her demeanor completely changed. She became cold and clinical, answering the questions like she'd rehearsed them. And when I asked her if she knew Sarah was pregnant, she stared me in the eyes and said no in such a bizarre way that all I could hear was yes."

Bill stood next to Seth. "Hm. You think she wanted to tell you something she couldn't?"

"Very much so. And that was another thing. There were cameras everywhere. Too many. She and the head nurse both had one in their offices."

Bill looked up at Seth. "In their offices?"

"I want to talk to the head of the Orbriallis."

Bill raised his eyebrows. "Dr. Owens?"

Seth shrugged. "You tell me. Is he still running things?"

"Believe it or not."

"Is he still a recluse?" Seth recalled the urban tales and scary stories he and his friends used to share about the Orbriallis Institute. But that had been about the founder, Geiger. Was it possible his protégé and successor was even more bizarre and haunted? He wondered if Bill had heard any new myths kids might tell these days and shivered. It wasn't unfathomable to think the Orbriallis suspicious. These stories had been circulating for decades, and most stories had some basis in reality.

Bill nodded. "Don't think we've seen him taking a stroll down Main Street since you left for college."

"Any stories about him?"

"Stories?"

"Rumors, you know…the stuff kids tell each other? I'm sure you've heard the ones about Geiger."

"Oh, yes. I know the ones about Geiger. But, come to think of it, no. I've not heard a single tall tale about Dr. Owens. And you know how people like to talk around here."

Seth nodded. He wondered if any local teens would know. Maybe he could swing back around to ask Jeremy. He seemed like the kind to pick up on town gossip. "Can you make some calls and arrange a meeting?"

"Yep. I'm on it."

Seth checked his watch. "Let me see the statement. I need to get over to the high school."

Bill walked back to his desk, grabbed a sheet of paper, and handed it over to him. "Tried to stick to what you mentioned last night."

Seth held the statement up, reading it out loud, "'The preliminary investigation into the suspicious death shows the victim, Sarah Elizabeth Grahams, 21, of Lost Grove, sustained unusual injuries related to complications during childbirth. It has been confirmed that Ms. Grahams was being treated at the Orbriallis Institute since her admission in January 2021 and was subsequently released January of this year, with no contact with friends or loved ones during her time of treatment or after release. All hospitals in surrounding counties confirmed Sarah was not treated there. The infant has yet to be found. Lost Grove police are treating this case as a potential homicide and kidnapping. Anyone with information that may assist with this investigation is asked to contact the Lost Grove Police Department phone number, etcetera. Spot on."

Bill grabbed the statement. "Great. I'll send it over to the *Gazette* and tell them not to post it until…when?"

Seth walked over and grabbed his coffee and the papers from Joe off Bill's desk. "I'm heading there now. Principal Bernthal said he'll ask Tommy to wait in his office until I get there. Doubt they could even get it typed up and released by the time I get there. Just want to make sure he hears it from me. Tell them to release it in an hour."

"Will do. You going straight to Mary Germaine's afterward or coming back to the station?"

"Depends on how long this meeting with Tommy goes. You have the copies of the crime scene—"

"Right here," Bill said and handed Seth a manila folder filled with color copies of all crime scene photos taken at Mourner's Beach.

"Thanks, Bill. I'll call you if Mary uncovers anything."

"What's this all about?" Tommy Wilder followed Sergeant Seth Wolfe out the front door of Lost Grove High, his heart thumping, terrified he was about to be arrested for something he didn't do. Or worse yet, something he did do that he didn't know about. He went to the police station yesterday and gave a full statement, answering all questions, holding nothing back, so he couldn't imagine what this was about. When the sergeant arrived, he told him to grab his stuff and follow him outside, his face unreadable.

"Why don't we head over to the creek," Seth said, walking to the side of the school nearest Main Street where a small creek ran by with plenty of tree coverage. "We used to hang out down here. Used to be a bench."

Tommy felt light-headed as they rounded the side of the school. He couldn't imagine what would necessitate a meeting like this, though, admittedly, his mind had all but shut down since he heard the news about Sarah.

"Ah, there it is," Seth said, spotting the bench. "Let's have a seat."

Tommy wove through the trees and stopped in front of the bench as Sergeant Wolfe sat down.

Seth looked up at Tommy, who was staring down at the bench like he was afraid it was covered in battery acid.

"This was one of our favorite spots."

The simple declaration felt like a knife slowly being inserted into Seth's side. "We can sit somewhere else if you like."

Tommy dropped his backpack to the ground, the same one he used as a student not that many years ago. "It's okay," he said and sat down, looking ahead at the creek. He could feel the sergeant staring at him, his body already turned to face him.

"I need to tell you something, Tommy." Seth waited for the boy to break his gaze from the creek and look up at him. "And I wanted to tell you before we release a statement to the press about it."

Tommy swallowed heavily, having a hard time keeping eye contact with the sergeant. "Is it about what happened to her?"

"It is."

Tommy looked down at his fidgeting hands. Endless scenarios had run through his mind over this past week. None of them seemed real. The way her body was found, it just wasn't right.

Seth had delivered tragic news to countless people over the years, but it never got any easier. Every person was different, every relationship unique. The reactions to the bad news were unpredictable at best but always supremely painful. There was no easy way around the hard facts, so Seth kept them as such. The boy looked back up at him. "Sarah died from complications during childbirth. We don't know yet what specifically caused the death, but it was likely either from severe blood loss or a heart attack."

Tommy felt like all the oxygen in his lungs had been sucked out. He stared into the eyes of Sergeant Wolfe, the words reverberating around him like an echo in a mountain range. *Did he say childbirth?* "I don't…" Tommy shook his head.

"I'm sorry to be bringing you this news. I realize it's going to be a shock," Seth said, his tone even and resonating with professional empathy.

Tommy pressed his eyes shut, tilting his head toward the ground. "I'm not sure…" His eyes opened, his eyebrows drawn into a tight knot. "Can you say that again?"

Seth felt like the knife in his side slid deeper. "Mr. Wilder, Tommy, Sarah Elizabeth died from tragic complications due to childbirth."

"She couldn't be…pregnant?"

Seth nodded. "I'm afraid so. And as of yet, we don't know where the child is or who the father is."

Tommy's eyes locked on a bright red maple leaf floating down the stream. He watched it swirl past, mingling with the long, flowing grasses. "There's a baby?" he squeaked.

Seth's eyes fluttered closed for a moment, feeling the pain in the young man's voice. "Yes. There is a baby, and we're hoping we find it healthy and safe."

Tommy's face constricted, the contours of the lines forming the epitome of anguish. His head and shoulders dropped simultaneously as he started to weep.

Seth took a heavy, pained breath as he reached over and placed a hand on the boy's shoulder. It was risky in the current climate to physically console anyone in these situations, but Tommy Wilder had no one outside of his younger brother to care for him. "I'm so sorry."

Tommy dropped his face into his hands. "She would never have…I don't understand."

"I don't fully understand everything yet myself. There's still so much we don't know."

Tommy gripped chunks of his long hair in his hands and squeezed. "Sarah wouldn't have done that. It doesn't make any sense," he said through tears.

"It rather defies everything we've heard as well. But it happened. We don't know where or how. We've checked with every hospital in a fifty-mile radius, and there's no record of her being at any of them. And she hadn't been deceased long enough for her to have come from anywhere farther."

Tommy shook his head wildly. "What the fuck? How is that even possible? And why would her body be on the beach?"

Seth shivered. A flash of him approaching her body taunted his mind. "I wish I had answers for you. Believe me, I do. But we'll get them."

"Why didn't you say anything about the baby when you found her?"

Seth pulled his hand back from Tommy's shoulder. "We didn't know. Not until the autopsy revealed it. There were no outward physical signs alluding to her pregnancy. And we were careful about when we planned on releasing the information. We had some leads we needed to follow, which we hoped would bring about a quick resolve. That didn't happen."

Tommy looked up at Seth, tears still flowing, his voice still shaking. "What if the baby is in danger? Why didn't you say something earlier? We could have…searched. Or something."

Seth had been beating himself up over this very thing the past few days, but the fact remained, there wasn't an infant crawling around the woods, lost. "We knew that if the baby was still alive, someone had possession of him or her and didn't want anyone to know. We didn't want them to panic and flee if they were close by. But we could only hold off for so many days, hoping we'd find that person first."

Tommy gripped his pant legs and gritted his teeth, trying to stop himself from crying. There was no way Sarah would have put herself in a position to get pregnant. She wanted to wait until she was older, having years of experience as a practicing doctor first. What could have changed in the short time that would have upended her dreams?

Seth could only imagine the confusion running through this boy's mind. Seth's own mind was a land of confusion, and he had never even met Sarah Elizabeth. Not really. What would Tommy do when they found out who the father was? If they found out. Seth shook his head. *When we find out.*

Tommy looked back up at Seth. "I don't know what to do. What do I do with this, this…information?"

Seth watched Tommy look around their surroundings, almost like he wanted to escape but didn't know where to go. "Take care of your brother. Focus on your job. And call me literally any time, day or night." Seth handed Tommy his card.

Tommy looked down at the sergeant's card, his cell number listed, wondering if he would call him. Who else did he have to call? He couldn't talk about this with his mother. His brother was too young to understand any of it.

Seth glanced down to his watch. He still had an hour before his scheduled time at Mary's. "Hey," he said, grabbing the boy's attention. "You want to go grab a coffee, breakfast, an early lunch? We could go to the Victorian Inn. It's usually pretty quiet at this time of day."

Tommy looked up, confused. "To…like, just talk?"

Seth smiled. "Yeah, just talk about whatever you want. Doesn't have to be about Sarah. Sports, movies, books."

The thought of having breakfast with a sergeant of the Lost Grove Police Department was nothing Tommy thought he'd ever do in this life. But in this moment, he was instantly grateful he was wrong. He wiped his eyes and nodded. "Okay."

Mary gently placed a china serving plate from her grandmother down on the lace tablecloth draped over her living room coffee table. Filling the plate were an assortment of crackers, nuts, and figs. A pair of teacups and saucers were already set, one in front of the love seat, the other in front of Mary's rocking chair. Between the cups was a small dish with an assortment of herbal teas and a ramekin of sliced lemons. Water was simmering in a vintage teapot on the stove, and a soy candle smelling of autumn was lit on the side table.

Mary stood back from the table, satisfied with her presentation. She knew it was overkill for Seth, but Mary had been so flustered and overwhelmed by Noble and his friends' surprise visit, she was doing everything she could to feel at ease. The thought crossed her mind that having tea and crackers while dissecting crime scene photos of Sarah Elizabeth's corpse might seem distasteful, but images of the dead didn't bother her. She couldn't imagine they bothered Seth. He'd been a homicide detective for twenty years. He would never eat if such things offended him.

Mary checked her family's grandfather clock for the twentieth time in five minutes, back when it was 9:20 a.m. Seth had texted her at 8:00 a.m., letting her know he was delayed having breakfast with Tommy Wilder and would be there around 9:30 a.m. Mary literally fumbled her phone, dropping it to the kitchen floor when she read the message. What on earth was Seth doing having breakfast with Tommy Wilder? Not that Mary thought Tommy would ever harm Sarah in any way. She had never seen such adoration. He had looked purely devastated when Seth spoke with him two nights ago. She was too far away to make out what they were saying.

Did Mary feel guilty for spying on Seth that night? A little. But then again, Seth was clueless about who Sarah Elizabeth's boyfriend was until she told him. Everyone was. Mary was just too curious to stay away. She didn't know how long Seth and Tommy had been talking, but she ran in a full-on sprint to get there. Mary was relieved that Seth didn't haul the boy away in handcuffs, and seeing Tommy break down in tears after Seth drove away broke her heart. She cried all the way home that night. She cried for the pain and loss Tommy was living through, and she cried because Mary knew she would never get to feel love and loss like that.

Heavy bass from a car approaching grabbed Mary's attention. Certainly, this couldn't be Seth. Mary walked over to her front window, pulled the curtains aside, and peered out to see a yellow sports car pass by her house. She looked both ways, and just as she was about to let go of the curtains, the Lost Grove Police Bronco pulled up and stopped. Mary walked over to the Victorian mirror in the entryway and looked at herself. Was she pretty? It had been so long since the question had crossed her mind; she wasn't even sure how to assess herself. Mary knew Story had her eyes set on Seth and that she herself was incapable of having a relationship, but that didn't stop Mary from putting on her favorite dress, some makeup, and a single spray of perfume.

Seth grabbed the folder of the crime scene photos, opened the door, and stepped out onto Merrill Lane. Breakfast at the Victorian Inn with Tommy seemed to be somewhat of a cleansing experience for the boy. Seth asked him questions about growing up in Lost Grove, what high school was like for him, and shared answers to the same questions in return. Tommy really started to relax and let go when Seth told him the story of the boy who got stuck in the cave. After walking Story through every step of the near-tragic time-traveling event, it was fresh in his mind. He reiterated to Tommy to call him or text him at any time and promised to keep him abreast of any new information in the case.

Seth opened the front gate to Mary's property and walked toward the front door, hoping for a minor miracle. The chances she would spot something that he and Bill missed were slim, but she was the only person in town who could recount seeing Sarah Elizabeth's body before they arrived at the scene. She and whoever it was who placed her body there, of course. Seth knocked gently on the door. Mary knew he was arriving, but he had an inkling she wouldn't react well to his usual officer-of-the-law greeting meant to echo throughout an entire house.

Mary opened the door rather quickly and smiled. "Hello, Seth."

"Good morning, Mary."

"Please, come in."

Seth nodded and stepped through the doorway, instantly catching the scent of a burning candle and, if he wasn't mistaken, perfume.

Mary shut the door and walked past Seth, motioning to her living room. "We can sit in here."

"That's a really nice dress, Mary," Seth said, motioning to her light brown and floral vintage dress that made him think she might ask him to a picnic.

Mary blushed as her heart fluttered, a sensation she hadn't felt in more years than she cared to remember. "I made it."

"No kidding!" Seth rounded the corner and noted the elegant setup for tea and crackers. "Are you…"

"It's for us," Mary said and walked between her rocking chair and the love seat. "I know you are going out of your way to do this here. I wanted to say thanks."

Seth smiled at Mary, wishing he hadn't eaten that breakfast burrito at the Inn. "That's very kind of you."

"You can sit over here." Mary pointed at the love seat and sat down in her favorite chair. "Oh, wait!" She popped right back up and shuffled toward the kitchen. "I forgot the water."

Seth lowered down on the sofa and set the folder next to him, recalling the case of Walter Speedman, a high school boy stabbed to death in an alley in the Financial District in San Francisco. He worked the case for six months, eventually catching who did it, bringing justice and some closure to the family. He became close with the Speedmans, Russell and Sienna, over the course of the investigation. That was the last time anyone had food and drinks laid out for him.

"Did you pick a tea yet?" Mary asked, reentering the room.

"Ah, sorry." Seth leaned forward and fingered the tea packets, picking out a rooibos chai. A memory of Story reading his tea leaves flashed in his mind. "This looks good."

Mary waited for him to open the packet and place the bag in the cup before filling it. She then filled her cup, which already had a bag of lavender tea.

Seth grabbed a cracker and ate it while he waited for Mary to return from the kitchen. He had no room left in his stomach, but he wasn't about to let Mary go through all this work for nothing.

"Of course I have to ask," Mary said as she returned to her rocking chair. "What was breakfast with Tommy about?"

Seth took a sip of his tea. "Let's look at these photos first. Then I promise I'll tell you."

"Of course." Mary felt a tingle of anticipation run up her spine. It wasn't that she was relishing the idea of looking at poor Sarah Elizabeth's dead body again, but the morning was seared into her memory. She had examined every part of Sarah's body, fighting off her urges, and wanted to help, to be a part of something.

Seth pulled the 8x10 photos from the folder. "Now, usually I would warn the person about to look at these, but you were there. And I really want you to take a moment before I hand you these to go back to that morning, retrace your—"

"I already have. All last night and this morning. I recall everything."

Seth raised his eyebrows. "Okay, then," he said and handed them over.

Mary placed the stack of photos on her lap and grabbed her tea, taking a sip as she looked at the top photo, a closeup of Sarah Elizabeth's face. The eyes were just as she remembered, milky and empty. Her lips, not unlike the color of the buds flavoring her tea, were a soft purple.

Seth took another sip and set the cup down. He folded his hands together, placed his elbows on his knees, and lowered his chin to his intertwined fingers. He watched Mary take her time with each photo, her eyes dancing across each horrific image, waiting, begging for the moment her eyebrows might lift with a revelation. Seth closed his eyes and internally chanted, *See something, see something, see something...*

"Well, this isn't right."

Seth's eyes popped open. Mary held an overhead photo of Sarah's body out toward him. "What? What is it?"

"There are no footprints," Mary stated.

Seth slowly nodded. "Right. We noticed that, too."

"No." Mary shook her head. "But there were."

Seth stood up, his heart jolting him into action. "Are you sure?"

"I'm positive. There were footprints, large ones, coming toward and then away from her body. I thought they could have just been leftover footprints from whenever, but they're not here now. So..."

Seth's eyes locked on Mary. "Jesus Christ. Whoever placed her body there—"

"Was still there. Watching me." Mary cocked her head to the side at the irony of her being the watched, not the watcher.

"And came back after you left to clear their tracks." Seth slowly sat back down, gaze falling to the ground. "Holy shit. I mean, we knew that someone placed her body there, but—"

"How did you know?"

Seth looked back up at Mary. "The autopsy. I'll... Please, keep going through the photos, and then I'll explain."

Mary sighed and took another sip of tea to calm her nerves. Seeing the picture brought back the scent of cold meat, the peculiar touch of soap, like someone had washed her clean before dumping young Sarah Elizabeth on the beach. "She smelled like soap," Mary muttered.

"Soap?" The admission threw him off, though it made sense given the state of the body when they found her.

Mary nodded. Recalling the scene made her teeth ache and her mouth salivate. The lavender tea was helping. She shuffled to the next photo.

"Do you know what kind?" he asked.

"No, not really. Ivory perhaps."

Seth marveled at how unaffected Mary was in this process. She had the level-headedness of a seasoned detective.

"Wait, hold on here," Mary said, setting her tea down. She stared at a photo of Sarah's left arm and shoulder. She brought back up the wide overhead photo from earlier, eyes darting between them. "No. No, no. What is this?"

Seth thought he might throw up in anticipation. Who was this woman, this old schoolmate of his, who kept unlocking secrets to this case at an eye-popping rate?

Mary held out her left arm, posing it like the photo. "No. It wasn't like this. Her left arm wasn't out like this."

Seth jumped up and walked behind her so he could see what she was looking at.

"It was on her stomach," Mary continued.

Seth narrowed his eyes, his mind racing. "It's a sign," he muttered.

Mary looked back over her shoulder at Seth. "What?" she asked. Her nostrils flared with the notes of basil, mint, vetiver, and sage, mixing in with the heady scent of adrenaline and testosterone.

"Mary, are you positive? And I mean one hundred—"

"Yes. No question." Her eyes noted the soft pulse in Seth's neck, the flush in his lips. Her jaw tightened to the familiar pain of her teeth shifting, only this wasn't a desire she'd satiate with blood.

Seth pointed at the photo. "Her hand. Her arm. It's pointing."

Mary returned her gaze to the photo. "It would appear that way, yes."

"I knew it! I told Bill that her body looked staged. Fuck. Can I…" Seth held his hand out for the photo.

Mary handed it over.

Seth knelt down and placed the photo on the floor. "Mary, can you put the rest of those down here, all next to each other?"

Mary's lithe body slipped from the chair to crouch next to Seth. "I'm like your partner," she enthused, watching him.

Seth laughed, his eyes on the photo. "You might as well be."

Mary laid down the rest of the photos, twelve in all. "What are you looking for?" she asked, settling onto her knees.

"I'm trying to figure out where she's pointing, which direction."

"South."

Seth looked at Mary, meeting her eyes. "How...?"

Mary pointed at the photos as she spoke. "Her head is facing the ocean, which is west. That obviously makes her feet east. And the town is south, so that makes this...well, southwest, I guess, not directly toward town."

Seth tried to set his internal compass to gauge what that meant. "Right. So, what's just west of town?"

"The Orbriallis Institute," Mary stated blandly, eyes still crawling over the photos on the floor. She could feel the ocean on her face, sense that human smell drifting toward her. The way it mingled with the briny bouquet of the sea air like a well-seasoned cut of meat. Mary bit the inside of her lip to make herself stop thinking such terrible notions.

Beside her, Seth stilled. *The Orbriallis*, he thought. Seth covered his mouth, while his entire body sprouted goosebumps.

Mary felt the shift and looked up to find a wary but determined expression burning in his eyes. "What is it?" Mary asked.

Seth closed his eyes as one hundred and one scenarios collided in the center of his mind. He already knew Sarah was being seen at the Orbriallis. Was this something more? Something different? Had she actually never left? Who would have staged this? Clearly someone with inside intel. But—

The sound of Seth's phone snapped him out of his trance. He pulled it from his inside jacket pocket, looked to see who it was, and answered. "Sasha," he said with plain inflection.

"Seth," she replied, mimicking his bored tone.

Seth caught the sarcasm and his own distant delivery. "Sorry, I just... We have a big breakthrough in the case."

"I know."

"What?"

"Did someone already call you?" Sasha asked, growing confused by the rapid-fire back and forth.

"What are you talking about? I'm talking about something in the crime scene photos that—"

Sasha interrupted. "I just got off the phone with the Coast Guard."

Seth's heart rate picked up even further. "And?"

"He's not on the fishing vessel, Seth."

Seth turned away from Mary, gritted his teeth so hard he thought they might shatter, and scrunched his face, trying desperately not to explode in a slew of expletives.

"I thought you'd be far more upset than this," Sasha said.

"I am," Seth squeaked out and then whispered, "I'm at Mary Germaine's and can't fully express the severity of my fury."

"Fully understood. And well stated."

"Is Bill there?"

"Yeah, he's in his office. Do you want me—"

"No. I'll be there in minutes. Make sure he doesn't leave—any of you."

"You got it," Sasha said and disconnected.

Seth pocketed his phone, let the muscles in his face ease, and spun back around to face Mary. "Sorry about that. And thank you. I can't begin to tell you how much help you've been. Again." Seth stood and straightened his pants.

Mary shrugged and smiled up at him. "I'm glad I could help. Do you have to go?"

"Very much so, I'm afraid. Between what you've helped me uncover and that phone call…let's just say it's going to be another endless day." He looked down at all the photos on the ground. "Shit."

"I can do it," Mary said and collected the photos.

"You're the best," Seth replied and whole-heartedly meant it. He walked over to the couch, downed the rest of his tea, and grabbed a handful of nuts, his appetite miraculously returning.

Mary stood and handed Seth the photos. "Seth?"

Seth stuffed the photos in the folder and tucked it under his arm, heading for the door. "Yeah, Mary?"

"You told me you'd tell me why you were having breakfast with Tommy."

Seth stopped mid-stride toward the front door and turned back around. "Right. I'm sorry. Um…so this is going to be released to the public any minute now if it hasn't been already, but we know how Sarah Elizabeth died."

Mary stood facing Seth, her hands clenched in front of her chest. "Okay."

Seth sighed, his vigor temporarily subdued at the macabre reminder of how Sarah passed away. "Sarah Elizabeth was pregnant."

"What?" Mary's voice lifted in shock.

"She died during childbirth in a…not pleasant manner. Her body was placed on Mourner's Beach not long after."

Mary felt a horrific pain in her heart for the girl she used to watch from afar. Tears welled up in her eyes. "The baby?"

Seth shook his head. "We don't know. There's nothing to indicate the child didn't survive. But there's also no trace of where the baby might be."

"Was she at the Orbriallis?" Mary asked, her face contorted with confusion.

Seth froze with his mouth open. "Um…"

"It's where she was pointing. And your reaction…I don't know." Mary shrugged.

"Mary, I've got to go. I wish I could say more, but there's still so many questions." Seth turned and walked to the front door, opening it to leave.

"Was it his? Was it Tommy's?" Mary asked, hovering directly behind Seth.

Seth turned back to her. "No. We'll check DNA to verify, but I'm pretty sure it wasn't."

Mary looked down. "This is all so terribly sad."

Without taking the time to think, Seth wrapped Mary in a hug. "I know."

Mary squeezed Seth tightly as an overwhelming urge started to overtake her. But it wasn't her usual craving. It was something else, something she hadn't felt since her early twenties. As she started to let go and pull back, all reason and sense left her body. She lifted on her tiptoes and kissed Seth directly on the mouth.

Seth was so stunned and baffled, he didn't come close to reacting by the time she stopped kissing him and pulled back.

"I'm so sorry." Mary covered her face and took a step back.

Seth's eyes fluttered as a less critical worry crossed his mind, that of a complicated love triangle. "Um, it's okay, Mary."

"No, it's not. I'm an awful friend. I know about you and Story."

Seth furrowed his brow. "About us?"

Mary peeked through her fingertips at Seth. "I promise I'll never do that again. I just haven't kissed anyone for… It doesn't matter," she said and covered her eyes again.

Seth's heart fell to his stomach. What a horrifically sad admission. He was afraid to ask how long she was about to say. He already felt bad enough about how people reacted toward her. "It's fine, Mary. Honestly. It was…well, it was really nice."

Mary peered out at him. "It was?"

"Look, I don't know how long it's been or why. But you're an amazing person, Mary. You're smart, unique, attractive…"

"You don't have to say that."

"I'm not!" Seth protested. "It's true. And I don't get the impression Story would care."

Mary shrugged, knowing he was right.

"And there are much bigger things to worry about right now, wouldn't you say?"

Mary nodded.

"Look. I promise I'll stay in touch, Mary. And honestly, I'm in your debt for your help. Thank you." Seth smiled and then headed toward his Bronco.

Mary shut the door and leaned back against it, a smile spreading from ear to ear.

What the Hell, Orbriallis?

The morning air was thick with mist and cold, the dense fog clinging to the towering cedar and redwood trees as if unwilling to let go. Emory felt like it was hiding something. His senses were on high alert, a feeling of unease settling in his gut. He kept glancing over his shoulder as they made their way from the school into town for lunch. The wind was biting, causing him to hunch his broad shoulders up around his ears. His dark brown hair, usually smooth and silky, was now ruffled and unruly, in contrast to his twin sister's tightly coiled Afro. Ember was ahead of him, walking shoulder-to-shoulder with Stan, texting madly to each other—her only form of communication these days, ever since the incident that sent them to Lost Grove just over two months ago.

Was she sharing what had happened over the weekend when they'd stayed overnight at the Orbriallis Institute for the sleep study? Emory remembered her wild and scattered reaction when he showed her the video on Saturday evening. She had been dismissive at first, but then her emotions had spiraled out of control.

So what, she'd said, her words radiating in his head as if they were his own, one of the many abilities the twins shared since childhood. *This looks medical. It's a medical research facility.*

He had told her to watch it again. Her brows furrowed, and she watched intently as confusion crept over her features. Suddenly, a frightening realization crossed her face, and he'd felt her fear prickle along his skin as if it was his own. All her thoughts came through inside his mind as they populated hers.

Why do they all look the same? They all look malnourished.

Vitamin D, Emory added amongst her rolling thoughts.

Why does he shake his head at you? Ember paused the video, pulling the video scroll back to watch the imperceptible shake of the head of the young man.

Emory had missed it too, at first. But having rewatched the video many times now, over and over, he knew the kid had been trying to tell him something.

He's shaking his head at you. Like, telling you to go or… Ember rewound the video again, catching more nuances. *They're like zombies. God, his eyes. He looks haunted. He's terrified.*

As the video played, Ember's heart raced with anticipation. The camera captured a blur of motion as the male nurse flung open the door and barged into Emory. He stumbled back, revealing a glimpse of the strange exam room in the basement of the Orbriallis Institute. The face of a female scientist floated across the screen, watching the commotion, before the camera steadied on the wall behind Emory. Ember replayed this part of the video over and over, straining to hear the muffled voices and decipher their words. Then she heard her brother tell the men he'd never been there.

A tingle of adrenaline shot through her. She knew what it felt like, the effort he put in, the strength it took to reformulate the thoughts of three grown men, erase himself, and the moment, from their minds. She felt the tingle, the energy, the thrill, but also the weariness that always followed. As Emory turned to leave, the camera caught the female scientist staring at him with a slight smile and an air of calculated interest. Ember paused the video repeatedly at this moment, studying every detail of the woman's face until she'd finally dropped the phone to her bed, tossing it away from her like the woman might leap out of the phone and grab her.

She knows you did something to them.

"I know," Emory said aloud. Unlike his sister, he hadn't taken a vow of silence. Granted, she believed her verbal words had caused irreparable damage when she spoke them last year to a fellow student, resulting in her gruesome death. But Emory was of the mind that with more practice, they wouldn't have to speak their mind-altering instructions aloud. For now, speaking the thought out loud acted as a strength-building conduit while they worked at internalizing their thoughts. If they believed they could silently mind-alter, truly believed, then it would come to be. Right?

Why didn't they do anything? Ember's internal pitch rose.

"I don't know. My guess? For the same reasons our entire care has changed. All the tests we've been doing. The overnight sleep analysis. It's bullshit."

But what is this kid? Why are they doing this to these kids? Are they like us? Will they do this to us? Ember asked him frantically while maintaining a level of control with her volume. Emory was happy to see her taking action, to be more aware, to practice, to find the natural balance they'd had for years before the incident.

"I don't think so. I mean, Mom and Dad wouldn't ever fall for this. Right?"

Mom wouldn't, Ember clarified. We have to tell someone.

"Who?"

Ember thought, and Emory saw every name and idea as it came to her.

I don't know. Someone, she'd said so desperately he wanted to kick himself for even involving her in this.

Emory looked up from the sidewalk, eyes on his sister and Stan. He had to say something. It now seemed so obvious. He wasn't sure why he hadn't thought of it sooner. The kids, these new friends of theirs, had been the ones to tell them all the strange stories about the town of Lost Grove and the less-than-savory rumors surrounding the Orbriallis Institute. They'd lived under its shadow all their lives. If anyone knew what to do with the video, wouldn't these fellow teens be the best ones to go to?

They stepped into downtown proper, kids milling about getting candy and treats for their lunches.

"Stan?" Emory said from behind.

Stan was waving ahead to Noble and Anya, already standing on the sidewalk outside one of the three cafes dotting the small downtown. Nettie followed a moment behind, cradling a soft drink. Stan thought she looked like she was recovering from the flu or something. "Yeah?" Stan replied, turning.

"I need to show you something," Emory said and turned his phone to her, having already pressed play.

Stan, with a smile on her face, fixated her eyes on the video. She watched, her smile slowly dissipating. "He looks familiar," she said, almost to herself. "What is this?" she asked, looking up before the video was over.

"This is in the basement of the Orbriallis Institute. Or one basement.

I found it this weekend when we stayed there. Do you know what it is?" Emory asked.

Ember was wide-eyed beside them. She dared a glance at Stan when the taller, poised girl glanced her way for confirmation.

Stan's face had hardened. She turned and waved once more to her other friends. "Guys!" she beckoned.

The other teens collected their things, heading over to the corner of the street in front of the pizzeria.

Nate jogged down the street from school. "Hey, do you know if the Moonlight has any sandwiches left?" he asked, missing the tense vibrations for a moment. "Whoa, what's going on?"

"Hold on," Stan directed, while the others came their way through a break in traffic.

"What's up?" Noble asked.

"Where's Zo?" Stan asked.

"She's with Mom, feeding Merryweather in the school parking lot," Noble replied, taking a bite of the sandwich wrap he'd bought from the deli.

Anya pocketed her phone. "Have any of you guys seen Ryker today?" she asked.

"Nah. He wasn't in English," Nate answered.

"I can't get a hold of him," she said to herself.

Nate looked at Noble and whimpered, "Tell me you didn't grab that because Moonlight was out of sandwiches?"

Noble nodded, taking another mouthful.

"Dammit. I was looking forward to their—"

"Take your mind off your stomach for a minute, yeah?" Stan instructed, nudging Nate. "Emory has a weird video to show us."

"Weird how?" Nate asked, switching his enthusiasm from filling his gurgling stomach to playing detective in the blink of an eye.

Stan gave Nate a sidelong glare. "Okay, tell us what's happening," she urged Emory.

Emory nodded, psyching himself up. "Right. You guys know we're being treated at the Orbriallis, right?"

Heads nodded, and Nettie snorted, who seemed to care very little about the topic of this conversation. The Orbriallis Institute was a sour flavor in her mouth, as weekly family therapy had taken its toll on her and the relationship she had with her parents and the non-relationship with her non-brother. She slowly sipped a ginger ale through a straw like she was going to vomit at any moment.

"This past weekend, we had these sleep analysis things. They're supposed to monitor—it doesn't matter. Anyway, I couldn't sleep, so I got up and wandered around. I got in the elevator, pressed a button, totally thinking it wouldn't take me anywhere, but it did. It took me down to this, I don't know, like a sublevel. So I wandered around. It's like a hospital and everything, so I'm not thinking this is wrong or whatever. But then I see this—well, fuck it, I'll just show you."

Emory prepped the video, holding his phone up as the teens gathered around him. All except Ember, who stood where she was. Emory wondered if she'd ever move again. Even Nettie leaned in, still taking short sips of her drink. Emory pressed play, and the teens watched. Nate leaned in, feeling this was pressing. Important.

Noble watched from over Stan's shoulder, glancing at Ember quickly before switching to the phone. *What's her problem?* he wondered.

Nettie looked away up the street and then back to the screen as it panned across all the young people, standing like drugged-up, mindless idiots, all with shorn hair, all dressed in the same standard-issue pajamas. Then the world shifted on its axis. Her sight grew dark, tunneling into focus on the haunted face of the young man taking up most of the video screen now. Her body felt numb, weightless. The can of ginger ale in her hand slipped loose, tumbling to the pavement. Sugary drink sprayed the shoes and legs of all her friends as she found air pushing at her lungs in a shrill cry.

"What the hell?" Nate whined. He turned to face Nettie just as she tilted sideways. On instinct, he reached out and grabbed her before she fell into the oncoming traffic.

Noble reached for her at the same time. "Grab her!"

"Nettie!" Anya reached over, holding Nettie's face in her hands, gently tapping on the girl's blanched cheeks. "Nettie, look at me."

"Jesus, what the fuck is happening?" Nate asked while shuffling the limp, shivering Nettie over to the small stone wall encapsulating the outdoor dining area of the pizzeria with Noble's help.

Nettie reached out suddenly toward Emory. "Let me…play it again."

"What?" Emory asked the crowd of teens.

Nettie reached for the phone. "Play it again!"

Emory, now completely second-guessing his decision, reluctantly hit play and turned the screen toward her.

Nettie gaped at the small screen.

"What, Nettie?" Anya asked, looking from her friend to the screen. As the video settled on a young boy's face, Nettie pointed and let out a stifled whine. Anya leaned in closer. Her breath caught in her chest as realization hit her. "Oh my God. It's him."

"It's who?" Nate asked.

Noble shuffled closer to Anya, still with a hand behind Nettie's back, taking in the video once more, looking for clues about what the hell was going on. He had a foreboding feeling this was going to be yet another in a long line of discoveries this past week had presented him.

Stan looked at all the faces of her friends, trying to understand what was going on. She cast a smile at an older woman walking by, as if to indicate everything was fine. She looked back to find Ember still planted to the spot on the sidewalk, eyes wide as she took in the scene. "What the hell is happening?"

Nettie was breathing too fast. She felt a weight pressing on her chest, like air had turned into smog, suffocating her.

"What do you mean, it's him?" Noble let go of Nettie, realizing that Nate fully had her, as he leaned down to get a better view of the video. He reached out and moved the indicator back so the video once again panned across, landing on the shocked, terrified face of a young man. Then he saw it. The undeniable resemblance to Nettie's not-brother living in her home. He flinched back. "The fuck?"

"What?" Nate asked with more urgency.

Noble pointed at the screen. "That's George Horne. The real George Horne."

Nettie fainted into Nate's shoulder.

Nate looked down at her. "What the shit, man!"

Ember chirped with surprise. It was the first sound she'd emitted since the incident. Even her sobs had been silent.

Stan took a deep breath. "Okay, someone needs to tell me what the hell is happening."

"Nettie." Anya gently slapped Nettie's face. "Shit, she's… We need to call someone…"

Noble was already running down the street. Miraculously, he spotted their small-town doctor, the guy who had delivered every infant in town since 1973.

"Anya, why the hell did she faint?" Nate asked. "Just because she saw a video of her brother?"

"She hasn't been feeling well," Anya replied, a half-truth. Nate had never believed Nettie's story about her brother. Well, no one ever did, not until days ago. Was it time to let everyone else in on their discovery?

Stan reached over and touched the side of Nettie's forehead. "Is she sick?"

"No, it's not like that," Anya explained with little effort to make her words cohesive. She didn't know how to explain what had been plaguing Nettie without rattling out the entire story, and she didn't much feel like now was the time to tell it.

"Well, what's it like, then?" Nate pressed. He moved his shoulder. Nettie's head lolled, so he had to catch her again, lest she topple forward.

"It has to do with my video, right? She said it's him. Does she know this kid?" Emory asked, looking at his phone, the image paused on the face of the young man. Staring at it, Emory felt like he sensed the dire fear the kid was radiating. He was trying to tell him to stay away—the imperceptible head shake, the widening eyes. He'd missed it in the moment, but now it plagued him that this kid had tried to warn him away.

"I…" Anya started, hoping to give them answers. All the questions, even the unspoken ones, overwhelmed her. Especially the unspoken ones.

Noble returned with the doctor in tow.

Dr. John Lancaster was a fit older gentleman of eighty years. "Let's set her on the ground," he instructed Nate. "When did she faint?"

"Like, a minute ago?" Nate responded as he gently laid Nettie's head on the ground.

Anya stepped away to call Nettie's father, Greg.

"Antoinetta." Dr. Lancaster firmly called her name, which elicited no response. "Lift her feet up, will you?"

Nate moved to her feet and lifted them up onto his lap.

"Antoinetta?" Dr. Lancaster called again. He leaned in to hear that her breathing was normal and not labored.

Nettie began to stir.

Noble raised his hands, running them through his hair while the others stood by, shocked by the turn of events. Stan watched Noble, concern ballooning on his face as he moved from the scene to go stand by Anya's side.

"Her father is on his way," Anya said to the doctor.

"Good. Okay, Antoinetta? You've fainted, dear girl. Has she been ill?" Dr. Lancaster asked the group, Nettie not yet cognizant.

Anya nodded. "Yes. She hasn't been feeling well. And she hasn't been eating."

"For how long?" Dr. Lancaster asked, attending to Nettie as she blinked back into consciousness.

Anya looked at Noble and then back to the group. Stan had not missed this minor exchange, beginning to put pieces together. Noble asked about cave systems and maps, particularly in town, behind the houses on Mulberry Street. Noble, Anya, and Nettie had been spending more time together than usual. She recalled the story of George Horne, the little boy who was taken by an evil spirit who lived in the cursed woods behind her house. What it all meant, she wasn't entirely sure, but something had clearly been building.

"A few days. Monday, since Monday evening," Anya finally responded.

Dr. Lancaster looked up at her, stern wrinkles drawing his bushy white eyebrows together. "She hasn't eaten since Monday night?"

Anya shrugged.

The doctor returned his attention to Nettie, who was finally coming back to reality. "Just stay still, dear girl. I'm Dr. Lancaster from in town. You had a brief fainting spell."

Tears started streaming down Nettie's face and into her ears as the reality of what sent her into a panic came back to her. "It's him," she mumbled. "Anya, it's him."

Anya nodded, though Nettie couldn't see. Instinctively, Anya reached out and grasped Noble's hand. He wound his fingers in hers and squeezed.

Has she really not eaten since Monday? Noble wondered, his heart jumping from the incident as much as the sensation of Anya's cool fingers. He looked up and into the eyes of Stan, standing across from them. *She knows.*

And Stan could see it too. She knew there was much more going on here, and he could tell she had deduced something, probably a good portion. Stan looked from Noble and Anya, a pleasant warmth filling her to see the two coming together, over to Nate. He was helping Nettie, holding her hand even as she cried, lying on the concrete sidewalk with his coat under her head. Maybe he should be a first responder. Of all the people here, he reacted with the most sense, the quickest instinct.

"We're going to wait for your father and his car," Dr. Lancaster said. "Then we'll take you over to the office and have a quick look. Does that sound okay?"

Nettie nodded, hands over her eyes. "Yes," she whimpered.

Stan crouched beside them, humming a lullaby her grandmother often used to soothe her when she was younger.

Within a minute, Nettie's breathing slowed, though she was still crying.

"Are we really entertaining the idea?" Noble whispered to Anya.

Anya shrugged, turning her face to whisper into Noble's ear. "He looks like George. Like the real George. I can't explain it."

"No, I think I get it," Noble whispered back. "Like, his face is right, and the one in her house—"

"Isn't," Anya said but kept her voice low.

Emory and Ember shuffled together in the background.

What the hell is this? Ember asked.

I don't know.

What she said, "it's him." What does that mean?

I have no idea, Emory reiterated. If the video wasn't confusing enough, this reaction and fallout were entirely unexpected.

Does she know the kid?

I don't know.

Is she going to be alright? You didn't do anything?

Do anything? Emory scoffed. *No, I didn't do anything. She just watched the video and freaked out when the boy came on the screen.*

I think the others know what she meant.

Don't, Ember. Emory warned his sister against looking into their thoughts. These were their friends. He had a strict rule of not doing that to friends.

But it's clear they know something. Noble and Anya. Anya for sure. Just a peek.

"No!" Emory scolded aloud.

The whole group, minus Nettie, looked over at the twins.

Stan, who had been watching the silent exchange from the start, stopped humming and glanced away from them just as Nettie's father pulled up in his car.

Anya let Noble's hand go and helped Nettie into the car. "I'm sorry, Mr. Horne," she said.

"It's alright, Anya. You did the right thing, calling me," Greg Horne replied, getting into the driver's seat.

Dr. Lancaster was already in the passenger seat, ready to escort them back to his clinic.

Anya waved as the car pulled away.

Lunch was done and over. The teens were late for their next classes, but no one moved.

The whole time, Nate pondered the information he had amassed. Much like Stan, he'd deduced a few things—rather easily, he had to admit. It was staring him in the face. Sleuthing without him? What were they thinking? But what was the mystery they were trying to uncover? It bewildered him to think they might indulge her in the fantasy that some monster had taken her brother in the woods.

Nate stood up, bringing his glance from Stan, over to Anya, then Noble (the traitor) giving him the evil eye, and lastly over to the Power Twins. "Okay, let me see this video again."

Emory fumbled into action, clumsily grabbing for his phone, finding the video, and offering it to Nate to watch. The others crowded in. Just as the video shifted to the nurse pushing the door into Emory, Nate pressed pause, his eyes narrowing. He looked side-eyed at Emory.

"It's weird, right? But, she, Nettie, she…what was she saying?" Emory asked the group.

"Yeah, Noble," Stan asked. "What was she saying? Better yet, what was it you said?"

"Yes, Noble," Nate stated loudly. "Please enlighten us on what's going on here."

Noble sighed. "It's her brother. Her actual brother."

"What…like, but what does that mean?" Emory asked while the rest of the teenagers had a stare-down. He slowly grabbed his phone back from Nate, who was glaring at Noble. Were the two going to fight?

Ember moved to sit on the stone wall.

"There's more to that video," Nate said, aiming his words at Emory.

"Yeah, there is," Emory barely answered.

"So let me see it." Nate held his hand out, more concerned about the rest of the video than about whatever Stan was pestering Noble about. He'd get to Noble later. Emory put the phone back in Nate's hand.

"What has been going on with you guys?" Stan asked Anya and Noble.

"Shit," Noble muttered. "Okay, look…Can I tell them?"

Anya nodded.

Nate peered up from the phone, now partially interested.

"Last week, Nettie's not-brother, the one she thinks is a fake, spoke some strange words at therapy. I stumbled on Anya trying to solve what he was saying, and she agreed to let me help. They weren't actually proper words, but we pieced it together, and the best we could make out was that he tried to say 'Papa LaRange.'"

"What the fuck does that mean?" Nate asked, the same thing Stan was thinking.

"I'm getting to it," Noble said. "I Googled it, and what came up was this story about a guy named Raymond LaRange. And it wasn't good. This guy was arrested in Ohio for molesting two girls, and apparently the girls were told to call him 'Papa LaRange.'"

Nate held his hands up. "How does this relate—"

"Shut up, Nate!" Stan ordered.

Noble nodded at Stan. "So, I told Anya this, and she asked if there was a picture of the guy. I showed her the police photo I found."

"The mug shot, you mean?" Nate asked rhetorically, glaring over the phone he had held up in front of him.

Noble rolled his eyes. "Yes, the mug shot. So we showed it to Nettie because she said she saw the guy who took George. The second she saw the photo, she freaked." Noble took a deep breath. "She said, 'That's the guy. That's the guy who took my brother.'"

"Who is this guy? I want to see him," Nate said, handing the phone back to Emory and walking over to the trio.

Noble swung his backpack around and brought out his iPad. He turned it on, found the old link, and shoved the tablet toward Nate.

Nate began scouring the news articles on Google.

Stan shifted her stance, legs wide. "You're telling me, a guy who molested kids in Ohio took young George Horne, even though *George* is still in their house?"

"But that's not the real George," Anya added.

Stan opened her mouth, but Noble jumped in.

"You have to know about the not-children," he said.

Stan shifted her gaze from Anya to Noble, blinking, eyebrows raised. "The not-children?"

"Of all the tales your family has, you *have* to know about the kids that aren't really kids. In the woods."

Stan's face grew stern. "I don't."

"Okay, fine," Noble said, hands raised. "And I'm not saying that like some culturally fucked asshole."

"I know you're not. But what you're saying, in general, is fucked," Stan said.

"Wait a second," Nate stated. "This guy was in Ohio, transferred to

Orbriallis within a year of his sentencing. So what the fuck? He's at the Orbriallis Institute?"

"What?" Stan asked.

"Yes. They transferred him to Orbriallis," Noble said. "What happened from there, we don't know."

Emory took a step forward. "Wait, they treat criminals up there?"

Anya nodded in reply. She had her arms crossed, feeling the chill of the day mingling with what they were discussing and uncovering. Things seemed to be syncing up, but why all of a sudden? What shift had occurred? She had a gut feeling there was more at play here.

"Okay, this guy, he comes creeping out at night and kidnaps little kids and does what with them?" Nate asked. "And, I'm sorry, but what the fuck are the not-children?"

"The not-children are his minions or some shit," Noble answered. "They follow him around everywhere. But they're not right. I mean, look at the kid living in the Horne house, right? He's a dimwit."

"Christ, Noble!" Stan scolded. "Do you hear yourself, the both of you? The Orbriallis doesn't make a habit of kidnapping people. It's a world-renowned medical facility." Stan was standing opposite him, arms crossed.

"I'm not suggesting they did. The Green Man did. And he's linked to being treated at the Orbriallis."

"Who the hell is the Green Man?" Nate asked.

"Sorry. That's the nickname of Raymond LaRange," Noble clarified.

"I thought it was Papa LaRange," Stan said.

"It is. They both are. The Green Man came from Nettie. And—"

"Are we sure this is her brother?" Nate asked.

"Look…just look at how much they look alike," Noble argued, thrusting his hand in Emory's direction.

"The kid on that video doesn't look like George," Stan continued. "George, who lives at 127 Mulberry Street, has a thicker nose, blonde hair."

"That's the point. They look different because there are two of them. But this one, the kid on the video, is Nettie's real brother. She's been telling the truth since the beginning, and no one believed her. They made fun of her. We all did at one time or another," Noble spewed, the passion coming from his own guilt.

Stan slowly shook her head. "I just…I can't believe that—"

"What did the nurse say?" Nate suddenly asked Emory.

Everyone stilled, pondering his left field question.

"The nurse?" Emory asked.

"Yeah, the nurse. The guy says, 'What the fuck?' and opens the door in your face. The video goes all crazy. What did he say? What did you say?" Nate pressed, picking up on where his friend was going with this wild, unbelievable story.

They're going to find out, Ember said inside her brother's head, resigned.

They don't have to, Emory responded.

Ember stood, grabbing the phone from her brother and handing it to Nate. Nate watched, and the others listened as the rest of the video played out. Emory felt fear edging into his thoughts. Can he make this all go away? Can he erase all four of their memories of this moment if things go wrong?

The video ended.

Nate looked up. "They let you walk? They seemed pretty upset you were there, and they just let you go cause you said…"

I said, "I'm not here. I was never here. You never saw me. You'll turn around and go back to what you were doing," Emory pronounced inside Nate's head.

"Jesus and fuck!" Nate stumbled backward.

"What?" Noble asked.

I've let him in on our little secret, Emory answered in Noble's mind.

Noble's eyes widened. His body completely froze over, not just prickled with goosebumps but a true cold, a freeze eclipsing the frigid air seeped under the cuffs and neck of his jacket. "What the fuck?" He met Emory's gaze.

"What is it?" Anya asked. Her eyes darted from Noble to Emory, over toward Nate, and back to Noble.

"Guys? What is going on? Is this some dude thing?" Stan demanded.

My brother's revealing his secret. Well, our secret, Ember added in Stan's mind.

"Ember?" Stan shifted her torso to look back at the girl, who didn't speak.

We can both influence ideas, thoughts, read minds, speak to you this way, Ember said.

Tell Anya, Emory instructed his sister, the others hearing it too.

Ember flinched. *I can't.*

Emory tried and found a wall. It felt liquid, like the dampening of deep water. When he turned his eyes on the girl with strangely colored hair, he found her looking at him, wondering what was going on.

The hair on Anya's arms shivered with her fae sense. Something was happening, and though she didn't know what, she had a feeling it was coming from the twins. "What are you doing?"

"I'm—" Emory started but was interrupted.

"I knew it!" Stan pumped her fist in the air. "They're speaking in our heads," Stan said with surprising nonchalance. "I once saw a medicine man do it. Not on me, but you could tell the person who was sick—they were unconscious for several days—heard him."

Noble threw her a glare. "You knew it?"

"Dude, something was off with them from the moment they arrived. That day on the bleachers, y'all two were like, speaking to each other, except neither of your lips were moving and I was like, this is some major league telekinesis shit, right here." Stan hopped from one foot to the other.

"Nah. No," Nate gasped, stepping back toward the group. "You're for real just going to be like, yeah, I've seen a medicine man do this, blah-de-blah? And you think this is fucking cool?" Nate bellowed. "Them talking in your heads? Just another day round the sun in this fucked up town?"

Ember moved closer to Emory, unsure of how this was all going to play out. *I hope we didn't screw this all up by letting them in.*

Stan frowned at him. "Isn't it? Can you honestly be that surprised given the things we've seen, heard about, witnessed?"

Nate moved closer, speaking low and harsh, because he noticed other people on the streets looking their way. "This is nothing like that. Rumors? Speculation? Folktales from your grandma, who I love, so don't say shit. He's— They're talking inside our heads." He pointed to his skull. "Noble? Back me on this."

Noble scoffed. "Like I have some control over the matter? This whole damn week has been a nightmare of finding out shit I didn't want to."

Anya remained silent, letting the others argue. If she drew attention to the fact that, unlike her classmates, she couldn't hear the twins when they tried to speak to her, and she was relatively certain they had tried, they would only follow it with questions and suspicion. She didn't want that from any of them, especially Noble. She focused, letting her mind drift, like she practiced when she was in the water with her mother as a kid, and suddenly heard something.

We're not trying to scare you. Hell, we'd like you to actually like us. But this is us, Emory explained.

Anya's eyes opened wide.

Emory noticed and focused his thoughts only on her. *You can hear me now?* She nodded.

Are you…can you do what we can?

She offered him a quick shake of her head.

You don't know how you were blocking us out, do—

"Ember, stop," Emory said aloud, leaving the conversation with Anya to another day and time. He'd felt his sister pushing into the thoughts of the others around them, not just speaking inside their heads.

"Both of you should stop," Noble suggested. "The talking up here"—he gestured to his head—"just stop."

Emory held his hands up. "Understood."

Nate sighed. "Man alive. What the hell is happening? You guys uncovered a sicko being treated at Orbriallis, who was the guy Nettie saw steal her real brother, while some not-child—that's what you called them, right? Not-children?—lives in his place. These two who have superpowers happened to stumble on some crazy ass shit going down in Orbriallis's basement and took video of Real George, who's now having weird experiments done on him. And one of our old classmates was found dead on Mourner's Beach after giving birth, and the baby is still missing. And she was being treated at the Orbriallis Institute! Am I missing something?"

"Are you talking about Sarah Elizabeth?" Anya asked.

Nate nodded. He pulled his phone from his pocket, tapped a few links, and swung the phone out for her to take. "Statement released this morning. I just saw it."

Noble leaned over Anya to look it over. "Wait, she was at the Institute?"

"For almost two years, yeah. So, did I miss something in this clusterfuck of batshit lunacy?" Nate asked again.

Anya looked up as Nate pulled his phone back, pocketing it. "How did no one know she was being treated there?"

"Maybe they kidnapped her like they did George," Emory offered.

Stan rolled her eyes. "We don't know they kidnapped George, and also, we can't go around believing all the conspiracy theories out of this one's mouth," she said, pointing at Nate.

"Not a conspiracy theory. These are facts staring us in the face," Nate countered with a level tone.

Stan narrowed her eyes at him.

"Okay, well, then there are a few more things. About the not-kids," Noble said.

"Great. Sure. Let's have it." Nate placed his hands on his hips.

Stan snorted at his stance.

Noble and Anya exchanged glances, and she proceeded. "When we talked with Mary—"

"Mary?" Nate immediately interrupted.

"Mary Germaine."

"The vampire?"

"Dude, come on. She's not a vampire," Noble argued, though he didn't understand why. He had thought the same thing himself. Even more so since the incident on the path. But he felt Mary deserved a break.

"Okay. Shut up, Nate," Stan instructed with a raised finger, looking at Anya. "You talked to Mary about the not-kids?"

"Yes. She's seen them. She says they live in the caves around here," Anya explained.

Stan began nodding her head. "This is why you asked me for spelunking gear earlier today."

"You asked her for her gear?" Noble interjected.

Anya wrinkled her nose, turning to face Noble. "I thought… Look, I feel it's worth looking into."

"I get that, but why the hell would you think you should go alone?"

Stan stepped between them. "Hold on. What caves? What are we talking about? Bring us into the loop," she said, twirling her finger around the group of friends.

"Nettie said she saw the Green Man—" Anya started.

"Raymond LaRange," Noble interjected for clarification.

"—come out of the woods behind her house. Specifically, she said he crawled out of a hole in the woods. So, I was thinking, there could be a cave system back there. If Mary says she sees them coming out of the caves, then maybe they live in them," Anya finished.

"The woods behind her house are the cursed woods," Stan said.

Anya shrugged. "I know."

"Yeah, but do you know about cave systems? Do you know how to use the gear?"

"Vaguely," Anya commented.

"You're not going alone," Noble stated. "I can show her how to use it."

"Like you're the only two who are going?" Nate guffawed. "I want to know what the fuck is down there."

I don't know how to spelunk, Ember communicated to the group.

You're not going, her brother commented. "At least not into the cave. If there is one. We can watch."

Stan sighed. "Well, you'll need a guide. If you plan to go into the woods, at least I know the signs to get us out."

"The signs?" Nate asked incredulously.

"My people have been living on this land for generations, Nate. We know what to look for. You don't."

Nate scoffed. "It's just behind her house. We won't get lost."

Stan offered him a look of bemusement. "I can guide us. I know the secrets of the cursed woods."

Anya simply nodded. She couldn't say that she too knew the secrets, and what's more, she'd be the safest of them all. She couldn't say that even out of water, her mother's kind, her kind, were predators, not prey.

"When are we going?" Nate asked.

"Tonight," Anya answered.

Stan nodded in agreement.

"Okay, yeah. We'll do it tonight," Noble said, pressing the bridge of his nose. "Were you really going to go down there alone?"

Anya opened her mouth, shut it, and shrugged. "You didn't seem to want to go."

"That doesn't mean you should go alone. If this guy is down there, or those creepy kids? Would you have told anyone where you were going?" Noble pressed.

Stan interrupted. "Dude, chill. She would have told someone."

"I would have probably told you," Anya added. "I don't want to go alone. It's just, well, you seem to have a lot on your plate—with the pressure of the race coming up, your sister to take care of, the stuff those guys said about your dad."

Nate cocked his head, looking over at Noble. His dad? What was that about? Was Anya talking about the guys that Noble got into a fight with? They said it was because they were saying inappropriate shit to her. He would press his back-stabbing friend about that later.

Noble didn't want to be reminded about that. The recent finds in his parents' closet stuck in his thoughts, plaguing him with unknowns. It had him thinking like a conspiracy theorist, and this, the unraveling mystery of Nettie Horne's brother, seemed to push his thoughts ever deeper into the macabre, sinister, and paranormal.

"Can you guys, like, hear thoughts from a ways away?" Nate asked the twins.

Both Emory and Ember nodded.

"Yeah," Emory confirmed aloud. "We can hear, like…" He paused, listening. "Some woman in that coffee shop is pondering ordering a mocha or an espresso. She thinks the mocha has too many calories."

"So, if someone was in the caves, within reason, you'd be able to pick them out?"

Emory turned to his sister and then back to Nate. "Sure, yeah."

"Good. You're coming then," Nate said.

"Oh, now you're okay with their powers?" Stan asked. "You were so offended—"

"I wasn't offended. I was just shocked that another person was talking inside my fucking head. The fact that you weren't maybe says something about you."

"Guys," Anya butted in, pointing at Ember and Emory. "They're literally standing right there."

Stan continued on, as if Anya hadn't spoken. "Yeah, it says that I'm more in touch with the world and all the possibilities—"

"Don't start with that shit. Let's get back on track here," Nate said, checking his phone. "Okay, so, sunset is at 6:25."

"I don't want Nettie to see us," Anya said. "Let's meet at the corner, the abandoned house. We'll trek in from there."

"Let's meet at five?" Noble asked the group.

They all nodded.

"Who wants to come with me to the library?" Stan asked the group.

"What for?" Nate inquired.

"A map of the cave systems in the area. I don't know if they charted this one, but I'd like to know what makes up the ones around here. We need to know if there's a link, in case we need another way out."

"For sure," Noble nodded.

"I'm game," Emory said.

Ember shrugged, nodding affirmatively.

"Yeah. Not like I'm going back to classes after this crazy shit. Let's do it!" Nate said, slapping his hands together.

The emotionally charged band of friends, new and old, made their way down the quieting streets as the lunch crowd fully settled back into the daily grind.

Inside the library, Story was busy cataloging old books with broken spines and worn-out pages for the library sale when her thumbs started itching.

She gave in to the sensation, scratching at the pad of her left thumb, which itched the most, and then put down her pencil. She stepped out of the small office, moved to the front desk, and watched the large wooden doors. Someone, no, many people were coming.

Story touched the computer to wake it, expecting questions would be on the lips of the people coming to see her. As she did, stepping closer to the desk, something inside her shoe dug into the bottom of her foot. She lifted her foot, slipping off the shoe and dropping the small pebble into her palm.

"Curious little pebble. Are you good news or bad?" she asked it as the library doors opened and the group of teens entered. "Very curious."

It's Complicated

Seth's eyes were glued to the computer screen, his brow furrowed in concentration. He was reading an article in the *New England Journal of Medicine* about a promising new treatment for childhood cancer developed by the Orbriallis Institute. The CEO, Dr. Neil Owens, had boldly stated that they would have a cure for this devastating disease by 2027. Seth had been researching the Institute for hours, searching for any hint of wrongdoing or illegal activity. So far, he had only found glowing reviews and articles praising their groundbreaking research. Seth hoped they weren't somehow involved in Sarah Elizabeth's death. It would be a shame to shut down a facility that was doing so much for so many people.

His thoughts were interrupted by a knock on his office door. Seth looked up to see Joe standing outside the door, a rare thing considering how little he used his private office. "Come in," Seth said, waving him in. Seth sat up straight and shook off the tension in his shoulders.

"It's almost three-thirty, boss," Joe said, motioning to the clock on the wall behind Seth.

Seth looked at his watch. "Shit. Thanks for alerting me," he said, shutting off his computer, cursing under his breath. In ten minutes, he was due at the Andalusian house to speak with Jolie and Noble. After a hectic morning, he'd returned to the police station to update the team on what he had discovered over at Mary's house, and then he doled out tasks. He needed Sasha to put out a BOLO on Peter Andalusian and told Joe to peruse social media for any nefarious stories on the Orbriallis. With his list of to-dos handed out to the other officers, Seth was halfway out the door, eager to confront Jolie and Noble, when Bill informed him of the obvious. Noble was at school, and Jolie was likely at work.

At that point, Seth returned to his office, grabbed his phone, and called Ross Ranch, asking for Jolie. When another ranch hand or worker finally found her, Jolie sounded as if she was prepared to receive grave news from her doctor. Seth hadn't revealed the severity of the situation, but had made it clear that he needed to talk to both her and Noble together. Jolie agreed to meet at 3:30 p.m., after she finished work, and promised to make sure Noble came straight home, which he should do anyway, if for no other reason than to drop Zoe off after school let out at 3:00 p.m. In the time he had to kill, he buckled down, shutting himself in his office for some long-overdue research on the Orbriallis Institute.

"You find anything?" Joe asked.

Seth stood up and shook his head. "Nothing damning. All awards and praise."

"The same thing on my end. Although there was an Instagram story I came across from this kid here in Lost Grove who claimed there were 'strange things afoot at the Orbriallis' and that he was 'going underground to investigate.'"

Seth glared at Joe as he put on his jacket. "Strange things afoot? Did he actually say that?"

Joe chuckled. "He did."

"When was this?"

"Today."

"Did you recognize him?" Seth asked, grabbing his keys.

Joe shook his head. "I don't think so."

Seth approached Joe, leaving his office. "I don't like the timing. Can you track him down?"

Joe followed behind Seth as he made his way to the station door. "Don't imagine it will be too difficult. His handle is Nate the Great."

"Handle?" Seth opened the front door, making his way toward the parking lot.

"His Instagram name," Joe clarified. "Doesn't matter. I'll ask around until I find him."

Seth opened the door to his Bronco. "Call me when you do. If it sounds even remotely legitimate, take an official statement. And if he's not eighteen, make sure he's got a parent present."

"You got it." Joe shut Seth's door for him and waved before sprinting back to the station.

"Come on in," Jolie said, opening her front door to let Seth in.

"Is your son home yet?" Seth asked, stepping into the entryway. Her tousled and wavy hair had the appearance of recently being let down, fingers run through it to relieve the tension of the day. He was guessing much of that tension was because of this visit.

"Not yet. He should be here any minute, though. We can sit in here." Jolie walked past Seth into the living room. Her feet were covered in thermal socks bunched up over the hem of her jeans. She wore a burgundy button-up with the sleeves rolled up, over a thermal.

Seth followed behind, disappointed to see an empty coffee table in front of the couch. Not that he expected Jolie to have tea and crackers set out for him. He just hadn't eaten lunch and was ravenous for food and another coffee. Mary's kiss came shooting to the forefront of his mind. It had been a pleasant kiss—unexpected but nice. It pained him to hear how little human contact she had.

Jolie sat down in the center of the couch in a rather deflated manner. "You want water or coffee or anything?" she asked, clearly with no desire to follow through.

"I'm fine," Seth replied begrudgingly. He crossed to the recliner chair on the far side of the room, angled it toward her, and sat. "So, when did you first meet your husband?" he asked.

Jolie looked over at him, raising an eyebrow. "You really want to know?"

"I do," Seth said, taking out his notepad and pen.

"Fine." Jolie sighed as her eyes fluttered. "In 2002, I moved up here to work at Ross Ranch. I was twenty-two at the time. I had been living in San Francisco, and a friend of mine there told me they were looking for a permanent horse trainer, so I applied and was immediately hired. I met Peter that summer. He'd been giving horse tours at the ranch, as well as being a summer trail guide at Devil's Cradle for a few years at that point."

Seth smiled. "That's funny. I was in San Francisco in 2002 going to college. You said Peter worked summers at the ranch. Was he not living in Lost Grove all year round?"

Jolie shook her head. "Just seasonal. Like you already know, Peter likes to travel, be on the move. Always has. We fell for each other pretty hard that summer, but he had another job lined up in the fall that was supposed to go until the following April. He came back in December.

Said he couldn't take being away from me any longer. He stuck around long enough for us to both know this was something serious. He took a couple shorter gigs out of state that next year, and then we got married in April 2004 and bought this house together."

Seth wrote the details and looked back up at Jolie. "So, it sounds like Peter has been taking odd jobs out of state pretty much since he got out of the military," Seth said.

"Is that a question?" Jolie asked, meeting Seth's gaze.

"Well, the background check that Bill ran back in 2015 didn't list any of these jobs, and I'm guessing I won't see any when we get back the one we requested on Monday. So, yes, I'd love to know what and where these jobs were."

Jolie shook her head. "Look, I don't know why you're here today, but I'm telling you now that Peter had nothing to do with those girls."

"To be clear, which girls are you referring to?"

Jolie rolled her eyes. "Can you not treat me like I'm an idiot?"

Seth held up his hand. "Not my intention in the slightest. Just protocol to specify names when we're dealing with a criminal investigation."

"The Fulson girl and Sarah Grahams," Jolie said, exacerbated.

"Kelly Fulson," Seth added.

"No, Victoria. You know, the other Fulson girl who died?"

Seth resisted the urge to smile, admiring Jolie's spirit. "I just want to know what jobs—"

The front door opened, interrupting Seth's question. "Hey, Mom."

"We're here!" a little girl's voice carried down the hall, elongating the words in a gleefully eerie voice.

"In here, sweetie," Jolie called out to her son and daughter.

Noble rounded the corner with his arm around his sister, his eyes catching Seth. "Fuck," he muttered.

Zoe skipped to Jolie. "Noble said 'fuck,' Mom!"

"That's nice, Zo. Why don't we go upstairs and check in on Merryweather," Jolie said, taking Zoe's hand as she stood from the couch.

Zoe looked over her shoulder at Seth. "Did Noble punch someone again?"

Seth laughed. "No, not that I'm aware of."

Noble playfully kicked Zoe in the butt as she passed by. "I didn't punch anyone, dope."

"You're a dope," Zoe said as she and her mom went up the stairs.

"Thanks, Mom," Noble mumbled, cursing her for not telling him that Sergeant Wolfe was the reason he had to be home and for leaving him here by himself. He turned to Seth. "Hey."

"Hi, Noble. Why don't you come sit down? I need to speak with you and your mother."

Noble looked toward the stairs and then back at Seth. "Should we wait for her to get back?"

"We'll wait for her to get back to talk about why I'm here. But I've actually got a couple questions just for you."

Noble walked apprehensively to the couch and sat in the corner farthest from Seth. "Okay."

Seth scooted up to the edge of the chair and leaned in toward the boy. "I'm curious if you and your friends ever hear or tell stories about the Orbriallis Institute."

Noble couldn't control his jaw from falling open. Had Stan told her dad, Wes, Lost Grove's medical examiner, about the video Emory took? Had Wes called Seth? "Um…what do you mean?"

"Oh, you know, stories, rumors, town gossip."

Noble felt like he was falling into a trap. "What's this about?"

Seth shrugged. "Just following up on some information that came my way."

"Are you talking about the nursery rhyme? Things like that?"

Seth laughed. "I completely forgot about that. What was it…" Seth looked down, trying to recall the rhyme. "'Little Lina, dressed in lace, went outdoors without a face.'"

The corner of Noble's lip curled upward. "Yep. Same one."

"Right. That kind of thing."

Noble shuffled around in his spot. Maybe he could actually find something out that would help them. "Well, we've heard rumors about some crazy experiments being done in the basement of the Orbriallis. Like 'off the record' shit. Have you heard anything like that?"

Seth furrowed his brow. "Hm. I don't recall anything like that, no. What kind of experiments?"

"I mean, I don't know any details, but it sounds like some weird science-fiction type stuff. What sort of stuff did you and your friends hear growing up?" Noble asked.

"Oh, how Geiger Orbriallis was a mad scientist and would do anything to cure his daughter's disfigurement. Like the rhyme. How Dr. Neil Owens never leaves the building. You hear anything about him?"

Noble felt like he was gossiping with Nate, not remotely what he was expecting. "Yeah. We'll hear rumors that someone spotted him in town, things like that. But no one believes it."

Seth held Noble's gaze. The questions seemed to have ignited something in the boy. Did he know more than he was saying?

Noble looked over his shoulder, his mother still nowhere to be seen. He turned back. "Have you ever heard stories of someone called the Green Man?"

"The Green Man?" Seth asked, his eyebrows squeezing even closer together.

Noble shrugged. "Just one of those Lost Grove myths. Apparently, there's this crazy guy who steals young kids in the woods. Like some dark fairy tale."

Seth slowly shook his head. "No, I've never heard that." He looked down and wrote the name on his notepad. He'd have Joe look into that, which reminded him. "Say, do you have a friend or know someone named—"

"Okay, Zoe should be occupied for at least ten minutes," Jolie said, reentering the room.

Seth and Noble both flinched, sitting up straight.

Jolie looked curiously at both of them as she sat down next to her son. "Have you already spoken to Noble about—"

"No," Seth cut her off. "I told you I needed to speak with both of you together."

All mysteries surrounding the Orbriallis left Noble's mind as a wave of anxiety overtook him. "What do you need to talk to us about?" he asked.

Seth looked from Noble to Jolie. "According to what you told me a few days ago, your husband and your father left last Thursday to Alaska for a job on a fishing vessel, correct?"

"Yeah," Noble said slowly.

"Yes. He's been up there many times for the same job," Jolie added.

Seth glanced down at his notepad for effect. "And you said the job started this past Saturday, correct?"

"Yes. Why are you asking the same questions?" Jolie was curt with her reply.

Seth looked from one to the other, gauging if they knew anything to the contrary. It didn't appear that they did. "I'm not asking. Just clarifying."

Noble's stomach churned. He thought he might actually be sick.

"Okay, and?" Jolie asked.

"And," Seth repeated, "Peter is not where he said he was going to be."

Noble gritted his teeth as tears of fear and anger built in his eyes.

Jolie shook her head. "What do you mean? How do you know?"

Seth balanced his gaze between mother and son, noticing the young man's jaw clench repeatedly as he went on to explain. "We got in contact with the company in Dutch Harbor where Peter's vessel was docked and would depart. His name was registered to the ship *Mary Lou*, so that checked out. But after not hearing anything for a couple days, we contacted the Coast Guard to reach the *Mary Lou* so we could verify he was on the vessel. From there, we hoped to get him to contact us to answer a few questions. The Coast Guard got a hold of ship captain Reginald Dupree, who stated that Peter Andalusian never showed up and was not, in fact, on the *Mary Lou*."

Noble's head fell as his eyes closed. He knew it. The money, the gun, the phone number, and the person on the other end of the line. He was positive his father was hiding something.

"Goddammit," Jolie exclaimed as she dropped her head into her hands.

Seeing Jolie's reaction, there was no mistake. She had no idea Peter wasn't where he said he was. But Seth watched Noble closely. He had immediately looked down and shut his eyes like his worst fears were realized. "Noble? Is this a surprise to you?"

Jolie flung her hair back. "Of course it is. What are you accusing him of?"

Seth ignored Jolie's reaction and watched Noble. His jaw moved left to right, and his eyes grew hard. He knew something.

Noble looked up. "I had no reason not to trust my dad."

Seth nodded, registering the past tense. He wouldn't get anything further out of the boy. Not here. Seth shut his notepad and put it and his pen in his jacket pocket. "Noble," he looked at Jolie, "Mrs. Andalusian, your husband is a person of interest in our investigation, and it is vital that we get in touch with him."

"Do you have any evidence?" Noble spouted.

"We don't need evidence for someone to be a person of interest. And that doesn't automatically make him a suspect."

"So, what is he, then? Why are you going after him?" Jolie fumed.

Seth gazed over at her, letting out a sigh. "Mrs. Andalusian—"

"Christ, would you quit calling me that? Just use my damn name."

Seth opted not to argue that "Mrs. Andalusian" was a version of her name. "Jolie, the facts are that your husband left town within hours of when Sarah Elizabeth's body was placed on Mourner's Beach."

"What do you mean 'placed'?"

"I'm assuming you haven't seen the news, then? Noble?" Seth asked.

Noble swallowed. "That she was pregnant?"

"What?" Jolie looked from Noble to Seth.

Seth nodded. "Sarah Grahams died during childbirth. Someone cleaned up her body and left her on Mourner's Beach. Not only did your husband leave hours after this occurred, this marks the second time the same pattern occurred. And the fact that Peter worked with both Kelly Fulson and Sarah Grahams makes him a person of interest."

"Worked with her? Sarah?" Jolie asked, pitch high.

"She volunteered with her church during the summer, taking kids to the day camp at Devil's Cradle. She took them on excursions led by your husband."

"That's not working together. Kelly—yes, we all worked together. But Sarah being a camp counselor for her church's summer day care program and my husband leading excursions now and then with the kids is not working together," Jolie stated.

Seth withheld a sigh. "Very well. Kelly Fulson was a colleague. Sarah Grahams was an acquaintance, at the very least, no?"

"Sure," Jolie acquiesced. It wasn't as if she wanted to be defending her husband right now. In fact, she'd rather like to punch him in the face. Jolie rubbed her face and ran her fingers through her hair. "So, what? What do you want us to do now?"

"Well, we've already issued a BOLO, so it's just a matter of time before we track him down."

"What does that mean?" Noble asked combatively.

Jolie stared out the window. "It means all law enforcement from here to Alaska will be looking for your father."

"That's correct," Seth said.

"What the fuck!" Noble yelled, standing up.

"Noble," Seth asserted his voice. "Please sit back down."

Noble quickly found the corner of the couch again.

"Look, I didn't come here solely to give you bad news and rile you up. The quicker we find your father, the better. I need to know if either of you has a better way of getting a hold of him." Seth looked from Noble to Jolie.

Jolie had her eyes shut and was shaking her head. "Noble, have you tried getting a hold of your father?"

"Not since he last called."

"I'm sorry, and when was this?" Seth asked.

Noble looked at his mom. "Um…last Friday?"

"It was Thursday night," she corrected him and then looked down. "He said he had just got to Anchorage and was planning on heading toward Unalaska in the morning."

"Unalaska?" Noble asked.

"It's an island, where the port is."

"Jolie," Seth said, getting her to raise her head back up and meet his eyes. "Is there anyone else that might know where Peter is?"

Jolie sighed. "Paddy."

"Paddy is who?"

"Paddy's a drunk," Noble said. "He's who my dad hangs out with when he goes to the bar."

"Paddy is also your father's closest friend, Noble," Jolie added.

"Like he would know anything."

Seth kept his eyes on Jolie. "Can I get Paddy's full name? And number if you have it."

Jolie nodded and pulled her phone from her back pocket. "Patrick Kipp."

"That's his real name?" Noble asked.

"Yes, Noble. And you'd be best not to judge people you know nothing about. He's a veteran like your father."

"I know," Noble said and looked away.

Jolie held out her phone to Seth. "That's his number."

Seth had his notepad already pulled back out and jotted down the number. "Thank you."

Noble was seething. How could his mom just hand over information to the police like this? He didn't know what his dad was involved in, but he wouldn't be giving the police anything. "I'm done," he said and stood up.

"Where are you going?" Jolie asked with motherly force.

"I'm meeting up with Stan to do some climbing."

"Now?"

Noble extended both arms, standing at the edge of the hall. "Yeah, now. You want me to just sit around here and be depressed about all of this?"

"Where are you climbing? The sun's setting—"

"Caves, not climbing," Noble interrupted.

"What?" Seth jumped at the mention of this boy going caving and at this hour.

Jolie narrowed her eyes at Seth.

Noble pulled his head back. "Um, yeah, we're going in the caves."

Seth's stomach clenched, and his skin prickled with goosebumps. Sweat formed at the nape of his neck. "Should you be spelunking in the dark?"

Noble shrugged. "It's dark in the cave. We have headgear."

"Well, where are you spelunking?" Jolie asked, Seth's clear worry rubbing off on her.

"Stan knows."

"And she's told her father the specifics?"

"Yeah, like she always does. I'll have my walkie. They're both charged," Noble explained to assuage further comments or demands from his mother. The walkie could reach for miles—some major-wave radio frequencies his father had picked up from somewhere—which now felt like another mystery. Where might he have gotten radios with that kind of range?

Seth methodically replaced his notepad and pen. "Be careful," he commented as he sensed the conversation between mother and son come to a close. Was she really going to let her kid go spelunking in the local caves just because he wanted to? And not know precisely where he was going to be?

Noble looked at Seth. "Do you need me for anything else?"

Seth looked up and shook his head. "Nope."

"Then I'm out," Noble stated and stomped down the hall.

Jolie ran her hands down her face. "I'm sorry. He's emotional. We're both—"

"It's completely understandable. I'm sorry to have to bring you this news. I truly am," Seth said. He felt like his voice was shaky and didn't want that to reflect on the end of this conversation. His reaction to the news that Noble was going wandering about cave systems had been oddly severe and immediate.

Jolie wiped fresh tears from her eyes. "So am I."

Noble trudged down the street with his spelunking gear over his shoulder. He was typing furiously into his phone.

What the fuck, dad! The police say you're not on your boat in Alaska, I got into a fight with some drunk asshole who called Zoe a murderer, and you're not answering any of my texts. Where the fuck are you? We need you. Now! 911.

Will the Real Paddy Please Stand Up?

"It's here."

Seth and Bill both looked from the board in Bill's office over to Joe, standing in the doorway.

"The pizza or the background check?" Seth asked, praying it was the pizza. After downing another double cappuccino on the way back to the station, he got the jitters and felt so lightheaded he thought he was going to fall over at any moment.

"Both, actually," Joe said, jutting his thumb over his shoulder.

Seth burst past Joe like he had been lost in the woods for days without food. The box from Lost Grove Pizza Company was sitting on a desk in the bullpen. The table light shone down on it like a beacon from heaven. He tossed open the lid and yanked a piece from the pie, not bothering with a plate or napkins. The smell of mushrooms and onions brought tears to his eyes as he shoved half of the slice into his mouth, grateful it wasn't scorching hot.

"You look like you just got out of prison and are having your first real meal."

Seth opened his eyes and glanced to his right. Sasha was standing right next to him. How long had he been savoring this bite? "Feels like it," he said after swallowing.

Sasha laughed as she grabbed a piece and placed it on a plate like a civilized human being. "So far, I got a hold of the ranch in Montana. The owner, Gregory Lansdale, says Peter hasn't worked there for three and a half years, but that he was a top-notch worker. Never had an issue with him."

Seth swallowed another bite. "Okay, thanks. These are all long shots, but you never know." Before he left the Andalusian home, Jolie gave Seth a list of four other part-time jobs that Peter worked over the years. She said that she wanted to speak with Peter as much as he did. There was no mistaking the ire in her voice. Peter would not be having a welcome home party whenever he returned to Lost Grove.

"Is it cool if I have a piece?" Joe asked, now standing on the other side of Seth.

"No, Joe. It's not cool," Sasha said.

"Of course," Seth countered.

Joe's eyes lit up as he reached for a plate, which Sasha pulled away from him. "Come on!"

Seth grinned as the two bickered back and forth. If they weren't both so thorough and accomplished at their jobs, he might be annoyed, but their playful chemistry brought much-needed levity to the office.

"Oh, hey," Joe said, finally with a slice of pizza and a plate to boot, "I printed out Patrick's background check for you." He made his way over to the printer, grabbed the sheets of paper, and handed them over to Seth.

"Thanks." Seth took a cursory look as he headed back to Bill's office with a second slice of pizza, spotting the military background and no report of criminal activity. "Bill, you gonna grab any of that pizza? It might be the best one ever made."

Bill, still at the Sarah Elizabeth board, chuckled and patted his overhanging belly. "No, I'm good. Just had lunch a couple hours ago."

"Your loss," Seth said, still reading the report.

"What have we got?" Bill asked, shuffling up next to Seth, putting on his reading glasses.

"Looks pretty clean. Decorated Army veteran, consistent line of employment going back to his honorable discharge from the Army. You sure this guy is the town drunk?" Seth asked, looking at Bill.

Bill shrugged. "I mean, he's been a park ranger for a good ten, twelve years now, so he can't be that bad. Just what I've seen and heard. He's reportedly at the bar every night and the last one to leave. Must sleep it off well."

Seth looked off to the side, something ringing in the back of his mind. "That's what it was." Seth looked back at Bill. "Didn't I see Paddy's name on the Kelly Fulson report?"

Bill nodded. "We interviewed him. Real brief. He was Peter's alibi for the night we believe Kelly Fulson's body was dumped."

"Hm." Seth set the report down on Bill's desk and flipped to the next page before taking another bite of pizza. "No, no. This guy worked as—" The ringing of Bill's desk phone interrupted Seth.

Bill walked over and picked up the receiver. "Chief Richards… That's right… Okay, hold on one second." Bill covered the receiver and spoke to Seth. "It's the Orbriallis. They say you can see Dr. Owens Friday morning at 10:30 a.m."

"Did you tell them—"

"Yeah, I stressed the urgency, believe me."

Seth shook his head. "If that's the earliest, obviously I'll be there."

Bill nodded and uncovered the receiver. "Yeah, that'll work… Okay, thanks," he said and hung up the phone.

"I'm telling you, Bill."

Bill sighed. "I still don't see it."

"Yeah, well—" The subtle ding-dong from the front door announced a visitor. Seth set down his plate. "Here we go." He turned around, expecting to see Paddy Kipp enter the station. Instead, Dr. Wes Hensley strode toward them, holding a folder. Seth had called Paddy as soon as he left the Andalusian home and was surprised that Paddy not only picked up after one ring but agreed to come right into the station without even asking why.

"Hey, Wes. You done for the day already?" Bill asked, stepping forward to shake Wes's hand.

Wes gripped Bill's hand. "Yep. Got the toxicology report at the end of my day. Figured I'd bring it by," he said, nodding at Seth and handing the folder to Bill.

"Wes." Seth nodded back, stepping next to Bill to look at the report. "What are the highlights?"

Wes huffed. "There are none."

Bill and Seth both looked up at Wes.

"Report came back squeaky clean. Not a trace of any toxins or illegal substances in her body."

"So, she definitely died during childbirth," Bill stated, looking for clarification.

"That's what will be in my report."

"Well, that puts that to rest. Now if we can just figure out where in the hell she gave birth," Bill said, walking back to his desk and setting the report down.

Seth patted Wes on the back. "Come over here, Wes. I want to show you something," he said, leading him over to the crime board. "I had my meeting with Mary Germaine this morning to show her these photos."

Bill joined them. He'd told Wes the day prior that Mary was the one who found the body and left the note on his door.

"We didn't just get one huge breakthrough, but two," Seth offered.

Wes looked at him. "I'm highly intrigued."

Seth pointed to the wide overhead shot of Sarah's body. "We had all remarked that morning about there being no footprints surrounding her body."

"Right," Wes said, looking back at the photo.

"Turns out there were footprints around her body, leading to and away from it."

Wes furrowed his brow. "How sure is she?"

"One hundred percent. Mary says the scene is ingrained in her memory."

"So…are you saying that someone came back—"

"They were there, Wes," Seth said. "Whoever placed her body there never planned on leaving a trace of themselves. Mary must have appeared before they could finish. He or she had to have hidden and waited for Mary to leave to finish what they started."

Wes looked at Seth. "Where the hell would anyone hide? The beach is wide open."

Seth shook his head. "It would have still been pretty dark at the hour Mary was out there. Lots of cloud cover, so moonlight would have been minimal. Whoever it was could have been as close as twenty-thirty feet away lying flat on the sand."

Wes shivered. "That's highly unnerving."

"It's also of interest that whoever was there clearly had no intention of harming Mary. It would have been the perfect opportunity if they felt they were compromised and in danger of being discovered."

"Sure. There was already one dead body there. Why not two? You still looking at Peter Andalusian?" Wes asked.

"Without question," Bill answered, much to Seth's relief, finally having Bill on board with Peter being their prime suspect.

"That's another thing," Seth said. "Before I show you revelation number two, we got a call from the Coast Guard today. They got in touch with the ship Peter claimed he was going to be on, and the captain confirmed he didn't show."

"Son of a bitch," Wes said slowly.

Wes felt for Noble. The kid was a saint as far as he knew, always taking care of his little sister, Zoe. He'd looked out for Constance frequently. Hell, he knew Noble would go to the ends of the earth for his friends. He was just that kind of person—polite when he was over, intelligent, talented. For all that, Wes felt like his father couldn't be all that bad of a person to have raised such a truly decent person. But circumstances being as they were, he was wondering if Peter's old days in the military had left more damage than the naked eye could see. Wes had seen the haunting trauma on childhood friends who no longer let him get close. It was proof that Peter could be hiding dark secrets. But murder? Jesus Christ, he thought.

"Talked to Jolie and Noble no more than a half hour ago. They were both shocked. I'm sure they felt embarrassed, betrayed, scared."

"Of course they were shocked," Wes replied immediately, shaking his head. "This case."

"What is it, Wes?" Seth asked, spotting the sour taste in his mouth talking about Peter.

Wes shook his head. "It's just…I've known the Andalusians since they both landed here in Lost Grove, back when Jolie was Jolie Williams. They're friends of our family. Noble and Stan have been best friends since they were in kindergarten. I know Peter's history in the armed forces and Special Ops, but I just don't see it."

Right when Seth had Bill agreeing with him, here comes Wes shedding doubt. "What makes you say that? Specifically."

Wes rubbed his chin, thinking back over the years to all the cookouts in both of their backyards, getting together on holidays. "I can't point to any one thing specifically, Seth. It's just the sense of the man. I wouldn't put it past Peter to defend himself and his family, at any costs, but an innocent girl? My sense of the man's soul doesn't align. That's all I can say."

Seth sighed. "I can respect that. I appreciate you speaking up."

"And it's not that I don't grasp why you're looking at him. The timing isn't favorable."

"I hope you're right. And I hope we'll know soon," Seth said and patted Wes on the back. "Now, look at this photo here. I had always thought the way her body was placed looked staged, not just dumped."

"It did feel that way," Wes agreed.

"See her arm, the hand? What does that look like to you?"

"Well, if we're going with the thought that Sarah's body was staged to tell us something. Or show us. It looks like she's pointing."

"Exactly. And much like the footprints, Mary insists that when she found the body, her arm was across her belly."

Wes tilted his head. "So, where is it pointing?"

"The Orbriallis Institute."

Wes looked back at Seth, his eyes drawn together. "The Orbriallis…I mean, we know she was being treated there."

"Right, but according to them, she left the facility earlier this year. So, if she was somewhere else, then why would the person who disposed of her body stage her to be pointing there?"

"Seth is all but certain that they have something to do with her death," Bill said.

Wes shoved his hands into his jacket pockets. "First of all, the Orbriallis doesn't have a maternity ward. And there's no way that any of the most esteemed doctors in the world would have performed a pubiotomy or a symphysiotomy."

"That's what I said."

Seth waved his hand in the air. "I'm telling you, there's something off about that place."

Wes frowned. "Seth, the Orbriallis has done more good for people than any research facility in the world. Dr. Owens may be a recluse, but the work being done there is groundbreaking."

"Well, I'll be talking to him on Friday, so we'll see."

Wes's eyebrows rose. "You've got a meeting with Dr. Owens?"

"This is a homicide investigation, Wes."

Wes shrugged. "Still. Let me know what he's like. I've only heard stories. We all have," he said, looking at Bill.

"I can't say I'm not intrigued," Bill added.

"Look, while we've got you here," Seth said to Wes, "what can you tell me about Patrick Kipp?"

"Patrick Kipp?"

"Paddy," Bill clarified.

"Oh, Paddy," Wes said. "Why are you asking me about him? Because I'm Indian?"

Bill laughed.

"No," Seth said forcefully. "Because you've lived here the entire time he's lived in Lost Grove, and I haven't. But now that you mention it, if there is anything that you might know because you're Indigenous…"

"Well, he's not a member of the Tolowa Dee-ni' tribe, so my family and friends on the reservation wouldn't have anything to offer. I don't think he's even from the West Coast," Wes said.

Seth shook his head. "No, he's from North Carolina."

Wes laughed. "Well, I can't give you any Native secrets, then."

"Look, just…what do you know about the man?"

"I know he's a park ranger at Devil's Cradle and that the man likes to drink. Come to think of it, he drinks with Peter Andalusian quite a bit. Is that why you're asking?"

Seth nodded. "Yeah. Jolie told me that Paddy is Peter's only close friend in town. I called him right after I left there, and he agreed to come in to answer some questions."

"He's on his way here now?" Wes asked.

"Yeah, I thought you were going to be him. I'll tell you what else is strange."

"What's that?"

"He didn't even ask me why I wanted him to come in."

Wes shrugged. "Maybe he's bored."

"That's what I said," Bill said.

"No, I don't think that's it. If he really is Peter's best and only friend in town, I have a hard time believing he doesn't know exactly what this is about. If he was Peter's alibi for the Fulson case, he knows damn well Peter left town the day you found her body. And here we are again."

Bill moaned. "I don't know. You might be giving him too much credit."

"Yeah," Wes said. "Maybe he doesn't even know about Sarah Elizabeth."

Seth glared at Wes. "Are you fucking serious? There isn't a resident in Lost Grove who doesn't know."

Wes shrugged just as the front buzzer sounded.

"Here we go," Seth tried again. This time, he was correct. Patrick "Paddy" Kipp strolled through the front door wearing a hooded forest-green sweatshirt over a grey T-shirt. Not exactly the warmest attire for a forty-degree evening. He had cropped black hair, looked about five-foot-ten, and appeared to be in great shape, the sweatshirt tight around his biceps and high trapezoid muscles. He nodded and smiled genially at both Joe and Sasha.

Seth looked back at Bill. "You good with me starting this interview solo? I've got a line I want to follow in mind."

"You're in charge of the case," Bill answered.

Seth, Bill, and Wes all walked out of Bill's office to greet Paddy. Seth extended his hand. "You must be Patrick."

Paddy shook Seth's hand, grinning. "How would you know? I'm not the only Indian in the room."

Wes chuckled.

"Just bullshitting," Paddy said. "But, seriously, don't call me Patrick. Gives me PTSD."

"From the war?" Seth guessed, the background check fresh in his mind.

"No, my parents."

"Where'd you serve?" Wes asked.

Paddy nodded. "Short stint in the Gulf. Two tours in Kuwait and Bosnia. You?"

Wes shook his head. "No. Decided to stick with dead bodies here instead."

Paddy laughed, a loud barrel-chested laugh. "Right, you're the medical examiner."

Wes narrowed his eyes.

"Seen you around town in your van," Paddy answered Wes's questioning gaze.

"Anyway, I'm just on my way out," Wes said, nodding at Bill and Seth. "Good to officially meet you, Paddy. And thank you for your service."

Paddy looked over his shoulder as Wes exited the station and then turned back with his eyes raised. "Wow, he actually meant that."

"Why wouldn't he have?" Seth asked.

"Oh, you know, Sergeant Wolfe, people aren't very patriotic these days, are they?"

Seth shrugged. "Depends who you ask. Anyhow, thank you for coming in on such short notice."

"Sure. It's my off day at the park. Didn't have anything else to do. Although," Paddy said, looking over at Seth's desk, "I haven't had dinner yet, and I am awfully hungry. You mind?"

Seth and Bill exchanged a quizzical glance.

"If it's no bother. I just got a whiff of that pizza the second I walked in."

"Joe? Sasha? You guys want any more pizza?" Seth asked.

Sasha shook her head. "I'm good."

Joe looked up at Paddy from his desk. "Go ahead, man."

"Hey, thanks, kid. You mind getting me a water?" Paddy asked as he meandered over to Seth's desk, helping himself to two slices of pizza.

Joe looked up at Seth, unsure of what to do.

Seth rolled his eyes and nodded.

Joe got up and headed toward the back room.

"Get me one too while you're at it, Joe," Sasha called out.

Paddy laughed and pointed at Sasha as he returned with his plate of pizza. "Okay, Chief, where you wanna talk?"

"Sergeant Wolfe will be the one speaking with you," Bill replied.

"Oh, I know."

"You said Chief, so…"

"Oh, right. Yeah, I know. But"—Paddy nodded his head toward Seth—"this guy. Am I right?"

Bill grimaced, not understanding what the man was trying to say. "I'll leave you to it," he said and returned to his office.

Seth grinned, already knowing full-well that Patrick Kipp was not just the town drunk. "Let's go into my private office," he said, leading the way.

"Here you go," Joe said, hustling up to give Paddy his cup of water, holding Sasha's in his other hand.

Paddy grabbed the cup and grinned. "You're a pal."

Seth held the door open for Paddy, who made his way in and instantly sat in the chair facing Seth's desk. "I've got to ask," Seth said, shutting the door and making his way over to his chair, positioning the tape recorder between the two of them.

"Oh, must be serious," Paddy said offhandedly.

"Weren't you even curious why I asked you to come in?"

Paddy chewed his pizza, nodding his head left to right. He swallowed. "Yeah, sure. I figured, why spoil the surprise, though?"

Seth wasn't a fan of Paddy's lackadaisical attitude, but he would give him the benefit of the doubt. For now. "You mind if I record this?"

"Do your thing," Paddy said and then took a sip of water.

Seth pressed record. "This is Sergeant Seth Wolfe of the Lost Grove Police Department. The time is 5:04 p.m., Wednesday, October 13th, 2023. I am in the room with"—Seth glanced up at Paddy— "Patrick Kipp, also known as Paddy, taking his official statement as to the whereabouts of Peter Andalusian."

Paddy nodded, his eyes wide. "Ah…Peter. Okay, sure."

"Mr. Kipp—"

"Ugh," Paddy groaned. "Not Patrick, not Mr. Please."

"Do you know Peter Andalusian?"

"Yes, I do."

"What is your relationship with him?"

"He's a friend."

"Is he a good friend?" Seth asked.

"Oh, yeah."

"Your best friend?"

"The one and only."

"Do you know the current whereabouts of Peter Andalusian?"

Patty swallowed another bite of his pizza. "He said he was going up to Alaska. He goes fishing up there every year. Loves it."

Seth could read most people. In fact, he would venture to say he could read ninety-nine percent of people. He wasn't sure if Paddy was clueless or just highly intelligent and gifted in the art of deception, but there was no give in his eyes. "When was the last time you spoke with him?"

"Mmm...think it was the day before he left." Paddy nodded. "Yep, last Wednesday."

"In person or on the phone?"

Paddy sighed after swallowing some water, setting his cup on Seth's desk. "Guess both. He called me and asked if I wanted to meet him for a drink. Then I talked to him at the Saloon."

Seth wrote down the details. "And what did you two talk about?"

"Why do you write notes if you're recording?"

"Helps me remember clearer—the act of handwriting."

Paddy raised his eyebrows. "I get that."

Seth looked back up. "Back to the Saloon. You two talked about what?"

Paddy shrugged. "Oh, you know, just day-to-day shit—what's going on at the ranch, the park, what have you. Asked me to watch over his family while he was gone."

Seth narrowed his eyes. "Why would he ask you to do that?"

"Why wouldn't he?" Paddy asked, his mouth full of pizza.

"I don't know Peter. You do."

Paddy chewed and swallowed. "Peter's a true family man. And not your standard nuclear family that speaks in pleasantries and platitudes." Paddy pounded his chest. "It's fierce, his love for them. Jolie is his rock. Noble and Zoe are everything to him. When he goes fishing or working a ranch out of state, he might be gone for a month or two. He wants to be sure they're being looked after."

Seth clicked his pen. "So, where were you Saturday night when Noble got into a fight with a drunk adult?"

Paddy splayed his hands out, his right hand holding onto a crust. "I can't be everywhere at once. But I will say Mr. Tacet and Mr. Weatherspoon won't be approaching Peter's family ever again."

"Did you threaten them?"

"Did either of them report a threat?"

Seth let the matter slide. In truth, he hoped Paddy did threaten the two pathetic men who not only harassed a child and exchanged blows with a high school student but directed unsolicited, salacious comments at an underage teenage girl. "Why does everyone think you're the town drunk?"

Paddy finished his water and set it back down. "Maybe I am."

"I don't think so."

Paddy grinned. "Well…maybe you're just a bit smarter than the locals."

"I am a local."

"Ha!" Another thunderous laugh from the bowels of Paddy's gut.

Seth leaned back. "What's funny about that?"

"You may be from here, boss, but you sure as hell aren't local."

Seth had the duplicitous feeling of not wanting to know how he knew that and needing to know. He kept his eyes on Paddy.

"You know," Paddy started, looking around the room. "Garbage can?"

Seth grabbed the small rubber garbage can behind him and slid it along the side of his desk.

"Thanks." Paddy tossed his plate and crusts into the can. "You solved a lot of big cases in the land of tech creeps. Tracked down that Jacobson crackhead who shot the two underage kids. You nailed that McCallum creep who had to have been a serial killer, right?"

Seth squeezed his pen tightly. In his twenty years in San Francisco, not a single person sitting across the interview table knew a thing about him. "What's any of that mean to you?"

Paddy shrugged. "Maybe nothing. Just good to know who's new in town. Especially someone wearing a badge."

"What else do you do besides watch over Devil's Cradle State Park?"

"Well, you know, I drink."

Seth shook his head. "No. There's a lot more to you than whatever image you've created for yourself here."

Paddy wagged his eyebrows. "Oh yeah? What's that, Chief?"

"You were an information security analyst in the city of tech creeps. Which kind of makes you one of them."

"That's slander, right there. Just because that shit comes easily to me doesn't make me one of those highfalutin mother fuckers."

Seth kept clicking his pen. "Maybe not, but you've clearly kept your skills sharp. And more to the point, I think you know everything that I need to know about Peter Andalusian."

Paddy leaned back in his chair and crossed his legs. "Maybe I do."

"Then where is he?"

"I told you. In Alaska."

Seth shook his head. "But he's not. The Coast Guard verified that this morning."

"Huh." Paddy looked down at Seth's desk. "I did not know that."

Seth hated that he couldn't tell if Paddy was telling the truth. He tapped his pen on his pad. "Do you know where else he might be?"

Paddy slowly shook his head and looked back at Seth. "Maybe he had a change of plans. There's at least two other ranches and an oil rig he works at periodically."

"And where might those be?"

"Oh, let's see here. There's a ranch in McCoy, Colorado, another one in Belt, Montana. Oh shit, he works at an oil rig in Anchorage. Might want to check there."

Fuck, Seth cursed internally. Every one of those locations matched up with ones Jolie supplied. One second it seemed like Paddy was playing games, toying with him; the next he's giving out helpful information. Seth set his pen down and leaned his forearms on his desk. "Hey, Paddy?"

Paddy raised his eyebrows. "Yeah, Chief?"

"Do you know why you're here? Why you're really here?"

"You mean, besides wanting to know where Peter is?"

"In conjunction with that, yes."

"Hmm." Paddy grabbed his chin. "Give me just a minute to think here. What could it be? What's happened since Peter left town? Goddamn, man, I just can't imagine."

Seth's patience was wearing thin, his suspicion from the start just verified. He knew exactly why he was here from the second Seth told him who he was over the phone. "Okay, so why don't we skip past the part where you pretend you know nothing about a dead girl found on Mourner's Beach," Seth said.

Paddy frowned. "Sarah Elizabeth Grahams? Why would I pretend that?"

"And I'll skip past the part where I remind you about the Kelly Fulson case and that we questioned both you and Peter."

"Ah, yes, Kelly Fulson. But I wasn't questioned. Peter was."

Seth let out an audible sigh. "It's in the report, Patrick."

Paddy narrowed his eyes at Seth. "I was asked to verify facts. I was not questioned."

"Did Peter have anything to do with the death of Kelly Fulson?"

Paddy let out another bellowing laugh. "Look, Wolfe, let's get something straight here. Peter Andalusian would never harm an innocent person. Much less a young girl. That I can tell you with the utmost certainty."

Seth sat back in his chair. "I'm not stupid, Paddy. Peter was in Special Ops, and his file is classified. Are you saying he's not capable of—"

"Harming someone? That's not what I said."

"Right. And are you telling me that no innocent people were harmed in Iraq, Kuwait, Bosnia?"

Paddy leaned over the desk, his eyes fierce. "Let's not bring the semantics of war into this, pal. Something you know nothing about. I'll cut you some slack not knowing Peter, but you best step away from the sacrifices we made for this country."

Seth's attempt to rile Paddy up had worked. "I'm not questioning your or Peter's sacrifice, Paddy. I'm simply looking at the facts that two young girls have shown up dead in Lost Grove over the past seven years, and aside from them both being pregnant, the only other similarity is that Peter Andalusian knew both girls and left the state the day each of them was found. You're a highly intelligent man, despite what anyone in this town thinks. Is what I'm asking crazy? Do you think I'm off base with the facts I have in front of me?"

Paddy slowly leaned away from the table. "All I'm telling you is that Peter would never harm an innocent girl. And he's not overseas anymore."

Seth leaned across the table, his voice low and severe. "If I find out Peter had anything to do with Sarah Grahams's death and you withheld any information that would have gotten us in touch with Peter, I'll arrest you as an accomplice."

Paddy held up his hands. "Whoa, whoa there, Chief. We're on the same side here. We both took oaths to protect this country, to protect our families and those close to us."

"Right. And Peter is very close to you."

"Ah, I see. And you think I'm protecting him?"

"That's right."

Paddy held out his hands as if waiting for raindrops to fall. "You might be right. But, hey…I want to help you! I'm serious. That's why I came in."

"Then give me something helpful!" Seth raised his voice, keeping it below a shout.

Paddy, unfazed, leaned back in his chair, crossing his arms. "I don't know where Peter is, and that's the truth. But maybe there's something else I can help you with."

Seth narrowed his eyes. Paddy was as serious as anything he had said since he walked through the front door. He was waiting for Seth to give him something. Something he could help with. Seth wasn't sure he was going to go this route, but he brought copies of the photos just in case. He opened his drawer, pulled out the wide overhead photo of Sarah Elizabeth's body, and slid it across the table. "What does that look like to you?"

Paddy looked down at the photo as he pulled it closer with the tips of his fingers. "That looks like the dead body of Sarah Grahams," he breathed.

"Does that strike a chord in you?"

Paddy looked up at Seth. "She volunteered at the park. She found a damn missing kid. She was a hero."

Seth was taken aback by the emotion in Paddy's voice. "And not only did you work with Sarah, Peter did."

"Your point?"

"Multiple people made statements they saw Peter having drinks with Kelly Fulson, who he worked with. Did he have a relationship like that with Sarah Elizabeth?"

Paddy leaned closer to Seth. "Did anyone make a statement to that effect?"

"Not yet, no, which is why I'm asking you."

Paddy thrust his finger on the crime scene photo. "Sarah was a child. A minor. Peter has a daughter. Not a fucking chance. And you don't need to show me this shit to make me tell you something that isn't true."

Seth held up his hands. "I'm not showing you this photo to upset you or to make you confess something. We both know that you will only say what you want when you want. But I believe you do want to help, Paddy. Because you know that Peter is waist high in shit right now. And the longer he stays away, the longer he goes without contacting me, the worse it will get for him. And you don't want that."

A sly grin rose on Paddy's face. "You're as good as they say you are."

"Look again at the photo and tell me, as a decorated soldier in the armed forces, someone with clear observational skills, what do you make of what you see?"

Paddy puckered his lips and looked back down at the photo. He tapped on the desk, taking his time, his eyes traversing the details. "Well, I would say her body looks staged."

Seth smiled. "That's right. It was staged. Her arm"—Seth reached over and tapped Sarah's left arm in the photo—"her hand…is pointing at something."

Paddy looked up, meeting Seth's eyes. "It would appear that way, yes."

"Paddy. Did Peter place Sarah Elizabeth Grahams's body on Mourner's Beach?"

Paddy didn't break contact or even blink. "That I can't tell you. But I'll say this. If Peter were to do something like this, then I would tell you that you're looking exactly where Peter wanted you to look."

Seth's heart rate ratcheted up a notch. "What does that mean?"

Paddy frowned, tilting his head to the side. "It means…if Peter were to do something like this, you would be looking exactly where he wants you to."

Seth closed his eyes, taking a deep breath through his nose so he wouldn't shoot Paddy in the kneecap under his desk. Opening his eyes, he unnecessarily clarified, "Can you please tell me what that detail means *about* Peter?"

Paddy nodded. "It means, when we were overseas doing horrible things to innocent people to protect your ass, if we were on a convoy together, and the truck in front of ours blew up, and Peter slammed on the brakes and jumped out of the driver's side door, leaving the keys in the ignition and the door five inches open, that wouldn't be a mistake. The keys, those five inches, are for a reason. And it's those decisions and that elite presence of mind that made Peter the best at what he did. Which is, of course, classified."

Seth and Paddy stared at each other, neither blinking nor breaking contact. Just as Dr. Bajorek's denial of knowing about Sarah Elizabeth's pregnancy was actually a confirmation, Seth was positive that Paddy just confirmed that Peter had placed Sarah's body on Mourner's Beach. But why would he even intimate such a thing if Peter had anything to do with her death? Even him dumping the body would land him in prison.

"Paddy," Seth started, "what can you tell me about the Orbriallis Institute?"

Paddy gave away the slightest grin. "Maybe someday you and I can grab a drink, and you can tell me all about that McCallum case—I'm just dying to know. And I'll tell you all about the Orbriallis Institute. But right now? My time is up. I gotta go, Chief."

If Seth thought he could say anything that would get Paddy Kipp to stay, he would. Instead, he watched him get up and leave his office, saying cheerful goodbyes to Sasha and Joe, slapping the latter on his back on the way out the door.

The Other Peter

Industrial, heavy-metal music blared through the speaker of the exquisite 2022 Alfa Romeo Giulia Quadrifoglio. The music rattled the eardrums of the driver. The crisp air conditioning blasted his face, shrinking the pores on his perpetually clean-shaven face. He adjusted his black sunglasses, shielding his eyes from the scorching rays of the sun. Brands and people's names meant nothing to him, so he didn't give a shit that he was driving such a luxurious vehicle or that his Northern California associate, Victor DesCombaz, gloated about how lucky he was to be getting the keys. What mattered was that he could drive the sports vehicle over 130 mph with ease. Honestly, it was the sonic assault of the music that elicited what Colin Renner would consider feelings, and those would be described as faint feelings.

Colin pressed his foot on the accelerator, speeding down the 101 freeway on his way to Lost Grove for the third time in seven years since he'd been assigned to serve as the Orbriallis Institute's ghost. His first trip was to introduce himself to the man in charge, a doctor. When his nameless contact for the nameless government organization presented him with his next contract, Colin ruminated on what an upper-echelon research facility would ever need with his services. It was an intoxicating mystery. Mysteries could be considered another thing that evoked "feelings." It wasn't the mystery of what the facility did, either. Nothing about their off-the-record research piqued Colin's interest. Dr. Neil Owens, on the other hand, was a person of profound intrigue.

The middle-aged, possibly elderly—it was impossible to tell—doctor invited Colin into his two-story residence at the top of the architecturally impressive hospital. He kept him there for two hours, serving Colin the best cognac he had ever tasted while fervently expounding on why the Orbriallis Institute was so significant. At one point, a strange woman in a veil wordlessly brought out a lavish spread of food. Colin paid little attention to what the enigmatic doctor was saying, more transfixed by what made this man feel so passionately. Looking out the floor-to-ceiling windows as the sun set behind the vigorous doctor, Colin wondered what it felt like to be passionate.

"And why exactly do you believe you would need a man of my attributes?" Colin made the mistake of asking.

Another deluge of emphatic lectures spewed from the doctor's lips. By the time the excellent doctor finished his explanation, it was well past dark. Dr. Owens stressed the importance of keeping his research secret and warned that if someone leaked even the slightest hint, he considered it treasonous. He likened it to the dropping of an atomic bomb, which Colin found appealing and also unnecessarily dramatic. He thought it a rather funny likeness. Because of the length of Colin's stay, he only grudgingly consumed part of the food set out for him. Not that the prosciutto-wrapped pork tenderloin and Roquefort cheese weren't exquisite, he just rarely trusted meals not prepared by himself. Colin almost meant it when he thanked the doctor for the cognac and his hospitality. He assumed he wouldn't hear from Dr. Owens again.

So when Colin's beeper sounded three years later with the proposed code if the need for his services ever arose, it invoked great surprise—and ultimately respect—from Colin. He left his Philadelphia hotel room and went to the center of a bridge over a deafening freeway to call the doctor on the burner phone provided. Despite Colin's request that the doctor only name the "candidate," a subject discussed at their initial meeting, Owens trampled over Colin's protestations, explaining exactly why one of his doctors had become a threat to everything he built.

Colin felt a growing sense of mutual respect for the impassioned doctor during this interminable explanation. Here was a well-respected doctor who was prepared to cut down one of his own for the greater good. Colin's thoughts wandered, as they frequently did, to the night when everything changed and the incident that propelled him into his current line of work, something that had come as a shock at the moment but made perfect sense after he had time to process it.

Colin had spent four years fighting as a Marine in Afghanistan. At the time, many people thought the war would never end, and Colin was quite content with that. Several peace negotiations and decisions were made to remove the troops from the country, yet year after year, they remained. Colin's lieutenant colonel trusted him and his two closest brothers, Grayson Hendrix and Josh Porter, with his most dangerous and demanding missions. They called themselves the Ministry of Justice. It was the beginning of the last week of Colin's service—this fact unknown to him at the moment—when the colonel approached the Ministry with a mission. He informed them the mission was not approved and that they would severely jeopardize their lives and careers if they carried it out. Colin could have found nothing more appealing.

To this day, Colin couldn't say whether the mission was to prolong or end the war. He only focused on the what and where, not the why. It was clear, however, in the colonel's mannerisms and tone that he was willing to commit career suicide to achieve it.

The penultimate event occurred when Colin, Grayson, and Josh were outside the house where the "candidate" and his twelve guards were holed up. They accounted for the thirteen men present in the compound before entry. What wasn't part of the mission, what the colonel didn't report to the Ministry, were the two women and one child also present. Colin recalled grinning, knowing the colonel wouldn't have been so inept as to have mis-scouted their mission. He had known from the beginning and believed he needed to leave that piece of information out for the Ministry to agree. The colonel judged correctly regarding Grayson and especially Josh, but it didn't matter to Colin.

When they saw the women and infant, the atmosphere around them shifted. Josh started by shaking his head and motioning that they had to call the mission off. What the fuck was wrong with him? The objective was the objective. Colin made this point very obvious with his eyes, which only raised Josh's ire, who began verbalizing his objections, compromising their position, their lives, and the mission. Colin pulled his twelve-inch tactical hunting knife and slit Josh's throat in one fluid motion.

Colin often recalled the look in Grayson's eyes at this moment, and it made him laugh. Grayson was so stunned, so shell-shocked, it was like he was staring at his own ghost. If the dark brown of his skin could have drained out to white, it would have. Colin sheathed the knife and grabbed Grayson's head with both hands, brought it to his mouth, and whispered, "Get it together. Now." Colin let him go and motioned that it was time to make their way through the underground entrance.

Grayson pulled it together enough to follow behind Colin. The mission plan was aggressive. Attack while they scrambled, and don't allow any time for planning or positioning. They each took out one of the two guards in the basement, the gunshots echoing off the stone walls. They made their way up the stairs, firing the entire time before rounding the corner. Colin dived and rolled, taking out two more guards before he came to a stop. He looked back to see that Grayson had foolishly stayed on his feet when they rounded the corner, taking a bullet in the knee.

Colin stormed through the house with ruthless aggression, putting bullets in the heads of the other eight guards, the "candidate," the two women, and the child. When he returned to get Grayson, his brother looked at him like he was the devil incarnate. Maybe he was.

It was less than twenty-four hours before the colonel, Grayson, and Colin were on a plane back to the States. The colonel's discharge was handled behind closed doors. The government never made the information available to the public, something of a minor miracle in the twenty-first century. Grayson Hendrix, who never looked at or spoke to Colin again—which was fine by him—was dishonorably discharged but given a hefty severance and top-tier medical coverage for life. What the Ministry had done that night, however frowned upon the decision and actions might have been, seemed to quietly please the unknown higher-ups, the puppeteers, in the government office.

Colin Renner's name was omitted from the report, a fact he found curious. Even more curious was his meeting with a man calling himself Jackson Fletcher, who neither claimed nor denied working for the government. It didn't matter—Colin knew who he was talking to. Who else would have direct contact with the commandant of the Marine Corps who had sent him to this secret meeting? Fletcher explained to Colin that there were few people in the world who possessed his iron will and blind dedication to this country. He elaborated that even fewer people would understand that the actions Colin took that fateful night were for the greater good.

The decision, not an offer, from that point on, was that Colin Renner would be a ghost—a ghost who didn't officially work for the government, who wasn't a former Marine, who had no past. He would live on the road, never settling in one place for more than a month. They gave him multiple cell phones, beepers, and computers, which were a means to receive missions securely. Colin would have a contact in every state—three in Florida, Texas, and California—through whom he could obtain his IDs, weapons, and any applicable gear needed. His mission would always be the same, only the location and candidates changing.

Colin felt like he had won the lottery in life. He was being heavily compensated for doing something he loved, something he would do anyway. Not only that, he was a ghost, free from the system, free from the law. They bankrolled his actions yearly at an obscene amount that allowed him to move whenever and wherever needed with no obstacles. The rest of the country would go to jail for twenty to life or be executed for what he was being paid to do. That was something that he could say made him feel. The power, the adrenaline, made him feel like what he expected kings must have once felt. He liked it well enough.

Fletcher told him that his willingness to "clip the wings" of a fellow brother and feel no guilt made him the most trustworthy person they could have for the job. Little did Fletcher know Colin had killed his own mother when he was sixteen by crushing up an entire bottle of her antipsychotic pills and mixing them into her vodka. He staged her suicide by placing the empty bottle at the foot of her recliner and felt absolutely nothing. He was born for this job.

When Colin translated his beeper code two nights ago to discover that Dr. Neil Owens needed another "cleansing," he felt like one must feel when reconnecting with an old friend after many years. Owens was the only other person he had met in his life who could understand him, who did what was necessary for the greater good. Colin even found himself eager to hear the good doctor's ramblings about why this contract was imperative. He imagined most people would find the story sad, heartbreaking. He found it too outrageous not to laugh.

Typically, there was only one candidate, so it elated Colin to find not one, not two, but three. A bereaved mother and father were duo candidate #1. This wouldn't be the first family he had to clip. But a police officer? A sergeant and former homicide detective? Candidate #2 was a first. But candidate #3 was the most intriguing of the lot. "Another you" is how Dr. Owens described the man. The irony filled him with adrenaline. He pushed the Alfa Romeo to 145 mph. He'd be in Lost Grove in less than an hour.

Just a week ago, Richard was filled with elation. He and Bess had bonded closer than they had been in years as they awaited the delivery of a granddaughter, one they could help raise alongside their beautiful daughter, Sarah Elizabeth. Sarah had not only fully recovered from her breakdown but was wiser and more confident than he had ever seen her. Since then, though, it had been an utter catastrophe, an avalanche of grief and suffering beyond his comprehension. His perfect daughter was dead. His wife despised him, blaming him for everything, despite the fact that this entire ordeal was her orchestration.

Now he was packing his suitcase in the guest bedroom she'd relegated him to, preparing for a forced vacation to step away from the mess he'd somehow created. How any of this was his fault escaped him, but according to Dr. Owens and Bess, he was the issue.

"When is this person showing up?" Bess asked, standing in the doorway.

Richard shrugged. "Dr. Owens just said sometime today. I told you that."

"I just don't understand why we have to go to this place."

Richard zipped up his suitcase. "Yes, you do. I've explained it to you at least three times now."

"He won't even let me see my own granddaughter!"

"Our granddaughter. Ours!"

Bess rolled her eyes. "The way you twist words. I think we should just go there and at least—"

"No! It's out of the question. You haven't let me hear the end of it for going over there yesterday, and now you want to just barge in there?"

"We have a right to see her."

Richard stepped closer to her. "I know. But—"

"Don't touch me," Bess said, holding her hand out.

Richard dropped his head back. "Would you stop with this? Dr. Owens said we should use this time to heal, not to rip each other apart."

"It's going to be a long time before I'm anywhere near healed, Richard," Bess seethed.

"I'll never heal from this," Richard countered, pounding his chest. "But we have to try."

Bess looked from his chest to his face. "That's as much passion as I've seen out of you in ages."

Richard closed his eyes, forcing himself not to respond. "Did you look up the resort?" he asked instead. Dr. Owens called an hour ago to give him the information on where they would stay and for how long.

Bess brushed the hair out of her eyes. "Yes. It's…really nice."

Richard smiled. "See. We don't have to look at this as a bad thing. I mean, do we really want to just sit around here for days in misery, waiting for the funeral?"

Bess looked out the window. "No."

Richard dared to take another step closer to her. This time, she didn't flinch. "Did you call them?"

Bess nodded. "I did. They confirmed we're booked for the next four days. We're in a luxury suite or something of the like—their best room."

Richard extended his hand and placed it on her arm. "I'm sorry…for everything. This is a living nightmare—all of it—and it would be much easier if we weren't at each other's throats."

Tears rose in Bess's eyes, the first tears Richard had seen in days. "I know," she said and dropped her head onto Richard's chest. "I wish we could just drive up there, the two of us. I don't see why Neil thinks we need a chaperone."

"Well, I stormed into his office a bit unhinged. And he knows you locked yourself in the bathroom."

Bess let out the faintest of laughs.

"I think he's worried one of us is going to break and tell the police everything. He's got his legacy, the entire institute, and everything they're doing at stake."

"Sarah would never want us to do that, so we wouldn't. We won't."

Richard smiled. "No. She would let us have it if we even thought about it."

Bess laughed and then sniffled, wiping her eyes.

"Why don't we—" The infamous Shave and a Haircut door knock interrupted Richard.

Bess looked up at Richard and placed a hand on his face. "I'm sorry, too."

Richard opened the front door to find a short, lithe, surprisingly young man standing there with a wide smile on his face.

"You must be Richard," Colin said, extending his hand. This was his favorite part. Seeing the unknowing looks on people's faces when he arrived.

Richard shook the man's hand. "That's right. You must be Dr. Owens's…guy?"

The man laughed. "Oh, I'm just his little gopher boy, running random errands and what have you. I'm sorry. My name is Josh. Josh Porter. Good to meet you. Where's the wife?"

Richard smiled and jutted his thumb over his shoulder. "Oh, she's just getting some last things packed." Richard noticed smoke wafting in the air behind Josh. He peered over his shoulder to see smoke coming out of the hood of a rather nice-looking car.

"Ah, yeah. My car," Colin said, looking back. "Think I pushed her a bit too hard on the way up here. I was at my grandparents' house down in Montgomery and knew I was running late."

Richard looked back at Josh. "Oh. So…"

"Oh, no worries. I'll just drive you guys up in your car. No big deal."

Richard grimaced.

"Oh, shoot. I hope you guys have a car."

Richard laughed. "Yeah, we have two."

Colin clapped his hands together. "Great. You choose which one. Doesn't matter to me. I'll drive it back once I drop you guys off. Should have plenty of time to get my car fixed by the time I come back to get you. And don't worry, I'll fill up the tank."

"That's a nice offer, but you don't have to."

"I insist," Colin said, wearing his best smile, the one he practiced after meeting Dr. Owens. The impassioned doctor had the grandest smile he'd ever seen.

Richard nodded. "Come on in," he said and turned, walking back into his home.

The smile on Colin's face dissipated in a flash. He walked in and shut the door behind him.

Spelunking After Dark

"What are we looking for, exactly?" Nate's voice echoed through the dense woods as the group trudged behind Mulberry Street. The biting October wind whipped through the trees, making their branches creak and moan. Twigs snapped underfoot as they searched for where Nettie saw the Green Man "come out of the earth."

"She said he came out of a hill," Anya remarked, ahead of the rest of them, busy scanning the trees and the houses to gauge the whereabouts of what Nettie could have seen all those years ago. Just dawning on her now, Anya couldn't believe she hadn't bothered to ask Nettie if she still saw him coming out from behind her house. That seemed like the first sort of question to ask, but she wasn't about to ask now that Nettie had taken ill. Instead, she'd spent her time asking Noble what to wear to go into a cave.

Anya looked over at Stan, all bundled up in thick overalls, an all-weather jacket with reflectors, and a knit cap, and thought her flimsy farm gear and rain boots weren't exactly up to snuff. Not to mention Noble's luxurious getup of sweat-and-rain-slicking cargo pants, hiking boots that looked like they did the work for you, and a thick coat lined by some weather-defying material. Anya felt cumbersome in thermal long johns, thick Carhartt overalls, her grandfather's old waxed jacket, and a knit hat from her mother. She shifted her focus from the couture hiking gear of her friends to finding the cave.

Stan walked just behind Anya, watching her head move like it was on a constant swivel. She casually picked up her pace and sidled up next to her friend. "I won't let us get lost," Stan whispered.

"Huh?" Anya asked.

"I won't let us get lost. You don't have to keep scanning the houses to make sure they're there."

Anya came out of her internal fog of thought. "Oh, yeah, no. I'm just trying to find this 'hill' she refers to," Anya replied.

"Okay." Stan smiled and veered off to look as well.

The library hadn't helped them discover any cave systems in town. A few just outside and several caves in the state park but not a thing alluding to their being anything like a cave system inside the town proper. Stan guessed that some caves on the outskirts had to link into the one they were now trying to locate, if there even was one. Not that she would suggest there wasn't. Her childhood was founded on lore, stories warning her against creatures, these very cursed woods they were now traversing. She was willing to believe the story, if not for the fact that two of the others in their present company could read minds and implant thoughts inside other people's brains. So who could deny Nettie's story?

Noble was about as far into the forest as Anya but a distance away, his emotions close to boiling over. The last thing he wanted was to lose it with everyone around. How could his father lie to them like this? What was he doing? That box in the closet…was it possible his mother had no idea all that money, the gun, were there? The questions were eating him alive. All the possibilities, every imagined scenario, just kept getting worse in Noble's mind. Why would the police want to question his father so badly in conjunction to Sarah Elizabeth's death when they knew she'd been at Orbriallis until a year ago? Yet that question felt like it was losing weight, some kind of thin veil of protection he was holding on to for his father. Was it possible his father was one of those serial killers who had a normal family and hid his alter ego so well his kids, even his wife, had no idea he was actually a sick and twisted murderer?

If she was discharged a year ago, he thought, *and he kidnapped her right away, there was time for her to get pregnant and deliver a baby—Jesus, stop thinking shit like that!*

Noble grabbed a stick, swung it against the brush with force, and then threw it into the woods. The sound of it made everyone look his way. "Sorry," he said.

Noble looked to his right, making eye contact with Anya. Her brilliant hair caught some last vestige of light, flaring bright orange in the dark wood. She smiled at him, and it struck his stomach like a clothesline, sending it flopping over and over, before she turned back to look at the houses, surging forward. He couldn't tell if she was nervous or excited, still not able to read her emotions or feelings. He desperately wanted that, to know what each smile meant, what her thoughts were when she looked off into space. Noble wanted to know her like he knew himself and be so open and connected there'd be no need to speak while still saying so much.

As Anya continued scanning the woods carefully, looking for any sign of a hidden cave entrance behind a hill, she felt like there was more to the raw, red edges of Noble's eyes and nose than the bitter temperature. It bothered her to think he might be suffering some unspoken pain that he was keeping inside. Her gut told her it had something to do with his father, or rather, the things people were saying about his father.

"We should work in a grid," Nate loudly announced to his friends as he scanned the forest like he was looking for a missing person or a dead body. He was wearing black leather gloves and a black jacket that he begged his parents to get him for Christmas last year because it looked like the one Jake Gyllenhaal's detective character wore in Prisoners while holding a flashlight at shoulder level pointing down.

Stan had been internally laughing at Nate since the moment he showed up in his detective gear and now couldn't hold in an audible laugh as she watched the way he moved through the trees like he was looking for minute evidence on the forest floor. Yet, as much as they made fun of him, he'd likely go on to be one of the more successful in their group of friends. He had genuine passion and tenacity, and unlike the rest of them, Nate knew what he wanted to pursue in life.

Emory and Ember, bringing up the rear of the group, clambered over twigs, vines, and moss, looking at each other occasionally and sharing internal thoughts of joy. Was this really that easy—these people accepting them, ushering them into their adventures with open arms like they were long-lost parts of the group, finally making it whole? That's how it felt for Emory. He'd remarked to his sister about the ease this group had with one another, how they all bantered as if they too could reach each other's minds. He felt like this group of friends was more connected than he and his twin sister, even with all their abilities. They got one another. And now, he felt like he might be included in that.

There is a word for that, he thought.

A word for what? Ember asked back.

A feeling of homesickness for a home you don't know.
I've never heard of it.

Emory pulled off his gloves and drew out his phone, the blue-green light blinding his eyes, which had adapted to the dark of the coming evening. He was thankful that Stan implored them to prepare for nearly freezing weather. The woods felt a good ten degrees colder than the town proper.

Fernweh, Hiraeth…maybe a mix of both, he said once his search had turned up the results for his question.

I've never heard of either of those words. What are you saying?

I'm just saying I feel like we were always meant to be friends with them, Emory explained.

Ember, never a fan of cold weather, crossed her arms tighter in her winter parka, not knowing what she felt. She still felt lost and, outside of her brother, completely alone.

"There," Anya said to herself, pointing into the woods. She rotated her torso, looking back to the Horne house, eyes focused on Nettie's bedroom window, and then in the direction she'd aimed her finger. From there, she walked a straight line deeper into the woods.

"Where is she going?" Nate asked the group. "Come on, guys. The grid!"

Stan rushed to catch up with her, seeing her make her way from the placid woods into the cursed ones. It wasn't something you'd notice offhand, the way the trees shifted—one moment normal, the next massive, eldritch living things, deeply rooted with a history all their own locked deep inside their sap and bark. The moss, thick and welcoming, enticed you to lie down and sleep a while. The vines thick, moving like snakes, twisted one way only to shift gears on a dime, confusing any unknowing adventurer. But the smell was a distinct giveaway. The closer you got, the sheer fecundity of the forest oozed a rich, damp, earthly smell laced with a scent too sweet to be natural, with an undercurrent of rot, like aged candied mushrooms.

Noble followed, jogging through the undergrowth, slipping on a felled tree, and quickly righting himself with ease. "Guys!" he said in a harsh whisper, urging the two to wait for the rest of them.

"What are you doing?" Stan asked Anya, finally catching up to her.

"There. See this?" Anya pointed.

She and Stan stared at a large mound of dirt and sticks.

"What is it?" Noble asked, approaching the girls.

The mound looked natural, likely built by an animal as some sort of nest or a beaver dam, though there was no water nearby.

"What is with this rogue shit?" Nate gasped, catching up as he deserted his methodical grid search.

Emory and Ember sped through the trees, reaching the rest of the group.

Anya looked deeper into the forest, shifting around Stan, who was examining the pile of mud, sticks, and fallen detritus. She moved on quickly, pushing deeper into the woods, her feet quiet on the forest floor.

"What is this?" Nate asked the others, equally entranced by the weird structure.

"It looks like a nest or something," Stan commented. She suddenly looked up. "Where's Anya?"

Noble turned from examining the massive nest to the direction he'd noticed Anya walk. Panic sped his heart into a galloping rhythm when he didn't see her and her vibrant hair. His eyes scanned the darkening woods. "Anya?" he called.

"Don't call out," Stan instructed him harshly.

"What the hell do you mean, don't call out? She's not—"

"You don't know what's in here, Noble," Stan admonished.

Nate narrowed his eyes. "What the fuck does that mean?"

"Guys!" Anya yelled out, waving from behind a fallen trunk of massive redwood.

Stan's eyes shot back and forth, finally catching a wisp of Anya's orange hair from beneath her hat. She had somehow gotten a solid hundred yards from where they were. Stan waved her arms in a massive slashing motion.

Anya frowned, not that the others could see it, and stepped back behind the fallen redwood, aiming her flashlight downward. The ground swelled, and she stood at the edge of an opening in the earth. It didn't look like a cave entrance you would find in a book or from Google results, and she imagined, because of how it was located just underneath the redwood and the slight, maybe two-and-a-half-foot-high entrance, it could easily be mistaken as a part of the giant tree. It was only because she was looking for it she even would have given it a second thought.

Instead of some hole in a rock face, this cave cut into the earth with a steep descent of crumbled stone and massive boulders. It certainly appeared that one could traverse it without gear, at least from up here. Anya shook her head in awe. This was it. Nettie was telling the truth.

She grinned, swinging her flashlight out of the hole and back toward the others, waving her hand in the air.

Noble was in the midst of a swift jog, pushing through the trees and brambles.

"Hey, let's not get separated now," Stan instructed, following and waving to the others to stick with her.

Nate scoffed. "We're not that far from the houses, Stan. I don't think we'll get…" He trailed off. He looked back over his shoulder but was stunned silent. The rooftops he'd spied only moments before were gone. There was nothing but woods now—a terrible, claustrophobic forest of trees, moss, lichen, mushrooms, and tiny flowers that shivered when there was no wind. "Stan? Where…? What the hell?"

Ember and Emory had stopped with Nate and were both following his searching gaze.

Stan circled back and came shoulder to shoulder with Nate. "What?"

Nate turned to her, mouth agape. "Where the hell are the houses?"

Stan scanned the horizon, noticing it too.

"What the fuck?" Emory said. He felt his sister move close, standing behind him. He could also tell she really wanted to reach out and take his hand, like she had when they were younger and she was too shy to go play on the playground without him.

"Shit," Stan spat. She moved first one way and then the other, staring between the trees and up to the sky. Not that there was much sky to see.

"When did it get so dark?" Emory asked.

Nate pulled his phone from his back pocket, checking the time. "It's only five thirty. It shouldn't be this dark."

"Yeah, man, and why does it feel like it's dropped another ten degrees from when we first got here?"

"Calm down," Stan implored. She looked into the woods to see Noble disappear behind the fallen redwood and then turned back to where the houses should be. She crouched on the forest floor, inspecting the tiny bits of moss, and stood back up, shifted to the right, and found what she was looking for. Two trees created a kind of periscope, and between them, she saw the houses. A sigh escaped her. "There," she said, pointing. "Close one eye, and look through the gap between those two trees. Right there. See those?"

Nate moved closer to Stan, following her instructions. His sight shifted slowly until the trees aligned just so, and there was the Horne house in full glory. "How'd you…?"

"Whoa," Emory sighed, peeking over Nate's left shoulder. Ember looked over his right, both greatly relieved.

"Come on, we gotta catch up with them," Stan instructed, already heading toward Noble and Anya.

Nate looked from Ember to Emory. "You good?"

"Yep, let's go." The three moved at a swift pace, not wanting to fall behind and get lost in this unnatural maze.

Unaware of the illusion the forest was playing, Noble and Anya stared down into the dark abyss of the cavern opening. Noble had to crouch to look inside and gauge the slope. It was steep, and the rock was loose. One could easily slide down it, hitting their head on boulders with one little slip. It smelled like metal, and he noticed shining stones of copper on the rock wall. The air was moist, still, and warm. There were hot springs in the state park. He wondered if some connected below as well.

"How the hell would kids crawl out of this?" he asked, standing up and unclipping his climbing backpack. The question brought to mind the image of little children clambering up the cave like little crabs, dark and demented faces covered in dirt, and mouths wide with sharp teeth. He shivered at the thought, grabbing glow sticks from his pack and snapping them alight. He tossed them into the cave.

Anya bent with him this time to look inside, the place lit with a sickly yellow green. "It is rather steep," she commented. "I can see a grown man could traverse it, but…"

Noble crouched back down and shuffled inside, kicking and shuffling his feet. "Stone is loose, too. Like really loose."

"Can we get down there?" Anya asked.

Noble fully removed his backpack, dropping it to the ground and unzipping it. "We can get down."

His confidence reassured Anya, and she squatted down next to him, watching as he pulled rope, carabiners, and harnesses from his bag. She glanced up at the snapping of twigs to see the others finally make their way over.

"Okay, so what the fuck?" Emory voiced, looking down toward the entrance. "Is that the weirdest cave y'all have seen because I thought caves were, like, in mountains and shit?"

"How did you even know this was here?" Stan asked.

Anya turned to her, realizing the question was for her. "I didn't.

Nettie said the Green Man—"

"Raymond," Nate corrected.

"Papa LaRange," Stan added.

"Came out of a hill behind her house when she was younger. That pile we stopped at, it looks like a hill from her window vantage," Anya described. "So, if that's the hill, there had to be something behind it. Right?"

Stan nodded, eyebrows raised. "Okay," she said, pulling her backpack off her shoulders and dropping it to the ground.

Noble unwound all the extra gear he'd brought for the others. "You guys really don't want to go down there with us?" he asked the twins, who told them earlier they would only go with them until they found the cave.

"If I'm being honest, hell no. But these woods, they're fucking creepy," Emory said.

"Doesn't look like any straight drops. More of a slide down with ropes and harnesses for safety," Stan said in a manner of comfort.

Ember was shaking her head, but she too didn't want to stay up here while everyone else went down into that cave.

"Nah. At least not here," Noble replied, turning on his headlamp and looking down once more. "Looks more like a rockslide, to be honest."

"Maybe a sinkhole," Stan commented.

"That sounds wholly unsettling," Emory remarked.

"We're good. We've got you," Nate said, slapping Emory on the back. "You've got us, right? Hear any weird shit down there?"

Emory hadn't been trying to listen, but Ember already had and replied in her brother's mind, *Nothing.*

"Nothing so far," Emory answered.

Nate nodded, pulling his lesser gear from his bag. "So, this seems weird and all, and maybe I should have asked this before, but what the hell are we looking for down there?"

"Signs of life?" Noble commented.

"Great, great." Nate nodded as if this all made sense and was logical for them to be doing. "Signs of what kind of life?"

"Kids?" Stan questioned.

Noble simply nodded, putting together ropes, tying knots, and adding carabiners to his belt. The methodical memory of prepping for a climb or a drop put his nerves at ease, erasing some of the tension in his gut and shoulders. If he focused, he could almost drown out the foghorn of betrayal from his father. *He lied. He lied to all of us,* he thought and then cinched a knot tight.

"And if we run into said kids?" Nate continued, wishing he raised this vital issue sooner.

"Yeah, I'm sorry, but do you really think there will be kids down there?" Emory asked.

Stan shrugged. "Dunno. But pay attention here. Anya, you watching?"

Anya stepped up next to Emory and Ember. "Yep."

"Step into your harness like this," she instructed, stepping into her own, showing them how it went on and then how it buckled. She'd laid out the two belts she had brought for herself and Anya and thankfully the spares she now set out for Ember and Emory.

Do you really think anyone is down there? Ember asked.

I really doubt it, Em.

Nate silently prepared himself. He put on his headlamp and switched it on, testing it. He didn't go climbing as often as Noble and Stan, and rarely did he go spelunking with them. The idea of crawling through tight tunnels underground made his palms sweat. "Just flying by the seat of our pants, then," he commented to himself, tying a knot in his rope and laying it in Noble's pile.

"It's a reconnaissance. No big deal. Let's just see what we see," Stan finally added.

Nate nodded, pursing his lips. "Right, okay. A reconnaissance for a child molester and his weird children that aren't actually children, which has yet to be fully explained."

Noble grabbed the ropes, finding the nearest tree to tie them around. "I don't know what they are. They just aren't right, not human. They're… something else."

"Something else, he says! That's great!"

"Shh," Stan scolded Nate.

"Look, all I'm saying is, do we have any idea what they are? Like, will they come at us like cave-dwelling cannibals or some shit? Do we have a weapon?" Nate continued.

"Do we need weapons?" Noble asked.

Emory let out a small laugh.

"What?" Nate asked.

He looked up, tapped the side of his head. "My weapon."

Nate blinked, looking at the others, then back. "Okay, now I want to know what the hell you can do. Are you telling me you can, like, explode heads or some shit?"

That made Ember and Emory laugh, Anya joining in.

"No. I can't explode heads," Emory said. "Just know that if there's anyone actually down there, we'll hear them, whether they're speaking or not."

Nate nodded. "Okay, that's both unsettling and somewhat reassuring."

"We've got your backs is all I'm saying." Emory hoped it would assuage some of the anxious feelings he and his sister's secret had left on this group of teens.

"Thanks," Noble said, resting a hand on Emory's shoulder in passing.

Maybe don't get too cozy with them just yet, Ember admonished her brother.

"Good?" Stan asked Ember, tightening the straps.

Ember gave her a thumbs-up and a smile.

"Anya, need yours fixed?" Stan asked, turning to find Noble already helping her adjust it. She smiled and turned back to Nate and Emory. "You guys good to go?"

Nate nodded, moving to the edge of the entrance and peering in once more. He clipped on his line. "Doesn't look too steep."

"The rocks are loose, and looks can be deceiving," Noble explained, handing a rope and clip to Anya that she attached to her belt. He followed with his own.

Stan helped Ember on with hers and then showed Emory. An exchange of awkward smiles passed between them. She liked his warm eyes and always felt a little disarmed when he looked right into hers. Ember had the same kind eyes, but hers were full of hesitation and wariness. Stan hoped she'd open up more as they got to know one another.

Nate took one step in before saying, "By the way, the cops came to my house earlier."

"What?" Noble squawked.

"Are you serious?" Stan asked, her brow wrinkled.

"Yeah, the one young guy, anyway," he continued as he descended.

Stan followed Nate side by side with Ember, who was clearly anxious about this whole endeavor. Emory was next. Though he didn't climb or cave, he'd done a few random indoor rock-climbing excursions with friends back in San Francisco. Anya went next, glancing at Noble as he stood waiting, face painted with concern, possibly anguish. His whole body shivered with riotous energy. She almost wanted to tell them all to stop and forget about it, so she could find out what was troubling him.

Noble gave her a reassuring smile, his face transforming the moment their eyes locked. For that brief moment, he had almost forgotten what Nate had said. As soon as Anya slid down, anxiety filled him back up. "What was he asking you about?" he called down from the entrance.

"He asked me about my post," Nate called up.

"What post?" Noble asked from above, still not moving.

"I posted about the Orbriallis. Said I was going underground to investigate. Get it?" He laughed.

"What did he want?" Noble raised his voice.

"Can we please be a little bit quieter?" Stan growled, negotiating the slope. It was steeper than it looked and slippery with moss and gravel.

Nate shrugged and then slipped on a sheet of stone. "Asked me what it was about. I told him it was just town gossip—you know, us kids getting up to shit. He seemed placated by that."

"So, you didn't tell him there actually is some weird shit going on at the Orbriallis?" Stan asked.

"Fuck no. This is my investigation," Nate said as he steadied his feet. "It drops even steeper for this last bit."

"Nate, this isn't some TV show or movie. This is a real problem…"

Their argument trailed off as Anya paused, ducking low so she could look out the entrance and still see Noble, standing there, bent over. "Are you coming, Noble?"

The soft way she asked prompted him to move, despite his heart racing in his chest. Why would the police be asking about some random social media story posted by a kid? It must have had something to do with what Sergeant Wolfe had asked him, but where was the connection to Sarah and his father? Noble ducked into the cave and made quick work to catch up with Anya.

"I am taking it seriously!" Nate was still hashing it out with Stan.

"Dude. Quiet," Stan barked.

"I think it's weird the police would ask you about that, Nate," Anya commented.

Nate grunted, leaping to the bottom. "It's totally weird."

"Do you think the Institute reported me?" Emory asked.

"Nope," Nate answered promptly. "They wanted to know what the strange thing was. Asked all about, 'What did you mean strange things were afoot?' and I was all like, 'You know, the usual.'" Nate unclipped himself, letting the spare rope coil on the ground. He helped Ember down, offering a hand to Stan, who smirked at him in a manner that suggested she was far more capable than he was in this situation.

Anya slipped on the steep transition, but Noble gripped her elbow. He'd made swift work down, more used to the feeling of letting go and knowing the rope had you. Noble let his mind focus on her, on keeping her safe, on the task at hand, while in the background a hundred fresh stories about his father, dead girls, and a shady institute played out in make-believe technicolor. He wanted to turn them off, make the horror stories stop whizzing around like a steel ball in a pinball machine, but it was no use.

It was pitch black at the bottom. Nate carefully meandered around. Noble unclipped himself and helped Anya.

"Check this out," Stan said. Her headlight swept across the cavern, disappearing into an entrance where blackness swallowed all the light.

Nate moved over to the new entrance. It was a tunnel, certainly big enough for children to walk through with ease, but a grown man would have to hunch over, nearly double.

I don't want to go down there, Ember said to both her brother and Stan.

Stan looked over at the twins. "Do you guys want to stay here?"

Emory looked around, back up, and out the entrance, far above them. He held his hands out. "I honestly don't know. Yes?"

Ember nodded profusely.

"You're staying?" Nate asked.

"I think we'll stay here," Emory responded. He couldn't leave his sister here alone.

Noble handed him a radio from his bag. "We'll be on sequence 1. If something happens and you need to call someone, switch to line 3. That goes to my home receiver. My mom will pick up."

Emory took the walkie, nodding, though he felt as if his stomach had been pulled up through his throat at the mention of needing to call for help.

"Okay, let's see where this goes," Stan said, excitement leaching into her voice. Sure, it was slightly horrifying. They were inside a cave in the cursed woods, but the adrenaline of the adventure, like every caving excursion, had taken hold of her body. "I'll be lead?"

Noble nodded.

"I don't want to be last," Anya whispered to Noble.

He smiled. "I'm last."

She smiled back and followed Nate into the tunnel. Noble waved at the twins and then was gone, sucked into the darkness of the cave.

"How would anyone negotiate this without light?" Nate asked, hunched over, his voice tinny inside the tunnel.

The floor of the tunnel was choppy and covered in dips, small holes, and tall ridges. One could easily trip and twist an ankle.

"Oh, shit," Stan said, stopping them.

"What?" Noble asked from the rear.

"Hole with water," she said and looked back at Nate and Anya. "Water in caves can be misleading. It might look like a little puddle but can be deceptively deep."

"Good to know," Nate said, raising his eyebrows.

"How big is it?" Noble asked.

"We can stride over it," she said. "Just be careful."

They continued on, crouched low, ambling down this tunnel with an unknown decline for a few minutes before exiting into a larger cavern.

Nate stood and stretched his back. This cavern had three more tunnels veering off in different directions. Stan went to one, shining her headlamp into it. It was dank and dripping with water. She didn't like the looks of it. A narrow crevice could be a death trap. No one was coming or going out of there.

Anya turned around and watched Noble pile three stones near the tunnel. He caught her watching him. "It marks the way out," he remarked.

Anya nodded. "Handy. I suppose leaving actual marks is frowned upon."

He smiled. "A big no-no."

"No one's going in and out of this one," Stan commented.

"No. Because they're definitely using this one," Nate said.

The others joined him at the entrance to a round tunnel, the floor smooth and worn like old stone steps. A doll was resting on the ground covered in soot near a small blanket, like a child had left it there to nap ages ago and never came back to play with it again.

"Jesus, I didn't really think…" Nate huffed, moving away from the entrance and wiping a hand across his forehead before pulling out his phone and snapping pictures.

Anya moved into the tunnel and squatted down over the doll. It was one of those dolls with eyelids that opened and closed. She picked it up, the doll squeaking with a long-lost voice.

"Leave it," Stan said, disgusted and discomforted by the strange appearance of this doll.

Anya tucked it back where it was and stood. "We're going this way, I assume?"

Stan nodded, passing her in the tunnel, which was wide enough for two people to walk side by side.

They came to a fork, with one part shrinking and looking like it inclined back toward the surface. The other continued on.

"Nate, you and I will check this one out, see if it leads anywhere, then double back. You guys check out that one," Stan instructed Anya and Noble, pointing down the path that looked normal.

"Okay," Noble agreed and held out his fist.

Stan knocked hers against his and climbed into the tunnel forking right. Nate and Noble exchanged a handshake typically reserved for track meets, and then Nate followed Stan.

Noble and Anya continued on the left fork.

"You okay?" he asked.

"Yeah, fine. You?"

Noble nodded.

"You seemed upset earlier," Anya stated.

"When?"

"When we first arrived, outside. You seemed, I don't know, shaken." Anya watched her footing, though the path looked well traversed and clear.

"Just stuff at home," Noble answered, not knowing why.

"About your dad?"

Noble looked down at the top of her head beside him. She looked up to meet his gaze, then back down at the ground. "Yeah."

Anya bit her lower lip a moment, deciding what to say, if she should say anything. "Do you know what people say about me and my mom?"

Noble flinched, frowning. "No. People say stuff about you?"

Anya smiled, nodding. She had never told anyone about her mother—what she was, what they were. It was too early to tell Noble everything, and maybe she never would, but she felt like sharing something. "They do. You know people talk because they see something strange or different. People here notice peculiar habits. There's no secrecy like there would be in a big city. Or, maybe not secrecy but, like, no hiding your weirdness. That kind of thing would go unnoticed in a big city because there are all kinds of people there, with all kinds of habits, peculiarities, fetishes, or whatever. But around here, you do one little thing, one small mishap or choice, and it becomes the talk of the town, and then it gets exaggerated. Next thing you know, people think you're a vampire or something, like Mary, you know?" Anya turned to find she was alone. Her heart thudded loudly in her ears. They'd been whispering, but now she raised her voice slightly and called, "Noble?"

Anya backtracked quickly, scanning the wall and the ground for a sign of Noble. She found a small tunnel branching off the one they were in and stepped inside. The smell of something rancid mixed with iron.

"Noble?" she asked again, voice echoing against rock as she crept forward. The darkness seemed to gulp up the light from her headlamp.

She looked up, feeling a shift of wind pass over the top of her. As her light came back down from the vast nothingness above her, it caught on something pale and white. She swung the light back but now saw nothing.

"Noble?" she asked, frantic to hear him respond.

"Anya?"

She heard him whisper. Her feet moved faster, the light bouncing on nothing all around. Another flash of paleness, like skin, and a shuffle of wind. Her visibility kicked in, the kind that came to her when she swam in the dark, deep waters with her mother. She saw Noble ahead and, above him, a figure darker than the darkness. A pale, gnarled hand with talons for fingernails reached out.

"Noble!" she shrieked, grabbing him toward her.

Noble fell into her. They stumbled back, but he kept them upright, a hand around her waist. Her fingers dug into his arms.

"What?" he asked once they'd steadied themselves.

Anya was looking behind him, eyes wide, sweeping the darkness.

"Anya, what?" he asked, looking over his shoulder and seeing nothing.

She was breathing fast, and her eyes looked black. Noble carefully released her.

"I thought I saw something."

"Seriously?" He turned and looked again.

"It's probably my imagination," she said, desperately wanting to believe it. "Where did you go? I was talking to you and then—"

"Sorry. I saw this, and it felt like there was a breeze."

"You scared me," she said, only now easing up on the hold she had on his arms.

"I'm sorry," he repeated, smiling and rubbing her arms before pulling her into a hug. It felt natural, and only after he did it did he realize how lovely it felt. He felt his skin flush around his neck, crawling into his cheeks. "I shouldn't have wandered off."

Anya liked the way his voice rumbled out of his chest and into her ear. He cleared his throat. "Come on, there's nothing in here. Let's keep going."

They held hands, Noble leading back out into the main path and onward. He was smiling from ear to ear. He couldn't stop himself. Just behind him, Anya was smiling, too. They walked this way in silence, each one wondering what to do next.

Should I kiss her? he thought. *Ask her out?* His mind was a race of scintillating thoughts when he stopped dead, shuffling backward.

Anya ran into him, felt him push her back. Neither one had bothered to notice the change in their environment, but now that they had, both their flesh burst with goosebumps. The tunnel had become something like a hallway. The walls had supports and were cut, not natural formations. But that wasn't why Noble had backpedaled.

"What the hell is this?" Anya asked. They'd come to a T, the tunnel jogging to the right.

Noble held up his hand to her, the other to his lips. He approached the corner and leaned his head around it. "What the fuck?" he whispered.

Anya moved up next to him and leaned out. The dirt-and-stone floor gave way to green-and-white checkered linoleum. Fluorescent bulbs glowed, lighting up the place, which was a little dusty but nevertheless clean. There was a door in the far wall and, above that, a camera. The little red light was blinking.

"What?" Anya elongated the middle of the word.

"It's recording," Noble said, motioning to the camera.

"Like, now?"

Noble leaned farther out, trying to get a view of the camera. "It could be."

"But who's watching? What is…? Where are…?" Anya couldn't think of the right question to ask because there were too many circling in her mind.

Noble moved back behind the wall, pacing. "I don't like this."

Anya pulled herself away. "No. It's not…right."

"No, it isn't."

"Guys?" Stan's voice was harried with worry. She and Nate had only gone so far before their path became too narrow. Not the thing a bunch of children would navigate regularly, let alone a grown man. They were heading back when she heard Anya call out for Noble, and it sent her stomach into her boots.

Noble rushed back, hands telling them to stop and be quiet. Stan was happy to see Noble alive and well, walking, talking, but clearly shaken.

"What happened?" Stan asked when she got close enough to whisper.

"We heard Anya scream," Nate added.

"Nothing. Guys—"

"Is that light?" Nate asked, noticing the unnatural fluorescents. He pushed around Noble, who grabbed him and hauled him back.

"Dude, stop," Noble urged.

"This is a fucking hallway," Nate noticed, still peering ahead. "This is man-made."

"Yes, and there's a door and a fucking camera down there," Noble explained in a loud whisper.

"What the shit?" Nate got away from his friend, galloping forward, and stopped at the corner before tipping his head around the edge to look. He pulled back, hands clenched and eyes wide. He mouthed the words, *Oh fuck*, before pulling out his phone once more and instinctively started taking photos and video.

"What is going on here, Noble?" Stan asked.

"I don't know," he said to his best friend. They looked at each other for a while before she, too, went to look for herself.

Stan saw the camera, its blinking light, the linoleum floor and felt like she'd fallen into a surreal film. This couldn't be real. She removed her headlamp and the elastic holding her hair up. She ran a hand through her hair and just as quickly put it back up and replaced her headlamp.

"What do we do now?" Anya asked the group.

It was Nate who found the words. "This was a reconnaissance. Now we know. I've got photos and a video. We need to find out what the hell that could be."

"How do we do that? I'm not walking up and knocking," Noble hissed.

"No, no. We've got to know where that leads to. There has to be something above. Get me?"

Noble began nodding.

"We need some maps and shit. We need to plot this, these tunnels. How do you guys do that?"

Stan's brow cinched tight. "Like we know? We don't map caves. We go into ones already explored."

Nate put his hands on his hips. "Alright. Here's the game plan, then. Get as many pictures of this cave on the way out as you can. We need proof. And don't forget to get pictures of that weird entrance. Then we find out how to map caves. We map this out, compare it to our town, and find out what the fuck is above us. And you know what? I'd be willing to bet my left testicle it's the fucking Orbriallis Institute."

A Roadside Tragedy

Seth woke with a start, his heart pounding, body covered in a film of sweat, images and memories of a vivid and stressful dream disappearing by the nanosecond. He strained his mind to hang on to the remnants. There was a game of chess, but it switched from him struggling to move his arm to play it to him being in the game stuck to a giant black square. Who was there? Noble was a chess piece, Paddy, Bill…yes, Dr. Bajorek was there. She was across the board, trying to tell him something, but the sound of her voice was a mile away. What else? Who else? Goddammit if it wasn't important. The Grahamses! They were knocked-over chess pieces, lying on their sides, their feet touching but their bodies stiff as a board. It was right after that. He spotted them, and then what happened? It was right there, mentally tangible but visually absent. And then his phone rang. His phone…

"What the hell?" He flopped over on his side and slammed his half-numb arm onto his side table, grabbing the phone. He looked at the screen and answered. "Hey, Bill, what time is—"

"I've called you three times in a row, Seth. This is bad, really fucking bad."

Seth sat up. "Sorry, I was completely—"

"It's Richard and Bess…"

Bill's pause was enough to stall Seth's breath in his throat. The ghostly image of the Grahamses as knocked-over chess pieces evoked an uncomfortable sensation that spread throughout his body.

"They're dead, Seth. I don't know what the hell…I'm here with Eddie. Wes is on his way. I just don't know what to make of this," Bill sputtered, his voice manic.

Seth gripped the side of his head, unprepared to delve into what the premonition disguised as a dream meant. He jumped to his feet to get dressed, looking at his watch: 6:10 a.m. "Bill, I'm getting ready now, but I need you to take a breath and start from the beginning."

Bill sighed. "I got a call from Eddie at five thirty. He said a call from dispatch came through from a trucker was heading up the Wildcat and spotted a car pulled over at a turnoff."

"Wildcat? Is it our jurisdiction?" There was an unincorporated area surrounding Lost Grove's city limits that was home to over 3,000 residents that fell under the watch of the sheriff's department. Seth needed to know who would be in charge of the scene. Bill informed Seth when he first joined the department that there had been heated discussions over the past few years about the unincorporated area becoming incorporated into Lost Grove.

"About half a mile out from it not being ours."

"Okay. So, what did the trucker do?"

"He saw the passenger leaning against their window and the driver's head against the steering wheel and what he thought was blood all across the back driver's-side window."

Seth sat on the edge of the bed and fumbled his boot laces. "Blood?"

"From a gunshot. I'm not an expert, but it looks like a murder-suicide," Bill said, staring at the scene.

Seth sat up and pinched the bridge of his nose. What the hell was happening?

"I just don't believe it. It doesn't make—"

"Okay, Bill, you got a call from Eddie, and then what?"

"Yeah, and I, uh…I met him up here. I shined my flashlight at the windshield, not recognizing the car at first, and almost had a heart attack seeing Bess's face. Her head is leaning against the passenger side, blood's covering the entire window, coming down the side of her face from the entry wound. Her eyes…they're open, but she's clearly dead…"

Seth could hear that Bill had already cracked. It was one thing to find a body on a beach with no apparent physical damage. But to see the aftermath of bloody violence…it was nothing TV, movies, or even crime scene photos could prepare you for.

"God help me," he said, turning away from the vehicle. "I was afraid to move my flashlight over to the driver's side. I thought I was going to see Richard sitting there, holding the gun in a state of mania. But he was hunched over, head on the wheel. So I rushed over, not knowing if he was—"

"Please tell me you didn't touch the car," Seth said, putting on his jacket.

"No. Even if I was about to, once I saw…the back of Richard's head…Jesus Christ."

"Have you or Eddie touched anything? Anything at all?"

"No. I just circled the car. Eddie's putting flares up now."

"You both have on latex gloves?"

"Yeah, we do now. And Wes should be here any second. Should I call Eureka PD, get their forensic team down here?"

Seth locked his door. "Yeah, give them a call. I'll have plenty of time to survey the scene by the time they get there. Did you see the gun yet?"

Bill glanced over at Richard's lifeless body. "No. I can't see either of his hands. His head…his body is covering—"

"It's fine. It's not going anywhere. Tell Wes not to open either of those doors until I get there."

"Will do. Should we call anyone else to—"

"I'm going to call Sasha and bring her with me. I'll call Joe and have him come into the station early to cover."

"Okay."

"I'll see the flares, but how far down are you?"

"About four miles from the coast, so roughly eighteen miles."

Seth got to his Bronco, thankful he didn't leave it at the station last night. "The only job you have to do now, both you and Eddie, is just keep everyone other than Wes away from that scene. I doubt there'll be much traffic heading down the Wildcat at this hour, but all it takes is one person. Don't let anyone stop or even slow down."

"Got it."

Seth started the vehicle. "I've got to call Sasha and Joe. I'll see you in twenty minutes."

Sasha was waiting at the curb, blowing into her hands and jumping from foot to foot when Seth pulled up. She didn't wait for him to stop before she pulled open the door and jumped in. "Holy shit."

"Holy shit, indeed." Seth stepped on the gas and headed for the Lost Grove entrance to the Wildcat Circle, the fifty-eight-mile scenic road south of town that looped from the coast up through Willow Creek forest.

"What do we know so far?"

Seth shook his head. "Not a lot. What little I got from Bill, it appears that the Grahams pulled over on the side of the road. Richard shot his wife, who was in the passenger seat, and then shot himself. But that could change drastically when we get there and investigate the scene."

"Did Bill say that's what happened?"

"That's his assessment. He said Bess's head was leaning up against the passenger window, blood coming down her face from an entry wound to the side of the head. He said that Richard was slumped, head on the wheel, and couldn't bring himself to describe the back of his head, which tells me he shot himself in the mouth and a good portion of the back of his skull is no longer there."

"What could change? Do you think it could be something else?"

Seth had had little time to ponder that question between calls with Bill, Sasha, and then Joe, but his gut instinct was that it felt off. "I don't think anything yet. But I look at every suicide as a possible homicide being covered up. Don't assume anything ever. Approach every crime scene like you know nothing. No matter what was reported, who says they saw what, discover the scene for yourself and take every precaution to make sure nothing is overlooked. You'll never get to relive that initial moment on the scene. Photos, videos, reports are all well and good, but the aura of the scene, the smell, the palpable emotion and tension in the air, what your gut is telling you, it's all vital in that moment."

Sasha appreciated everything Seth had done for her since he arrived. Early on, she admitted to Seth that she desperately wanted to move on to a bigger city, to a bigger department. Ever since then, he used every opportunity he found to teach her, to prepare her for what she might encounter if she ever got the chance to make the move. "There hasn't been a scene like this in the years that I've been here. And from overhearing you and Bill talk since finding Sarah Grahams, it doesn't sound like there ever has been. At least not in the recent past."

"Aside from the Kelly Fulson case, the worst this town has seen in decades in terms of violence are from accidents, hunting, farming, hiking." Seth looked over at Sasha. "How do you feel?"

"About the scene?"

"Yeah."

Sasha watched Seth while he drove, periodically looking over at her. "I'm ready."

"It's impossible to prepare yourself to see this level of violence firsthand.

No matter how much you've trained, read, seen photos…seeing it in front of you is something different. Not everyone can handle it."

"This won't be the first time I've seen someone close up after being shot." Verbalizing the words brought Sasha back to a night from her past, the feeling of horror still attainable.

Seth looked over at her, eyes narrowed. "You want to tell me about it?"

Sasha puckered her lips, the memories flooding back to her as vivid as if it happened last week.

"You don't have to, of course."

"Nah, it's fine." Sasha brought the heel of her boot up to her seat, leaning her arm across her knee. "It was back in Cleveland. Angel and I were outside a nightclub, trying to figure out where to go next. There was a big-ass fight inside, and they cleared us all out. Nothing we hadn't experienced before. But then this car pulled up, and you could just tell. The speed, the pace, the angle it came in at, I knew it was bad. This dude gets out and just makes a beeline to this other dude standing about three feet in front of me, and bam! Shoots him right in the head. Blood, fucking tiny bits of skull, all over me and my girl. First thing I did was wrap Angel up to protect her. She had dropped to the ground, screaming her head off. And then this other girl makes a commotion. Turned out to be the girlfriend of the guy that just got shot. She ran up to the dude with the gun, screaming, crying…"

The story wasn't a shock to Seth. He'd sensed Sasha had a leather tough shield from the moment he first met her. It wasn't her height, her build, or the tattoos on her neck. It was in her eyes. The eyes were always the telltale sign.

Sasha shook her head. "This motherfucker shoots her right in the stomach. For no fucking reason. What was she gonna do to him? Scratch his face with her long-ass nails? I watched her slowly die in front of me. Ambulance was too late. Worst thing I've ever seen."

Seth looked over at Sasha. Her whole demeanor, her voice, her body, had gone back to Cleveland. Which wasn't a surprise, because he felt like he was back in San Francisco. "That why you left and came here?"

Sasha laughed. "Nah. Wasn't me. I was fine. I was finishing up at a community college there, where I got my law enforcement degree. It was Angel. A couple years earlier, I was about twenty-two at the time—she was thirty—we took a road trip up the West Coast. She had seen some story or something about Lost Grove and was dying to visit. And I'm not gonna lie, I fell in love with the place too. But that night outside the club really shook her up, ya know? I wanted to stay in Cleveland, join the force right away, but I knew Angel needed to get out. I hit up three stations on the coast, and Bill just happened to have an opening. So, here I am."

"And now you want to get out?" Seth stated more than asked.

Another long sigh from Sasha. "You know I do. I feel like I can't do enough here, be what I wanna be."

"Does Angel know this?"

"Yeah…I mean, she's known it since we got here. Shit, since before we even left Cleveland."

"And?"

"And…I think if we can live in a decent area in a bigger city, she'll be okay. I do."

Seth nodded. "There are plenty of nice areas in San Francisco. I can make some calls."

Sasha jerked her head toward Seth. She had been hoping this might come up but didn't want to push it. "For real?"

Seth looked at her and smiled. "For real. And I get it. I knew since I was probably in…ninth grade, maybe, that I needed to leave Lost Grove to make the impact I wanted to make. And I did."

Sasha felt a deep empathy for him. She knew he was out of place, despite being born here. "You gotta wanna go back, right?"

It was Seth's turn to laugh. "I think about it every day. I honestly thought I was going to die from boredom until a week ago when Bill called me about Sarah. But…my parents are older now, and even though I know they don't need me to stay here…it's tough. And…" Seth's mouth hung open for a moment before it slowly closed.

Sasha grinned. "Story Palmer?"

Seth shot her a look.

"Hey, man, you know I understand. I just told you why I'm in this town."

Seth looked back at the road ahead. Would he really consider staying here? Whether it was for Story or his parents? Would Story consider leaving Lost Grove? Why was she even here in the first place? Questions for another time.

"So, what's the worst thing you've ever seen?" Sasha bounced in her seat, an eager grin on her face. "I told you mine, and I *know* you've seen some shit."

Seth's grip on the wheel tightened. A wave of shivers rolled down his body. His stomach immediately felt empty. He hadn't talked to anyone about what he'd seen just weeks before coming back to Lost Grove.

"Sorry if that's too personal. I know that—"

"No. You have every right to ask."

"I do?"

"Partners need to talk," Seth said, feeling a tug of longing for his last partner, Kendra Washington. She was only twenty-nine when he left, but she was sharp as a razor and had instincts decades beyond her years.

"'Partners.' That's dope."

Seth took a deep breath and forced himself to loosen his grip. "There are a lot of parks in San Francisco. Maybe you've even been to some of them on your West Coast trip."

Sasha just smiled, not wanting to interrupt him.

"Some are nicer than others. Most are hotbeds for recreational drug use. And with any big city, and plenty of smaller ones, drugs are an issue. Many of the homicide cases we got called to involved drugs, whether it was people on them or deals gone wrong."

"Who was your partner?" Sasha always imagined he had a partner, like in TV shows and the movies.

Seth smiled. "Her name is Kendra Washington. She—"

"Kendra Washington," Sasha repeated the name, drawing it out with emphasis. "Tell me your partner wasn't a sister."

Seth laughed. "Assuming you're referring to an African American, then yes."

"'African American,' he says, sounding all politically correct."

"My partner was a Black woman, yes."

"That sounds more natural."

Seth glanced over at Sasha. "She was young like you. Still is. She was only twenty-five when she made detective and got paired up with me."

"How old is she now?"

"Just turned thirty last month."

"You still talk to her?"

Seth nodded. "All the time. She calls me about every case, picking my brain, talking it through."

"I bet she wants your ass back there."

Seth sighed. "That she does."

"I'm sorry," Sasha said. "Didn't mean to interrupt. I wanna hear this before we get there."

"Anyhow, the local city parks aren't necessarily the safest places, but there weren't a lot of actual homicide calls to the parks over the years. So, when we were called to a scene at Dolores Park this past May at five in the morning, it was something of a surprise. When Kendra and I got there, the officer who responded to the 911 call met us. He was a young guy, couldn't have been over twenty-three years old. His face looked like all the blood had drained from it, and his eyes…he was gone. He just pointed toward the forensic team and coroner and started walking. All we'd heard was that there was a body, so I asked him what happened. He just muttered 'woman.' By the time we made it across the park, he started crying and mumbling to himself. I had to ask the paramedics to look at the kid."

"Jesus," Sasha uttered.

"The look on the coroner's face wasn't much better. His name is Rich Stevenson. I worked with him countless times over the years. We had seen some grisly stuff, and I can't say that I had ever seen him emotionally fazed before that morning. Despite all these warning signs, and all my years on the force, nothing could have prepared me…" Seth swallowed, trying with all his might to keep his emotions at bay. "As Rich led us over to the body, he said the woman had overdosed on heroin. Before he could get out the rest of the story, maybe because he couldn't bring himself to verbalize it, I saw the child."

Sasha's face tensed, a heavy frown forming.

Seth had a vise grip on the wheel. He released his right hand to wipe at his eyes and face. "She was eight months old and"—Seth motioned toward his bicep—"had two heroin needles sticking out of her."

Sasha covered her mouth.

Seth took a long breath in through his nose and slowly blew it out through his lips. "Haven't really talked about it since."

"What the fuck," Sasha breathed.

Seth nodded. "Yeah."

They sat in silence until Sasha spotted the flickering red light in the distance. She pointed ahead. "We're here."

"So, now that we've both put ourselves in the right frame of mind…"

Sasha let out a laugh of relief. "Right. This shouldn't be so bad."

"Just remember what I said about the scene, the moment, your gut."

"I got it."

Seth pulled over in front of the first flare and stopped the car. He removed his gloves, pushing them into the pockets of his coat, and pulled out a pair of latex gloves from his center console. He handed Sasha a pair before they both got out.

Bill walked up to meet them, hands in his jacket pockets, shoulders pressed up to his ears. He seemed more settled since their phone call. "Scene's been kept clean. No lookie-loos."

Their breath clouded the air, shifting upward and disappearing. Seth couldn't help but find the image metaphorical. If he'd been here in the moment, would he have seen Bess and Richard's spirits leave their bodies in a similar fashion? He wondered if Story could see something like that. She probably could.

Time to focus, Seth thought. "Good. Sorry, I didn't think to stop for some hot coffee." Seth spotted Wes standing in front of the Grahamses' car, about twenty feet away, camera around his neck, taking photos.

"Not a worry. I wanted you out here the second I pulled in with Eddie. I just don't like this." Bill shivered visibly.

Seth crouched down as Bill spoke, pulled out his flashlight, and shined it from the pavement slowly up onto the dirt shoulder and up to the back tires.

Sasha crouched down next to him. "You looking at tire marks?"

"Mm-hmm." Seth slowly stood up, tracing backward from the back left tire with his flashlight. "What do you see?"

Sasha looked at all four tires and then followed the tracks back to them. "Looks like they pulled over and then at some point turned the steering wheel back, like they were going to drive out again."

"Very close." Seth walked closer, keeping the light on the dirt just behind the back left tire. "See the dirt just to the left of this tire? And see how the back wheel is just slightly to the right of the track leading up to it?"

"Yeah."

"That turn of the wheel you noticed happened the second the car came to a stop. They pulled in and yanked the wheel to the left, causing the back tire to skid."

"Okay, yeah, that makes sense."

Bill shuffled near but gave Seth the distance to do his job. The circumstances notwithstanding, Bill felt a touch of pride when he saw Seth at work. From the young man trapped in a cave to a top-notch detective in record time. Now here he was, back home, and on Bill's squad.

Seth slowly approached the car, his light moving up to the back driver-side window, and saw blood spatter across the top third of it at an almost horizontal angle.

Wes walked around to join them, decked out in his forensic disposable Tyvek suit that rustled like fallen leaves. "Seth."

"Wes. See anything that stands out?"

"Well, I haven't come across a murder-suicide before, but the blood, the wounds, the positions of the bodies seem pretty clear." Wes pointed toward the driver-side window. "Looks like Richard shot Bess when she wasn't looking at him. The entry wound is in her temple. Whether she knew what he was doing is hard to tell. Her hands are in her lap, so it doesn't appear she was trying to stop him or struggling at all. From the blood spatter on the back window here and the exit wound in the back of Richard's head, it looks like he was sitting up straight, put the gun in his mouth, and pulled the trigger."

Seth nodded, agreeing with how Richard was sitting and the angle of the gun. He walked up closer to the window, shining the light on the back of Richard's head. Or what was left of it. "Had to have been pretty powerful from the size of that exit wound, which is what I'm guessing we'll find when we open that door."

Sasha stood behind Seth's right shoulder, peering over at the exit wound, the blood inside glistening from the flashlight. She felt a slight tightening of her chest but didn't feel sick or like she wanted to look away.

Seth leaned back from the window, taking in a broader view of the scene. He flashed the light along the outside of the door, then leaned down, and slowly ran it from the back of the car to the front. Blood spatter all looked to fit with Wes's thoughts. He stood up and made his way around to the front of the car, checking the ground in front and underneath it before sweeping over to the passenger side.

Sasha followed behind him. Bill and Wes remained at the driver's side. She didn't notice any steam coming from the hood or anything leaking from the engine, guessing that's what Seth was looking for.

Seth shined his light on the window, immediately pointing to the bullet hole. "You find the bullet yet, Wes?"

"Yep. It's about two meters behind you in the woods, marked and sectioned off. The trajectory lines up with her entrance wound and the exit there," he said, pointing.

"And the second one?" Seth asked, stepping forward and shining the light in the back window behind Bess.

"I'm assuming it's lodged in the roof above the back seat. I see a hole there that could be it."

Seth nodded. "Aside from the blood, the back seat and floor look pretty clean." He pulled the handle to the back door to find it locked.

"You expecting to see something other than the bullet back there?" Bill asked.

"Don't know yet," Seth answered cryptically and then circled back to the driver's side. He checked the handle to the back seat and then the driver-side door. "Shit."

"I got it," Bill said and headed toward his vehicle.

"Guess you don't just wanna break the window in," Sasha said.

Seth looked over at her, catching her smirk. "That would be highly frowned upon by Wes and the forensics team."

"Speaking of which, they should be here soon," Wes said.

"Good. Let them do their thing, Wes, but make sure you've got everything you need before they disrupt anything."

Wes nodded.

Bill returned, slid the jim in, and had the door unlocked in a matter of seconds.

"Impressive," Seth muttered.

"The height of our action around here," Bill responded. "Typically."

Seth slowly opened the door, squatting down. It didn't appear Richard's body had any weight in that direction, but the last thing they needed was for his body to fall out and what was left in his skull to pour out. He shined his light to the floor first, the glint from the gun catching instantly. "Holy shit."

"What is it?" Bill asked.

"Huh," Seth uttered to himself as he started putting pieces together. He looked over his shoulder, Bill, Wes, and Sasha all waiting to hear what was so surprising. "Well, this is the first time I've seen a Luger P08 as the firearm used in a crime."

Seth pushed the door open farther so they could all get a good look at the historic pistol used in the first two World Wars.

"I'll be damned," Bill said.

"That has to be old as fuck," Sasha said.

"It is," Seth replied.

"First World War, right?" Wes guessed.

"First and Second," Seth answered. "The Walther P38 replaced it, but it was still used."

"What do you make of it?" Bill asked.

Seth looked up at him. "As shocking as it is to see, in theory, it actually might make more sense."

"How so?"

"One thing I'm really struggling with is imagining Richard having the balls to purchase a gun. But this pistol has to be a war trophy. Do you know if Richard's father or grandfather was in the war?"

Bill shook his head. "I don't, but should be easy enough to find out."

"Exactly. I'll get Joe working on that. And if we find out this was a family heirloom passed down from generation to generation, it would explain why Richard was a gun owner. Frankly, I would have bet my life savings he wasn't."

"That's a pretty big hole for such a small gun," Sasha observed.

"The Luger used nine-millimeter rounds, same as a lot of guns now."

"Ah, well, that'll do it, then," Sasha said.

Seth dropped to his elbow to get a worm's-eye view of Richard's face. His eyes were open, and if Seth were to describe the look in his dead eyes, it was one of fear. Or maybe he was just reflecting his own feelings on Richard. He got to his feet, tapped the unlock button for the remaining doors, and moved out of the way, looking at Sasha. "Go ahead."

"Yeah?" she asked, eyebrows raised.

Seth nodded, and Sasha crouched down to investigate.

Wes followed Seth around to the passenger side.

Seth opened the back door, and after Wes took some snapshots, he leaned in and peered over the seat to get a better look at her. His nostrils flared with the familiar, sickeningly dry, sweet metallic scent of recently shed blood. It was drying and just turning ripe.

"Bullet wound looks as expected for a nine-millimeter. Close range. Some residual scorch marks from the muzzle flare," Seth commented, leaning farther still over the seat to take in her position. There was something about her hands he didn't like.

"Doing my job?" Wes commented, his voice light with humor.

Seth smiled. "Habits die hard."

He continued his observation of Bess's folded, polite hands settled in her lap. Her clothes weren't wrinkled, rumpled, or out of place. She looked neat as a pin. She looked staged or like she hadn't seen it coming. *Did Richard shoot her and then make her look presentable?* Seth wondered.

It wouldn't be too uncommon.

Wes shifted aside for Sasha to look. She bent over at the waist, hands on her knees, scanning the scene. Seth took a glance in her direction, noticed her swallow a couple times in rapid succession, and turned back to his job. She wouldn't puke, but she was struggling with the smell.

Avoiding the blood spatter on the driver's side, Seth observed the front seat. Bess's purse was on the floor by her feet near the door. *Odd position*, he thought. His experience with women showed them getting into the car bag first, which meant it ended up on the interior, next to the middle console, not by the door. There was a cup of coffee in one of the cup holders. He wondered how much coffee was left in it and where they got it from.

Seth slid out, and Wes jumped in for a quick observation of Bess's gunshot wound, snapping off a multitude of pictures.

"Good?" Seth asked Sasha.

She nodded. "I'm good."

"Do you mind popping the trunk?" Seth asked her.

Sasha obliged, jogging back around to the front and pulling the release. She, along with Bill, made her way to the rear of the vehicle. Seth held his hand under the lid and looked at Sasha. "What do you think we'll find in here?"

Sasha smiled but realized quickly that he was actually testing her. She swallowed, thinking through what she knew of the case. After a concentrated moment, she said, "Suitcases?"

The corner of Seth's mouth lifted at the same time as he lifted the lid of the trunk. "And the winner is?" Three suitcases were neatly organized like a simple game of Tetris.

Bill leaned in to look. "Would have to be Ripley's, yeah?"

Sasha looked at him. "What?"

"Ripley's Resort," Seth answered for him, a smile rising on his face as memories from a fourth grade summer vacation flooded back to him. "It's the only destination on the Wildcat that requires luggage."

Seth leaned in and unzipped one case. It was neatly packed, all items perfectly folded and placed in with intention—flowery tops, knitted sweaters, pairs of jeans, and chinos. Bess's suitcase was neat as a button. She took her time packing, everything set deliberately. It reminded Seth of the house—all things in order, neat and tidy. Sasha, curious now, opened the smallest case to find another well-organized, compartmentalized litany of makeup and beauty products.

Sasha picked up one bag, turning it over to inspect all the facial creams. "Trying to maintain that youthful glow," she commented before setting it back.

It didn't surprise Seth to see all those accessories. Bess struck him as a woman who had all the creams that claimed to defy gravity and ease wrinkles. She came across as a woman who was angry that she was aging. His mother, far older than Bess, looked about the same age or younger than Bess. It all came down to that phrase, aging gracefully. Embracing it versus fighting it. And good genes, he supposed. He really needed to check in on his mom and dad.

Seth stepped back and removed the latex gloves, the snap of them sounding louder than it should.

"What are you thinking?" Bill asked.

Seth sighed and glanced at him. "It looks like a murder-suicide."

Bill measured Seth's expression. "But you're not sure."

"It all makes sense on paper. Grieving parents. Their only child died in a ghastly manner. A missing grandchild, odds not looking good. And they're both staring at a likely prison sentence for obstruction of justice, if not more, and neither are cut out for prison. Well, maybe Bess, but…"

"Jesus, I can't believe this." Bill sighed, looking at the car, then back at Seth. "Lay it out for me—your hesitations."

Sasha shuffled closer.

"Let's start with Richard. The thought that he jerked the car off the road in, what, a rage? The thought of him catching Bess off guard or getting her to accept her fate? If the seats were reversed, I'd feel differently. I could see Bess pulling the trigger, but Richard?"

"Was she really that much more agro than him?" Sasha asked.

"Yes," Seth, Bill, and Wes all answered simultaneously.

"Damn. Okay, then."

Bill stroked his beard.

Seth shook his head. "The psychology feels off to me."

"Grieving parents—grieving people—do strange things," Wes added from the back passenger-side door.

"Agreed, they do, but examine that," Seth countered. "They have a potential grandchild out there, alive, in need of a home. Yes, it's looking grim because we have no leads and no idea where this baby could be, but it's hope. More than anything—and I've worked a couple of missing children cases—parents hold on to hope in a way you wouldn't believe. The things they'll say and do, you, as a police officer, know it verges on delusional, but it's all they've got. Focus on aspect number two. They haven't buried their daughter yet. She's dead, yes, but they haven't laid her to rest."

"Unfinished business," Sasha added, nodding along with Seth's train of thought.

Seth nodded at her. "Typically, when people organize a suicide, they wrap things up. And let's talk about a planned murder-suicide. If that was Richard's idea, why do it with a gun?" Seth pointed to the trunk. "You've booked a nice getaway. Go have a lovely time, an enjoyable meal, all the extravagances, then take some pills and lie down with each other for the long sleep."

"So it wasn't both of their ideas?" Bill asked.

Seth pointed at him, nodding from side to side. "Then take this scene in. What's with the skid to a halt? Are they arguing? And what about? This suicide idea was not in both their heads. You don't argue if you're off to a nice last hurrah to end things."

"Maybe it was just murder, then. Richard murdering Bess," Sasha commented.

"And guilt makes him take his own life? I can see it. He's clearly downtrodden, grieving. Maybe he's finally sick of dealing with her shit," Seth added, scratching at the stubble on his jawline.

"But you're not seeing any of these scenarios befitting of the Grahamses, though, are you?" Bill surveyed the scene.

"Put aside the gun and the fact that Richard is the one wielding it. They were running away—"

"With three suitcases?" Bill interjected.

"She has all her essentials," Sasha added.

"In which case, I can understand him taking the gun," Seth continued. "Or they were getting away for a moment. Most likely going up to Ripley's Resort. So, why bring a gun? More than that, why have the gun on your person? He didn't get out of the car, grab it from the trunk, get back in, and shoot his wife."

"Maybe he felt they were in danger," Bill said, shrugging.

"From what?" asked Sasha.

Seth looked at Bill, his gut tickling his senses. "I actually think you might be onto something."

"They were certainly on edge," Bill said. "More so than us just pressing them, I thought."

Seth couldn't help but smile. "You've got more intuition than you think you do, Bill."

"I don't know about that."

"Here they are," Wes said.

"Bill, you good staying here to oversee this?" Seth asked.

"No question. You gonna head to their house?"

Seth nodded, proud of Bill's instincts in a situation he'd never been in. He turned to Sasha. "Sergeant Kingsley, how about I drop you off so we can both get properly ready? Then we'll meet back up at the station before we head to the Grahamses'. Sound like a plan?"

Sasha held her fist up. "Hell yes, partner."

Seth met her fist, and they headed back to his Bronco.

Seth's Bronco rolled to a stop in front of the Grahamses' house, and he took a deep breath, exhaling a long sigh. Physically, he felt refreshed and refueled after taking a shower and getting some much-needed coffee before heading into the station. Mentally and emotionally, he was drained. The recent deaths weighed heavily on his mind as he processed what they meant for his investigation. Richard and Bess, two of the people who really knew what happened with their daughter, were dead. The knowledge he had hoped to glean from them was now gone, like a puff of his hot breath in the cold air. The sudden revelation that Richard had fired an antique Luger pistol in a spur-of-the-moment decision—a fit of rage?—only added to Seth's inner turmoil, churning like a turbulent sea.

It wasn't that Seth didn't grasp that people could do things completely unexpected or that the most rational person on earth could snap. He also had a gift for understanding people, reading them, gauging their characteristics, applying traits and tendencies he'd seen in others quickly to those he just met. The Grahamses, especially Richard, just didn't fit the profile of a murder-suicide with a high-caliber handgun. If he found them in their home dead from an overdose, whether it was mutual or a murder-suicide, he wouldn't have been surprised. Or if they fled, which it looked like they were thinking about doing on some level, that would almost be expected. But not this.

The shock of their deaths was almost enough to overshadow the already confounding and infuriating case of Sarah Elizabeth Grahams.

But that was just it. The deaths of Richard and Bess Grahams were linked to the Sarah Elizabeth case. Two more bodies would soon be on their way to the county morgue for a routine autopsy and then shoved into cold lockers, next to their daughter. A whole family in this small town had been wiped out in a week. By whom?

There was still the Orbriallis Institute to deal with, the cryptic words of Dr. Bajorek looming in the back of his mind, and a missing infant that was torn from Sarah Elizabeth's womb in a location they were no closer to finding than they were a week ago. And Peter Andalusian, their prime suspect, whose best friend all but admitted Peter had dumped her body, was untraceable and could be anywhere in or out of the country. None of this spoke to his personal dilemma of time traveling, not to mention Story's body-mind transference into Sarah Elizabeth's past.

A knock at his window startled Seth to where he actually jumped. He turned to see Sasha laughing at him. He gave her a thumbs-up before grabbing a new set of latex gloves and exiting the Bronco.

"Man, you looked like Angel when we watch horror movies. That girl jumps!"

"Glad I could entertain you," Seth said as they headed toward the house.

"You were clearly deep in thought. Anything come to you?"

"Just more questions."

"Seems to be the theme of this case."

They walked onto the front porch, and Seth tried the front door. "Okay, why don't you do a circle around the house, check for any windows that open. There's a sliding glass door in the back that leads into their kitchen area. Call out if something is open. Otherwise, come back up here. I'll be working on the lock," he said, opening up the leather case and pulling out two metal tools.

"And here you said people didn't need to protect their homes in Lost Grove."

Seth grinned as Sasha checked the front living room windows and then made her way around the right side of the house. The unease of this development was killing him. Everything felt off. If only he could grab some thread to follow. Seth unlocked the door handle rather quickly but found the deadbolt locked, a more challenging affair. He found his frustrations unleashed in a series of expletives mumbled under his breath.

Sasha peered in a locked window on the side of the house. It looked like a guest bedroom. A closet door was open with men's clothing on hangers. The bed was unmade, but the room wasn't decorated and showed no other signs of being lived in. She reached the sliding glass door, which she also found to be locked. The drapes, though, were open, and she had a clear view into the kitchen. The counter was a bit of a mess, with three glasses, two plates, four boxes of crackers, and snacks scattered about. She also spotted a laptop on the other side of the kitchen underneath an open cupboard. She found three more locked windows on her way back around to the front.

"No luck, I assume," Seth said, hearing her approaching.

Sasha climbed the stairs to the front porch, sidling up next to Seth, who was still trying to pick the deadbolt. "Nope. But a lot of open window shades and blinds. Looks like they were in a bit of a hurry before they left."

"Mm," Seth murmured.

"Are you—"

"I got it," Seth said just as he gave a sharp twist to his tools in the keyhole, unlocking the deadbolt. "Was just waiting for you."

Sasha appreciated Seth's dry humor, wondering where it had been since he joined the team. Maybe it was being back on a proper case that brought out the old part of himself that he left in San Francisco. She followed him through the front door and stood next to him while they both surveyed the living room on their right, the small den to their left, and the short hallway to the kitchen in front of them. "You were just here a couple days ago. Anything look different?" she asked.

"Not much, no."

"This living room is just too clean and…formal. Kind of creeps me out."

"I have fond memories in that room of getting Bess and Richard to break. I say that with no jest toward their memories. It's where I felt that spark come back to me, made me feel like I was doing something, moving the needle." Now, that needle was skipping.

Sasha didn't sense that spark now. He looked tired and frustrated.

"We need to search every drawer, under every chair, behind every book."

"For anything specific? Or just something suspicious?"

"Both. I want to see if we can find a suicide note and any trace of that gun. If it was a personal family heirloom, there could be an entire box filled with effects. Why don't you take the den, and I'll take the living room you don't like."

"On it."

After tearing apart both rooms, they moved on first to Sarah's bedroom, which was unchanged since Seth last saw it. After digging through her drawers and her closet, they moved on to the guest bedroom across the hall.

"I can't say that I'm surprised," Seth said, seeing Richard's clothes and the unmade bed. "They were fracturing when Bill and I questioned them."

"Looks like Bess had the upper hand in the relationship."

Seth nodded. "That would be accurate. Check the dresser. I'll check the closet."

Sasha took her time going through each drawer, reading papers, checking receipts, feeling around the sides and tops of the dresser and drawers in case something was taped.

Seth finished searching the closet and moved to scan under the bed.

When Sasha opened the last of the nine drawers, she cleared her throat. "Uh, Seth?"

Seth popped up and peered over the mattress at her. "What have you got?"

Sasha held up an open, aged wooden case with a green felt interior, and a large empty spot where the Luger was housed.

Seth jumped up and slid across the bed, grabbing it from her. "Son of a bitch."

"You were right. There's all sorts of old shit in this drawer, all military stuff. Check this out," she said, handing him a small notebook, paper aged to a wheat brown.

Seth opened it up and read the top of the first page. "Lieutenant Commander Theodore Grahams."

"I guess that's one thing off the list," Sasha offered.

"I guess it is," Seth replied quietly. He had to rethink everything he assumed about Richard. Maybe he really did have it in him. Maybe he thought this was the quickest way out. But why were Bess's hands in her lap? Why was there no sign of movement or hitching up in her clothes? Even if Richard had tried to make her look presentable, there would be a sign of movement, a tug to her shirt or pants that Seth didn't see in the car. Was she just sitting there as Richard peeled off the road to a sudden stop, remaining still as he pulled the gun? From where? Under the seat? His jacket?

"There's a laptop in the kitchen. Should I see if I can get in and check recent emails, search history, documents?"

Seth shook his head free of the cataclysm of questions assailing his mind. "Absolutely."

Sasha sat at the small kitchen table working her way through possible passwords when Seth entered. He finished searching the master bedroom—a neatly made bed, the lingering scents of perfume, face creams, and lotions. Bess's clothes were in the closet. Her jewelry box looked untouched. All the rings were pushed into place in a neat row. Gold and pearl necklaces hung from their jewelry tree, and delicate tennis bracelets were all lovingly placed onto the soft velvet interior. If they were running, wouldn't they bring her jewelry to pawn? Maybe he was thinking too much like a hardened criminal and not like a religious married couple who recently lost their only daughter. Seth started rummaging through the kitchen cupboards and drawers.

"You happen to remember Sarah's birthday?"

"June 8th, 2002," he replied, increasingly frustrated at the lack of clues in the house. Seth felt like the case was spiraling out of control. Had he lost that much of his instincts, that much of his training and experience in just the four months he stepped away from being a homicide detective?

"Elizabeth0608! We're in."

Seth spun around and rushed over to the table, pulling one of the other chairs around to sit next to Sasha. "Great work."

"Thanks. Looks like Safari is still up, multiple tabs here. Email, nice! Let's see whose computer this is." Sasha opened the first email on the page. "It's addressed to Bess."

"Go back for me," Seth said and then pointed at the screen. "There. Open that one."

Sasha clicked on it. "Ripley's fucking Resort. It's a confirmation email."

Seth leaned back in the chair. "They booked a trip, despite us telling them they couldn't go anywhere."

"It's not even under a code name or anything."

"Scroll down to the dates."

"Wednesday, October 13th, through Sunday, October 24th. Goddamn!"

Seth put both hands on the table and dropped his head. "A week-and-a-half trip. So, why pack up and only drive halfway there? What the fuck happened?"

"It does feel odd. I can definitely understand wanting to get away after what happened to their daughter, notwithstanding you telling them not to leave town, of course. But why bring the gun? Was he planning to see how the weekend went before deciding to use it?"

"Or they were afraid of something, like Bill mentioned. But if that was the case, where's the leap to murder-suicide?" Seth stood up. He paced around the kitchen, slamming a drawer shut as he passed. "What the fuck? Something's missing. What is it?"

Sasha turned round and looked at him. "We'll figure it out. I'm sure you've solved crazier shit than this."

Seth looked back at her. "I'll be honest. I don't know if I have."

Sasha went back to scanning the history of the computer. "She was just looking at their website yesterday morning."

"I want to know what Richard was looking at, searching, texts… Fuck, his phone!"

"He had to have had it on him. Call Bill."

"Already doing it," Seth grumbled, holding the phone up to his ear.

Sasha clicked on browser history. "No cleaning lately."

"Huh?" Seth asked, looking up.

"They haven't cleared their browser history or cookies. Everything is still here."

He nodded. "Bill, did you find their cell phones yet?"

"Yeah, we got both of them bagged up."

"Good. I want those back at the station. We need to scour every text, search history, notes, everything."

"Was planning on it."

"Anything of note from the forensics team?"

"Nothing to report. Dusting for fingerprints, swabs, the works. Though what it will report…"

"You don't think anything will come back as not matching the Grahams?"

"Can't say I expect it, no."

"Look, is there a laptop in the luggage?" Seth asked. He flicked on the garage light and listened to Bill walking, asking a few of the team if they saw a laptop.

He surveyed the garage.

"No," Bill said, his voice strong on the line. "No laptop. Is there not one at the house?"

"There's one here. Bess's. Confirmation email for Ripley's. They were planning on staying there for a week and a half."

"Well, what the hell happened then?" Bill asked, his pitch rising.

Seth shook his head. "I don't know, Bill. We're scouring the house for anything at all. We did find something, though."

"What's that?"

"Case for the Luger and loads of military documents and photos for Theodore Grahams. Guessing it was Richard's great-grandfather. He served in World War I."

"Well, that's something. Anything else?"

"Nothing of any outward significance."

Bill sighed. "Jesus, Mary, and… How the hell is the town going to take this?"

Seth heard unspoken words behind Bill's plea. *Where are you with this case? Why haven't you brought in a suspect? Are you even doing your job?* He knew Bill wasn't thinking any of those things, but his old boss would have. His own conscience was railing him about his lack of progress.

"—someone to go speak with her," Bill interrupted Seth's tirade of berating slander.

"Hmm?"

"Richard's mother, what good it'll do in her mental state. It should be me, I suppose. Maybe she'll recognize me. I don't know." Bill sighed.

Seth registered the stress this was placing on his boss, the chief of police. This was a little town, and all the inhabitants meant something to him. Hell, they were starting to mean something to Seth. He needed a break in this case. Seth needed a clue, something to point him in a solid direction. The Orbriallis? Dr. Bajorek? Another doctor he didn't know about? A lover? Peter Andalusian?

"They'll be wrapping up here, then I'll send them your way."

"Yeah, okay."

"I'll head into the station to start up the reports."

"Okay," Seth said and ended the call.

In the garage, he moved to the other family car, tried the handle, and felt relief when it popped open. The inside smelled of leather and an air freshener assaulting his senses. He checked the glove box, the floors, the cup holders, the center console. They revealed the usual—manual, registrations, a few random receipts from the grocery store, loose change, a parking pass for a garage with the name Booker & Morrow Finance. This was obviously Richard's car.

Finding nothing in the back seat, Seth slammed the door. "Fuck," he cursed out his building dissatisfaction. He forced himself to take a moment to count to ten and even out his breathing before heading inside.

"You find anything else? Maybe a suicide note?" he asked in vain.

"Sorry. Nothing major."

Seth grunted, looking around at the mess. The three glasses caught his attention. He moved over to them and looked inside. Two tall tumblers looked like they'd held water. A third, smaller glass, which he leaned down to smell, may have held juice.

"What now? Are we waiting for forensics to get here?"

"Yeah," Seth responded on autopilot.

Sasha moved around the room, stopping in front of a cross on the wall surrounded by a quote from the Bible. "'Be still, and know that I am God.' Huh."

Seth looked over at the wall. "You religious, Kingsley?"

"Can't say that I am. Not in the good old-fashioned sense. You?"

He laughed a little.

"What? You one of those types who says I'm spiritual, more than religious?"

Seth was about to respond when he stopped himself. Was what he'd experienced spiritual? Was time traveling spiritual? Religious? Lunacy?

"Oh, Christ. I didn't mean to offend you if—"

"No, I don't have a clue what I am or believe," he said, meaning it. "My mom goes to church. Presbyterian."

"But you never went?"

"Not really," Seth replied, his mind preoccupied with visions, body transference, and spells.

Sasha turned from the wall. "My parents were Baptists. I used to go when I was younger, but I never…ah, doesn't matter," she mumbled, feeling stupid for bringing it up.

Seth ground his teeth, jaw pulsing quickly. He couldn't believe what he was considering. "Kingsley, you good to stay here and wait for forensics?"

"Yeah, of course. Where are you going?"

Seth headed for the front door, trying to think how to phrase this. "I've got a few questions I need answered. Let me know when things wrap up. Head back to the station when they're all done here. Bill's starting the reports," he instructed as he headed out the door.

"Sure…thing," she said to herself, now alone, wondering what in the hell just popped into her partner's head.

Maps of the Underground

In a single motion, Nate catapulted himself up the steps of the front porch of the Andalusian house and through the door, shutting it behind him.

"Guys?" he called, removing his coat and backpack and setting them on the bench in the foyer.

"Kitchen," Stan called.

Nate was buzzed on information and adrenaline. He'd been waiting all day to speak with the others about what he found out last night after they all parted ways from their spelunking escapade.

Anya, sitting on a stool at the kitchen island, looked up from her phone as he walked into the open and airy, modern family kitchen. She was still wearing her knit cap, hair tucked up under it to keep it from getting wet in the unexpected sleeting rain.

"Alright, assholes, we need a team powwow. Right now!" Nate exclaimed, circling his hand in the air with urgency.

"Dude," Noble scolded, pointing to Zoe, who was just outside the kitchen, crouched down by a small bird cage.

Nate scoffed, waving the younger girl away like she wasn't listening. His sister, Cheshire, was never listening, always engrossed in a video game. But Zoe Andalusian was not his little sister. She heard more than her brother and parents probably wanted her to hear.

"Also, dude," Stan remarked. "Powwow? So culturally inappropriate."

"Oh, Jesus." Nate sneered at her and rolled his eyes. "We need to fucking talk. Is that better?"

"Language man, seriously," Noble warned his friend as he moved around the kitchen with ease, pulling out a sheet pan and parchment paper. He wasn't sure why he kept up the protective shield for his sister. They all swore, including their parents.

"Can we do the pizza bites?" Zoe asked, standing from where she was whispering to the baby owl.

"Yeah," Noble agreed, heading to the freezer to grab the box.

Zoe went to the oven, set it to preheat, and then read the note their mother had left. "She went back to meet the vet," she said.

"Is it Zephyr still?" Noble asked, the old horse causing recent issues up at the ranch.

"Yep," Zoe said and grabbed a juice box from the fridge.

"Okay, can we like…" Nate waved his arms at Noble to join them at the island to talk.

Noble glared at Nate and then looked at his sister with a smile. "Zo, can you go watch TV or something?"

"I've got to feed Merryweather."

"Can she wait five minutes?"

Zoe sighed and walked out of the kitchen to the attached living room, turning on the TV.

"Okay, what?" Noble asked as he ripped open the bag of pizza bites, poured them onto the pan, and shoved it in the oven.

Nate held his hands out. "Bro, can you stop moving around for two minutes here?"

Noble spun around from the oven and crossed his arms. "I'm done. What is it you're so eager to share?"

"Okay." Nate looked from Noble to Anya to Stan, making sure he had everyone's attention. "What do we know about Emory and Ember? Like really know about them?"

Noble leaned back against the counter. "They moved here from San Francisco."

"For treatment at the Orbriallis," Stan added.

"They are telekinetic," Anya contributed. "Or is it telepathic?"

Nate leapt. "Exactly! And that's like it. We know fuck all about them. So—"

"I wouldn't say that," Stan interrupted.

Nate ignored her and continued, "Yesterday, we find out they can read minds and implant thoughts into other people's brains. Not to mention they reveal this after they showed us a weird-ass video of young people getting hooked up to machines and shit. One of them possibly being the actual George Horne, right?"

Brows raised, Anya asked, "What's your point?"

"Yes, what is your point?" Stan asked. "Aside from the Orbriallis doing weirder shit than even the urban legends tell us."

Nate shook his head. "No, no, forget the Institute for a minute. Look, I did some research last night about the Institute, yes, but also on the Graffs. And guess the fuck what?"

The others allowed him the pause for effect, Stan biting her thumbnail in boredom. He always made something out of nothing, and she was sure this was going to be another one of his stories linking rumors and myths together to create a plot that fit his conspiratorial needs.

"They murdered a classmate," Nate whispered.

"What?" Anya exclaimed.

"I'm sorry, what?" Noble reiterated.

Stan scowled at Nate. "Dude, why the fuck would you even joke about something like that?"

"You think I'm joking?" Nate asked, raising his eyebrows.

Noble shook his head. "Seriously, man. Like they would even be going to school here if that was true."

"Well, they *are* going to school here, and this *is* an actual court case, you guys. A girl—her name was Cassidy Zimmer—was stabbed multiple times in the face, chest, mouth, eye—"

"Wait, wait, fucking wait," Stan interrupted, pushing off the pantry cupboard to move closer to Nate. "You're trying to tell me they stabbed—"

"Okay, no. Just hold on. Let me start this over."

"Please do."

"This better not be bullshit," Noble said. "These are our friends."

"That's why I'm bringing this up!" Nate protested. "Now, listen. A girl, Cassidy Zimmer, who they went to school with, died from multiple self-inflicted stab wounds."

"Self-inflicted?" Noble asked, his face contorted.

Stan sighed. "Suicide. A girl commits suicide, and you start this story with Emory and Ember murdering her. What's wrong with you?"

"Yeah, Nate," Anya said, "that's not something to speculate on. And it's mean."

Nate looked up at the ceiling and sighed. "Guys, I'm not trying to be mean or…" He looked back down and made eye contact with each of his friends as he spoke. "Just give me the table for two minutes here. I'm sorry I started the story wrong, and admittedly confusing, but I'm not making this up. I'll try to explain better. Just don't interrupt. Let me finish, and then you can yell at me all you want if you think I'm full of shit."

Stan looked over at Noble, gauging his thoughts.

Noble shrugged. He had little energy left in his body to argue about this with everything going on with his dad. He looked over at Anya, who nodded. "Okay, go ahead."

"Thank you," Nate said and regained his composure, trying to get the story straight in his head. "So, Ember and this girl, Cassidy, they're in the same chemistry class together. This is just last year. And they've had some ongoing issues with each other for years. So, during this particular class, they apparently got into some big argument, exchanged some harsh words, and the teacher made them both stay behind and clean the lab. The teacher left them there alone to go do whatever, and the next person who enters the room is Emory, who apparently was running like a madman toward their classroom, with no way of knowing what was happening. He says he walked in the room to see Cassidy stabbing herself like a crazy person and tried to stop her. The teacher hears all the commotion and comes back to see Emory covered in her blood because he'd been trying to help her, the articles say. Flash forward to yesterday when Emory tells us, what? That he and his sister can make people do things, like walk into traffic or slap themselves. And we know that's not bullshit because they were in our fucking heads talking to us. So, while the defense is arguing that Cassidy stabbed herself, the prosecution argues, who in the fuck would just randomly, for no discernable reason, pick up a pair of sharp-ass scissors and stab themselves in the face and neck over and over until they were dead? Put two and two together, and you tell me that Ember didn't make that girl do that." Nate paused, looking around the room.

Noble was just staring at him, his face pale and eyes wide. Anya was staring down at her phone, tears on her cheeks, scanning article after article about the stabbing of Cassidy Zimmer. Stan was chaotically looking from her phone to Noble to Nate, her breathing heavy.

Noble stared at his friend, wishing he could argue with him, tell him the idea of such a thing was insane, but everything this past week was insane. It was all really happening. After what seemed like an hour to find his voice, he simply muttered, "What?"

"I know, dude. This is why I wanted all of your attention," Nate said before taking a deep breath. "This is from news reports, okay, which you guys are clearly looking at," he said, looking at Anya and Stan.

"Twenty-three times," Anya moaned in a hushed voice.

Noble looked at her, his mouth parting, his stomach churning at the thought.

Nate shook his head. "I know. It's even too much for me. And here's the thing, the witnesses who were called in the case said they saw Emory running down the hall toward the class, and how strange it was that he was running before anyone else knew what was going on. Why was he running if he didn't somehow know what his sister had planned? That's the thought, right, from all these people who don't know what they can do," he said, tapping his temple. "But now we do."

Anya gasped and put her hand to her mouth, carefully setting down her phone. Noble couldn't help himself then. He moved away from the counter, reached across the island, and pulled her phone over to him. His thumb flicked across the screen, reading so quickly he wasn't even sure he was absorbing this correctly.

"But there's no evidence," Stan said, her eyes engrossed in the article on her phone. "No fingerprints of Ember's on the scissors."

"That's what I'm fucking saying!" Nate held his hands out to her, brows raised. "We know. We know what they can do, right? Emory said it himself. I mean, what girl, what person, would stab themselves in the face twenty-three times, Stan? She did it, though. She did it because they, Ember at least, told her to. She brainwashed her to do it."

Stan lifted her eyes methodically from her phone and met Nate's eyes. "We don't know that, though. We don't know if they can do *that*."

"Oh, come on," Nate huffed. "They spoke in all of our heads! Just yesterday! I was there, remember?"

"I know! I'm not arguing that. But saying hello in our heads and making someone do something like…I mean, it's against nature. I find it hard to believe anyone, no matter what their, like, powers or whatever are, could make a person stab themselves—in the face, no less."

The doorbell rang, making both Stan and Anya jump. Noble moved around the island and peeked down the hallway toward the front door. "Fuck! That's them," he said in a loud whisper.

"Language," Nate mocked him.

Noble glared at him. "You dropped this bomb. What the hell are we going to do?" he asked, looking at Stan and then Anya.

Stan ran her hand through her long black hair. "Well, we certainly can't pretend we don't know."

"Why not?" Anya asked, dreading a potential confrontation.

Stan looked at her. "We'll never be able to hide the looks on our faces."

"And, even if we did, they'll read our fucking minds," Nate added soberly.

Noble looked into the living room, meeting his sister's look. She hadn't been watching TV, he realized, or had until the emotions of the teens shifted the vibes in the house. Zoe had always picked up on stuff like that, even as a toddler. He smiled at her, hoping it was reassuring, and looked back at the group. "Well, I've got to answer the door. Just… don't be aggressive about it," he said, staring at Nate.

"Like I would," Nate responded, sneering.

"Right," Stan and Anya echoed each other.

Noble left the kitchen and opened the front door.

Emory stood from a crouched position, shaking the rain off his jacket on the front porch. He forced a smile at Noble, stepping through the open door. "Should I just hang this up, or…"

"Yeah, you can hang it there." Noble pointed to the hooks on the wall. "Where's Ember?"

"Ah, yeah…" Emory turned and his already diminished smile vanished even more.

Noble looked down toward the ground. "Come on in. We're in the kitchen."

Emory followed behind Noble, instantly sensing cold apprehension from him.

Noble entered the kitchen, ignoring the others, and headed across to the living room.

If Emory thought there was tension coming from Noble, the kitchen was a pressure cooker. Anya had her head down, staring at her phone. Nate stood at the opposite end of the kitchen island with his arms crossed and a severe look on his face. Stan offered a breathless greeting with a nod of her head before looking down.

"Oookaay," Emory said to the room.

"Sit," Noble told his sister, grabbing the remote and turning up the volume. "Stop listening."

"You're the ones talking so loud."

Noble offered her a brotherly glare that made her sit and pay attention to the television. He returned to the kitchen.

"Where's Ember?" Stan asked this time.

Emory met her gaze. "She's not coming. She's, um…she's scared."

"And why would she be scared?" Nate asked with no subtlety in his undertone.

Emory raised a brow at his question. "I'm not sure—"

"Is she scared of the Institute and what they're doing to you there? Or is she scared of what we might know about her?" Nate asked.

"Nate," Noble scolded him.

Emory's face fell slack, his brow wrinkles unraveling, eyes falling to the ground.

Anya glanced over at him and could feel a sense of peace, a resounding weight lifting off his shoulders.

"Both," Emory said. He looked back up at Nate. "So, you finally looked us up?"

"Yeah, I looked you up," Nate responded.

"What happened?" Stan asked.

Emory looked at her. "How much have you read?"

Stan shook her head. "Nate literally told us like two minutes before you showed up. Just a summary. I only had time to look over a couple of headlines."

Emory gave Nate a sharp look. "You clearly have formed an opinion."

Nate relaxed his stance. "Look, after what you told us, showed us yesterday, it's hard—"

"No one's formed an opinion," Noble interceded.

"Uh-huh." Emory refrained from dipping into any of their minds, looking around the room at all of them. "This is why I wanted to tell you guys when we first met at the bleachers that day. I was actually about to, but Em jumped at me in my head. She was terrified. I thought it would be better for y'all to hear it from us than read some bullshit article online."

"You were right," Stan said. "The news is bullshit. And none of us should blindly believe what we read. Especially these days."

Emory nodded at Stan. He then stuffed his hands in his pockets as he looked at the rest of them. "Y'all actually want to hear what really happened, or the rest of you already made up your minds? Because if so, I can leave right now."

"No," Anya protested. "I want to know."

"Yeah, man," Noble said, "we're all friends here."

Nate let his arms drop. "A good investigator never believes hearsay. We need to hear it directly from the source."

"Are you kidding?" Stan said.

"'We'?" Noble asked, brows raised.

Emory shrugged. "Well, shit, he's the one that discovered it, so…"

"I'll put everything I read aside," Nate said. "Sorry if I was a dick."

Stan huffed. "That's a first."

"Shut up!"

Emory let out a stifled laugh. "Alright, alright," he said, approaching the kitchen island, while Nate and Noble stepped up to form a circle around it. "I'll tell y'all the truth from the beginning. Just let me get through it, though, yeah?"

"Of course," Anya said. The rest nodded.

"I won't say a word," Nate added. Stan gave Nate a skeptical glare. "I won't!"

Emory placed his hands on the island and leaned in, looking first at Noble. "Let me start first with a question. Noble, we all know you got into a minor scuffle last weekend. Some drunk dude said something to you, your sister, creeping on Anya. What did you feel in that moment?"

An understanding of why the question was asked struck Noble in the solar plexus. "Well, I hit him."

"Did you want to do more?"

Noble imperceptibly nodded. "I wanted to keep punching him."

"Right," Emory said, not breaking eye contact. "Ain't nothing wrong with that. Looking back, were you thinking clearly during the scuffle?"

Noble shook his head.

Emory looked around the table, settling on Stan. "Any of the rest of you even been in that situation? Bullied, called names, attacked?"

A soberness overcame Stan, and she knew Noble would know why. "Well, I'm Indigenous. A lot of people have said a lot of stupid, insensitive shit over the years—and 'Indian' isn't one of them."

"Right. That shit builds up in you."

"Definitely," Stan said, a fierce edge in her voice.

"What about you, bro?" Emory shifted his attention to Nate.

The self-righteousness clouding Nate's mind had disappeared by this point. "I already get what you're saying, man. But, yeah, I've wanted to pound some people before. This mother fucker, Paul Ficks, tripped me during a state track meet our freshman year."

"I remember that," Noble said.

"I had daydreams for years about getting him back. I envisioned smashing his head on the locker room door."

"Jesus, Nate," Stan said, genuinely shocked. Nate put up a tough front, but when it came down to it, he was jelly.

"Fuck that guy," Nate spit, putting an end to his answer.

"What about you, Tinker Bell?" Emory asked, looking to his right at Anya. "You seem pretty tame, but you got any dark thoughts in there?"

Anya looked from Emory down to the counter. Had he called her Tinker Bell because she was the quiet one of the group or because he sensed something else in her? "People say things about my mom. I don't like to talk about it. I don't. I just…I just want those people to disappear."

Emory reeled back. "Daaamn. Okay. That's the darkest thought of all of ours. Disappear someone. But I get it." Emory pushed himself up, bringing his attention back to the group at large. "Now that we're all in the right mindset, I'll tell you about me and my twin sister. We've been able to speak to each other, in our heads, since we can remember. It's been as natural as y'all speaking verbally. That's all it was, though, talking with each other. For years, that's what it was. As we got older, sixth grade was the first time we started to be able to hear what each other was thinking, without speaking to each other. Like our inner thoughts. It was like discovering you could speak German but never having learned it."

Stan felt a stronger connection than she already did with the power twins. Her grandmother could read minds, tell people things about themselves that they hadn't even come to terms with yet.

"It was amazing at first," Emory continued. "It was like a trick, a game we could play with each other. But that shit got old real quick, let me tell you."

Noble and Nate both laughed.

"Especially when we hit that age when we were looking at other kids differently, feeling that tingling down below."

Anya stifled a giggle, knowing that feeling all too well lately.

"I don't want my sister knowing all that. We tried to set some rules, some boundaries. We did our best, but sometimes that shit just came flowing across like a river. It was in middle school that other people's thoughts started creeping into our minds. That was fun—still is. Sorry, guys. I promise I'll stay out the best I can. We promised never to do that to our friends, and that's a promise we take very seriously, even if we slip now and again."

Stan grinned, finally able to put an action to what she sensed when she was around Ember, her peeking into her mind.

"It was early high school when we started thinking critically about our gifts. If we could hear each other, hear everyone else, and speak to each other, couldn't we speak in other people's minds? The extent of our grand plan was to convince our parents to let us stay out till midnight at a friend's house or to not be mad about our grades."

"That would be awesome," Nate let slip, before covering his mouth. "Sorry."

Emory snickered. "And that was it, guys. That's all we did and all we knew—little nudges here and there to get an extra dessert, to go see an R-rated movie, that sort of shit. So, believe me when I tell you that what happened to Cassidy Zimmer was so off the fucking charts, so unbelievable, that we both still have doubts. More importantly, let me tell you about Cassidy Zimmer."

The group all leaned in closer to Emory.

"That bitch bullied my sister for years. Years! Since sixth grade, man. You think this generation is woke, hashtag 'me too', hashtag 'black lives matter'? Shit. I'm not saying we haven't progressed. We have. But I think we all know that some people are never gonna change. Just the way it is. Cassidy Zimmer was one of them." Emory adopted a girl's voice, "'Nappy-hair bitch, dyke, rug-muncher,' you name it. Ember heard that shit for years. And then Cassidy had the audacity to feign a crush on me, just to piss Ember off. Came after me with doe eyes, brushing her tits against my arms. I wasn't having it. But that didn't stop her. In ninth grade, Cassidy played out this whole act like she changed. She was sorry. She was young and stupid. Bitch, you're in ninth grade. You're still young and stupid.

"Anyhow, she fooled Ember into buying it. Cassidy invited her over to her birthday party. My sis, man, she was so happy. She's always been quiet—not silent like now, but quiet—so she didn't have that many friends. Me? I've always been a talker, as I'm sure y'all can tell, so that wasn't a problem for me. I was skeptical but gave that girl the benefit of the doubt. What happened? Ember got over there, and Cassidy and all her little minions played this little game where every time Ember joined a group, one by one, they'd all leave. It took about an hour for Ember to get the message. She walked home in tears."

Anya wiped tears from her eyes, her heart breaking at the thought.

"But, unlike me, Ember let that shit build. Insult after insult, 'nigger' after 'nigger'—"

"No!" Noble spouted.

Emory nodded. "You better believe it. Not around her friends. Not in class. But whispers by her locker, passing her in gym class on the track, like stealing a candy bar when you think no one's looking. So, whatever happened that day, that day y'all read about, I still don't know what was said because Ember hasn't spoken since, but I know it was bad. Real bad. I couldn't get the words out of her head, but I sure as shit got the emotion. The anger, the shame, the embarrassment."

"All I know is that she screamed something at her. Whatever was building in Em for all those years, six years of constant abuse and bullying, she let it out with her voice and with whatever the hell is in us. From there, it was a fucking mess. I felt it from the other end of the school, ran faster than I ever have before. I thought Em was in danger, being attacked. I couldn't place it but knew it was bad. When I stormed into that room..." Emory closed his eyes. "My whole life flashed before my eyes. Our lives. Ember was catatonic Cassidy...as much as I hated her...fuck, man. I tried to stop her. It was like trying to hold back a lion, man. It wouldn't have mattered, anyway. Even if I had got those scissors away from her the second I walked in..."

Emory shook his head and let out a long sigh. "That's it. Ember had no idea. Neither of us ever could have imagined. Which is why it's still hard to believe."

"This is why she doesn't talk?" Anya asked.

Emory nodded. "She hates herself. She's terrified of herself. I've tried. The doctors are trying...or at least they were...but I don't know if she'll ever forgive herself. And all for something she didn't even know was possible."

The group sat in silence. A silence of understanding, empathy, and self-reflection. Nate was the first one to speak. "You know what?" he breathed. "Hundreds of kids every year commit suicide from being bullied. Boys, girls, no one is safe. I'm not saying this to be cold or callous, but... I'm not saying anyone deserves what happened to her. I'm not. But...it feels like the world was delivering some karma."

Emory shrugged, still not knowing what to make of what he'd been living with for almost a year now.

Stan nodded. "I wish I could disagree with you, Nate."

"I'm so sorry," Anya said through tears. "No one should have to go through what your sister did."

Noble walked around the island, not caring what anyone thought, and wrapped Anya in a hug.

Emory slowly nodded, looking around the room, spotting Zoe peek around the couch. He poked in her mind for just a moment, worried the girl was terrified, but she wasn't. He felt empathy stemming from inside her. Emory winked.

Zoe smiled and slunk back down to hide herself.

Nate couldn't take the tension any longer. He clapped his hands loudly. "Okay! Who wants to talk about those caves?"

The entire kitchen broke into a short fit of laughter, a needed release.

Emory appreciated the levity but didn't want this hanging over his or Ember's heads. "Look, guys. I want to move on and talk about the caves and all, but I just want y'all to know, Em and I really feel at home here—not in Lost Grove, but with you guys. So, if anyone has any more questions, get 'em off your chest now, because I don't want to be worried that anyone looks at us or thinks of us in a certain way."

"I'm good," Nate quickly said.

Stan nodded. "I've got nothing else. Not now anyway."

Emory nodded at them both. "If something comes up later, Stan. Just ask."

"I will."

"Noble?" Emory asked.

Noble let out a soft laugh and shrugged. "Man, I've had so much going on in my life the last week, shit I'm not sure about, confused about…so, yeah, I'm good. I think we all are."

Anya nodded. "Yeah."

"So," Nate started and let out a massive sigh, shaking out his arms, "before we get into the caves, although I believe this all to be linked, Emory, you said, 'The doctors are trying, or at least they were.' Something like that. Did something happen there?"

Emory nodded. "Yeah, something happened. We've been seeing doctors there for a couple months, and everything seemed…normal, I guess. Questions about how we felt, did we feel guilty, remorse, all that type of shit. Trying to get Em to talk or write about how she felt. Anyway, one day we arrive for treatment, but our regular doctors are nowhere to be seen. Instead, it's the head of the department who wants to see us, Dr. Bajorek. She sees us one at a time, but she didn't want to talk about the incident at all. She was asking all sorts of questions about us, our history…I don't know, it was weird, it felt different. I wanted to poke inside her head to figure it out, but I make a habit of not using my 'powers' for that, especially in places like that."

"Careful. Makes sense," Nate said, nodding along. "Was the doctor weird?"

Emory shook his head. "*She* wasn't, no. She's actually really smart. And she seems genuinely caring, which not all the doctors do."

"So, how was it weird?" Noble asked.

"I'm getting to that." Emory took a deep breath. "So, we talk to her, and only her, for a couple days, and everything seems alright. But then on like the third day, I go into her office and there's this older woman there with her. And she's just sitting there…in the darkest corner of the room."

"What the fuck?" Nate exclaimed.

Emory nodded. "Right? I gave Dr. Bajorek that exact look, like 'What the fuck?' and she says, 'Oh, she's a colleague, here to observe.' I'm like, 'Nope, not buying this shit.' The whole mood in the room was off. But I sit down to vibe it out, and then…I can feel it. I'm sitting there, doing nothing because it's clear something odd is happening, and I can feel this older woman crawling around inside my skull."

"Oh my God," Anya said, covering her mouth.

"You mean like you can?" Stan asked.

Emory nodded his head from side to side. "I mean, yes, but not like my sister. Not the symbiotic sort of connection we have. It's this creepy, crawling sensation. And I know I can't keep her out, because that would prove what they want, what they're clearly trying to figure out. But I also want to keep her out, because that too would prove what I can do, but I don't know if I want to prove that. So, I'm stuck hoping nothing goes on. And then, bam! I'm sitting outside of the room, and it's been hours and I have no idea where the time has gone."

"Fucking hell," Noble said, leaning his forearms on the counter.

Emory sighed. "So now Ember is afraid of them. I'm afraid of them. They are doing shit to the other kids in the basement. I don't know what they want to do to us, or what they'll ask us to do, but I want to find out. I don't want to end up like that kid in the basement, drugged up, terrified, and alone. We've been keeping this secret from people since we were kids," Emory explained.

Anya knew that feeling. She empathized with it. The secret of who you were, of the base being that made you, that no one could understand. What if the Institute knew what she was? Would they run experiments on her? Slice her open and peek inside to see what made her and her mother tick. Anya shivered to think about it.

"I'm not letting some assholes in lab coats run experiments on me or my sister. Not now, not ever," Emory said.

Nate pointed his finger in the air. "This even more proves my point. That weird underground horror movie hallway definitely leads to the Orbriallis."

Stan scoffed. "I think we should maybe be sure of that before—"

"Oh, I'm sure, Hensley."

"Okay, Abbott," Stan mimicked. "But we're here to verify that, so hold your balls together in the meantime."

Nate grimaced. "Huh?"

Zoe, sensing this was her moment, turned around on the sofa. "Noble, can I feed Merryweather now?"

Noble startled, having been so sucked in by the course of this conversation. "Yeah, sorry, Zo, go ahead."

Zoe leapt from the couch with excitement.

"Oh, shit," he said, dashing to the oven to pull the pizza bites out.

"Alright," Nate said, "if you want to prove what I already know, we need a map."

Stan moved to her backpack and grabbed her laptop. "We can do it online."

"Nah. We need a paper map. Do they still sell those at, like, gas stations and shit?"

"I think we have one," Noble commented, setting the hot pan on the butcher block next to the oven.

"Where?" Nate asked.

"I don't know. In the garage somewhere maybe," Noble answered.

"Noble, I need you to hold her," Zoe called for his attention.

"I'll hold her," Anya offered, leaping from the stool.

Zoe beamed a wide smile and set about instructing Anya how to hold the owlet while she fed it with a syringe.

"Okay, right, map." Noble headed for the garage, followed by Nate and Stan.

The Andalusian garage smelled like all garages—gasoline, rubber, leather, aluminum, and childhood memories. There was a red-and-yellow Big Wheel hanging from hooks in the ceiling. A hand-me-down from Noble to Zoe, though why they still had it is a mystery. Zoe's banana-seat bike from when she first learned to ride remained shoved in a back corner, the streamers in the handles still shimmering though tattered.

Noble moved to the small worktable running along one side of the garage and began opening drawers. Nate followed suit while Stan stayed in the doorway, huddling in the warmth while the cold air from outside leaked under the garage door, breezing in, pushing to get inside and chill everyone.

Having a moment to herself, so to speak, Stan had a cyclone of mixed thoughts and feelings running through her mind. Stan had bonded with Ember so quickly, formed an opinion of her from what little she knew, which had just been thrown into a blender. Stan still believed in the connection they formed, and didn't think less or more of her. It was just so difficult to sort through an event based on a reality she never knew.

"So," Nate said as he looked, "I've got to ask. What is going on with you and your dad?"

Noble's shoulders tensed.

"Come on." Nate sighed. "You think I, we"—he pointed to Stan in the doorway and back to himself—"wouldn't catch those slips. Anya said those guys said something about your dad. But you told us they'd been throwing unsolicited flirtations at Anya."

"So what?" Noble asked, pausing in his search to look at his friend. "Are you going to tell me you don't know what they said?"

"No. I know what they fucking said, and it's total bullshit."

"What did they say?" Stan asked.

"People are saying Peter is a killer. That he disappeared the day Sarah was found, same as that girl eight years ago. What's her name…Fulson."

"Are you serious?" Stan pushed away from the doorway but kept her arms crossed against the cold. "Fuckers. Fucking fuckers always throwing judgment. That loser is bona fide white trash."

Nate ignored her, staring at Noble. "Sure, they're assholes. But more to the point, you've been acting weird. And now you just mentioned you had a bunch of confusing shit happening to you this week. Like, man, what the hell is going on? You don't actually think what people are saying about your dad, do you?"

"He was questioned in the Fulson case. Did your sleuthing uncover that?" Noble was quick to remark.

"It wouldn't. The case is still open," Nate remarked, his tone neutral.

"Well, he was. And he is gone. He left that morning, and it turns out—" Noble cut himself off. He turned back to start looking for the map.

"Turns out?" Stan prompted.

Noble slammed a drawer. "He's not where he said he was going to be."

Nate let this information pool in his bank of clues.

"Your dad is not a murderer, Noble," Stan said. Her tone was ferocious.

"Yeah, but he's something," Noble responded. "I can't explain it."

"Dude," Nate finally said, stepping toward his friend. "You should have told me. You should have told us. But mostly me."

Stan snorted.

"I know all the details of the goings-on around here. Keep that locked up here in the vault. If you told me what more was going on, we could find a reasonable explanation, or something closer to it. Instead, you've kept this all to yourself. Even this Nettie bullshit! I'd have had this locked down and puzzled together in a way that kept her from knowing anything about it until we had concrete evidence to give her."

"Like I could have known she'd identify a convict from Ohio as being the guy who took her brother." Noble huffed as he shut another drawer and turned to face his angry friend.

"She's really fucked up about this," Stan added.

"I know she is!" Noble exclaimed. "Did you forget I was there when she fainted? That it was me and Anya who showed her the picture? You know what she asked me? 'What do I do with this?' Of course I know it's fucked her up, even more so than the fact she's been living with this truth for eight years. Can either of you fathom that aspect? We all thought she was insane."

Stan looked at her feet. "I know. I've been struggling with that."

"You should have told us, is all I'm saying." Nate turned back to search for the map. "You should tell us about your dad. We could likely figure it all out and then how stupid will you feel when I put it all together, and you were freaking out over nothing."

"Jesus, Nate." Stan huffed. "You don't have all the answers."

"I have a lot of them."

"Your ego knows no bounds," she said, leaning back against the doorjamb.

"I'm confident in the deductive knowledge I have."

"Guys, we're not talking about my dad. This is about finding out about Raymond LaRange and a kidnapped kid. Can we focus on that for now and, when you solve it, oh great one"—Noble offered Nate an extravagant bow—"maybe I'll be willing to talk about this shit with my dad. But not now."

Nate shuffled through some random tools on the tool bench. "Yeah. Cool, fine."

They fell silent, searching for the map and consumed in their own roiling thoughts.

"Found it!" Noble finally enthused, pulling a sheaf of old, folded papers from a box tucked away in the Andalusian garage.

Nate stepped forward and took it from him. "This is perfect," he explained, unfolding the maps of Lost Grove and the surrounding areas, their argument already forgotten. "Yeah, yeah. See, all the roads and stuff."

"I still think we could have done this on my laptop," Stan commented from the doorway.

"*So* not as cool," Nate said, making his way back through the boxes and junk toward the house.

Voices from inside carried down the hall from the kitchen into Noble's ears. His sister, busy chatting Anya's ear off. He smiled and followed Nate and Stan back inside, switching off the garage light and shutting the door.

Zoe lifted the baby owl from Anya's hands and cuddled it close to her chest. The little bird squawked but settled into her palms, enormous eyes blinking closed.

"Mom told you not to handle her too much," Noble instructed.

Zoe ignored him, patting the soft head with her small index finger.

"Okay," Nate said, spreading out the main map of Lost Grove on the wide kitchen island. "We need markers or something."

"Zo? Can I use your markers?" Noble asked.

"Whatever," Zoe replied, focused on Merryweather.

"Hot, hot," Stan said with an open mouth, having eaten one of the scalding pizza bites.

"You never let them cool." Noble laughed before running upstairs to his sister's room and grabbing her set of markers.

When he returned, Stan was tossing another pizza bite into her mouth.

"Alright, kiddos," Nate started, taking the markers from Noble. He selected a bright red one from the glass jar, popped the top off with his thumb, and hovered over the map.

Anya leaned over the island counter from the opposite direction, searching for Mulberry Street. "Here," she said, her index finger landing at the point where the Horne house would be.

A wave of guilt tempered Anya's excitement. Nettie hadn't been in school today, and it was becoming more and more obvious how transformative, how traumatic, all this information was to her best friend. Not that she didn't know that going into the endeavor, but one can never fully guess how a person might take a blow of knowledge such as this. There was no "when you find out your brother was taken by a child molester and no one believes you" handbook.

"That's the Horne house, so…" She trailed her finger back into the woods.

Nate followed the path of her finger with the red marker while Noble plucked a few pizza bites from the pan into a bowl. He pulled a jar of homemade ranch dressing from the fridge, dolloped a spoonful on the side of the bowl, then set it on the island counter. Zoe climbed onto a stool, the owlet still in her arms. She'd also somehow managed to secret a book under her arm and eagerly opened it and began reading.

Noble glanced over at his sister, juggling a book and an owl. He swore it was the book she was adamant to return to the librarian but had since been carting it around with her everywhere, studying it. He made a mental note to find out what book it was she was so obsessed with.

Emory leaned over the island counter, watching. When the others returned from their excursion through the cave system and told him what they found, he'd been perplexed. When he saw the pictures and video, the more surreal it became. Had he dreamed it? Their entire excursion? When they'd walked out of the cursed woods, it seemed to him it had been Anya leading more than Stan. No one seemed to have noticed that minor detail, but he had.

"So, here would be the cave entrance," Stan added, jabbing her finger on the spot.

She had her phone out, the app that tracked walking or hiking routes open. Noble grabbed his phone, too. After what they found in the cave, both Stan and Noble launched the app in an attempt to measure distances and mark landmarks. Since the app had gone in and out of service, Noble marked the distances and directions in his phone to make sure their calculations would be as close as possible to accurate.

"I have a question." Emory stated.

"Yeah," Nate said, eyes locked on the map. He grabbed a black marker. It was actually midnight blue, he discovered, and began mapping the cave system with Noble and Stan dictating, arguing, over the directions.

"When we find out where this is, or what it might belong to, what then?"

Nate peeked through his lashes at Emory. "Not sure."

"Oh, okay," Emory said, nodding. These kids sure flew by the seat of their pants, and he loved every second of it.

They kept on mapping, twisting, curving midnight-blue marker paths onto the map until they got to the hall, door, and camera. Nate marked an X and stood up. All of them looked over the map.

Noble leaned forward, his index finger pressing a spot on the map, away from the X. "This is the Institute."

Nate nodded, thinking. "Yeah, but…"

"It's not part of the Orbriallis basement," Stan said.

Anya sat back and then forward again, examining the map.

"No, it could be," Nate said. "Our measurements could be off."

"That's like…" Noble inspected the map, trying to work the measurements and the distance in his head. "A quarter mile. So, like a 400-meter race."

"Hold on," Nate said, pulling out his phone and opening the map app. "But, guys, check this out." He held out his phone, zooming into the Orbriallis Institute.

"Okay, we know where it is. What's the point?" Noble asked.

Nate narrowed his eyes at him and looked back down at the phone. "This is the point, jackass." Nate zoomed out to show the area surrounding the Institute. "There's literally nothing else around the Orbriallis. No houses, no stores, nothing."

"I think he's right," Anya said. "Because there's something else."

Everyone looked at her, and Stan asked, "What would that be?"

Anya trailed her fingernail on the map between the mark depicting the Orbriallis and the X marking the weird door in the cave. "This is a decline, you can see in the map the elevation marks. This," she said, tapping her fingernail to the X, "doesn't have to be anything but an entry point. There could be an inclined elevator just inside this door that goes up," she said, tracing the short distance to the Institute, "and it lets you out into the lowest basement of the Orbriallis. There are places with longer underground passages. Disney World has a massive tunnel system under the park, so visitors don't see all the behind-the-scenes stuff."

"We're equating the Orbriallis Institute to Disney World now?" Emory joked.

"No, it's true. I read about that," Nate jumped in. "And they are massive. They're like, big enough for floats and shit. Disney built them first, then built the park over it. Technically, the park is like the third floor of a massive building, because, being in Florida, they couldn't dig below the water level."

"That's both cool and creepy," Zoe commented, still absorbed in her book.

Noble glared at his sister, re-questioning how much she had actually heard of all their conversations this past week.

Anya smiled. "Kind of is, isn't it?"

Nate scoffed. "Hell yes it is. But it proves the point. There's literally nowhere else that entrance could lead to. And there's no way there's just a random hallway with a camera and lights not going somewhere. Guys, it's the Orbriallis." He capped the midnight-blue marker, tossed it in the air, and caught it.

"What's the purpose of it, though?" Stan asked, not only for the others but for herself. She had a hard time with it. "It's not like this cave system was super easy to get in and out of. It's dark as shit. They haven't installed lighting, at least not until you find your way to the creepy entrance. So, what's the reason?"

"I don't know the reason," Anya started, "but it proves what Nettie was saying and links the Green Man—"

"Raymond LaRange," Nate cut in.

"To the Orbriallis Institute."

"Yeah, and does a nefarious supervillain always have to explain themselves at the end of a movie? No," Nate answered. "So why should a super hospital? Better yet, why should the government?"

"We don't know they're still operating the Orbriallis." Noble paced to grab a pizza bite.

"I guarantee it!" Nate proclaimed.

"Damn," Stan said. "I hate to admit it, but Nate's right. There's nothing else this could be."

"Fuck yeah!" Nate said, pumping his fist in the air and then holding it up to Stan for a high five, which she reluctantly reciprocated.

"Okay, this is dope and all, that we have proof," Emory said. "But back to my question. What do we do with this? What's the purpose?"

Nate capped and uncapped the marker, finally setting it down. "What did you think we'd do?"

"No idea. Just seemed like we're trying to find either the Raymond guy or a way to get the brother—what's his name?"

"George," Anya answered.

"George out," Emory finished.

"Or proof." Nate's smirk grew wider. "Which we now have."

"Proof to do what?" Emory asked, not sure what Nate was so excited about.

Nate huffed. "Go to the police. What do you think?"

Emory shook his head. "No way, man. If they get that video, the Orbriallis will know it was me. We'd be fucked."

"Then we just show them the video and tell them they can't have it. Or, shit, send me the video and I'll tell them I found it online. On the dark web."

"The dark web?" Noble asked, an eyebrow raised.

"Yeah, they won't have a clue what to do with that."

Stan slapped her head. "Nate, don't say anything about the dark web. My God. But didn't Nettie's parents already get the police to look into the Green Man years ago?"

Anya nodded. "Yeah, it was Chief Richards that came to check it out. But he didn't find anything and dismissed the whole notion."

"But Nettie didn't have what we have now," Nate said.

"Look, I want to take these guys down, believe me," Emory said. "But do we have enough?"

"Yeah, I think we do. We've got all the articles online about LaRange, we've got the video, we've got all the photos we took inside and outside the cave, we got the maps and the coordinates…"

"I think it's enough where they'd actually take us seriously." Anya finished Nate's train of thought.

"How could they not?" Noble asked, agreeing. "These things, especially now that we know the cave leads to the Orbriallis Institute, are too coincidental. They'd have to look into it. Wouldn't they?"

Nate tapped the marker on the counter. "But who do we take it to? That young cop, the one who questioned me about my social media, he wouldn't get it."

"Why not tell your parents?" Emory asked.

Noble couldn't begin to answer that question for himself.

Anya shook her head. Her mother would tell her to stay away from messes that weren't her own. Her father would say the same. "My parents wouldn't believe me."

Stan shrugged. "My dad might. Gran would."

"Story," Zoe said. She was still leaning over her book. The owlet had hopped onto the table and was watching all of them with gigantic eyes.

Now it was time for all eyes to shift to Zoe.

"What?" Noble asked his sister.

Zoe raised her head, taking the last pizza bite, dipping it in the remaining glob of ranch dressing from her bowl. "Ms. Palmer. You should tell her. She knows everything. She'll know who to tell."

"The librarian witch?" Nate scoffed.

"No, wait." Noble stopped his friend from saying more. "She might be right. Story, Ms. Palmer, she does know everything. Like, she knew what we came in looking for yesterday. And this one time in the street, she gave Zoe a pair of shoelaces, and the next day her laces broke. You guys were there when she made Zoe that bracelet that, like, totally mellowed her out. And Story is close with Mary. So, there's something there…"

"I was thinking of someone with a little more authority," Nate slowly remarked. "Can we get back to the police?"

"But you just said you can't bring it to the young guy," Stan said.

"And Chief Richards already looked into it," Anya reminded them.

"Yeah, but you just said that we have more now, so—"

"Seth," Noble reluctantly spit out.

"Who?" Nate asked.

"Oh, the nice sergeant," Anya said. "He helped us after Noble punched that jerk."

"Oh, the new guy?" Nate asked. "The one with dark hair, good-looking, kind of—"

"Ah, Nate has a crush," Stan said.

"That's cool, man," Emory added.

"No, assholes. I'm just remarking—"

"He asked me about the Orbriallis," Noble said, wishing he didn't have to bring this up.

"What? When?"

"He was here," Zoe said.

"Thanks, Zo," Noble said.

Nate held out his hands. "Okay, everyone else, stay quiet. Noble, what the hell?"

Noble sighed. "Sergeant Wolfe came by to—"

"His last name's Wolfe?" Nate asked, impressed.

"Dude." Noble held his hands up.

"Sorry, go on."

Noble detested lying. He couldn't recall the last time he had ever lied in his life. But throwing his dad under the bus to all his friends was not something he was going to do. "Sergeant Wolfe came by and while my mom was getting Zo settled, he asked me if we ever heard any stories about the Orbriallis."

"What?" Anya asked.

"What the hell?" Nate added.

"He said he was following up on a lead or something. Anyway, I think...no, I know he would listen to us. He's very serious."

"Well, yeah," Stan said. "He was a homicide detective in San Francisco for like twenty years or something."

Nate's eyes nearly popped out of his head. "What! Are you fucking serious?"

Stan nodded. "Yeah, he and my dad went to school together."

Nate shook his head like he was trying to rid his mind of a demon. "You're telling me that you knew we had a real-life homicide detective working...wait, what the fuck is he doing here? And why is he a sergeant? He would run circles around Chief Richards."

"I don't know, Nate. You'll have to ask him."

Nate pointed at Stan, sneering. "Oh, I will. But more to my point, you knew who this guy was and just sat here while we were trying to figure out who to tell?"

Stan shrugged.

"Well, that settles it. Let's go to the police station."

Nate grabbed the map, folding it. "I agree. Let's do this."

"Now?" Stan asked.

"Hell yes, now," Nate said. "When the hell else?"

"Zo, put Merryweather away," Noble instructed.

"Why?"

"Because you're coming with me, us. I'm not leaving you here."

"Mom will be home soon," Zoe protested but picked up the owlet and got down from the stool.

"Just, please."

"Okay," Zoe said, giving in quickly because deep down she was hoping this would be the outcome.

"Will we all fit in your car?" Stan asked.

"Yeah, we'll fit," Noble said.

As they all pulled on their coats, Nate offered brief "oohs" and "ahhs" and random tidbits as he read all about Detective Seth Wolfe's escapades on the SFPD. He remained glued to his phone as they piled into the car.

The atmosphere was electric. The sleet had stopped, and an icy wind rushed around the houses, looking for something to blow down. As they turned onto Pixley Street, toward the station, Noble's Crosstrek sputtered.

"What the hell?" He pressed the gas and got nothing. The lights flicked off and on, and the car died.

"What is it?" Stan asked, leaning forward.

Noble pulled the car over to the side of the road with some effort as the power steering was gone. He hit the brakes, putting the car in Park. "My car just died."

"How the hell did it die?" Nate asked from the passenger seat, finally pulling his gaze from his phone. He leaned over, looking at the instrument panel.

"Told you we should go to Story's," Zoe said from the back seat. She was already unbuckling her belt. She opened the door and sprinted out.

The teens all looked out the windows to their left. A classic white Victorian surrounded by berry vines, mint, rosemary, and lavender rose above them.

"Well, shit," Nate said from the passenger seat.

"What?" Emory asked, not at all familiar with who lived in the iconic home.

Noble sighed, unbuckling his seat belt. "This is where Story Palmer lives."

"We appease your sister for like one minute, Noble," Nate said, unbuckling, "then we walk to the station. It's only five blocks from here."

"Agreed," Noble said as he got out and followed his sister, who was already knocking on the front door. He paused at the iron gate as the others made their decisions to join him.

The Visionary

Seth couldn't believe it when he pulled up in front of the address Story had given him. The house she had purchased was the subject of much speculation when he was younger. He wondered if she knew whose home this used to be. Maybe Mary had told her stories.

Seth took a deep breath, feeling—which was a shock to him—as if he'd made the right decision calling Story. He was in a state of desperate mania when he got to his Bronco and dialed her number. He almost ended the call after two rings, doubting his strange intuition, but when she finally answered with, "I could feel you were going to call," he felt a calming sense of relief. He asked if she was working, to which she replied, "What happened?"

Seth wondered if he would even have to tell her anything. He said there had been a drastic turn of events and that he needed to speak with her. "If you're at work, I can wait until you're off," he lied, needing answers.

"No. I don't think it can," she replied. "Meet me at my house. I already have coverage lined up."

Could this really work? Was he wasting time going down a path that would have had him thrown off the force in San Francisco if anyone found out? What would Bill say? Did it matter if it actually produced results? His gut told him this was the right thing to do. Time to find out if his once ironclad instincts were still intact.

He approached the Victorian home, which resonated a flare of gothic aura and was far too big for one person, with a smile contradicting his inner turmoil. Story opened the front door and quickly adopted a look of quaint confusion. She was radiant in a cream-colored, ankle- and elbow-length floral dress, making her black hair more striking than usual. Her necklaces, bracelets, and rings shone, and for the first time, Seth got a clear view of the tattoos adorning both forearms.

"I can't say I expected to see you smiling," Story said in greeting.

"I'm not," Seth replied, stepping onto the porch.

"Your face would say otherwise."

"It's just"—Seth motioned at her home—"this house. Do you know who lived here before you?"

Story shrugged. "I don't recall the name on the closing paperwork, but I know she had a powerful energy and resilient spirit. Did you know her?"

Story's description surprised Seth, but he didn't doubt it. "I'm not sure anyone really knew her. At least no one in town. Her name was Lina Orbriallis."

"As in…"

Seth nodded. "Yes. She was the daughter of Geiger Orbriallis, the founder of the infamous Institute. She walked throughout town often, but no one ever saw her without a black veil covering her face. There were, of course, rumors, stories—fact or fiction no one knew for sure—that she was born severely disfigured. Her disfigurement supposedly drove Geiger to push his research and experiments to groundbreaking levels, trying to fix her, so to speak."

Story's face had grown grim. "That's terrible. No wonder she needed strength and resilience. I can only imagine everyone stared and spoke in not-so-subtle whispers about her."

Seth looked down. "You're not wrong. We were…stupid kids. I mean, we never pointed or called her names, nothing mean-spirited. We just believed rumors. One of them, ironically, was that she was a witch."

The frown etched into Story's face was short-lived as a grand smile rose. "I knew it."

Seth laughed. "I don't doubt it."

"What happened to her?"

"I…I actually don't know."

"I'm sorry. Please, come in. I know you're here for something far more serious."

Seth stepped through the doorway, doubly interested in seeing the interior. He had so many memories as a kid of what it might look like, and now, it was Story's home. It was quintessential Victorian, tall ceilings, lead glass windows, a massive, caramel-coated door leading into a welcoming foyer, a softly curving staircase leading up to the second floor. The wood was of a beautiful, rich color, while the walls were a soothing cream shade and there were plants all around. He couldn't keep his lips from curving into a smile, his shoulders easing down from around his ears.

"Is it what you expected?" Story asked.

"Yes. No… I'm not sure, to be honest," Seth said, still taking in everything. What was she doing in a house like this all to herself? Perhaps she'd been considering a husband and children when she made the purchase. Seth wondered if he'd considered children. He had, though so much time had passed without a partner with whom he could see himself raising them that the idea needed to be dusted off. No, more than dusted off. It needed to be pulled down from the attic, vacuumed, dusted, and wiped down with a rag and cleaning solution.

"Come, let's sit." Story led the way into a sitting room.

At first glance, Seth wondered where they would sit, exactly. Floor-to-ceiling windows let in the light, which was why the sitting room had become host to a ludicrous amount of plants. Vines clung to the walls, drifted down the shelves, wound around the books, and crawled along the floor. Massive leaves wiggled as the two people entering disturbed the air, but it felt to Seth as if they were twitching at the approach of their caregiver.

Books lined the shelves of the elaborate Victorian built-in occupying one and a half walls. Piles of books littered the floor, some acting as perches for small pots and baby plants. The floor, what he could see of it, had a beautiful inlay pattern, a mix of tile and wood. The sort of craftsmanship of the historical homes throughout Lost Grove.

Seth approached a settee in a dusty midnight blue but decided against it when he noticed it covered in books. It didn't matter because Story carefully removed them, placing them on the floor to join the many others, and sat there herself.

Seth sat down across from her in a vintage armchair, all light-hearted pleasantries upon arrival leaving his body as the reality of why he was there overtook him.

"I would hope that after our night on the beach, any lingering hesitations to speak plainly would have disappeared. So, please, speak freely and openly. I'm here for you," Story coaxed.

Seth paused, not because of a fear of voicing what was necessary but because of the intimacy of her words. Their night on the beach? He supposed that was accurate. And the way she said that she was there for him carried a deeper weight than just this moment in her sitting room.

"Right," he said, pushing on. "I can't give you the details of the recent turn of events, but you'll find out soon enough." His lips quivered into a lopsided grin.

Story nodded. The news would spread in this small town.

"It's just…I feel like I've hit a brick wall in this case. I encounter more questions and flat-out mysteries with every thread I follow. There's a missing infant and we have no clue where she is or if she is even alive. Our prime suspect, or at least the one person who I know has answers, is a ghost. Not literally," he said, realizing who he was speaking to, "but he's nowhere to be found and apparently can't be traced. Unless I hire a bounty hunter. Even then…"

Story could see the mental and emotional strain emanating from Seth's body, almost as if it was a visible layer of sweat pouring down his face. A wavering energy of deep blues denoting a sense of anguish or despair. The urge to reach across the space between them and grab his hands was overwhelming.

"And I think the one thing that has been holding me back, which has been a constant mental distraction, or like a hurdle, or, or, like a giant metal ball chained to my ankle—"

"Your time travel." Story helped him to get to his point.

"Yes." Seth nodded. "And…I think my avoidance of dealing with it, or my preoccupation of trying to understand it, is clouding my judgment and killing my instincts."

"And?"

"And," Seth sighed, "I think I need to embrace it. I'd like to try to have a…a vision."

Story met Seth's eyes and smiled. She had hoped this was why he wanted to speak with her. His resistance to embrace his abilities was understandable, especially coming from his line of work, but it was difficult to watch, knowing she couldn't push him.

"Do you think that's something—"

"Yes, Seth. It is."

"So, what exactly do we do?"

Story closed her eyes, collecting her thoughts. "Well," she said, opening them back up, "there are some things I'll need to collect. Here at the house. But the biggest question is one of proximity."

Seth cocked his head to the side.

"To Sarah Elizabeth."

"Like the beach?" he guessed.

"The beach is too distant now. I've been doing this my whole life, and it was incredibly difficult for me to connect that night."

Seth swallowed, sensing where this was going.

"It would be the best way," Story said, reading his expression. "I don't know the legality or logistics behind it, but if you want to have the clearest, most powerful vision…you need to be as close to her body as possible."

Seth ran his hand over his mouth and chin, his stubble having grown into a beard. He knew Sarah's body was still at the county morgue with Wes, tragically joined by the bodies of her parents. How would he even approach Wes on the subject? Foremost, he needed to make sure Wes was back at his county office. He looked at his watch. It had been hours since he left the scene.

Seth stood up and grabbed his phone from his inside jacket pocket. "I need to make a call. And then would you be willing to make a trip to—"

"Of course. I'll gather up everything we'll need now."

Story exited the room to gather whatever was needed for this… ritual? Seth didn't know what to call it. Having tapped on the name, he brought his phone to his ear.

"Seth," Wes answered.

"Wes. Are you back at your office yet?"

"Yeah, been here for a while. Just finished my initial examination of Bess—a rather surreal experience."

"I'm sure. Look, I need to come up there to…um…is it okay if I come by?"

"Hm. You know you don't need to ask."

Seth gripped his temples. "Well, that's the thing. I sort of do. I can explain when I get there."

After a brief silence, Wes said, "Okay. Come on up."

Seth ended the call and let out a long sigh.

Seth pulled his Bronco into a spot in the Coroner's Public Administration parking lot and turned off the engine. The ride up was rather silent. Story told him when they first got on the road that he needed to find a place of calm inside himself and focus his mind on what he was looking for, what he was hoping to find, and who he needed to see. Seth found Story's presence helped him feel more at ease, able to hone in on what he wanted. That didn't stop an overriding anxiety from swelling inside his chest. He figured it stood to reason. The notion of lying down next to a dead body to transcend to another realm, dimension, or time would do that to you.

"Are you nervous?" Story asked.

Seth looked at her for the first time in what felt like an hour but was more than likely fifteen minutes. "I think I'm more nervous about approaching Wes with this than actually going through with the…ritual or whatever."

"I think we'll call it a process," Story offered.

Seth laughed. "I suppose that sounds less sinister."

"Not that rituals are negative."

"And I'm sure I don't have a clue what a real ritual even is. So there's that."

Story reached over and grabbed Seth's hand. "I believe this was all meant to happen, just as it is. I knew you were calling. And I knew what you wanted to do. And I have a feeling your discussion with Wes will go much smoother than you think."

"Only one way to find out." Seth got out of his vehicle and led the way around the building to the back entrance of the coroner's office, through the linoleum-tiled hallways to Wes Hensley's office. He looked back at Story as they approached the door, needing to see the positivity in her eyes. She smiled and ran her hand down his back.

Seth knocked once before entering.

Wes stood with his back to the door, placing papers in a folder, and didn't bother to turn at the knock. He wasn't expecting anyone else coming to see him. Office hours were over, and everyone had left for the day. "Seth, come in." Wes hated the amount of paperwork his job entailed. Hated that it still involved using so much actual paper instead of being computerized. But that was the way of things. He grabbed the files he'd been working on and turned, placing them on his desk. "Here I thought it was going to be a slow day—oh. Hi," Wes said in greeting to Story. He looked from the town librarian to Seth.

"Wes, this is Story Palmer. Story, this is our chief medical examiner, Wes Hensley." Seth made introductions as he gently closed the door.

Wes wondered about the hesitation in his old friend's voice over the phone. This was definitely not a straightforward visit. He extended his hand. "Pleasure," he said.

Story took it, smiling. "You're Constance's father," she said more than asked.

"That's right." Wes nodded. "Take a seat. Or is this…?"

Seth adjusted one chair in front of Wes's desk but waited for Story to sit before sitting himself.

"I figured when you called you had questions about"—Wes glanced over at Story, then back to Seth—"this morning."

Seth huffed. "I have endless questions about that whole scenario, but that can wait till after. Wes, I need to ask you a huge favor, and it's going to sound…rather unorthodox. And I will fully respect whatever decision you make, but I really…really need to make this happen."

Wes considered the two people sitting before him. He heard the talk around town about the librarian, Ms. Palmer. Everyone thought she was a witch, and there wasn't much he could say to that. There had been several small, seemingly insignificant moments in passing that had built a case in favor of her being a witch. About a year ago, he was walking in town with his wife to get lunch at the cafe. He saw Story exit the library, walking with purpose, then a slight jog, as she ran to kick a ball back toward Madeline, the little deaf girl. A truck exceeding the speed limit zoomed past just as she prevented the ball or child from galloping into the street. She'd turned and walked back to the library. He noted the scenario because it just felt too out of place.

There was another time waiting in line at the pharmacy. Story had been in line as well when two quarreling siblings caused a scene. The older one pushed the younger, who fell, but instead of hitting his little head on the counter, the bag of cotton balls in the display fell, cushioning his blow. Wes thought nothing of it at the time, but in retrospect, there was no way the bag could have simply fallen from the display shelf. The store clerk had overpacked the shelf so the bags were firmly in place.

Not to mention the more personal interaction he'd had with her. One night on Main Street, he'd come from a dinner by himself, needing a moment after a chaotic argument at home regarding the twins. It was the first time he'd met Story Palmer. He'd read the local announcements of her new appointment as the librarian. He smiled in passing, as everyone in Lost Grove did, and she responded in kind but also stopped on the pavement. Wes had felt like she would say something like, "Have we met?" or "Do I know you?" Instead, she said, "It's the woman running the daycare. She's the one biting your little ones."

Wes had continued to smile and asked her to repeat herself.

"It's called cute aggression. Though I believe there is more going on with the woman caring for your twins at the daycare than meets the eye. I'm sorry, this is very forward of me."

"How did you know we have twins?"

The smile she'd offered him reminded him so much of the smile his mother would give him when she offered information he didn't think she could know or intuit. He'd been so thrown that he'd excused himself. But she'd been right. The woman who cared for children at the daycare had a checkered history. She was even charged with child endangerment when she took a toddler from a previous preschool job home with her.

Wes looked from Seth to Story and then back to Seth, a premonition of sorts forming in his mind. "What is it you need?"

Story slid forward in her chair a little.

"We need to be in a room with Sarah Grahams," Seth answered, watching Wes absorb this information, waiting for a response or a sign of how he felt.

Wes sniffed and pushed back from his desk, standing. "Back when we lived on the reservation, these people would come to our home. They'd knock on the door and ask for my mom," he explained as he pulled his lab coat from the back of his chair and put it on. "I always remembered their faces. Every time the knock came, I opened the door to the same desperate expression. Like wind or water, grief has a way of carving itself onto the sufferer. Shall we?" Wes opened the door.

Seth rose from his chair, bewildered. Story stood with a smile as they followed him out and down the hall.

"My mother, she rarely gave in to their requests. No solace comes from speaking with the dead, not really. But one time, this *one* time, she did it," Wes continued, opening up the door to the autopsy room and flicking on the lights. "She agreed to help the family sitting at our small kitchen table. Everyone on the reservation knew the family, but not just because we keep an eye on our own. In fact, this was one influence for me to pursue this career. But that's not the point of this story. My mother said she'd see if she could speak with Charley. That was the name of their teenage son. A number of misdeeds had been performed on their son, and the police weren't doing much about it."

Wes pulled a stainless steel gurney from the wall, moving it around the room and situating it under a cold locker.

Seth watched Wes move, performing this task as if what Seth asked was the most natural question on earth. Had he misunderstood him?

"So, she used a lock of Charley's hair, performed a ritual to see if Charley would tell her who had done this to him."

Seth glanced over at Story, hearing Wes mention a ritual, but her eyes stayed glued on the medical examiner.

Wes grabbed a hold of the lever and let his hand rest there as he continued, "I remember watching from outside the kitchen, hanging back in the doorway. The way my mother started breathing…God it terrified me. Then she started yelping, crying out. I was petrified, cemented to the spot where I stood. Charley's mother started crying. My dad, I could tell he was uneasy. He began shaking my mother, speaking in our language. It seemed to take an hour, but I knew it was seconds before it was over. She opened her eyes, and they locked right on me. She told me to leave. I don't know what she saw." Wes pulled the cold locker open and slid a body inside its bag easily onto the gurney.

"Did it help?" Story asked.

Wes turned to her. "Hm?"

"Did they find who hurt him?"

"Ah. No. No, they didn't," Wes answered, unzipping the bag and pressing it down so Sarah's face was exposed. "What my understanding was, is that it was someone passing through. Someone who likely did this all across the States but had never been caught, or at least, not for Charley's murder. Nothing to link him." Wes crossed the room to the door. "You know where to find me if you need me." He left them alone in the room.

Seth stood frozen in shock. How did that go so easily? Did Wes even know what they were going to do? Did he trust him that much? Or was it something about Story being there? Did he understand her in a way that Seth never could? Wes directed almost his entire story at her.

"You'll probably want to remove your shirt," Story instructed, keeping her eyes off the corpse. She set her satchel on the only unmovable table in the room and grabbed another gurney, pulling it away from the wall and settling it next to Sarah's.

Seth turned around, pulling himself out of his stupor. "Why?"

"You'll probably sweat a lot," Story responded, returning to her satchel on the prep table. She stood with her back to the young woman lying cold, motionless on a gurney not eleven feet away from her. Story wasn't afraid of the body. She wasn't afraid of the spirit. This wasn't Story's time with the deceased, however. She didn't want what remained of Sarah to take Story's presence as an influence. This was about Seth and his abilities. Like a coroner placing a scalpel, bone saw, and forceps on the stainless steel table, Story pulled her tools from her large satchel—silver burning bowl, resin, leaves from a salvia plant, crow and owl feathers, a small mirror, and salt—laying them out with care.

Seth watched while he removed his belt and unbuttoned his police-issue long-sleeve shirt, leaving him in a tight white T-shirt. He placed it on a nearby chair, hanging it over the back to avoid wrinkles. He turned to survey the room.

Sarah Elizabeth looked serene and pale with death, and the empty gurney next to her did not look inviting. Seth could already feel the cold steel on his skin. He shifted his gaze back to the young woman painted with the blue-white pallor of a life snuffed out.

Story placed resin and salvia in her ornate silver burning bowl, striking a match. The sound snatched Seth from his clouded thoughts. He didn't want to do this. But he felt he needed to.

The resin in the bowl took the flame, burning a cool blue that lit the plant material. Smoke rose into the recycled, clinical air of the medical exam room. She took the bowl in her hands, turning to find Seth waiting by the door.

"Ready?" she asked.

Seth took a deep breath, rubbing his hands together. The room was chilly in just his undershirt, and he felt his skin rise with gooseflesh. He moved to the empty table, mentally and emotionally psyching himself up. "Ready," he replied.

Story gave him a reassuring smile as she approached. "Go ahead and get on the table."

Seth sat on the table and then stretched the muscles in his back, feeling the stress and anxiety building between his shoulder blades. He could smell the resin burning, a peculiar scent that was both sweet and sulfuric. It left a thick coating on his tongue. "What is that?"

"Salvia and copal," Story answered. She stood close.

Seth could feel her warmth radiating onto his knees. The smoke billowed into his face as she wafted it toward him with the feathers. "And those are?" he asked.

"Take deep breaths," she instructed, her lips tilted with the hint of a smirk.

Seth did as instructed. After several deep breaths, he formulated the question another way. "Are these hallucinogens of any kind?"

"Salvia has historically been used to achieve an altered state of consciousness," Story replied.

Seth shut his eyes. "Great."

Story smiled. "It's not a drug, Sheriff. Just a plant."

He liked the way her voice calmed him. When he opened his eyes to find hers locked on his, a wave, like the way your stomach drops on a roller coaster, rippled through him.

She took his hands and rested the bowl in his palms. "Keep breathing."

Seth took another deep breath, closing his eyes, calming himself. Either nothing would come of this or something would, and he didn't know which he wanted more or which frightened him more.

Story returned to the table with all her magical materials. "Are you hungry?" she asked.

Seth raised a brow. "No. Nauseated more like."

Over her shoulder, Story offered him a smile. "Nerves are normal."

Seth nodded. "Why do you ask?"

Story turned to face him. "We usually fast for this ritual."

"Usually...okay. Should I have?"

"We don't really have the time."

"I know, but should I have?" he asked again, a nervous laugh escaping.

"No. It's not a prerequisite. Only, it helps." Story turned back to her bag, removing the last elements. She tipped salt into her hand.

"Helps how?" Seth asked, still breathing in the smoke of resin and salvia leaves.

Story threw the salt over her left shoulder, and it landed on the ground, sprinkling under the gurney Seth was sitting on, bouncing off his shoes before she responded. "It's a physical attribute, something you feel within your physical body. So, being hungry is a good way to stay connected to your body."

"Oh. Good." Seth huffed. "So, what should I do to stay connected to my body?"

Story pondered, grabbing a small glass bottle. "If you find yourself wanting to return to your physical form, it always helps to think of loved ones—parents, lovers, children—or concentrate on a physical desire."

Seth considered, swallowing as if it would rid the thick, acrid scent that clung to his mouth from the resin and leaves, but it didn't. "Physical desire?"

"Yes, you know. Pain, hunger—"

"There you go, mentioning hunger again. I really feel like I've skipped a step."

Story smiled. "You haven't. Keep breathing that in."

"Is pain really a desire?" he asked after a moment.

She shrugged. "To some."

The comment felt reasonable until his brain processed it. He looked up, watched her fiddle with the feathers, laying them out on the table facing certain directions. "Do you mean sexually?"

She turned at his words and, after a beat, shrugged, nodding her head left and right. "Sex works."

"No, I mean—"

"Sexual desire is a good one to think of. It's a strong physical pull."

Seth produced a quick smile. "I only meant, if that was what you meant by some people finding pain desirable."

"Ah," she said and removed the small cork from the bottle containing oil of lavender, bergamot, and sage. "Yes and no. Physical pain is sometimes desirable for those suffering mental pain. You're on the right track, Seth. You'll be fine."

"I don't feel like it."

Story considered him for a moment. "Let me ask you this, when you were first getting started, as a detective, I bet you had nerves. But I bet they were nerves of excitement more than a doubt of self, am I right?"

Seth wanted to say no because he didn't want to sound like he had an ego, but she nailed it. He'd never felt the nerves of not being able to do the job, just excitement to solve the case. Her smiling face told him he'd given himself away.

"Like detective work came naturally to you, this will too. It's part of you, though you've so rarely exercised it, you might as well say you've never exercised it. But it's there. Have confidence in your ability."

"This is nothing like detective work," he said.

"It could be. Think of it like finding clues. It just so happens that the clues are on an existential plane."

Seth released a tense laugh.

Returning to the gurney Seth was sitting on, Story doused the oil onto her right index finger and made a circle on the table, all the while murmuring the protection circle spell in her native language, French.

Seth took in a breath, about to ask what he might expect, but the air he pulled into his lungs felt insufficient. He took another, also feeling like he just wasn't getting enough air. He cleared his throat, tried again.

Story continued to draw the protection of the elements within the circle, the pentagram connecting all points.

"Story?" Seth set the silver bowl down next to him. But Story did not respond. She was busy reciting.

"Montrez à cet homme la réponse à ses questions,
Fournissez-lui des conseils sur le chemin qu'il parcourt.
Permettez-lui d'utiliser ses pouvoirs
et libère ce qu'il a gardé caché."

"Story?" Seth asked for her attention once more. He really couldn't breathe now. Every time he tried to inhale, it felt like his chest wouldn't expand enough. There simply wasn't enough air getting in. "I can't breathe."

"Entend ces mots, ceux qui marchent de l'autre côté
Viens à lui, Nous t'invoquons.
Vie, mort, renaissance
Présent, passé, futur convergent," Story recited and finally opened her eyes.

"Seriously," Seth gulped.

Story moved to stand in front of him, placing her hands on his thighs. "It's okay."

"But I can't…get a breath," he stuttered.

"Seth, it's normal. It's okay."

Seth shook his head, watching her take the bowl and move away. "Are you sure you put the…right dose of…stuff in there?"

Story returned to him, taking his left hand in both of hers. "Yes, I'm sure. Nothing will harm you. You can't breathe because that is how you found your gift the first time."

Seth drew his eyebrows together. His left hand clenched at his thigh just above his knee. He hated the feeling as it was, but now she'd reminded him of the panic, the claustrophobia of the cave.

"Look at me." Her calm voice drew his attention, hypnotizing. "You're going to lie down now," she instructed, helping to lower him onto the table.

The steel was icy against his back. His flesh broke out in goosebumps once more, and he felt his body shiver, despite his efforts to control it. "Story?"

"I'm here," she said, leaning over him. Her hair framed her face, and the smell of her perfume mingled with the smoke. "Seth, you have to let go."

His body shook. "Let go of what?" his teeth chattered.

"Of your body, Seth," she said. Story leaned down. Her hair brushed his face. Her breath whispered in his ear. "Lâcher," she said in French. *Let go.*

Seth blinked out of sleep, out of the darkness of his shuttered eyes. The cold hospital ceiling came into view. Ceiling tiles, a vent pouring out cold air. His mouth felt dry, tongue thick, and his neck stiff. He rolled his head to the left. Story's bag and things remained on the table. He was in the mortuary, and nothing had happened.

"Well, fuck. That was useless," he remarked, rolling his head to the right, more to ease the tension in his neck. Mistakenly, he opened his eyes and looked at Sarah Elizabeth. She remained in repose, her lips washed-out rose, a hint of blue under her eyes. As he was about to look away, a shadow of movement stopped him, and instead of looking away, he watched as Sarah's head slowly dropped so that she was now facing him.

Seth's muscles tensed. His stomach clenched. Sarah's eyes gently opened.

"Shit!" Seth bolted upright.

The gurney swayed. His boots clanged on the metal like an inept steel band drummer. He was half-on, half-off the gurney when her arm slipped out of the bag, flopping down to her side. Seth catapulted himself off the metal table, sending it clattering and bouncing off the table at the far end of the room. Some detective instinct in him looked at her loose hand—the casual, almost balletic grace in it—and followed the direction across the floor, toward him and beyond. The door to the room was partially open, and outside, there were no lights.

Seth moved to the door, gripped it with his fingers, and, with a caution that was more instinct as a police officer than fear, carefully opened it. His body pressed to the frame, leaning out just enough to see down the hall back toward the office, and swiveled to look down the other way. A light was on farther down. There was a room. Seth assessed it and stepped into the hall. He moved down toward the light and experienced a most distressing sensation. He felt tipped off his axis, like the building was upside down, gravity pulling him upward, while his feet remained stuck to the linoleum. A strong compression clamped down on his skull and he had to shut his eyes to endure the pain. When the sensation left, he found himself in a different hallway. This one had rich wood floors, warm light, a homey feeling overriding the underlying smell and aesthetic of an institution.

Doors came at intervals on each side of the hall, all of them bright with light or pitch black, none emitting a sound. He picked up his pace, striding down the hall, moving so fast he almost missed the door where, at last, a sign of life presented itself. Seth paused, turning back at the sound of a child's laughter. He quietly backtracked to a door with soft light emanating from within and the sensation of life.

Seth peered inside. The walls were a mural of animals and plants, a wild rainforest ripe with leopards, snakes, bright toucans and parrots, and monkeys swinging from vines. The floor was a plush carpet, green and brown, like grass and dirt, to match the mural. An assortment of toys, a bead maze in primary colors, rainbow stacked donuts, and a xylophone were all pushed close to the wall. Just off center on the floor sat a baby doll. So where did the giggle come from?

Seth opened the door, stepping inside. On the floor around the doll, a complex puzzle with scattered pieces was being assembled. He was so busy looking at it, he failed to notice the baby doll turn and look up at him. The doll smiled, dimpled cheeks round and bright, hands slapping up and down, clutching a puzzle piece in one chubby fist.

A sense of trepidation took hold of Seth's bowels. This was not a doll.

"Hi, Seth," the baby garbled. There was a slight speech impediment, most likely because of youth, causing the *th* in Seth's name to sound like an *f*.

The baby jostled once more, bouncing on its butt, waggling its chubby arms.

Seth was overcome with a feeling of the uncanny, the surreal. *This is a dream.*

"It's not," the baby said.

Seth opened his mouth to speak, not a single word available.

"You've gone ahead, not back," the baby said.

A baby this young forming full sentences scrambled Seth's brain. He was so baffled, his body was incapable of sorting out what emotion he should be experiencing.

"Ahead?" he managed to ask.

The baby looked down at the puzzle and put the piece clutched in its chubby hand into place. "You're looking for Neil Owens."

Seth narrowed his eyes. "I was looking for Sarah Grahams. I'd like to talk to her or see what happened."

The baby spread its small stubby fingers, reaching out for another puzzle piece, which it promptly stuck in its mouth. After a moment, the baby removed the saliva-covered piece of cardboard, eyes roaming the ground, seeking a place for it. "But you went ahead," the baby replied. "So, you get to talk to me."

Seth looked around, leaned back out into the hall, peering up and down. *Think,* he told himself.

"Cleo," she answered.

Seth moved closer, squatting down to be on the baby's level. "Cleo. That's a nice name. Do you know Sarah Grahams?"

A garbling chuckle of infant laughter bubbled into the room. Cleo bounced on her butt again, rocking her whole body. She dropped the puzzle piece and reached for Seth, hands opening and closing.

"You want me to pick you up?" Seth smiled as he reached over and picked her up. Cleo wiggled in Seth's arms until he shifted her to his hip. She was so small, so precious, she should be cradled and supported, not holding herself up and grabbing onto him like he was a fleshy jungle gym.

Cleo grabbed Seth's hair, the soft curls at the back of his neck alluring in their texture and color. But then she leaned over, looking down at the puzzle from this higher vantage.

"Gah," she said, leaning farther down, her chubby hand clawing for a piece on the ground. Seth bent with her, and she picked it up, then slotted it into place. She repeated that with another seven pieces before she fidgeted in his arm, indicating she wanted down. Seth sat her back in place on the floor.

"Thank you," she said.

"You're welcome. Cleo?" Seth prompted the baby to pay attention, which felt beyond abnormal. *Why am I talking to her like she's a twelve-year-old child, not a baby?* he thought. "I need to find information about Sarah Elizabeth Grahams."

"I know," Cleo answered. "I told you. You're looking for Neil."

"Neil Owens? Head of the Orbriallis Institute?"

Cleo's whole body rocked, which Seth took to be her form of a nod. "The Green Man will lead you to him."

Seth's brow wrinkled in deep confusion. "The Green Man? Cleo, who is—" A cold hand cut off Seth's next words. It clamped down on his calf, fingernails digging into his flesh.

"They did this to me," said the corpse, clinging to him. The face was swollen with exposure to the water, her flesh mottled in veins of blue and green. Seth tried to place her face while she reached another hand up, grasping hold of the pocket of his pants. Then it hit him. It was Kelly Fulson. He felt himself sink. A flash glance at Cleo, who was shifting her little body, crawling toward him. Seth caught a fleeting glance of a woman in a black veil walking through a door hidden in the wall before he found himself plunged into the roiling, blustering depths of deep, dark water.

His body was pushed and pulled, the undercurrents warring with the weight of Kelly Fulson clinging to him. Bubbles floated past him, and he looked down to see she was speaking, though the words came out only as a muted sound. He kicked, hoping to pull them both to the surface, his lungs burning. A speckle of light danced above him. He was too far down. He'd never make it before his lizard brain begged him to open his mouth, to suck in air.

Somewhere, he recalled what Story told him. Think of loved ones. Seth recalled his mother, doting and fierce. He thought of his passions, of solving this case. His legs kicked, his arms swung, clinging at the elusive grip of the water. Was he supposed to feel this? Was it supposed to feel this real? Could this kill him? He had to get out of this, back to his body. This wasn't real. This was just an out-of-body experience. So why did it feel like he was dying? Panic surged forth, overcoming his reason, his thoughts of parents, family, lovers.

And then a hand gripped him. He looked up and saw a boat far above, but there was no way the person could have just stuck their hand in the water and taken hold of him. Regardless, he clung to that hand with desperation and pulled. Whoever held him had a firm grip and lifted him with a fierce tug.

Seth jolted, gasping, on the steel table. The bright lights of the autopsy room greeted him. He sucked air into his lungs. His shirt and pants clung to him, thick with sweat.

On the floor next to him, Story bolted upright, stumbling a little as she stood too quick from her trip into the Otherworld. "Seth, you're okay," she said, grasping for him as he flailed. "I'm here," her soft, velvet voice cooed.

Seth latched onto her biceps, pulling her close while also steadying himself. He felt off-balance, lost in the recovery of the weightless support of water and the real world of gravity.

Story took a hold of him and brushed a cool hand across his forehead to get his hair out of his face. Seth could have died with the relief and comfort that cold hand brought. He leaned into her, his head falling onto her collarbone as he struggled to regain his breath. When he inhaled, her subtle flower-and-vanilla scent wound its way into his stomach, reminding him he was alive and human and very much aware of this woman's warmth, scent, and proximity.

From the corner of the room, Wes offered a small bowl of cold water and a washcloth that he laid on the table beside Seth.

It took a moment of concentrated effort, but finally, Seth looked up at him, able to control his equilibrium. He saw Wes staring at Story with a new sense of, what was it, wonder, intrigue, fear, or respect?

"Here," Story said, moving to grab the washcloth. She wrung it out and pressed it to the back of Seth's neck. It felt like heaven.

"You look a mess," Wes said to dilute the thick air of discomfort hanging in this cold exam room.

Seth laughed and cast another glance in his direction as he swung his legs over the side of the table. "I feel it," he said as he reached up and pressed both of Story's hands and the cool washcloth against his neck. "What...what happened?"

Story gently extricated her hand and the cloth, dunking it back into the cool water, wringing it out, and handing it to Seth. "Another energy that is connected to all this wanted your attention."

"I—"

"Don't formulate it into words just yet," Story interrupted. "You need time to digest everything. There's no rush." She cleared her throat, stepping back and rubbing a hand over her shoulders. "Do you mind if I take a moment?"

Seth looked up and noticed the sheen of sweat at the base of her throat, the drained pallor of her lips. "No," he said, shaking his head.

Story turned to Wes. "Is there a bathroom?"

"Just down the hall, turn left," Wes said, indicating with his hand where she should go.

Alone now, Wes walked closer to Seth. He held out a bottle of water.

"Oh, Jesus. Thank you." He hungrily took the bottle, screwing open the cap and chugging so hard the plastic crinkled.

"She's good," Wes mentioned. He was observing the tools of Story's trade laid out on the table where he normally placed surgical instruments.

Seth gulped down the last bit of water, wiping his mouth with the back of his arm. "Story?"

Wes nodded before turning to his former high school baseball teammate, leaning back against the solid stainless steel table. "She asked me to get the water, rag, and bowl. When I brought it all in here, she was lying down, there, on the floor. Forty seconds later, you both came to. She was in and out with you in just under two minutes."

Seth turned to look at the clock on the wall, indicated by the subtle movements of Wes's eyes. "It's been an hour and a half."

"Yeah. Took my mom hours. She said it took time to find the other side, the one time she'd talk to me about it."

Seth turned back, feeling a crick in his neck from lying on the hard table. The sweat on his body was drying, cooling him in the already chill examination room. A creeping sensation rippled up his back, but he didn't want to turn and look at Sarah Elizabeth's body.

"I covered her up," Wes said, sensing the shift in Seth's body language. He visibly relaxed.

"Did you…talk to her? Find her on the other side?" Wes asked.

Seth shook his head and pushed off the table, stretching. "I wasn't looking for her. I was…hell, I don't know what I was doing."

"I thought it was going to be her—Story—that was going to travel. When you brought her in here, I just figured…but it was you."

"Yeah." Seth groaned. "I could have made that more clear. It's just, well, I didn't really know if it would work."

"But you can do it? Spiritwalk, that is."

Seth shrugged, looking at the door to see if Story would return. He felt she'd better explain what it was he had done here. "I don't know what it's called."

"When did you have your first—" Wes cut himself off, exuding a subtle laugh. "I'm asking too much. Pressing too hard. I did it with my mother, too. Always wanted to know what she saw."

After a long moment of consideration, Seth answered, "The cave."

Wes regarded him, knowing the story of the boy in the cave and how he came to be rescued.

"I had a vision. At the time, I thought it was a dream. I thought I was dying." He laughed. "But then the other day, there it was. The whole scene. Every nuance, every breeze, every staccato crash of the waves. Everything was identical to what I'd experienced, envisioned, while trapped in that cave."

"Do you mean the scene? Her scene on the beach?" Wes asked, gently pointing to the deceased.

Seth dared a glance at the body, wrapped back up, sealed for preservation until the funeral home came to collect her when Wes signed his release of the body. "Yeah," he said with a grimace.

"Jesus." Wes shifted, folding his arms tight across his chest, his shirt protesting against his wide, solid shoulders.

Seth had just enough presence of mind to ask, "Did you find out anything yet? You said you examined Bess."

"It's still early on. I need to do a full autopsy, but my initial examination has all signs pointing to what it looked like—a murder-suicide."

Seth nodded. He had expected nothing else, despite his trepidation.

"I'll call you with updates as I make my way through the process. I'll let you get yourself together," Wes said and exited the room.

Seth sat in silence, the visions, the experience still vivid, the opposite of a dream escaping consciousness after seconds upon waking. "Dr. Neil Owens," he said to himself.

Story sat on a chair in the blink-and-you'll-miss-it waiting room outside Wes's office, meditating, waiting for Seth to come out. She had gone in to gather her things and could tell Seth still needed time to himself. She didn't mind some time alone, either. When she felt the troubled spirit walk through the room, she knew there was more attached to what Seth sought. Her instincts told her he needed her help. He was easy to find. Their connection was linked. Her younger sister, Asterin, would have smirked and said, "I told you so," for she believed that love was a strong fate line that influenced most actions or inactions in the daily lives of people, witches or not.

The trail leading to Seth had been strange. Story traversed a hall and was briefly pulled into a birthing room, the occupants chaotic as if something had gone drastically wrong. There was a teenage girl in the doorway who watched her fly by, a look of astonishment on her face that Story didn't like. Occupants of the past or future should not have seen her, but this girl had. Then she used the power of imagination, the power of her feelings, the strange tingly emotion she had every time she saw Seth Wolfe on the street, or the warm glow she felt on her skin when he laid his eyes on her, and she found herself in a boat on the ocean thrusting her hand into the sea. His hand latched onto hers, and she pulled her spirit back to her body, trailing his with her. She felt it had been an intimate encounter that only she had wittingly been a part of, and she needed time to remove herself from those emotions.

The door creaked open, and Story stood up, jacket slung over her arms, scarf hanging loose around her neck. "You okay?" she asked Seth.

He nodded and gave her a faint smile before turning to Wes, who was seated back in his office. "Thank you, Wes. You made this…much easier than I was expecting."

Wes stood, coming to the doorway, and nodded at him. "Don't mention it. I think we all share something now, an understanding of the beyond," he said, looking from Seth to Story.

"We do," she responded with a smile.

"I'll be in touch, Seth. About the rest," Wes said.

Seth nodded, walking slowly past the office to join Story.

Story turned to Wes. "Oh, how are the twins?"

Wes opened his mouth, a slow smile taking hold of his lips. "I'm sure you know."

"I do. But it's polite to ask. I'm glad the issues at the daycare were resolved."

Seth raised his brow at Wes, who returned his look with an expression of maybe some other time. Seth turned to grab his coat and stumbled over his own feet, just catching himself on the arm of the chair.

Wes moved to help but found Seth had control of himself. "You need a drink."

"You need an elixir," Story corrected politely. "I'll drive you back to my place. You look dead on your feet," she said, holding out her hand for his keys.

"I'll be alright to get us there," Seth said.

"Sure?" she asked.

He nodded. "Can't have you driving the police car."

"Ah, right. Yes," she said, forgetting for a moment that they'd arrived in the police-issued Bronco, not his personal vehicle. Though for the amount he drove it around, it almost felt like it was his personal vehicle.

Seth turned to Wes before leaving. "Thank you. Sincerely."

Wes nodded. "You're welcome, Spiritwalker."

Party at Story's

Arriving at Story's home was a glorious, welcome relief from the sleeting, chilling rain. Seth couldn't recall another year such a desperate chill took hold of Lost Grove. They'd had lovely, fluffy snowfall now and again in the past, but nothing as monstrous as this fall since the colossal storm passed through two weeks ago.

Seth entered behind Story, shaking his jacket off. "Should I hang this…?"

"Just there," Story instructed, pointing to the coat rack in the vestibule. She walked off into the home, leaving him to remove his coat. Story typically exited out the back way, with a much smaller mudroom where she hung her coat and satchel or left her muddy boots from gardening. She hung her things, then fixed her hair as she made her way back to find Seth observing her dining room with a faint smile.

"Thinking of the other witch again?" Story asked.

Seth laughed. "No. I mean, she did pop in my head, but I was more just taking in another room in your home." The formal dining room held a massive wood table partially covered in a drop cloth. The 1980s wallpaper half peeled off to reveal a stunning hand-painted wallpaper beneath. It appeared as if Story was trying to preserve the original wallpaper as best she could while removing the outdated, more modern one.

"And you're thinking what?"

He looked over at her, surprised to see her face and posture exuding timidity. Story always came across so assured and in control. She was biting her bottom lip, which somehow made her even more alluring than usual. "I think the house suits you. I've only seen two rooms, but its aura feels very Story Palmer."

Story giggled. "Look at you using words like *aura*."

Seth shrugged. "What can I say? Between this case, my…experiences, and your influence, I feel a very changed man."

"And you look it. In a good way."

Seth's motioned to the dining room and then across to the sitting room. "Did the home come furnished, or did you—"

"It was fully furnished. I took the long drive to Lost Grove, just me and my car and anything I could fit in it. Mainly clothes, books, and accessories," she said with a grin.

"Right, from Nova Scotia." Seth itched the side of his head. "So, what on earth brought you here?"

Story's grin grew wider, thinking that her sister, Asterin, would say "true love" or something of the like. "Let's just say a number of signs pointed me here."

Seth nodded. The explanation made perfect sense to him. Six months ago, he would have thought the response was a flight of fancy, but now he could see himself deciding outcomes based on a sign. Look at what they'd just done. "Would you mind if I clean up? Wash my face?"

"Please," she said, pointing down the hall. "Bathroom's second door on the right. Should be towels in the linen cupboard. I'll be in the kitchen just past there when you're done."

Seth nodded a thank you and meandered down the hall. He liked the way the wood floors creaked under his feet. The bathroom was luxurious, smelling of soap and jasmine, with a black-and-white tile floor, a clawfoot tub, a white porcelain sink, and bronze fixtures. The light was soft. A small rectangular window with a complex latch sat up near the ceiling. He quietly shut the door, admiring its glass handle.

"Are these all original to the home?" he wondered aloud as he unbuttoned his shirt and spun the hot water lever on the sink. A wooden wardrobe set into the wall held the fluffiest towels he'd ever seen. He pulled one from the shelf and jumped when he heard the tinkle of a coin falling on the tile. He looked down to see a copper penny turned green spinning round and round.

Seth bent and grabbed it, holding it between thumb and index finger, and set it on the edge of the sink, where steam was now rising. He turned on some of the cold water, taking in his worn-looking reflection in the slowly fogging mirror. "Jesus, you need some sleep," he admonished himself and removed his shirt and undershirt.

With the bar of soap smelling of eucalyptus and citrus, he washed his face and neck and then dried himself off, feeling refreshed. Seth grabbed his undershirt, which was still damp from his vision. The thought of putting it back on made him cringe. He considered just throwing it in the open wastebasket but thought it would be a strange sight. He folded it up instead and put on his long-sleeve police shirt.

Seth exited the bathroom and backtracked to grab his pen and notepad from his coat, setting his undershirt at the foot of the rack. He then followed the sound of china into a kitchen that somehow remained periodic whilst also being stunning in both size and modernity.

"I made you a coffee," Story said with her back to him.

"Thanks." Seth moved toward her, to the massive island that looked like it was something from an industrial kitchen. He imagined women around it with rolling pins, flour dusting the top and clouding the air. "Was this all here when you moved in as well?"

Story turned with a mug, placing it on the island near her. "No. I've done some updating over the past three years." She smiled at Seth and then turned back to finish making her own cup.

Seth wondered where she got her money from. The house itself must have cost a fortune, and he shuddered to think how much the kitchen updates cost. He walked around to find a stool he was glad to sit on, still shaky on his feet. He set his pen and notepad aside, pulling the warm cup into his hands. "I thought you were making me an elixir."

Story moved back over to him, stirring a small spoon in her cup. "There's more than sugar and cream in there."

"Ah," he said, lifting the cup. The coffee had a deep roast that tickled his nose. He took a sip, savoring the perfect sweetness, the creaminess just right. There was a hint of fruit, a touch of something bitter beyond the coffee bean itself, and a sprinkle of molasses. All of it combined into a strange but delicious cup of coffee.

Story sat next to him, hooking her heels on the bar of the stool. She cupped her own coffee below her chin, hiding behind the mist rising from the warm drink. They savored their drinks in silence, while Seth pondered his experience, constantly distracted by the house and the woman who lived in it.

"We don't have to talk about it," Story said before a sip of her coffee. "I want you to know you don't have to share, is all."

Seth looked at her. "No, I need to. I think it would help, to be honest. I don't think I can make sense of it. Besides, I'm used to working with a partner, so using you as a sounding board would be helpful."

Story nodded and set her cup down. She ran her hand over the smooth, time-worn marble countertop, then drummed her nails on it in a pretty little rhythm.

"What did you see?" Seth asked.

Story peeked at him beneath her bangs. "I was in a boat, a small boat, surrounded by a vast ocean. And I saw your hand, reaching up and out of the water."

His brow wrinkled. "That's all?"

She raised an eyebrow. "I had a path to get to you, but what I saw is not what matters. This was your quest." She didn't want to go into the details of how personal, how intimate, her journey in locating him had been for her. "What did you see?"

Seth, mid-sip, quickly put down his cup. "I didn't think anything had happened at first. I was in the morgue. Sarah was next to me. Then… then her head turned to look at me. But not intentionally. More like it fell. And then her eyes opened. I jumped off the table so quick…I mean, call me a hardened homicide detective, but dead bodies aren't supposed to move, you know?"

"Not typically." Story smirked.

"Her hand," he said somberly. "It fell out from under the sheet, and it was pointing me out into the hall. I figured she was trying to tell me something. It's not like I know how these visions work."

"No one knows how they work. All visions are unique to each individual. They've been different for me nearly every time I try one. Dreamlike. Surreal. Too real."

"So there's no one way? I feel like Sarah always received her visions in a singular fashion," Seth commented.

Story tipped her head. "How much have you come to know about her visions?"

He shrugged. "Not much, just…"

"Intuition?"

Seth sighed, smiling. "Yeah."

"So you left the room?"

He nodded and took another drink of his coffee elixir. "I left the room, into the hall, and there was this moment that felt like I was being compressed and moving at the same time. I thought I was going to vomit. But I ended up in a different hall. There were doors on each side, sometimes lit up, sometimes dark, but nothing in them. Then I heard this giggle, a baby giggle. So I turned back at the sound and opened the door to this room where light was coming from. It was painted with a mural of a rainforest. The floor was thick carpet, lush and green. And there was a doll on the floor. Well, there were a lot of toys, old-fashioned ones, but there was this doll sitting in the middle of the floor surrounded by a puzzle. At least I thought it was a doll because it was too small. I mean, a baby would have been too young to be sitting up on its own, supporting its own weight. Does that make sense?"

"I think so," she responded.

"So, I looked around to see where the giggle came from. But then the doll moved. She turned around and looked at me and said, 'Hi, Seth.'" He huffed and shook his head at the haunting memory. Or was it the future again?

"The baby spoke?"

Seth nodded. "Yeah, but it was very proper, beyond the years of any infant. She said, 'You've gone ahead, not back.' Jesus, the way she spoke. And then I looked down to see that she was putting the puzzle together. Not like one of those wood baby puzzles, a proper 500-piece puzzle."

"What else did she say?" Story asked, sipping her coffee.

Seth sighed and ran a hand through his damp hair. "I don't remember the order in which this all came, but she told me I was looking for Neil Owens. Have you heard of him since you moved here?"

"The man who runs the Institute?"

"Indeed. But no one knows him. No one sees him. He's still running the place, but hell if anyone outside the Institute has seen him. So, I tell the baby, who's completely unperturbed by my presence, I tell her I'm looking for Sarah. And she smiles, this adorable cherub smile, and bounces on her butt, and she tells me, 'But you went ahead, so you get to talk to me.'"

Story's brow knitted together, and her eyes drifted to the countertop. After a moment, she looked back up at Seth. "You went forward in time. She knew you wanted to go back, to see who had done this to Sarah, but instead you'd gone forward."

"Is that what she meant?"

"I believe so. It's hardly up for much interpretation," Story explained.

"I don't think a young child, granted her abilities, would have any concept of subliminal nuances, you know, read-between-the-lines sort of thing. I think she was literally telling you you'd gone ahead in time."

Seth rubbed his eyes.

"Did she tell you her name?"

"Cleo," Seth responded. He ran a hand down his face and rubbed his bearded chin.

"Cleo, Cleo," Story repeated, tapping her index finger to her chin, pondering over the name. What could it mean? Why had someone chosen it for this gifted child? Story was relatively certain she knew who the baby was, who she belonged to, but it wasn't time to voice this.

"Does that mean anything to you?" Seth asked and took a healthy drink from the much-needed elixir, which was already helping to bring him fully back to his senses.

Story shook her head, coming back to the present. "Could. Cleo means celebration, glory. I don't know…"

Seth wanted her to voice her thoughts. He could tell she had many of them.

"What happened next?" Story asked.

"I asked her if she knew Sarah, and she went all happy and bouncy again."

"Of course she did," Story said, a subtle lift at the corner of her mouth.

Seth wrinkled his brow for a millisecond before it came to him. "I was looking for Sarah, but I went ahead, so I got Cleo. Her baby?"

"It certainly seems like it."

"Holy shit." Seth fell forward onto his elbows, resting on the island countertop. "Why can she talk?"

"That I don't know. I get the feeling things got a little mixed up. Your belief in yourself still rests in the fantastical, so perhaps your vision was more dreamlike, not an actual direct link, like the one you had in the cave," Story reasoned.

"So, I moved ahead in time but also wasn't actually speaking with a baby?"

Story smiled. "Think of it this way. You know Sarah in death. You know she has a baby. So when you go in search of answers, the ones that come fit inside the forms you have preconceived inside your head. That is not to say it wasn't her daughter you spoke to, just you spoke to her in the guise you could picture. A baby. The very baby you are looking for and hoping to help."

"And the other woman was Kelly," Seth whispered, his eyes drifting toward his coffee elixir.

"The one who pulled you into the ocean where I found you?" she asked and took a sip of coffee.

He nodded. "It took me a second to recognize her, but it was definitely her. She was telling me, 'They did this to me.'"

Story swallowed. "And who is Kelly?"

Seth looked up at her. "Oh, right. She, um, Kelly Fulson was a young girl from Lost Grove, around Sarah's age, who disappeared a little over eight years ago. She was missing for sixteen months before she turned up dead at the edge of a local farmer's property."

Story's senses percolated as her eyes widened.

"Yes. And here's the other thing. Kelly was also pregnant."

"Oh my God. Was her child missing, too?"

Seth shook his head. "It was still inside her. She was seven months pregnant."

Story covered her mouth. "Do you think…"

"I do now. I had a strong gut instinct telling me the cases were linked. But now? After she showed up in my vision, coming from the past, even though I was in the future…they have to be."

Story set her coffee down and dropped her head into her hands.

"What?"

"Nothing," she sighed, looking up and moving her hands to the side of her face. "I fear I may have fudged it all up."

Seth smiled at her word choice. "Fudged it up, how?"

Story's mouth pursed into an enticing, demure pout. "I asked for past, present, and future in the spell. I invited them all in. I shouldn't have done that to you."

"How would you have known—"

"I wouldn't, but that doesn't excuse the mistake."

Seth laughed. "It worked out, though, didn't it? In a way, it worked out."

"It could have been better," Story said, standing and taking the cups to the sink.

Seth watched her rinse the dishes, place them in her dishwasher, and wipe her hands. "You're exacting about this stuff, aren't you?"

She turned to him, eyes wide. "Of course. One needs to be exacting with this sort of stuff," she said, playfully mocking his use of words and returning to sit beside him.

"It's funny to think how I would have treated this case back in San

Francisco. I wouldn't have believed."

"I dare say the obscenities of this case are the only reason you are even contemplating there's truth to what you've seen," Story whispered.

Seth met her eyes, caught the dancing fire inside them, though there was no candlelight to reflect off them. "It is true what they say about you."

Story hesitated, wanting to hear him say it, wanting to hear him acknowledge what she was. "What do they say about me?"

Seth found himself unable to speak it aloud. All the logic in his personality demanded he not utter the word, but he knew it needed to be said. His mouth opened, paused, breath held tight in his lungs before at last he uttered, "Witch."

Inhaling slowly, Story leaned back from the man in front of her. Humor tugged at the corners of her lips, but she was filled with a sense of relief, joy even. "Ah, the infamous phrase that had women tortured and murdered for centuries."

"You are one. And not like, not like the people who…"

"Those people are witches, too. Just a different kind." Story leaned forward, hands together, resting on the counter.

Seth laughed, losing control of his laughter for a moment before reeling it back in.

"It's only natural to question things. To lack belief. The same as it is for many to believe entirely in long-dead gods and false prophets. But you believe in yourself, don't you?"

The question gave Seth pause. Did he believe in himself? His solve rate was nearly flawless. He had confidence in how he carried himself, how to handle intense situations. "Yes. I believe in myself."

"Then the other part of you is something you need to believe in, too."

It felt like he did and also like it would take time for him to truly understand and accept what he was capable of.

"So, you know what you need to do now, yes?" Story asked.

"Yeah, I guess so. Talk to the elusive recluse, Dr. Neil Owens. Oh! Cleo also mentioned something about a green man showing me the way." Seth noticed Story visibly stiffen. "What?"

"She said the Green Man?" Story asked.

Seth sat up, alert. "Yes. What…does that mean something to you?"

Her hesitation was palpable. It made him tense, his body alert, senses heightened.

"When I first moved here, I saw something I couldn't explain."

Story's voice wavered before continuing. "Even now, it gives me chills. There is a man who stalks the woods, but there is a preternatural, ghost-like quality to him."

Seth's brow knitted tightly, his hands moving to the notepad cast aside on the top of her kitchen island.

"I've sought him out, to curse him," she explained, catching Seth's eyes so he could understand what she said next.

"Curse?" he asked.

"That is not a light thing for my kind. It is not something you put out in the world. But I am willing to do it because this man felt like the incarnation of horror. He's a predator."

"A killer? Does he live in Devil's Cradle?" Seth asked after a moment's pause. Her eyes bored into his, delivering some unsaid meaning, telling him and not telling him so many things. He flipped open the pages of his notepad. "Give me a description of him," he said, readying his pen.

Story reached out and held his hand. "I've searched for him for three years. Mary has seen him as well. He can't be found, he can't be called out…we can't find him. I can't find him. I have tried everything in my powers and the powers that be, but he will not show himself to me again. You won't be able to find him. Not unless he wants you to see him. He only shows himself to certain people."

Bile rising, Seth wanted to push the question down, so fearful was he of her answer. "Who does he show himself to?"

Story hesitated before responding. "Children."

A knock on the door startled them both out of their conversation. Story frowned but rose and moved to answer it. Seth, feeling the timing was quite ominous, followed her.

The massive front door opened to the soggy, frigid world outside. Zoe, cheeks red with cold, beamed up at Story.

"Ms. Andalusian, to what do I owe the pleasure?"

Zoe leaned to peer around Story, spotting the police officer behind her. With a massive grin on her face, she turned back to her brother, who was just coming up the stairs, his face painted with his charming, polite smile. "Told you," she said to him.

Noble's face faltered for a moment when he noticed Sergeant Seth Wolfe standing next to the librarian. "Uh…"

"Mr. Andalusian? Is something wrong?" Story asked.

"Yeah," he muttered.

This shifted Story's kind expression. She looked between the children, toward the road to the other teenagers, and reached out a hand to Zoe. "Zoe, are you alright?"

"I'm fine. But they need to talk to him," she said, pointing at Seth.

Noble managed to remove himself from his bamboozled daze. "Oh, I mean, nothing's wrong. No, something is wrong, but no one's hurt or in trouble," Was it a coincidence that Seth Wolfe was here? It had to be. But why had his faithful car stopped just outside the house of the neighborhood witch? And why did his sister know they should come here?

"Someone might be in trouble," Anya said from behind him.

A small hum, more like a song, escaped Story's throat. "Well, come in. It's far too cold outside. I'll make you all hot chocolates, and you can speak with Sergeant Wolfe. Yes?" she asked the last of Seth, who could do nothing but nod.

"Is this about your father?" Seth asked Noble in a quiet aside.

Noble shook his head.

"Jackets can go there." Story pointed to the coat rack and led Zoe into the kitchen.

Noble couldn't help but think of Hansel and Gretel, the witch leading his sister away into her magical house.

"Sergeant Wolfe?" Nate stood at attention, holding out his hand. "It is an honor to meet you. I've read about your cases down in San Francisco. Nate Abbott."

"Uh-huh," Seth said, taking his hand.

Stan jumped in. "Hi, Mr. Wolfe."

"Sergeant," Nate corrected.

"Constance, hello!" Seth exclaimed, his eyes wide. "Jesus, you've grown."

"You should see my brothers," she commented.

"Sergeant Wolfe?" Nate started again.

"Call me Seth," Seth said, slapping Nate on the shoulder, urging him onward. "Let's go inside, settle into a nice place to chat, yeah?"

"Yes, of course. Yes," Nate agreed.

Seth turned to the last of the teenagers and felt a pang of recognition. "I'm sorry, we haven't met. I'm Seth Wolfe."

"Emory Graff," Emory said, placing his hand in the police officer's. Was he surprised to see a touch of recognition in the man's eyes? Not really. San Francisco was a big place, but the way Nate acted, it seemed like this guy was the real deal.

The name jogged Seth's memory. A case about three students involved in a stabbing. There was no evidence on the two accused, and he thought the whole thing was a shambles, a media circus. "Come on in," he said.

Noble had preceded everyone, quickly following his sister. He walked through the entrance to see her concentrating on a jar of milk. Her cheeks puffed out, and the milk bubbled.

Zoe stopped, releasing a spit of laughter, until she looked up to see her older brother watching her.

Noble, falling into yet another stupor, looked from the jar of milk miraculously bubbling to his sister and then over to Story.

Story said nothing, simply pulling the milk away from Zoe and pouring it into a copper pan.

"You know trumpet vines are highly toxic. They're poisonous," Stan remarked upon entering. She'd noticed the array of flowers and plants, particularly the bonsai trumpet vine in the foyer.

Story smiled over her shoulder. "I have oleander and hemlock in the garden. Are you fond of poisonous plants?"

Stan wrinkled her nose. "No."

"Ah." Story grabbed a wooden spoon and stirred what was in the pot. The kitchen bloomed with the scent of vanilla, chocolate, cinnamon, and cream.

"Your friend ran out to your car to grab something," Seth said to the kids, entering behind Emory.

Emory looked around and let out a quiet whistle. "This is nice."

"Thank you," Story responded, a brilliant smile lighting up her face. "I was just about to ask what brought you all here."

"I told them to come here," Zoe offered, nibbling on the edges of a cookie.

Noble didn't see where the cookie had come from, but there was now a plate of them on the island. How had he missed them? Why was milk bubbling not on a stove? Was he hallucinating? He shook it all away, trying to focus. "We were on the way to the police station to see Sergeant Wolfe when my car died."

Story raised her eyebrows. "I see," she said and turned back to the stove, winking at Zoe as she did.

"To see me about what?" Seth asked.

"Okay, alright," Nate huffed, jogging into the room with a backpack slung over one shoulder. "Is this going to be the incident room?"

Stan rolled her eyes.

"Incident room?" Seth queried.

Nate began unpacking. "Emory, pull up the video," he instructed, while he retrieved his tablet. He turned it on, made sure all the right tabs were open, then set it on the island with relish. Next, he removed the map, unfolding and spreading it out, nice and smooth. He took Emory's phone and placed it on the island with reverence. "Guys, phones," he prompted the others.

Stan and Noble brought out their phones, pulling up the images from the cave, along with Nate.

"Set them here," Nate instructed.

Seth crossed his arms, spread his feet wide like he would during a briefing back at the SFPD. Humor lit up his eyes, and a faint smile curled his lips. He looked in Story's direction, caught her smiling back before she pressed her lips together and grabbed several mugs from the cupboards.

Nate took all the phones, laid them out one next to the other. He surveyed the island countertop, adjusted the map a little, then stood back. All the items faced Seth. Clues laid out for him to review.

"Alright, let's start," Nate said.

"Okay," Seth commented.

"Are you familiar with the Horne family?" Nate began.

Seth shook his head. "Can't say that I am."

"So, nine years ago, Antoinetta Horne, we call her Nettie, swore she saw a man peering in her little brother George's window every night, trying to climb in and steal him. Her parents said she was being overimaginative, but Nettie kept saying, 'There's a man trying to steal George.' So, they go to the local police. According to Anya, by way of Nettie," Nate explained, pointing.

Anya raised a hand to wave at Seth, who responded with a nod and a smile.

Nate continued, "Chief Richards went to the Horne house and had a look around. Checked for any vagabonds in the area."

"Vagabonds?" Stan asked, voice thick with sarcasm.

Nate ignored her and plunged onward. "He says there's nothing to worry about. But Nettie keeps insisting. One night, when Nettie was sick, the man came and took George from his bedroom and replaced him with another George, almost identical."

"I'm sorry," Seth said, stopping Nate. "You're saying a boy was kidnapped and replaced with another child? An identical child?"

Nate raised a finger. "That's...let me get to that. So, in comes this new kid who can't talk, can't eat, doesn't even know how to communicate. George was five, so this was a strange turn of events, right? Doctors end up diagnosing New George—"

"Not-George," Anya corrected.

Nate looked at her.

Anya stepped forward. "We call him Not-George."

"Right, doctors diagnose Not-George with late-onset autism. But Nettie doesn't give up. She knows this isn't her brother. She knows that the Green Man took her brother."

Seth practically leapt forward. "What did you just say?"

"The Green Man?" Nate sputtered. When Seth turned it on, his intensity was overwhelming.

Seth looked over at Story, standing stock still with two mugs in her hands. He approached Nate, leaning a hand on the island countertop. "She saw the Green Man?"

"Holy fuck, you already know about him? Man, I thought we were—"

"Nate, I need you to focus. I need you all to focus," Seth said, looking around the room. "Have any of you seen this man?"

They all shook their heads. Then, Noble said, "But we may know where he came from."

Seth's eyes locked on his. "Explain."

Nate kicked back into gear. "Okay, alright, so, last week, Nettie was at family therapy up at the Orbriallis when Not-George said something. Now, this kid doesn't talk, right? He makes noises and gurgles and shit, but no words. So, when he said this, confused as it was, Nettie was sure he was saying something."

Seth's blood ran cold. Orbriallis, Green Man, stolen children.

"She enlists Anya's help to find out if they can make sense of what he said. Anya was in the school library when Noble happened along. He was all like, 'I can help,' so he does some research and…" Nate paused, grabbing his tablet and handing it to Seth.

Seth hesitated to take his eyes off the kid but eventually looked down at the screen.

"'Man and Mother Brought Up On Charges of Sexual Abuse,'" Seth read the article's heading aloud.

"You can see all the tabs of the articles we found. The third and fourth tab are the important ones. They're the ones that mention the nickname Papa LaRange."

Seth lifted his gaze to the kid, his eyebrows lifted with enthusiasm.

"In his search, Noble finds out that the kid who mumbled Bah Bah la Ranch, was saying Papa LaRange. And why is this case in Ohio related to a missing kid out here in Northern California?" Nate reached across the island to tap on the last tab. "Raymond LaRange, aka Papa LaRange, as the girls were instructed to call him, was found unfit for trial and remanded to a state-of-the-art facility, the Orbriallis Institute."

Seth contained the shivers coursing through him and felt the soft, reassuring touch of a warm hand on his arm. Story handed him a fresh cup of coffee, which he promptly took but immediately set down.

Nate held up his hand, locking eyes with Seth. "I can see what you're thinking. Where is this going? Alright, so, Anya and Noble are like, 'Could this be what Not-George said?' Well, Anya's all like, 'Is there a picture of the guy?' There is, by the way, on tabs two and six."

Seth tapped and scrolled, bringing up the man's face. Story looked over his arm. A sharp intake of breath drew Seth to look at her, but she turned away. She'd intimated that she couldn't find the Green Man, but she had to have seen him at least once to know he was a predator, as she'd described him. Seth set that aside to revisit.

"Noble and Anya show Nettie and—" Nate slapped his hands.

Stan jumped. "Jesus, Nate. The theatrics."

He turned to her. "Whatever. Your dad works for the police."

"What?" Stan asked, bewildered.

"Yeah," Nate replied, as if that was an answer, and then turned back to Seth. "Nettie said that's—"

"Hold on." Seth stopped him and turned to Anya and Noble. "You showed your friend, Nettie, this picture?" He held the tablet turned around so they could see.

Noble nodded.

"Yes," Anya replied.

"And she recognized him?"

Anya huddled the warm cup of hot chocolate close to her chest but responded. "She said, 'That's him. That's the man who came to George's window.' She saw him countless nights. You have to understand. She saw him multiple times. And he saw her. He'd wink at her, she told me. It was almost like he was taunting her."

"She was petrified," Noble added. "I mean, she turned white. It was the freakiest thing. You hear people say they turned white as a sheet, but to actually watch it happen is…"

"Okay." Seth set the tablet next to his forgotten coffee. "This man, Raymond LaRange, is a sexual predator being treated at the Orbriallis Institute. But your friend says she's seen him outside, roaming around?"

"At night," Anya confirmed.

"Recently?"

"I don't think since Not-George showed up, but…"

Seth locked eyes with Story. So much to be said within them. Namely, he got the impression she believed what these kids were saying. "And you want me to check and see—"

"Oh, no. There's more," Nate enthused. "We haven't even talked about the not-children."

"The not-what?"

"His children, the ones who follow him around," Story answered. "You went to see Mary."

Noble's shock prevented him from an immediate response. "Um, yes. I…I knew she knew about the not-children. So I thought, maybe she knew more, maybe she knew the Green Man. So, we went to talk to Mary. But she said she didn't know where they came from, only where they stayed."

"In the caves," Stan added.

Seth sighed. "The caves." Noble was heading to the caves the evening he'd gone to relay the news that his father, Peter, was not on the ship he'd promised his family he would be on. That was the same night his officer, Joe, had seen a social media post by one "natethegreat," saying he was going underground, that something was afoot at the Orbriallis. "You're Nate the Great," he said, staring at the boy.

Nate's eyes opened so wide it was like someone told him he had just won a million dollars. "I am," he said dreamily.

"So, anyway," Stan said, redirecting the attention, "Anya, who's closest to Nettie, had this idea. Turned out she was right."

"And that was?" Seth prompted.

"Nettie always said she saw the Green Man come out of a hill behind her house. He and his not-children."

"I'm sorry, why are they not-children?" Seth interrupted.

"Because they're not right. They're not…real," Noble explained.

"That's exactly what Mary says," Story commented.

Seth blinked this away. He didn't have time to fit the details of beings that look like children but aren't into his thoughts right this second. "So, you went to find a hill behind her house, then?"

Nate stepped forward and tapped on the map.

Seth approached.

"Anya found a cave system that, from Nettie's window perspective, would have made it look like LaRange and his child-things were coming out of a hill. But Mary was right." Nate grabbed one phone after the next, laying them out on the map in front of Seth. He tapped on one image, enlarging it.

Seth looked down at a small baby doll covered by a blanket, its eyes half-closed, lashes dusty with dirt.

"That wasn't all we found. There's also this." Nate lifted his phone and held it out for Seth to watch the video he'd taken.

Seth watched the small screen display a cave held up with beams. *An abandoned mine?* he wondered. He'd never heard of anything being mined in the area and, in all his caving adventures, never come across something like this. The video wobbled. He could just pick out the excited breathing of the person operating the camera. If he had to guess, it was Nate. Now the camera shifted. Seth spotted Nate pressed against the stone wall, and carefully, the phone maneuvered around the corner. As he watched, Seth actively had to register what he was seeing. There was a hallway, fluorescent lighting, linoleum floors, and a door. The last thing he caught was the blinking red light of a security camera in the upper corner.

Seth took the phone from the teenager's hand, pausing the video.

"We have a bunch of photos," Nate said, his body buzzing. "And that's not the only video we have. Look, we tracked the route we took through the cave," he explained, tracing the line with his finger across the map before stopping and tapping the X. "It ends here, at that secure door. Can you guess where this is?"

"I don't need to guess," Seth said.

"There's nothing else around it. This door has to lead into the Orbriallis Institute. And check this," Nate explained, grabbing Emory's phone.

"Emory and his sister Ember are being treated at the Orbriallis. They're undergoing these sleep studies, right? So, one night, this past weekend, Emory can't sleep. He goes wandering around the place, not thinking much of it, and then he catches this shit." Nate handed the phone over to Seth, who pressed play.

He watched as young people were loaded into pods, connected to wires, and injected with serums, but it was the kid who looked at the camera, shook his head in one imperceptible nod, that made his skin prickle. "What the hell is this?"

"It's in the basement," Emory explained. "I didn't know it was off-limits. I pressed a button. The elevator took me there. If it was meant to be restricted, I shouldn't have been able to go down there."

"They didn't want you there, and yet they let you go," Seth commented.

Emory opened his mouth to say something but found he couldn't explain it to this adult, to this figure of authority.

"That kid," Nate said, leaning over and tapping the phone. "That kid is George Horne. Here." Nate turned to Anya. "Show him your pictures."

Anya removed her phone from the island and pulled up images of Nettie and her brother as children and showed it to Seth. She then found one of Not-George, a family photo from Christmas a year or two ago. She showed that one to Seth as well. Each time, he scrutinized them.

"Emory, tell him about your treatment," Nate urged, seeing this all coming to a standstill.

"My sister and I were transferred here for PTSD, because of the case that I'm pretty sure you're aware of," Emory started.

Seth looked up from Anya's phone. "I recall it."

"What!" Nate exclaimed. "Oh, right. You guys were both totally in San Francisco at the same time."

Emory chuckled and nodded. "Right, well, everything was normal at first," he said, looking back at Seth. "We talked about our feelings, our anger, who we were outraged with. My sister, she won't talk, so they work on trying to make her come out of her shell. But then we show up one day and start having these one-on-one sessions with a Dr. Bajorek."

"I've met her," Seth said.

"Then you know she's the real deal. I'm thinking, this is interesting. But the thing of it is, she's not asking the right kind of touchy-feely questions. She's asking me about ink blots, she's asking me to look at Zener cards."

"Zener cards?"

"The things from *Ghostbusters*," Story explained. "You know the scene where Bill Murray holds up a card, and he has two students trying to guess what's on it. Star, triangle."

"Yeah, okay. So she's asking you what? To guess cards?"

"She's checking to see if I can guess the card by reading her mind," Emory said.

Seth absorbed his words but couldn't find reason amongst all the details he'd just received. He took a step back, leaning against the countertop behind him.

The teens all waited for what he'd say, how he'd respond.

How did this kid, George, fit in with Sarah Elizabeth? *By proxy*, Seth thought. The Orbriallis is doing something to young people, children. Sarah Elizabeth was being treated there, got pregnant… What did her child have to do with all this?

"Follow the Green Man," Story said.

Seth, and everyone else in the room, turned at the sound of her voice.

"That's what Cleo told you to do. You can follow him both literally and figuratively," she further explained.

Seth began nodding. "All this evidence backs up my suspicions about the Orbriallis Institute."

"So it seems," Story concluded.

Nate, whose eyeballs had been flashing between the two adults, was puzzling it together. "Oh shit! Does the Institute have something to do with Sarah Elizabeth?"

Seth ignored him, continuing to hold his gaze on Story, feeling like there was something there, a piece of the thread he was following just within reach. He didn't want to break it. "There's someone missing, though."

"Who?" Story asked.

"The person who put her on the beach for me to find. They staged her, they had her hand pointing toward the Institute. So how do they know? What do they know?" Seth asked.

The kitchen was heavy with concentrated ruminations when a knock on the door threw them all out of their internal thoughts. Seth felt like the next shoe was about to drop as he followed Story to answer the door.

The Other Shoe

"Dad!" Zoe squeaked, running to her father.

Peter Andalusian caught his daughter with a grunt as she barreled into him. "Hey, sprite," he said before leaning over to kiss her on the temple. Standing back to full height, he locked eyes on whom he knew was Sergeant Seth Wolfe, giving him a subtle nod.

Seth returned the nod in its subtlety. Mr. Andalusian had clearly come back to town to see him, the communication in the quick glance said everything. He wasn't surprised by the height of Peter, Noble being over six feet tall himself, and his wet, dark-blonde hair was the same shade as the daughter he held in his arms. He was clearly still fit, as Seth imagined many former Marines would be.

"Dad?" Noble came up the hallway, spotting his father. His stomach instantly churned like a large vat of butter.

Peter looked past Seth and nodded at his son, feeling his apprehension from ten feet away.

"Oh, hey, Pete-dog!" Nate shouted, coming up behind Noble with Anya, Stan, and Emory in tow.

Peter's eyebrows rose as the onslaught of Noble's friends trickled into the hallway. "Nate, Stan, Ms. Bury," he said with a wave. "New friend."

"Emory," he introduced himself, raising a hand in greeting.

"Do come in," Story suggested, standing aside for Peter and his daughter to step out of the vestibule and into her house.

Noble and Peter met in the foyer, the father reaching up and placing a loving hand on the back of his son's neck. "Hey, kiddo." Peter saw his son's jaw flex. "Sorry for the intrusion," he said to the room, meeting Story's eyes. He offered a warm smile. "I was on my way to the station to see Sergeant Wolfe, but it appears this is where I was meant to be."

"Did your car stop working?" Zoe asked.

Peter looked down at his little girl. "Did my car stop? No. I saw Noble's car out front."

"But how did you know to knock on *this* door?" Seth asked.

Peter looked up and met the detective's eye. "Intuition. It's the only home that made sense. Zo is always at the library, and Noble must have driven her here."

Seth felt a guarded sense of ease. Peter's demeanor was calm, almost acquiescent. "You know the neighborhood better than me."

"That wasn't always true."

Seth shrugged.

Nate leaned over Noble's shoulder and whispered, "What's going on here?"

Noble shrugged Nate away from him.

Peter smiled, letting out a huff of amusement. "But my intuition, which is usually spot on, didn't tell me *you'd* also be here."

"I guess here it is, then," Seth said, nodding toward the sitting room stuffed with books and plants. "That okay?" he asked Story.

Story nodded. "Of course. I'm sure you two have lots to discuss."

"Dad?" Noble leaned forward to grab his father's attention.

"S'okay," Peter reassured his son, pressing Zoe toward her brother.

"Is anyone hungry? I can fix a snack," Story said, gently ushering the Andalusian children and the teens back toward the kitchen while Seth escorted their father into the sitting room.

Seth really wanted to put the man in handcuffs and take him down to the station for questioning, but Peter was here of his own free will. That and the expression on his children's faces were enough to be comfortable doing this here. The look Noble gave his father—anger, distrust, but also love, the hurt of betrayal—gave Seth pause, and it was a look he didn't think he'd soon forget. *I've become a softy,* he thought. *That or this is just the way small-town detective work goes.* Taking statements from witnesses at their home and interviewing murder suspects in a witch's sitting room. This was just part and parcel to not only this case but Lost Grove life.

Peter, smiling at the decor, sat in the lounge seat. "Lot of the same stuff here."

Seth furrowed his brow. "Meaning?" he asked, shifting the chair opposite Peter to face him, and settled himself on its edge.

"Well, I helped Lina move out a few years back. I'm sure you know who that is," Peter said, meeting Seth's eyes.

"I do."

"Do you know where she lives now?" Peter playfully challenged Seth.

"Does it matter?" Seth asked, not in the mood for games.

Peter lifted his eyebrows. "Oh, I think it might. But, seeing as you're in no mood to guess, which I fully understand given this long-awaited moment, I'll just tell you. She lives in the two-story penthouse of the Orbriallis. Dr. Owens forced her into it, claiming he needed the help, as he was getting on in years, which is bullshit."

"How so?"

"I mean, he is getting on in years, but…have you not met him yet?"

Seth simply sighed in response.

Peter held his hands up. "Okay, I get it. I'll just say that you'd agree with me. So"—Peter relaxed further into the chair, ready to get to it—"here we are."

"Here we are." Seth leaned closer to Peter. "I had a perplexing conversation with your friend, Paddy, the other day."

"I heard," Peter replied.

The two men stared at each other. Like most good detectives, Seth knew that one of the best ways to get someone to talk was to let them do it. Sit in silence. Wait them out. They'll fill the silence because most people can't handle the quiet. Peter, he knew, was not most people. He'd have to prompt this conversation into being. "Is that why you're back?"

"We were waiting for you to connect the pieces."

Seth didn't like that he was being played by Peter and his friend. "Withholding evidence?"

Peter tilted his head to the side. "This whole situation is very delicate. Very complex."

"I've gathered," Seth said, his expression growing more stern by the second.

"I have to admit, I'm a little surprised," Peter commented, looking around the room.

Seth followed his gaze. "By?"

"That you haven't put me in handcuffs."

The bluntness of it drew Seth's attention back to the man in front of him. "It's still on the table, believe me."

"I understand. But in all fairness, I'm glad you haven't. I was coming to see you in the slim hopes of avoiding that process."

"Am I making a mistake not putting you in handcuffs?" Seth asked.

Peter smiled. "Very much not."

"Convince me."

Peter nodded. "Paddy gave you an idea of what I may know, what I may have done. I'm here to tell you in my own words. I'm here with hope." Peter paused. "No, I'm here knowing you'll listen."

"And you know this, how?"

"Paddy's good at reading people. And we did our homework. You're a smart man. Your record is clean. You have a solve rate unlike most. What was the percent?"

"You know the percent." Seth smiled, not joyously.

"I do," Peter answered and paused. "That's why I know you'll listen, and I know you'll want to do the right thing. And look, let me clear the air. I know what I'm about to say involves illegal activity. Highly illegal. I have no dreams or notions that I won't serve time for my actions. When it comes time for that, I'll do what is necessary. We just needed your eyes on the Orbriallis before I could come back."

"Why did you believe that? You couldn't have just come forward and saved me and my team a heap of fucking time?" Seth asked, stern, but his voice low.

Peter held up a hand in defense. "I apologize for that. But you wouldn't have believed me."

Seth scooted forward in his chair. "How the hell do you know?"

"I wouldn't have. And even if you did, it wouldn't have solved my very large problem."

"Larger than the hole you're in now?" Seth asked.

Peter kept his eyes measured on Seth's. "You have no idea. But I'll get there. As I said, I'm here to talk. And I promise you I will hold nothing back and answer every question you have."

Seth acknowledged this with a brief nod, believing Peter's intention. "Let's start with the night and morning in question. Tell me what happened. I want to know every detail of your movements that night."

Peter resettled himself to get into the details. "I'll start by making it clear that I work for the Orbriallis Institute. Paddy and I both, in very different capacities. I started working there in 1999. When I got out of Special Ops, I hit up Paddy—already out of the service—looking for a solid gig. He told me to come up to Lost Grove. He said he'd get me a job as a tour guide and introduce me to some folks at Ross Ranch. After I got settled in for a few months, Paddy approached me and told me there was an opportunity to make some more money. He said it was a unique job, a sort of freelance type situation. That's when he set me up for an interview with Dr. Neil Owens."

The chills that ran up Seth's spine were so potent, his right shoulder jerked in a spasm.

Peter could have seen Seth's visceral reaction from a hundred yards away but continued on as if he hadn't noticed. "Dr. Owens told me my time spent with the Marines, the duties I carried out in Special Ops, along with the sterling recommendation from my commander, made me an ideal candidate for a very special job."

Seth couldn't hide the perplexed look on his face.

"Now, I know what you're thinking. You're thinking the same thing I was when he laid this all out to me. What the fuck does a world-renowned research facility need with someone with a Special Ops background?"

"That would be almost word-for-word accurate," he confirmed.

"My job was to facilitate cash flow from government funding to the Institute, to facilitate reports from the Institute to the government agents controlling said funding. I facilitated the movement of patients in and out of the Institute."

Seth shook his head. "Why would they need—"

"Because, unbeknownst to the public, there is a sector of the government funding under-the-table research and experiments, led by Dr. Owens and a special team. Now, I have no knowledge of what they are, but I would bet my balls that one of said experiments involves fertility."

Seth dropped his head into his hands and ran them through his hair. If Peter Andalusian was to be believed, this would confirm Seth's growing suspicion that Sarah Elizabeth never left the Institute. And although he wanted to wring Peter's neck for the dangerous games he was playing, he did, in fact, believe him. What in the blue hell was going on at the Orbriallis?

"You see now why I said you wouldn't have believed me," Peter said. "Not back then. But I believe you've seen enough, learned enough, and uncovered enough where you do believe me now. Is that accurate?"

"Get back to the night in question," Seth said, ignoring the question.

Peter nodded. "Fair enough. So, that night I got a message on my phone. It's an alert letting me know I'm needed. I keep a burner in my closet. So I got up and made the call. I was told to come in. That's it."

"What time was this?"

"10:15 p.m.," Peter answered.

"Is it typical to be called at that hour? Did you have a feeling about this call?"

"I will say that the timing of when I'm called is never predictable. I might get two calls a week or two calls in six months. So, no, there was nothing suspicious about getting the message when I did. I arrived and parked in the underground garage, and entered, expecting a standard assignment. But when I walked in, I was met by…Dr. Owens has a nephew, a huge son of a bitch that you would not want to—"

"Seamus?" Seth asked.

Peter paused, his mouth open. "Ah, so you have been there."

"I have."

Peter nodded. "Good. That's good. But you haven't met Dr. Owens?"

Seth stared at Peter, his mind swirling in the background. Just after Sarah Elizabeth's child from the future had instructed him to look for Dr. Owens, another person was suggesting the good doctor was a person of interest. Seth was far past the point of ignoring coincidences in this case. "Not yet. It's high on my list." Seth was still withholding what he would divulge to Peter, waiting to get a better grasp of what he had done and how much more he knew.

Peter narrowed his eyes, trying to read between the lines. What did Seth already know? His silent reaction to Dr. Owens was loaded. "We'll have to talk about that," Peter said. "But back to last Wednesday night. Seamus was there to meet me. He took me to one of the medical wards, still in the lower levels, the sublevels."

"Okay."

"We went into a room and—" Peter stopped. "There was a table, and on the table was Sarah Elizabeth. I almost exploded."

"Did you recognize her?"

"Of course. I'd seen her around town and worked with her at the summer camp. So I turn to Seamus and ask him where the fuck Neil was. He said the doctor was too distraught by the tragic turn of events. I think I said something along the lines of, 'I don't care if he's saving the president's life right now, I want to see him.' I tell him I'm not doing it. But that's not an option. I know the job. I better get it done. Seamus says this with a hint at the gun in the holster on his hip. I felt sick. I felt a lot of things. But I also had a plan. A plan that Paddy and I put in place eight years prior after having my hand forced in a similar situation."

Seth stroked the lengthening stubble on his chin, quickly organizing this watershed of information into the correct mental files. "To get back at them."

Peter smiled. Paddy was right about this guy. He didn't miss a thing. "It's never gonna sound right for me to say, but this was our moment."

"What was her state?" Seth asked.

"Cleaned, wrapped up, and ready for me to do what was needed. So I covered her with the sheet they had her wrapped in and carried her down to the garage. I put her in a Sprinter van. License 4LLT067."

"VIN?"

"453BMHB66H3386050."

"You memorized them?"

"I did. I put her in the van. The orders were explicit. Dump the body deep in the ocean, far enough where there was no chance she would wash back up on shore. On my way to Mourner's, I call Paddy and tell him what's up. So he knows things are about to start. I pull over on the side of the road and pull the van up into the sand, hidden from the road. Not that anyone is up that early. Save for farmers, and they've got farming to do. I carried her out to the driftwood. It seemed—I don't know—peaceful."

"She was nude under the sheet?"

"Yes."

"And you staged her."

Peter nodded. "I could have left the sheet, but they'd have wondered where it was. I tried to give her some decency. Kept her legs together. Then I heard someone running up the beach. So I drop and crawl back toward high ground, slide down a small dip, and plaster myself to the ground. I heard the footsteps slowing down. I know this person sees Sarah now, but there's nothing. No response. No scream. So I lift my head over the edge, and there's Mary Germaine, bending over Sarah, looking at her like…like she's a sculpture to be admired.

"I thought for sure she was going to pull out her phone and dial 911. But she didn't. She just jogged off like she had stumbled upon someone's lost sweatshirt. I wasn't sure if she didn't have reception or what. I scrambled over, keeping low in case Mary looked back, but she was fast and out of sight within a minute. I finished the staging. Her arm extended, hand in a gentle point, as much as I could get it to look like she was pointing. I stood and looked across the inlet, right at the sun hitting the top of Orbriallis Tower, and I swear I hoped it would catch flame. God, I wanted it to."

"What would you have done if Mary had called 911?" Seth asked, a dark feeling sitting in his gut.

Peter looked down for the first time, contemplating. "I don't know," he said, looking back up. "I had done what I set out to do. For the most part."

"Then what?" Seth prompted after Peter went quiet, not wanting to imagine how things could have turned out for Mary.

"I returned the van and the sheet. It was probably taken down to the incinerator or thrown in the wash to be carted off to the industrial laundry service that morning. I don't know. I asked to see Neil again. Seamus said he'd gone to bed. Then I was dismissed."

"And this is when you left town. Presumably not to Alaska," Seth said, without a trace of humor.

Peter held both hands out as if to say, *What does it matter?* "But here's the other thing. I have two kids. I know what my wife's body looked like after giving birth. That belly doesn't just disappear, it takes on an interesting quality. I knew Sarah was pregnant, and now I know everyone is looking for a missing baby. I promise you, if that child survived, it's up there, probably being watched over by Lina."

Seth let out a long sigh through his nose. He wanted to go storming into the Orbriallis and search every room on every floor. But was Peter's testimony along with the facts they currently had on the case enough to procure a warrant? For the entire facility? "What about the vehicle?" Seth asked after a moment. "Is it still in the Orbriallis parking garage?"

"I guarantee the one I used to transport Sarah is long gone."

Seth nodded, already guessing that would be the case. The amount of information he'd digested today bounced around in his skull, but he felt alive and on high alert, not bogged down. Whether that was a natural high or the elixir Story had put in his coffee, he wouldn't argue with it.

"I know what you're thinking," Peter said, "but I'm telling you now that you'll never get the warrant you're looking for. We don't have enough evidence. And even if I were willing to go on record, which I can't do right now, I don't officially work there. There's no paper trail that links me to the Orbriallis. I'd just sound like a madman. I also wouldn't be the most reliable witness, given what I've done."

Seth gritted his teeth. "You came to me to tell me all of this, but you won't go on record?"

"Look," Peter said, lowering his voice, "this isn't the first time I've had to do this with a body. I'm guessing you've put that together by now. And this isn't the first time I've tried to arrange things in a way to have it all come exploding back on Neil Owens and the Orbriallis. But this time, you received my message loud and clear. My family and I are in grave danger. I can't risk going on record if there's a chance that Owens doesn't go down. It's not the way."

Seth leaned in even closer, their heads within inches of each other now. "How are you in danger? It's my job to protect everyone in this town. If you're telling me—"

"Sergeant Wolfe, something is very wrong with Neil Owens and the Orbriallis. I'm not discounting the astonishing work they do above ground, so to speak, but the shit being funded by a very small sector in the government is important enough that they would kill to protect it. Neil, himself, made that very clear to me when I tried to quit after the Kelly Fulson incident."

Seth's heart beat heavily against his chest. Pieces were coming together at a blistering pace, and with them, a cloud of impending danger was rolling over Lost Grove. "Tell me about that."

Peter nodded, his gaze bending toward the floor. "The first time they asked me, it was a young woman named Daisy Sutherland. I didn't know who she was when I saw her. I had to wait for her to be found, for her family to claim her, to find that out. I told Neil it would be wrong for him to think he could make a habit of asking me to do such a thing. Ten years went by. I carried out my regular orders. I wanted to believe it was a one-time thing.

"But then eight years ago, I got a message, made a call, and was asked to come in. I can't describe the pit in my stomach when I walked into the room, saw the body all wrapped up, and just knew. It came with a warning this time, too." Peter met Seth's eye. "Make sure it doesn't come back. Neil wasn't happy about my choice with Daisy. He wanted this one to disappear. I had the boat. I'd rented it for the kids,. For Jolie's birthday. But I…I couldn't just do what they asked. I unwrapped the body to see who it was—" Peter cut himself off, fists clenching.

"Seeing this young woman I'd known and worked with. A person I drove home when her shit car wouldn't work or shared a drink with at the bar. A woman who had fallen off the face of the earth. This entire town, including me, thought she'd been kidnapped, killed, lured by someone on the Internet into something that ended terribly. And lo and behold, the young woman I thought went missing is lying there, blue to the gills, with a baby in her belly."

Seth gave him a moment. "You meant for her to wash back up on shore?" he finally asked.

"Yes." Peter nodded. "I knew it would be up the coast. I knew she'd be in the water for a while, but she'd come back up."

"But it never came back on the Orbriallis," Seth said, frustration seeping in, anger growing.

Peter shook his head. "It was too much to hope for. Regardless of how it was going to turn out, I went back to see Neil, and this time, I wasn't taking any bullshit excuses. I told him I was out, that I was done. He betrayed my trust and broke our agreement."

"But you didn't have one," Seth guessed.

Peter frowned. "Exactly what he told me, along with a thinly veiled threat that if I were to speak up, or ever try to leave, my family would be in danger."

Seth let that stew. He wondered if he himself was in danger.

"Paddy and I," Peter continued, "we've been collecting some information on the doctors and nurses that work within the government sector of Orbriallis."

Seth leaned forward, their foreheads almost touching by this point. "What sort of information are you talking about?"

"I've spent the past few years getting to know a few of them, the doctors. Watching them. Seeing how they move, who they go out with, if any of them break the rules a little and, occasionally, say something they really shouldn't. Nothing damning, but a little over the line, considering what must be dictated in their contract."

"Okay. Go on."

"With those few, I've gotten a little buddy-buddy. You know, have a little chit-chat around the figurative water cooler. Things have not always been copacetic among the doctors working under Neil. I believe there are a few who'd be willing to speak out about the research happening there, but they'd have to be assured of security, and we would have to move fast. Getting them to talk and following through with action would have to come one right after the other."

Seth nodded. "Understood. It would be a volatile situation."

"Yes. And they may be hesitant to speak because of a scenario that happened twelve years ago. One of the head researchers was there one day, gone the next. They were told he was let go. A few weeks later, they see something on the news that shocks them all. A family discovered in their home after worried calls from relatives sent officers to do a wellness check, all dead. Murder-suicide."

Seth's chin slowly lifted, followed by his torso as he sat upright. He felt his skin tingle.

Peter noticed. "I'll give you one guess whose family it was."

"The researcher's."

"Dr. Theodore Chirishnaya, wife, Alyssa, two kids, Anthony and Neve." Peter finally felt like he could sit back. He saw this news percolating with Seth and noticed something more. His eyes flinched around the edges.

"How?" Seth finally asked.

"Doctor suffocated the kids, stabbed his wife, then shut himself in the garage and let the car run," Peter explained, wondering what it was Seth knew that he didn't.

"The case of this doctor, was there anything to refute that it wasn't a murder-suicide?" Seth asked, his voice and words careful.

"Not according to the officers working it."

Seth scooted forward in his chair. "But do you or Paddy have anything to refute it?"

"A little," Peter admitted. "The papers picked up on the story of the defamed doctor because testimony coming out of his former employer, the famed Orbriallis Institute, was that they had released him from their employment because of poor standards. Pills went missing during his hours of work, and patients' treatments were suspended or short-changed. But his family seemed happy. Reports from neighbors and relatives contradicted any tension."

"Neighbors and relatives miss a lot of shit that goes on behind closed doors."

"No doubt," Peter agreed. "But Paddy got into his personal computer. Traced all the quote-unquote 'deleted emails.' There was no sign that this guy was off his rocker or that there was any strife within the family. We also found a first draft of what appeared to be a resignation letter. We can't be certain, but he may have resigned, not been let go."

"What made him a threat to Dr. Owens?" Seth asked.

Peter shrugged. "Disgruntled, is what I hear. Making noise. Upset with the way something had turned out."

"Maybe about dead bodies piling up?"

Again, Peter shrugged. He waited for Sergeant Wolfe to continue, but when it was clear he was deep in thought, Peter said, "Look, if there's something you're not telling me that could be helpful to our cause here, let me have it."

Seth held Peter's gaze, giving nothing away. The news would be released later tonight if it hadn't been already. And if there was a sector of the hospital running dangerous experiments, kidnapping children from their homes and plugging them into machines for God knew what, impregnating them with…he couldn't even fathom, and that sector was responsible for Sarah's death, and the person running that sector was Neil Owens, then it was that person Seth wanted to put in prison. It was that person he needed to charge in order to close this case.

"Bess and Richard Grahams are dead," Seth said, eyes watching for the reaction of Peter Andalusian. He watched the tension in the face go slack, the jaw relax.

Peter closed his eyes and dropped his head. "How?"

"Murder-suicide."

That made Peter's head snap back up.

"Found them on the road out of town, packed up and ready for a long getaway at Ripley's Resort. Gunshot wounds to the head. He pulled the trigger on her, then put it in his mouth."

"Richard?" Peter said.

Peter's clear disbelief almost made him smile. "Yeah." He waited a time, watching Peter, before asking, "Could Neil have been responsible for this?"

Peter contemplated his words. "I think you know the answer to that by now."

Seth sat up. "I know they knew more about their daughter than they divulged. How much more is what I'm asking you."

"They would have to know a lot. I'm guessing you're not of the mind that this is something Richard would do."

"You also seemed surprised by it," Seth remarked.

"And I am."

Seth swallowed. The dangers connected to anyone touching this case were rising by the second. "I have young officers working this case. The chief of police is working on this case. It's my job to protect them if they're in harm's way."

"No offense to Bill or your officers, but they aren't the threat here, Sergeant. You are," Peter said. "I think we both need to be looking over our shoulders and sleeping with one eye open until we can figure out how to go about this."

Seth motioned for Peter to get closer to him as he dropped his forearms to his knees. Peter adopted the same pose, huddling closer. "That's the third time you've said 'we,'" Seth said. "Let's put aside the fact that you've committed multiple felonies and that I have no reason to trust you. What exactly do you have planned?"

"You may not trust me, Sergeant, but you believe me," Peter said.

"I had my reasons for believing most everything you've said before you showed up at Story's doorstep. Just spill it."

"You need concrete evidence to take down Neil Owens. And at this point, we both need him to be taken down before anyone else ends up in a peculiar murder-suicide. Paddy and I have a plan on how we can get into the Orbriallis without anyone knowing—"

"Breaking in?" Seth cut in. "You think I'm going to risk my career by breaking into a medical facility? One purportedly being funded by the government?"

"If it means saving your life, and saving the lives of my family, yes, I think you would consider it."

"You may have done your research on me, but you don't know me."

Peter scoffed. "What's that got to do with it? If you believe everything I'm saying, and I'm sure much of it backs up what you've already put together, I don't see any other way of doing this. I know where they keep the files that I take to their government contacts. We get our hands on those, we've got evidence."

"Unlawfully obtained," Seth countered.

"The information we get could be brought to someone else in the government. When I deliver those packages, I'm not taking them to 1600 Pennsylvania Ave. I take them to different places. I take them to different people."

"Always different?"

"No. I see the same few guys each time. But you know my meaning."

"Yeah, I'm starting to."

"This isn't something the entire government is in on," Peter continued.

"It's more like an *All the President's Men, Seven Days in May* type of deal," Peter explained.

Seth lifted his brows. "I don't follow."

"*Seven Days in May?* Kirk Douglas? Burt Lancaster?"

Seth shook his head.

"Well, shit, alright. You should watch it," Peter said as an aside.

"In my spare time," Seth replied, the first touch of a smile shading his lips.

Peter noticed this and was grateful. They were building something. Not trust by any sense of the word, but a discussion of intellect, of shared thoughts. "We get it into the right hands, and we might not see it broadcast across the evening news, but something will be done about it."

Seth caught Peter's eye and held it.

Peter half shrugged. "We can hope something will be done about it."

Seth couldn't believe he was sitting here, in a witch's den, with someone who should be in jail, discussing breaking and entering. Yet Peter was right. He believed what he was saying. Between the evidence he had put together, his conversation with Dr. Bajorek, and his vision with Sarah's child telling him he was looking for Neil Owens, not to mention the strange news the local teens had brought him, everything was pointing at the Orbriallis. He also couldn't dismiss what his gut was telling him about Richard and Bess. They had been murdered. Murdered for knowing too much.

"What's security like?" Seth caved in and asked.

"Security is tight. It's like Area 51 tight. No personal phones allowed in. When we enter, there are lockers where we put our things. We walk through a scanner. The security is made up of people like me, ex–Special Ops. We get patted down. There are cameras everywhere."

"I noticed that when I went to speak with Sarah's doctor."

Peter pointed at him, acknowledging this. "The researchers only use what stays there. When they leave, that's it, they don't take work home with them. I have a little more leniency. I'm meant to look like a normal guy. But that doesn't mean I don't have to walk through scanners. I still get patted down by Seamus every time I enter."

"And you're saying you've got some way to get through all of this?" Seth asked, an eyebrow lifted in skepticism.

"I'm not saying it will be easy."

Seth sat up and stretched his back, his muscles tight from hunching over. "Look, I've got to at least try to approach this lawfully. I do have an appointment with Dr. Owens tomorrow, and I'd like to see where that goes before considering drastic measures."

"I'm sure he's been waiting for you. Probably surprised you haven't shown up yet. Not that you'll get a goddamn thing from him."

"Like I said before, you don't know me."

Peter smirked. Paddy was right. He did like this guy.

Seth leaned in one last time. "Look, the fact that I'm even letting you go right now is going to be very hard to explain to Bill and the rest of the team. I'm finding it difficult to explain to myself."

"I'm cooperating?" Peter offered.

"Something like that," Seth said. "I will have someone on surveillance, watching every step you make."

"I would expect as much. And honestly, my family could use it."

It took Seth a second to register that he was talking about being in danger. "I will do anything to protect your family. Noble and Zoe are amazing kids."

Peter nodded in thanks. "I appreciate that. And look, I'll have Paddy watch over you. He is a surveillance expert and—"

"Please don't."

Peter shrugged. "Look, it's in my best interest to make sure you're safe. You're who we've been waiting for. Someone intelligent with a will of steel. Someone with enough experience to take down someone like Owens."

Seth shook his head. "I want to follow up on a couple of things. Can you get me a list of names of the doctors and nurses who might testify?"

"I'll have Paddy drop something off. Should he bring it to the station?"

"Yes. That would be safest, right?"

Peter nodded in agreement and laughed a little as Seth stood. "What?"

Peter looked up at him, eyebrows tilted inward. "I didn't expect…this."

"We're not done."

"I know." Peter stood and held out his hand. "Thank you."

Seth shook it, exchanging a firm grip.

Story's singsong voice pulled the men's attention out toward the foyer. "And wrap up, kids. It looks even more dreadful out than earlier." As Story walked past, she looked into the sitting room, ushering the teens along as if there was nothing to see. She locked eyes with Seth and registered all she needed.

Seth wondered what she'd garnered from their exchange. Probably more than he ever could read or register in their passing glances, which made him smile.

Zoe skipped in, and Noble stood in the doorframe between the foyer and the sitting room. "I have to take everyone home," he explained.

Peter nodded. "Zoe? Want to come with me?"

"Yep!" she replied.

Peter ushered her into the foyer, following his son.

Seth followed them out into the crowded foyer and vestibule. "Nate, one moment."

Nate swung on his coat as he hurried over to Seth. "Yeah?"

"I want to give you my number. We need to go over this evidence more, but for now, I need you to hold on to it," Seth said, pulling Nate aside a little farther into the foyer so others didn't fully overhear the exchange.

"Of course!" Nate said, eyes wide. He pulled his phone out and typed in the sergeant's number.

"Call me if anything comes up. If anything…strange happens. Yeah?"

"Yeah," Nate enthused, feeling thrilled and having trepidations. He wondered what exchange Sergeant Wolfe and Peter Andalusian had shared.

"Good. Thanks." Seth patted him on the shoulder and sent him off. "Oh, and Nate?"

Nate stopped and turned back around. "Yeah?"

"You did a really good job in there," Seth said, smiling at the eager youth.

Nate grinned from ear to ear. "Thanks. Thank you!"

The children went out the door. Peter exchanged a "Be careful" with his son and watched him head into the frigid rain, all hunched and rushing toward Noble's car. Though Story had said the car would likely start just fine now, it still surprised Noble when he turned the key in the ignition and it roared to life.

"…and she's so cute, Dad! She is SO cute," Zoe enthusiastically explained the owlet in her care to her father. He was listening as he bundled into his coat and then buttoned Zoe into hers because her hands were too busy emoting with one and clutching a book in the other.

Peter exchanged a pleasant thank you and goodbye with Story, leaving with a look and a knowing nod toward Seth.

Story shut the door and turned back to Seth.

"I should be going," he said, having already grabbed his coat from the hook.

Story asked, "Are those the boots you wear every day?"

Shrugging on his coat, Seth looked down at his boots. "Yes. Why?"

"Take them off," she said, walking past him and back into her home.

"But I have to go," he commented, but she had disappeared down the hall. He bent and unlaced them, pulled them off, and followed the sounds of her into a large room with one small window and cabinets all around. It looked like a butler's pantry, except for the assortment of bizarre containers and elements inside.

"Here," she said, extending her hand to take the boots. She had in her other hand a dangerously pointed knife.

Seth handed her his boots. "What is… What are you doing?"

She turned one boot over and began carving into the sole. "Protection."

"It looks like you're ruining my boot," he said.

She carved into the tread at the toe of the boot a symbol and poured a glittering, sand-like substance over it. She repeated it with the other, spit on them both, and handed them back to Seth.

She smiled. "Now you can go."

Seth leaned over, put on his boots, and tied the laces. When he stood, Story grabbed his face and pressed her lips firmly against his. They were soft and warm.

"To seal the spell," she said once she'd pulled away.

His lips tingled, and his nose warmed as if he'd just come in from the cold. He wasn't entirely sure if she was joking about the spell. Likely she wasn't. His lips tasted of cedar and juniper.

"Be careful, Sergeant Wolfe," she said.

It was the first time she'd used his correct moniker, an indicator that she was being serious. Seth nodded and zipped up his coat.

"I'd like to know what that's like when it doesn't involve a spell," she said.

Seth met her gaze, her warm eyes lit from within, a smirk on her lips, and felt himself grin in return.

Face to Face

"Hello, Dr. Bajorek. This is Sergeant Seth Wolfe from the Lost Grove Police Department calling. I'm sorry to bother you with this, but I need to verify some dates with you regarding the contact made between your team and Grady-Angel House after Sarah Grahams left your facilities. There was something you mentioned at the very end of our last conversation that made me think you might be the one I should speak with. I'm ready to listen when you have the information."

Seth disconnected, hoping his message was clear yet veiled enough in case someone else was listening, which he assumed they were. He set his cell phone down on his desk next to Dr. Bajorek's business card. He would have called her cell directly if it weren't for the information he received the night before from Peter Andalusian. Seth was positive that the doctor would pick up on his phrasing. Especially after receiving the list of names from Paddy.

Paddy, who was still in the bullpen cavorting with Seth's team like they were the best of friends, had brought over the list Peter promised at 9:30 a.m., along with a box of pastries. He was even deft enough, with the rest of the team hovering around, to proclaim the sealed manila envelope was a list of names of all registered campers at Devil's Cradle State Park in the past month. "Anything to help the investigation," he said proudly, winking at Seth. Thanking him for his cooperation, Seth immediately withdrew to his private office, ripping open the envelope like a child attacking a present on Christmas morning. Only one name mattered, and seeing Dr. Jane Bajorek's name among the five others confirmed everything he suspected.

Seth already had her business card in his left breast pocket, hoping it would prove him right, and he wasted no time in making the call. Knowing he likely wouldn't receive a return call until later this evening, Seth busied himself with reading through Paddy's report on the Orbriallis employees. The cover page had six names divided into two columns, four under the heading "Positive" and two under "Maybe." The pages after that offered a comprehensive breakdown of the five doctors and one researcher, along with editorialization of thoughts and impressions on each.

Seth was on page four, Dr. Victor Strauss, cross-referencing Paddy's report with information on the Internet, when his cell phone rang. He glanced down, eyes going wide at the name Dr. Jane Bajorek. Seth glanced at his watch: 9:53 a.m. It had hardly been twenty minutes.

Seth picked up his phone. "Sergeant Wolfe."

"Hello, Sergeant. It's Dr. Bajorek returning your call."

Seth heard a forceful wind in the background, crackling in the receiver. "Thanks for calling back so quickly."

"I've been awaiting your call."

"I thought maybe that was the case. I need to speak with you. Outside of the Orbriallis." Seth hoped he wasn't pushing too far, assuming too much.

"Yes. I understand."

The response was succinct, but all Seth needed to hear. "I'm glad. Look, I think—"

"It would be best if it's not in the public eye," she said, finishing his thought. "I'd like to see where you found her body."

Seth clicked off his pen and set it down, closing his eyes. Was he never to escape that spot? "Tell me the time."

"One thirty p.m., during my normal lunch hour. We won't have long."

"There's an outlet next to Mourner's Beach. You'll see my silver Mercedes parked there. When you make your way over the dunes, you'll see me by a large piece of driftwood."

"I'll see you then."

Seth stood in the spot that might as well be the landmark of his life—his life and Sarah Elizabeth's death. He had his hands tucked in the pockets of his winter police-issued coat, shoulders up to his ears. Temperatures were predicted to drop into the mid-twenties tonight, and it didn't feel much warmer in the middle of the day. He looked down the coast at the thick, ominous, almost pure black clouds headed their direction. This uncharacteristic cold spell, accompanied by sporadic bouts of rain and hail, felt like they were summoned by the circumstances infecting their small town.

Feeling an immediate premonition, Seth turned toward the road to see two figures with long black hair descending the dunes. Seth's breath caught in his chest and a knot formed in his stomach, briefly thinking he had made a terrible mistake until he recalled the portrait of Dr. Bajorek's mothers on the wall in her office. What on earth was the doctor doing bringing one of them with her? Had she been in for treatment at the Orbriallis? Or on her way to receive treatment?

Dr. Bajorek closed the gap between them, as one of her mothers lingered behind, her head swiveling up toward the clouds and then out toward the water. Jane, wearing a long black coat and scarf, extended her hand. "Sergeant."

Seth shook it. "Doctor. I appreciate you coming to see me."

"I appreciate you calling," she said, her glance drifting to the sand. "This is the spot, then."

"It is."

Jane squatted down and gracefully ran her fingers over the sand. "Dear Sarah. So incredibly gifted. And no one will ever know."

"I don't think that's true," Seth countered, watching her.

"Not enough people. Not near enough," she said, standing back up.

Seth turned around and nearly leapt backward. Dr. Bajorek's mother was standing inches away from him, her head cocked unnaturally to the side. "Hello," Seth offered. "Sorry, I didn't notice that you had…"

"This is my mother, Apolonia," Jane said, unfazed by her mother's behavior.

Seth couldn't pull his eyes away from this strange and unfathomably beautiful woman. Her large, round brown eyes, accentuated by long black lashes, were entrancing. Her high cheekbones and full lips filled out her exotic features. Like in her picture, she didn't look even ten years older than Dr. Bajorek, if that. She wore only a thin, beige, long-sleeve shirt, clearly with no bra underneath, and seemed immune to the cold.

Apolonia grinned as her eyes bore deeper into Seth's.

"Mamo, nie rób tego." Jane spoke in Polish, narrowing her eyes at her mother.

Seth's heart rate had ratcheted up, and he felt himself beginning to sweat, an inexplicable arousal developing.

Jane slapped her mother's arm. "Co powiedziałem? Jesteś tu z jednego powodu."

Apolonia smacked her back and flung her hand up in the air. "Nigdy nie pozwalałeś mi się bawić."

Seth looked between the two women, feeling as if he had entered yet another dimension.

"I told you before I came here. Now do what I asked of you," Jane said to her mother.

Apolonia grunted and took a step back from Seth, eyes still on him, but now serious and probing.

Seth wiped the sweat from his forehead. "I'm sorry. I don't think I understand—"

"I apologize, Sergeant. Just give my mother a moment, and I'll explain."

Seth stared at Apolonia, who stood frozen across from him, her arms stiff at her side, only her eyes active. Where before he saw nothing but sheer beauty, he now sensed something feral, dangerous. Seth opened his mouth but found himself unable to speak. Suddenly, he twitched, squinting his eyes, feeling a tickle inside his skull. His vision faded when an image of a house appeared to him. An old wooden house sat in the middle of a dark wooded area. Then, just as quickly, it was gone, and his senses returned. He sucked in a breath like he had been underwater for a minute and was back looking at Apolonia, who had taken another step back from him, her body half-turned, eyebrows furrowed.

Apolonia turned to her daughter. "Jego intencje są czyste. Ale on ma coś. Coś innego."

Seth turned to Dr. Bajorek. "What the hell is going on? What did she say?"

Jane grabbed Seth's shoulder and smiled. "She said your intentions are pure. But that you have something. Something in you like she does."

Seth narrowed his eyes and looked over at Apolonia, then quickly back to Dr. Bajorek, brows raised. "Wait. You mean I'm possessed?"

Apolonia threw her hands up and spun around, furious. "Powiedziałeś mu?"

"Yes, I told him," Jane said to her mother, letting go of Seth. "I told him because I could sense it. And I was right."

"Agh!"

"Was I not right?"

Apolonia dismissed her daughter with a wave of the hand and sauntered out closer to the shore.

Jane looked back at Seth. "I am truly sorry. But I had to be sure."

"Of what?"

"That I could trust you. My mother," she said, nodding in her direction. "Both of my mothers have abilities beyond their afflictions."

"I could feel her. She was in my head," Seth said, still slightly panicked.

Jane nodded. "And I think you might have been in hers based on her reaction. Did you see something?"

"What? I…" Seth shook his head, trying to regain his composure. "I saw a house. Almost like a cabin. It was in the woods, and nothing else was anywhere in sight."

Jane looked at Seth, not responding at first, and her eyes watered. "That was our home," she whispered.

"Home? You mean…in Poland? Was it Poland?" Seth asked.

"Yes." Jane nodded and wiped her eyes. "I'm sorry. We must talk. And quickly."

"Right." Seth had almost forgotten why he was here and what was at stake. He glanced over at Apolonia, staring out at the ocean. Seth closed his eyes and brought the image of Sarah Elizabeth's body on the beach, in the spot he now stood, back to his mind. Her contorted, staged body, one leg crossed over the other as if it would conceal the atrocities performed just hours prior. Her lips slightly parted, giving the impression her last breath was a soft exhale, not a shriek of unimaginable agony. Her eyes… her eyes haunted him more than anything—still open, the life behind them still lingering like a spirit watching over him at the moment he first examined her body, and still even now. Seth opened his eyes and turned back to Dr. Bajorek, his entire demeanor severe, his mind refocused.

"Let's talk about Grady-Angel House," he said.

Jane kept her eyes locked on the sergeant's. "There was no Grady-Angel House. I tried to convey that to you the best I could, given the circumstances."

"And you did. Enough to make me question the validity of just about everything I'm looking into. Why did you?"

Jane weighed her words. "I sensed there was something very wrong with what happened to Sarah, and I have my reasons for wanting to know exactly what that was. I knew I wouldn't get my answers inside the walls, so I put my faith in you."

Seth considered the significance of her words. If they were to be believed, which his gut said they were, then one of Sarah's own doctors didn't know how she died or how her body ended up in this very spot. "To clarify the implications of there being no Grady-Angel House, can you confirm that Sarah Elizabeth never left the Orbriallis?"

Jane nodded. The desire to know the truth of what happened to Sarah only slightly outweighed the guilt and fear of peeling back the curtain and defying orders.

"Which clearly means she became pregnant while at the Orbriallis and carried the baby to term while under the care of you and other doctors there," Seth continued.

"Yes." The word came out hoarse. The phrase "under the care of" felt like a knife twisting inside her heart.

"And the baby is alive and safe?"

Another nod.

Seth let out a long sigh. Hearing the confirmation from someone besides Peter Andalusian was a massive weight off his chest. "This, of course, begs the questions of who the father is and how this happened while Sarah was being treated for sleep and psychological issues," he said, trying but failing to keep the frustration out of his voice.

Jane looked down and pulled her coat tighter around her body. She expected these questions, but she hadn't planned on the internal conflict of divulging information about secret government research being so strong. If she was wrong about her suspicions of Dr. Owens, she would torpedo her career, along with those of every other doctor in the special research unit. Jane looked up and over to her mother, whom she could feel tugging at her. Apolonia looked back at her over her shoulder and nodded.

Jane looked back at Seth. "Sarah did come to us for the reasons I told you earlier. Her abilities were special. Groundbreaking. As her mental health improved, these abilities flourished. Because of these abilities, among other factors, Sarah was chosen as a potential candidate for a very special fertility program."

Seth, brows pinched, shook his head. "Fertility program? What… what does that mean?"

"It's part of our cutting-edge research. I truly cannot say any more than that."

"I need to know who the father is. Can you tell me that much?"

Jane brushed her hair out of her face and behind her ear. "There is no father. So to speak."

Seth squinted and looked over at Apolonia, relieved she hadn't moved. What in the hell was going on at the Orbriallis? Some sort of artificial insemination, in vitro, or God knows what else. Seth looked back at Jane, whose eyes were trained on the ground. It was clear she was racked by guilt. "What were you told about Sarah's body being found here on the beach?"

Jane quickly looked up. "I think this conversation would be better served if you told me what it is that you know."

Seth nodded. He knew he would have to give Dr. Bajorek something eventually. "I have firsthand testimony that Dr. Neil Owens ordered the disposal of Daisy Sutherland, Kelly Fulson, and Sarah Elizabeth Grahams's bodies, one to look like an accident, the others were never supposed to be found."

Jane's eyes had grown wide as the sergeant spoke. She sneered as she turned and cursed. "That son of a bitch! I knew something was off. I knew it, and still, I went ahead and…"

"Something was off? What do you mean by that?" Seth asked.

"We were told…" Jane could hardly bring herself to repeat Neil's bullshit stories. The guilt for believing them was near paralyzing. Her suspicions being confirmed were of little comfort. "He said that Daisy's eggs weren't taking. And that after several failed attempts, they amicably agreed to part ways, that she was no longer a part of the program."

Seth had an impulse to console the doctor. Her pain and anger were palpable.

"And Kelly…poor, sweet Kelly. It happened in the middle of the night. Not unlike Sarah. We were told that she insisted on leaving. That she was overwhelmed and needed to step away to be with a close friend. We were assured it was a temporary absence and that she would be back within days. When her body was discovered, it was all chalked up to suicide."

Seth could feel the permanent cloud of confusion in his mind dissipating as the puzzle pieces were dropping into place. "Which brings us back to Sarah. What were you told about how she died?"

Jane looked back up into the sergeant's eyes. "That she died during childbirth."

"At the Orbriallis?"

"Yes."

"And what were you told about her body being discovered?"

Jane sighed. "We were told that someone within the facility stole her body and that it was being internally investigated."

Seth raised an eyebrow. "But the authorities weren't being told. And no one thought—"

"We're all under strict contract, and much of our research is highly classified. We were given direct orders to follow the story put forth for us. The story you initially heard."

Seth let out a long sigh. "I have to ask, is it common to deliver children there?"

Jane shook her head. "No, not at all."

"Do you have trained obstetricians there?"

Jane narrowed her eyes. "There are a handful of doctors who are capable of delivering a child."

"Who was the doctor who delivered Sarah's baby?"

Jane recalled the look in Dr. Kierslav's eyes the morning after the delivery. She knew that something terrible had transpired. All that Dr. Owens could focus on was the child, how perfect and strong she was, how responsive and self-aware, a resounding success. Dr. Kierslav looked like he had seen a ghost, a demon that sucked his soul from his body. "What happened to her? What do you know?"

Divulging the grim details of Sarah's death to Dr. Bajorek presented Seth with a dire conflict. On one hand, she was a doctor who could very well expound upon what and why the procedures were performed. It might also force her hand to reveal who that doctor was. On the other hand, it was still an ongoing investigation, and regardless of how little fault may fall upon her, she was still under suspicion.

"I know I need to bring someone to justice for Sarah's death, and I need more than the one witness I currently have whose testimony may not hold up in court. Would you be willing to testify that—"

"Sergeant, we must be going. I've already put myself and both of my mothers in danger by being here."

Seth felt a wave of guilt for bringing about this meeting. It was necessary for the investigation. Richard and Bess Grahams were already potential victims of a double homicide, and they didn't know near the incriminating information that Dr. Bajorek did. "I sincerely apologize that you're in this situation. If you feel that you or your mothers are in any physical danger, I can—"

Jane leaned in and spoke with quiet conviction. "I chose to come here, Sergeant. I believe Dr. Owens needs to be taken down, but you would have to have concrete evidence that would leave absolutely no doubt in a jury's mind for me to agree to testify."

Seth cursed inwardly. The last thing he wanted to do was entertain the thought of Peter's break-in proposal, but she was right. He needed hard evidence. He needed to see Dr. Owens. "Look, I've been given a list of other doctors and researchers who are believed to be disgruntled with Dr. Owens. I'm guessing the names won't be a surprise if I share them with you."

Jane tilted her head to the side. "Where are you getting this information? The same person who told you about the bodies?"

"Człowiek, który wykonuje polecenia doktora Owensa!" Apolonia yelled from down near the shore.

Seth looked from Apolonia back to Dr. Bajorek. "What did she say? Can she hear us?"

Jane nodded, her eyes on her mother. "She said it's the man who carries out Dr. Owens's orders. And yes, she can."

"Does she… Do you know who that is?" Seth asked.

Jane looked back at Seth. "I do. Can he be trusted?"

Every logical part of Seth's brain wanted to say no, but his gut said the opposite. "He can. He believes his family is in grave danger as well, and he's trying to find a way out."

"You believe that?"

Seth nodded. "I know it. And if it weren't for him, Sarah's body would have been dumped in the middle of the ocean, never to be seen again."

Jane lifted her eyebrows. "He's the one who put her body here?"

"Against explicit orders. He's been in hiding ever since. But now he's back to protect his family, and we need things to move quickly."

"Then you better find evidence. Because the rest of the people on your list are terrified right now. They wouldn't even consider talking to you without it."

"So, you know who they are?"

Jane let out a huff. "I have a pretty good idea. It's time for us to go."

Seth nodded. "Thank you for coming here."

Jane offered a faint smile.

Seth turned to his right and jumped back, startled yet again by Apolonia, who was standing close enough to smell him.

"Mother!" Jane warned.

"On jest przystojny. Chcę go," Apolonia said, her eyes again locked on Seth's.

"I'm sure you do, but you can't. We have to go now," Jane said, beginning to move toward the dunes.

"It was nice to meet you," Seth offered.

"Teraz mamo!" Jane yelled.

Apolonia leaned toward Seth and did, in fact, smell him before following her daughter.

Seth swallowed the lump in his throat and then called out, "Dr. Bajorek!"

Jane turned to face him but kept walking backward.

"I asked you if I was possessed! You never answered!"

Apolonia turned back toward Seth. "Nie opętany! Można zobaczyć!"

Jane translated. "She said you're not possessed. But that you can see."

And with that, the mother and daughter crested over the dunes and out of sight.

Seth stepped into the elevator on the ground floor of the Orbriallis, followed by Seamus, who scanned his keycard and pressed the button to the penthouse.

"I'm surprised my great-uncle is willing to see you," the Irishman said.

"Why is that?" Seth asked.

Seamus casually leaned back against the side of the elevator, smiling at Seth. "He's a busy man. And he's not really the sociable type, ya know?"

"I've heard. I am the police, though."

Seamus shrugged. "No offense, but he's made the heads of foreign countries wait to see him. And who are you?"

Seth's nerves were already on edge, and the elevator's ascent, along with the giant standing across from him, weren't doing his stomach any favors. Was Seamus the person who he and Peter needed to be looking over their shoulders for? God, he hoped not.

Seamus let out a burst of laughter as he lunged toward Seth and pretended to give him a series of uppercuts to the stomach. "I'm just playin' with ya, brotha. I like you," he said, slapping Seth on the shoulder and flopping back against the rear of the elevator.

Seth let out what was likely the most ludicrous laugh ever to leave his mouth. "Right. Good. Yeah. Probably shouldn't pretend to assault an officer of the law, though. I mean, in general."

"Agh!" Seamus waved off the notion as if it were a foolish suggestion. "So, what are you plannin' to talk to the big boss about? The girl still, is it?"

"Yeah, just some follow-up questions after talking to her doctors," he said, unsure why he was divulging anything.

"Suspicious, you said it was. Or, no, you said somethin' funny." Seamus turned his head toward Seth, his eyes looking up, trying to recall the phrase.

"Did I?"

"Ah! Criminal. That's what it was. Criminal death." He laughed and elbowed Seth's arm like they were in on a joke together.

Seth nodded. "That it is. Not really a laughing matter, though."

"No, sure. But the way you said it was."

Seth stared at the doors, his eyes wide. Was the elevator moving slower because of Seamus's weight?

"You know"—Seamus leaned over to Seth and lowered his voice—"me uncle's got a bottle of the most expensive cognac in the world. Tastes like heaven on your tongue, it does. You tell him I said you need to try it."

"Sounds lovely, but I am on duty."

"Duty?" he exclaimed, leaning back. "You hear what I told you? The most expensive in the world. You just forget about that duty business. I won't say a word to—"

The ding from the elevator mercifully sounded.

"Oh, shit, we're here," Seamus said.

The foyer of the Orbriallis had impressed Seth, but it paled in comparison to when the elevator doors opened, revealing Dr. Owens's…mansion? Everything dripped with luxury—books, grand piano, atlas globes, velvet and leather, rich-colored wood, and an intricate herringbone floor.

"Opens right to it," Seamus needlessly remarked before walking in.

Seth stepped in behind him and skimmed the immense living quarters before his eyes settled in on who was undoubtedly Dr. Neil Owens, making his way toward them in an immaculate silver business suit, black button-up, and a white tie, extending his hand.

"Sergeant Wolfe, a pleasure to meet you," Neil said, taking Seth's hand between both of his.

Seth nodded, assessing the man's face. What he heard was correct. The man could either be a really old fifty or a really young eighty. Either way, between the tan, wide, bright eyes, and tight skin, he looked fantastic. "Thanks for seeing me on such short notice, Dr. Owens."

"No, no, not at all. Please, come in and have a seat." Neil waved him in and led the way to a sitting area with a marble-and-glass table encased by two luxurious sofas and two stately armchairs.

"Neil, you need me to stick around?" Seamus asked, still standing by the elevator.

Dr. Owens waved his hand at his great-nephew. "No, of course not."

Seth walked around one armchair and looked back at Seamus, who was smiling at him from within the elevator.

"Please, have a seat anywhere," Neil said, sitting in his favorite armchair at the far end facing the elevator.

Seth opted to sit in the armchair opposite Dr. Owens. It was roughly seven feet away, but sitting on the sofa felt too intimate, too chummy.

"I hope my staff has been cooperative during the investigation," Neil said, a look of concern on his face.

"They have indeed." Seth pulled out a small digital recorder and carefully set it on the table. "I hope you don't mind, but I prefer to record all my interviews and meetings. I don't like taking notes, it pulls focus from properly communicating," he lied. The impulse to pull out his notepad and pen was severe.

"I couldn't have said it better myself," Neil replied, extending a hand toward the device. "Record away."

"Thank you." Seth leaned forward, pressed the record button, and looked at his watch. "This is Sergeant Seth Wolfe. The date is Friday, October 15, 2023. The time is 3:53 p.m. I'm here with Dr. Neil Owens, who's agreed to see me at the Orbriallis Institute in his…"

"My home," Neil offered. "I've got an office, but I thought it would be more comfortable to have a chat in here."

Seth leaned back. "I appreciate that. Your home is quite immaculate."

"That's very kind of you. Can I get you something to—Lina!" Dr. Owens called out.

Seth looked over at the door that the doctor yelled toward, surprised he was ushering Lina Orbriallis to join them.

After a weighted moment where both men sat smiling at one another, the door opened. Lina entered the room wearing a long, green Victorian dress and her black veil.

"Ah, very good," Neil said, looking from Lina to Seth. "What can I get you? Water? Tea? Coffee?"

"Coffee would be great. Thank you," he said to Lina. It was hard to tell through the veil, but it didn't appear she had aged much since he was in high school. And it had always been difficult to see where or how she was disfigured, if in fact she still or ever was.

"You look familiar," Lina said.

Neil rolled his eyes. "Lina, please don't disturb the sergeant."

"It's quite alright," Seth said, keeping his gaze on Lina. "I grew up here, but I left when I was eighteen. You were still living on Pixley at the time. A friend of mine lives there now."

"Is it the woman who bought my home?" Lina asked.

"It is. She loves the home. She's kept it in tremendous shape."

Lina hung her head. "I miss my home."

Neil sighed audibly. "Lina, can you please just get Sergeant Wolfe his coffee?"

Lina looked back up. "Your father. He owns the drugstore."

Seth nodded. "He does. Unfortunately, he had a pretty bad stroke a few months back and isn't well enough to go back to work. I've been helping."

"I'm sorry. Your father was always very kind to me."

Seth smiled, his heart warming at hearing that.

"Please send him my regards."

"I will. I promise."

"Cream or sugar?"

"No, thank you."

Lina turned to Neil.

"I'm fine, thank you, Lina."

"I did what you asked. I've kept—"

"Thank you," Neil loudly interrupted, holding up a clenched fist.

Lina turned and left the way she came.

Seth noted the curious exchange, recalling what Peter told him the night prior, believing that Lina would be the one watching Cleo. Seth had the desire to bust through the door and search the rest of the penthouse.

Neil folded his hands in his lap. "So, how can I be of assistance, Sergeant?"

Seth casually leaned forward, dropping his forearms to his knees. "I was hoping you might be able to shed some light on Sarah Elizabeth Grahams's treatment here."

Neil frowned. "I'm afraid to say that I don't personally treat any of the patients here. I meet them on intake. I read the reports. But I don't deal with any of our patients on a day-to-day basis. I would never have the time. That's why I hire the best doctors and researchers in the world."

"Right. But you did meet Ms. Grahams, yes?"

"Yes, of course. I spoke with her a handful of times during the years she was here, just to check in and make sure she was happy and comfortable. To ensure she was satisfied with the doctors treating her. Her parents are friendly donors to our research every year. So, I suppose I may have checked in on her progress a tad more. Political brown-nosing, you could call it. Ridiculous to think that now. Poor girl."

Seth kept eye contact with the doctor. He either hadn't heard or was pretending he hadn't heard. "It would seem you haven't heard the news about Sarah's parents."

Neil's brow creased. "Whatever do you mean?"

"Mr. and Mrs. Grahams were found dead yesterday morning."

Neil brought a hand to his chest. "Dear Lord, what happened?"

"I'm not at liberty to say. It's still an ongoing investigation."

Neil pulled a handkerchief from his breast pocket and brought it to his chin.

Seth noticed the subtle shake in the doctor's fist, his eyes darting left and right, searching for reason. There was nothing disingenuous about his reaction. "They were found together on the side of the road. On the Wildcat loop."

Neil's eyes narrowed. "Wildcat," he whispered. "Wildcat."

"It's a road leading out of town. Goes south."

Neil nodded. "Yes, I know of it. On the side of the road?" he asked, looking up at Seth for the first time since hearing the news.

"In their car," Seth clarified.

Neil dabbed his brow with the handkerchief. "This is…just a terrible tragedy. First their daughter, now…"

"Yes, it was all very surprising. I'd like to get back to Sarah, if you don't mind."

Neil cleared his throat and began folding his handkerchief. "Of course."

"You mentioned you checked in on Sarah more than most. Would you say she was satisfied with her treatment?"

Neil carefully returned his handkerchief to his breast pocket and forced a smile. "Oh, yes, very much," he said. "She had nothing but glowing things to say about the Institute and the doctors who treated her."

"How many doctors did she have?" Seth asked.

"Well, she had a primary doctor. Dr. Bajorek, who I know you've spoken with."

Seth kept his expression neutral.

"She would have been seen by specialists in our sleep analysis division. Dr. Bajorek could supply you with a list if you think it pertinent."

"Perhaps, yes. The more information I can get, the better. Anyone who came into contact with her. As I'm sure you know, the circumstances of Ms. Graham's death were highly suspicious, and we're approaching the case as a probable homicide."

Neil shook his head. "It's just terrible. I think the news devastated everyone here who knew her. The tragedy, of course, is that she was fully on the road to recovery. So many tragedies. I can't imagine what happened to the poor child. We will, of course, do anything we can to aid your investigation, which is why I canceled my meeting with the board of trustees to speak with you today."

"I appreciate that," Seth said. Dr. Owens gave nothing away in his body language or his voice in response to the mention of a homicide. If Seth didn't know the things he did, he would have assessed the doctor's reaction as genuine. The man was stoic.

"Dr. Bajorek has been forthcoming and helpful, I would assume?" Neil asked.

"Yes. She's been nothing but professional and open with me."

The door creaked as Lina backed in, holding a small serving tray.

Seizing the moment, Seth asked the doctor, "Do you know if any of the sleep specialists Sarah would have seen were male?"

Neil tilted his head to the side. "They certainly could have been. Why do you ask?"

Lina stepped between the sofa and armchair Seth sat in, crouching down to set the coffee on the table.

"As I'm sure you're well aware, Sarah was pregnant, and we have every reason to believe the child could still be alive."

Lina's hand faltered as she set the porcelain cup on the glass, causing a rattle.

"Thank you, Lina," Seth said, turning to her, trying to read her expression through the veil.

"You're welcome," she muttered and walked out twice as fast as she'd entered, which could be attributed to her not carrying a cup of hot coffee, but Seth thought otherwise.

"I can assure you, Sergeant Wolfe, there is no chance something of that nature would ever occur here at the Orbriallis. We have cameras everywhere and monitor them twenty-four hours a day."

Seth sipped his coffee and inadvertently let out a murmur of delight. Apparently, Neil's expenses didn't stop with the cognac. "Well, that's relieving to hear. Still and all, she became pregnant somehow, by hook or by crook, and then died during childbirth."

Dr. Owens's face was granite solid, not a flicker of an eyelid, not a swallow. "And I genuinely hope you find out who it was and what happened. We all do."

Seth took another sip of coffee. "Speaking of which. Do you ever treat pregnant women here?"

"Treat, no. Study, yes," Neil said, his voice brightening. "We help women, and families, with the fertilization process. We conduct studies on women who are pregnant, as well as the drugs they take during their pregnancy and how they affect them. Our goal is to improve these drugs, improve the fertilization process. We want every woman who wants to be pregnant to give birth to a child, to have that opportunity. We have made great strides in helping to solve the issues of infertility."

The man's passion for the good work they actually did at the Orbriallis was palpable. "All of this to make it safer?" Seth guessed.

"Precisely!" Neil exclaimed, thrusting his finger in the air.

"Well, that's certainly commendable work. I would imagine in your studies of pregnant women you've had individuals here at late stages in their pregnancy?"

"Of course. Every stage is vital in our research."

"Have you ever had a patient go into labor?"

Neil laughed. "Thankfully, no."

"Would you and your staff be prepared if such an occurrence were to present itself?"

Neil splayed his hands out from their folded position. "We have the best doctors in the world here, Sergeant. Many would be more than capable of handling such a situation."

Seth nodded. "Makes sense. It's just that you said 'thankfully' that hadn't happened."

"Well, it wouldn't be an optimal position for the mother, and their health and safety is the number one priority."

Seth smiled, holding the doctor's gaze. It was truly impressive and terrifying that he could answer such questions without a hint of falter in his voice or manner. "Getting back to Sarah."

"Of course, of course," Neil said and leaned back in his chair.

"If you've read the reports, then you'll know Sarah Elizabeth was being treated not only for her sleep issues but for the visions she was having. Visions believed to be from the future. Believed by her doctor."

Neil smiled. "And you think this, what, strange?"

"It's unusual," Seth said. "Not that people claim to have them but that a doctor would not only believe them but treat them."

"And that," Neil emphasized, pointing at Seth, "is what makes the Orbriallis Institute special. When Geiger Orbriallis founded this Institute, he set about to solve the impossible, cure the incurable. And the only way he saw fit to do that was to believe that anything was possible. And he was right. I've carried on Geiger's vision, no pun intended, his mission, to explore everything, to push the boundaries of science and medicine to places no one believed they could go—to make the blind see, to make the deaf hear."

Seth's heart jumped at the statement, and yet again, the passion hit home. His mother, Amaranth, was always on his mind.

Dr. Owens leaned forward. "Have you ever had an experience you can't explain, Sergeant?"

"I can't say that I have," Seth quickly lied.

Neil gave the slightest smirk at Seth. "If you say so."

Seth came here to corner the doctor, not the other way around. He hurried on. "Dr. Owens, is there anything at all you can tell me that you think would be helpful to my investigation? Anything that her doctors may not know or be aware of?"

"I wish I did. I've racked my brain since first hearing the news, trying to think if there's anything we could have done differently, anything that we might have done that put her in a dangerous position. But her treatment was resoundingly successful. She was beaming in her exit interview."

"And when was that?"

Neil lifted both hands in the air. "I couldn't possibly know the date off the top of my head. I'm sure you already have that by now, do you not?"

Seth nodded. "I do. But sometimes you ask different people the same question, and something different will pop up. Not just a date but sometimes a memory. Thinking back, is there anything you see now that you didn't see in that exit interview?"

Neil furrowed his brow, looking straight ahead but in thought. Not the typical action of someone lying or trying to cover their tracks. "You're very good, Sergeant. That's a highly intelligent and intuitive way of posing a question, I must say. And quite accurate. Did you study psychology?"

Seth couldn't hide looking impressed. "It was my second major."

Neil raised his eyebrows. "I wish I could say something is occurring to me now in hindsight, but I can't grasp anything. I'll think over everything again tonight, wipe the slate clean, so to speak. I'll be sure to reach out if anything, even if it seems unimportant, comes to me."

"That's all that I can ask," Seth said and reached for his recorder, turning it off. "Thank you again for your time."

Neil stood to his feet. "Absolutely."

Seth finished the coffee, not wanting to leave a drop behind, and stood to leave. He rounded the armchair and then quickly spun back around. "I'm sorry. There was something I forgot," he said, sitting back down, pressing the record button again.

Neil, having already taken steps to usher the sergeant out, sat on the sofa next to Seth.

Seth looked at Dr. Owens, smiling. "Are you treating a patient by the name of Raymond LaRange?"

Neil's eyebrows lifted a smidgeon before quickly shifting course to narrow them. "Who?"

Seth had him. It was nothing anyone would hear on the recording, but the falter in the doctor's eyes was as good as an admission. "Raymond LaRange. He was a convicted sex offender whose IQ was so low that they deemed him incapable of understanding his actions. He was transferred here from Ohio in 1992."

"1992?" Neil scoffed. "No wonder the name didn't ring a bell. What on earth is this about? Certainly nothing to do with Ms. Grahams."

"No. No, it's not. It's in relation to another case I'm working on."

Neil swallowed and tried to cover for it by looking intrigued. "Well, that must be quite the cold case. I can assure you whoever Mr. LaRange was, he's certainly not being treated here now. We haven't had a patient here longer than three years."

"Even for the criminally sentenced?" Seth asked. He thought it strange that a man sentenced to a mental facility for molesting two underage girls would find his way back into society within three years.

"Ah, well," Dr. Owens stumbled. "It was so long ago. Remind me, if you know, of the sentencing?"

"He was deemed unfit for trial. Remanded to a local psych hospital, and then transferred here." Seth noted how Dr. Owens flinched when he used the words *psych hospital*, as if the phrase was barbed and below the status of his highfalutin facility.

"So, not sentenced? We do have sentenced criminals here, but I don't exactly place them in the same context as patients. You asked if we were treating this LaRange fellow, so I assumed he was a patient. That was some time ago, regardless." Neil smiled beatifically.

Seth couldn't help but notice how the smile felt like it had been orchestrated, practiced over and over in a mirror to mimic that of a pleasant, esteemed doctor. The smile didn't reach the man's eyes. "No, it was a sentencing. The thing is, I've found prison transfer papers and official intake forms. It all being a legal matter, those records are public. But I can't find a trace of any discharge paperwork or orders."

"Well, I'm not sure what to say. I'll have my staff search the archives and turn over everything we have on the man."

"That would be a tremendous help," Seth said.

Neil continued to smile unconvincingly. "Any way we can help."

Seth clicked off the recorder and stood back up to leave. At the elevator, he turned around to shake Dr. Owens's hand. "We'll see each other again, I'm sure."

Neil shook Seth's hand with conviction, a confident smile back on his face. "I look forward to it."

The Green Man Strikes Again

Noble was alone in the kitchen, putting together the meal his mother had prepared for him and Zoe, his mind a chaotic war zone of thoughts—the Green Man, the Orbriallis, not-children, the eerie and dangerous powers of Emory and Ember, his father, and possibly magic? Their parents had gone out for dinner, his dad cryptically telling him there were things he needed to discuss with his mom. The tension between his parents, though they tried to hide it, was affecting Zoe more than him. Noble was curious about how the conversation with his dad and Sergeant Wolfe went last night.

Noble dropped the diced carrots into a bowl and tossed the salad with a store-bought vinaigrette dressing as he pondered what his parents were currently discussing. Where his dad was this past week was likely top on the list. Noble had fought the urge to confront him about it, mainly because Zoe was always in earshot, but also he wasn't sure it was his place to raise the issue. It felt like something solely between husband and wife. Or did he have the right to question his father now that he was eighteen?

Noble washed his hands and wiped them on the kitchen towel, hearing the buzz of his phone, followed by the subtle ding. He grabbed it off the counter on his way to lure Zoe out of her room with the promise of spaghetti and garlic bread.

Nate: If you have enough, cool.

This was Nate's response to Noble saying he was making spaghetti and Nate was welcome to some since he was on his way over.

We have plenty.

Noble responded and shoved his phone in his back pocket, heading for the stairs. As he passed the front door, he unlocked the bolt. When his parents left for dinner, Noble noticed his father turn the deadbolt as he walked past, following his mom out into the garage. He found the action curious. They rarely had the door locked while home.

Another buzz and ping drew his attention as he vaulted the stairs. He figured it was Nate commenting on Noble's culinary prowess, but it was from Emory.

My sister is a frazzled, paranoid mess and
I'm exhausted trying to keep her out of my
head. Can I come over? Like, please!

Noble paused at the top of the stairs and let that thought sink in. What would it be like if Zoe could infiltrate his mind, talk to him, harass him, read his thoughts? It sounded like a living nightmare.

Yeah dude of course!

Noble replied and headed down the hall to his sister's room. "Zoe? I made spaghetti and garlic bread. Cheesy garlic bread! Actually, Mom did, but I have it ready," he said with a broad smile as he pushed the door to her room open. His smile evaporated.

The portrait of a horror film painted itself before him, frozen in time. The killer at the window wearing a mask that seemed to resemble the face captured years ago from arrest and trial photos printed in black and white. Images that were recently planted in Noble's mind. The age difference was apparent, but there was no mistaking the man staring back at him. Holding Zoe in his arms, he had one leg partially out the window. This was Raymond LaRange. This was the Green Man.

Zoe looked dazed, almost asleep, with her arms and legs hanging limp. A surge of fear and adrenaline flooded Noble's bloodstream like a dam breaking loose. That jittery tension tingled through his body and settled in his limbs, making him tremble.

Raymond locked eyes with the boy called Noble the minute he barged into his target's room. He'd already had a freakish time subduing the young girl, and now, as he tried to press his intentions into the mind of the teenage boy, he struggled to gain any mental footing inside Noble's brain. It wasn't at all like the woman covered in tattoos who lived in Lina's old house. She was strong. She didn't let him anywhere near her mind. But these children, they had a roadblock he'd never encountered.

Noble felt his body go numb. A sensation worlds different from the thrill of a race but not altogether dissimilar. What he felt now was like the moment before the bang signals the release of anxious feet but on steroids, kicked up to eleven, overdosed on caffeine and speed. His stomach rolled in circles like the dryer at a laundromat, but his muscles tensed. Instincts took over as Noble rushed the Green Man, murder seeping into his mind, whatever it took to protect his sister.

Raymond dropped Zoe to the floor and took the brunt of Noble's lowered shoulder to his abdomen as he tried to bring his leg back into the room to gain balance. His ankle caught on the windowsill, twisting, sending sharp, radiating pain up to his knee.

Noble wrestled the devil masquerading as a man to the ground, throwing wild punches at whatever body part he could reach. Raymond's face was the primary target, but it was too far away. During a moment of sheer mania, Noble registered the Green Man pushing Zoe out of the way. Was he trying to protect her?

Raymond struggled to his feet, backing away from the erratic swings and the young man's attempt to pull him back to the ground. He clenched his fists, extending his arms forcefully toward the floor, trying once more to influence the teen's actions. He felt a tendril connect and dared to close his eyes to solidify his hold.

Noble was up to his feet in a swift move that seemed to defy physics. Seeing Raymond LaRange in a baffling pose that looked like he was trying to spontaneously combust, Noble thrust his fist forward, connecting half of his fist with Raymond's cheek. It knocked the Green Man backward into Zoe's dresser, the books neatly organized on top spilled off. Gaiman, Lewis, and L'Engle weren't the only casualties. Zoe's favorite ceramic sculpture, a Cheshire Cat holding an open book with a wide grin, fell to the ground, breaking into three pieces.

As Noble moved forward, Raymond nimbly leapt over the bed, trying to put some distance between them so he could work his magic, still hanging onto the boy's mind by the thinnest of strings. When Noble vaulted the bed in pursuit and swung again, Raymond dodged out of his way and grabbed a hold of the boy from behind. He pressed his forehead into the back of Noble's head, yet again meeting an unfamiliar roadblock.

Noble, feeling a sensation similar to Emory poking around in his brain, yanked himself free and thrust his elbow into Raymond's jaw, sending him stumbling backward toward Zoe's desk. As Noble closed in on him, Raymond grabbed every object he could from the desk and tossed them at the boy to keep him at bay. Noble held his arms up to block the books, pencil cases, and coffee-mugs-turned-marker-holders from hitting him in the face. "Fuck off!" he shouted and ran at Raymond.

With luck and timing, Raymond shifted the weight of his body to the right. Noble went rushing past him and landed half on the desk, his head slamming into the edge of a bookshelf. He turned around in such a daze that he only had time to register the fist coming at him, knowing he didn't have time to dodge it before lights danced in his vision, followed by blackness.

Nate climbed out of his mom's car, shoulders lifted to his ears, and squinted his eyes. After a short but vicious storm in the late afternoon, the skies were clear, but that somehow made the cold more prominent and biting. The weather app told him it was going to drop into the low twenties tonight. Was this really Northern California, or had they been teleported to Alaska? He thrust his hands in his pockets and jogged toward the front door of the Andalusian home, failing to notice that someone was waiting there.

Emory turned at the sound of the car door shutting and watched Nate make his way up the pathway. When he got to the stairs, Nate flinched back, just noticing Emory standing there.

"Holy shit! You scared the dick out of me."

Emory laughed. "Sorry, man. Is it always this cold here?"

"Fuck no! I don't know what's going on. What are you doing just standing here?"

"I knocked, but no one answered," Emory explained.

"We don't knock," Nate scoffed and, in a single motion, strode forward, opened the door, and entered the Andalusian house. He kicked off his shoes and pulled off his coat. "Noble!" he shouted.

"Is something burning?" Emory asked, sniffing the air while removing his shoes as well, following Nate's lead.

Nate smelled and wrinkled his nose. "Smells like it," he said, walking down the hall to the kitchen. Smoke was drifting out of the oven. Nate grabbed the kitchen towel and opened the door, keeping his head back. He pulled a sheet pan of burnt garlic bread out of the oven.

"Damn," Emory said, wafting a hand through the air.

"What the fuck?" Nate set the pan down before calling out again. "Noble!"

"Did they go out?"

"No." Nate pushed past Emory and headed for the stairs. "Zoe!" he called as he took them two at a time. Emory was close behind.

Nate moved down the hall, peering into Noble's room.

"He's not here," Emory said from behind.

Nate moved further down the hall. Warm light spilling from Zoe's room drew him toward it.

Noble could hear someone yelling. They were yelling his name. His head pulsed in pain, and a strange sticky sensation covered the right side of his face. His nose felt stuffed with snot, but as he drew in a breath, he realized it smelled like iron. Blood trickled down the back of his throat, and with it came the dawning realization of his last moments before blacking out. He struggled to open his eyes and sit up.

"Holy shit! Noble?" Nate shuffled through the mess on the ground to his friend. A gash in his forehead was still leaking, though most of the blood had already streamed down his face and onto his shirt. His nose looked busted, and a bruise was already forming like a ripening plum under his left eye.

"Jesus." Emory shuffled some books out of the way and made his way over.

"Where's Zoe?" Noble struggled.

"Dude." Nate grabbed a hold of the front of his shirt. "You're jacked up. Stay still."

Noble latched onto Nate's arm. "Where the fuck is my sister?"

"I don't know!"

Noble grimaced, his face twisting into sheer anguish. His hand hovered over his head wound and then gripped his hair. "He took her," he moaned.

Nate's skin prickled, his heart hammering in his chest. "Who took her?"

"The Green Man." Noble gulped in air, tears streaming down his face. "Raymond LaRange. He was standing right there," he said, pointing.

"Are you sure? Those photos were like thirty years—"

"Yes, I'm sure!"

"Okay. Okay. Emory, come here. Sit with him," Nate ordered as he stood and moved to the window, removing his phone from his pocket and swiping through the names until he found the one he needed. He tapped it a few times with shaking fingers before the phone registered that he wanted to make a call. He held the phone to his ear, hand trembling, listening to the ringing. Once, twice, three times. "Come on," he growled.

"Sergeant Wolfe," Seth greeted from the other side of the connection, sitting at his desk, mulling over Paddy's report.

"Sergeant! Someone's taken Zoe Andalusian. Shit, the Green Man, Raymond LaRange. He took her, and Noble's bleeding all over, and—"

"Calm down," Seth instructed as he stood to his feet. "Where are you?"

"The Andalusians'."

"Where is Peter?"

"I don't know. No, um, Noble said his parents went out for dinner."

Seth was already moving. He booted his chair backward, making his way into the main office. "Is Noble okay? Does he need an ambulance?"

"No. Maybe. He's really upset," Nate said, looking at Noble hunched over, demoralized. Nate's eyes stung with tears brought on by fear and adrenaline. "Jesus, is this really happening?"

"Nate, I need you to stay calm. Address Noble's wounds. Do you know how to do that?"

"Yeah. Yeah," Nate said, sniffing and swiping at his eyes.

"I'm on my way," Seth said and disconnected. "Joe," he snapped, not realizing his youngest officer was already standing, waiting for an order.

"Yes, sir," Joe said.

"I need you to get over to the far end of Mulberry Street by the woods. Keep an eye out for a man carrying a young girl, twelve years old."

"A girl and a man, okay." Joe grabbed his coat from the back of his chair. "Doing what?"

"The girl will either be passed out or thrashing around trying to get free," he explained as they made their way out of the station.

"Jesus."

"I want you to get out of the car and look around. Check behind the houses. And keep an eye out in the woods."

"Yes, sir," Joe sounded off, rushing to his car.

"And, Joe," Seth called out before jumping into the Bronco.

Joe spun around. "Yes?"

"If you see this man, I need you to apprehend him. Use your taser, your baton if you have to, but do not draw your firearm."

Joe's face quickly changed from fear to conviction. "I got this."

Nate turned his ringer on in case Sergeant Wolfe called him back. He pocketed his phone and walked over to Noble, kneeling next to his best friend. "Emory," he said, looking up at their newest friend, "can you go get some towels and ice?"

"Yeah." Emory stood and disappeared back downstairs. He was shaking all over, reminded of the last time he'd seen someone covered in blood.

Nate shuffled closer in front of Noble.

"I couldn't…I didn't protect her," Noble said, his voice hardly audible.

"We're gonna find her," Nate said confidently and then placed his hand on Noble's shoulder.

Noble looked up and got a reassuring smile and nod from his childhood friend.

"Yeah. We're gonna find her. We know where that asshole lives, remember?"

Noble swiped at his nose and winced, inhaling sharply.

Nate grimaced. "Yeah, you maybe got a broken nose there."

"It's not broken," Noble said, unsure if that was true. He tried to shift forward, to stand.

"Wait, just wait," Nate instructed.

"I have to call my dad," Noble said.

"I called Sergeant Wolfe. He's on his way."

Noble let out a weighted sigh and relaxed back down. "Yeah?"

"Yeah. He'll call your dad," Nate said.

Emory entered the room, dropping some kitchen towels to the floor. "Here," he said, handing a package of frozen corn to Noble. He wouldn't normally do something this intrusive, but Noble was so shaken and worried, Emory offered just the slightest bit of respite. He built the notion in his mind—calmness, warm sunshine on meadows, gently lapping waves on the shore, a pleasant breeze.

Calm. He directed the thought into Noble's head and watched as his new friend leaned back against the desk drawers.

Noble held the frozen corn to his nose, feeling pitiful but somehow level-headed. For a minute, he really thought he was going to lose it. His little sister was gone and he could have stopped the person, but he'd failed.

No one will blame you, Emory said inside his head.

Noble glared up at Emory. "I blame me."

"Huh?" Nate looked from Noble to Emory. "Oh, you were…right."

Emory held Noble's gaze and nodded. "Yeah. I know what that's like."

Noble's face relaxed, and he offered his new friend a half smile.

"Let me try to get some of this blood off," Nate said. He took one of the wet towels Emory had brought and dabbed at Noble's head, rather inexpertly.

Noble flinched away and took the rag. He pressed it to his face, wiping away the drying blood that had carved a course down his eyebrow, cheek, and jaw. When he pulled the towel away, he noticed how red it was. This was doing him no good. Noble pushed up to standing.

"Be careful," Nate said, helping him to his feet.

"I'm good," Noble said, though his brain felt like it teeter-tottered inside his skull. Careful of his movements, Noble made his way through the books on the ground to the doorway.

A forceful knock on the front door rattled the entire house, and a voice called out, "It's Sergeant Wolfe!"

"Come in," Nate bellowed and made his way past Noble and down the stairs.

Seth entered the house, catching a whiff of burnt bread and a cold tension typical of a home after a crime. He could never tell if it was the blood permeating the air, but violent crimes always had this metallic smell. He saw Nate shuffling down the stairs and met him there.

"Thanks for coming so quickly," Nate said, standing at attention.

"Where's…" Seth caught the movement at the top of the stairs and looked up to see the bloodied face of Noble Andalusian. "Jesus." He took the stairs quickly, Nate following behind, and eased the battered boy toward the light in the hallway as Emory Graff slowly approached. Seth had looked further into the case involving the boy and his sister last night. He had questions, concerns that would have to wait for another day.

Seth observed the cut on the top of Noble's forehead as he rested his hands on either side of the young man's face. He tipped his head up and looked into his eyes. The left one had a bulbous purple lump growing under it. "You know what day it is?"

"Friday," Noble answered.

"What's your mother's middle name?"

Noble narrowed his eyes. "River."

"Really?"

"Yeah," both Noble and Nate replied.

"What do you last recall?" Seth asked as he continued his examination.

Head wounds caused a bloody scene, and the cut was pretty deep.

"Getting hit in the face," Noble responded. "Look, I'm fine. We need to find Zoe."

"We will."

Noble pulled away, sick of being looked over. "That sick child molester has her. He took her!"

"I know, Noble," Seth said calmly. "Nate told me."

"I tried to—"

"Noble, I need you to walk me through what happened," Seth ordered.

Noble nodded and led them down the hall to the bedroom, stopping in the doorway. "It all happened in Zoe's room."

Seth looked over Noble's shoulder. It looked like a tornado had swept through, books and knickknacks strewn everywhere. Despite the mess, it looked like a little girl's room but also a lot like Story's house. Shelves were lined with books and plants that trailed long vines down to the floor. Trinkets, such as a snow globe, a porcelain unicorn, and a fishing hat filled the room, reflective of the young girl's personality.

"I came up to get her for dinner," Noble said, stepping inside.

Seth followed, looking around. Blood spatter on the desk, bookshelf, and floor showed where the skirmish had likely ended.

"He was over here, holding her, stepping out the window."

An icy wind blew through the room.

"Have any of you touched the frame or the glass?" Seth asked.

"No," Nate said from the door.

"No," Emory added, standing next to him.

Seth looked back at Noble and pulled out his notepad and pen, clicking it. "Now, I need to ask. In all of your research, have you come across any recent photos of Raymond LaRange?"

Noble squinted at him. "No."

"Because the photos you showed me, and everything I found researching him, is from three decades ago."

"It was him!"

Seth held up his hands. "I'm not saying it wasn't. I just need to know how similar or different he looked."

"That's what I was going to ask," Nate mumbled.

Noble gave him a quick glare before looking back at Sergeant Wolfe. "He looked older, but I know it was him."

"Okay," Seth said. "I'm sure you don't want to think about the man's face, but I need you to recall every detail you can."

Noble nodded.

"How tall was he?"

"Shorter than me. Not like we were ever just standing up straight next to each other, but I would guess maybe five-ten."

"Hair?"

Noble raised his hands and held them about six inches from the sides of his head. "It was out to about here. It was crazy. Like he stuck his finger in a light socket. That was like the main difference. I think."

"What color?"

"It was blondish brown, I guess."

Seth finished jotting notes and looked back at him. "That's great. Any facial hair?"

Noble shook his head, then nodded. "A little. Stringy. Like he was trying to grow a beard but couldn't."

"What was he wearing?"

"He was in this dark, like…" Noble waved his hands around. "I don't know, like a painter's outfit."

"A jumpsuit? All one piece with long sleeves?"

"Yeah, exactly."

Seth wrote it down, nodding. "Now, can you try to describe his face? Any distinguishing marks? A crooked nose, connected eyebrows, piercings, things like that."

Noble stared down at the ground, recalling the moment he opened the door. "Insane. He looked totally unhinged. Nothing specific about his face. I mean, he was gaunt and…gross. But it was his eyes. He had crazy eyes. And his skin was kind of, well, it was actually kind of greenish."

"No shit," Nate commented. "The Green Man," he whispered to the room as if it all made sense now.

"Not like the Incredible Hulk or anything, just like he was sick or… lacking a lot of nutrients or something. Still, green."

"Green skin. That's a new one," Seth said as he transcribed Noble's description. His mind was running amok, trying to make sense of who they were dealing with, why Zoe was the target, and how LaRange climbed the house and got into the window without Zoe screaming. He stopped and looked up.

"Noble, to be clear, you said you were coming upstairs to get Zoe to come down to dinner?"

Noble looked back up. "Yeah."

"And you hadn't heard anything? A yelp? Commotion? Did you hear a vehicle outside?"

Noble thought back to making the salad in the kitchen. He wasn't playing music. The TV wasn't on. "No, it was silent. Nothing outside, and, like, no sounds at all in the house. It…"

Seth lifted an eyebrow, waiting for Noble to work through his memories.

The frozen moment in time flashed across the back of Noble's eyes. "She was out."

"Zoe?"

"Yeah. When I opened the door. He was holding her, half out the window, and she was…it was like she was asleep in his arms."

"Did you notice any abrasions on her face or on her body?"

"No."

"And he wasn't holding anything else? Anything sticking out of his pockets?"

"No. And"—Noble grimaced—"when we were fighting, there was this moment when he pushed her out of the way. Like he was trying to make sure we didn't hurt her."

Seth clicked his pen off and on. "Is there anything else at all that's coming back to you? Take your time."

Noble rubbed the back of his neck, rolling his head from left to right. "I can't think of anything," he said, leaving out the strange feeling of his mind slipping away from him.

Seth pocketed his notepad and pen. "That's great, Noble. Very helpful. Thank you."

Noble looked out to the roof where the Green Man had gained access to Zoe's room. "Did you call my mom? Dad?"

Seth followed Noble's gaze out the window. "We had an officer following them. They'll get an escort back here."

Noble looked over at Seth, eyes alert. "He's taking her to the caves. He has to be."

"I was going to say that," Nate added.

"What I was thinking," Emory said.

"First things first, guys," Seth said, looking at all the boys. "We need to get a search party out there to find him before he gets to wherever it is he's going. That's the priority. If we focus on one spot, we open multiple doors for him."

"Where else would he go?" Noble countered. "It's not like he has a house here."

"Look." Seth placed his hand on Noble's shoulder. "It's not that I haven't thought of this. I have Officer Casey positioned over at Mulberry Street right now, okay?"

Noble's brow relaxed. "You do?"

"I do."

"Is that the young dude who asked me about my post?" Nate asked.

Seth nodded. "Yes. Officer Joe Casey."

"Good thinking," Nate commented, nodding at Sergeant Wolfe.

Emory silently laughed.

"But we need to spread out and cover the entire town. If we come up empty, I promise I'll go into your cave myself. Sound like a plan?"

"Yes, sir," Nate replied.

Emory nodded.

Noble sniffed. It was a sloppy, moist sound. "Can I clean this?" he asked, pointing to his head.

"Yeah, let's take a better look at it," Seth said, ushering him back into the hall and following him into a bathroom.

Noble turned on the hot tap, splashing his hand through the water.

"Let me get a picture," Seth said, pulling out his phone.

Noble stood in the bright bathroom light, turning this way and that as Seth snapped photos of his injuries, and then he washed his face. He dried off, then leaned forward into the mirror to look at the cut on his forehead, hidden in his hairline.

"Let me see," Seth said, examining the wound and taking new photos now that they cleaned it up. "I think you might need stitches. Or staples."

"I'm fine. I don't want to go to the hospital," Noble said.

"I already radioed for an ambulance. They'll decide that."

Noble sighed and turned back to the mirror to look at his nose. He grabbed some tissues, gently wiping away the blood congealed inside his nostrils.

Sirens outside grabbed their attention, and they all moved to the stairs. Noble pushed past them as the front door opened and Jolie Andalusian swept into her home. She saw her son and rushed to him, wrapping him in a motherly hug, one hand holding the back of his head as Noble leaned into her shoulder.

It wasn't the first time Seth noticed the natural love and comfort this family displayed to one another. He made his way down the stairs, Nate and Emory following behind.

Peter Andalusian stepped inside, his eyes surveying the occupants in rapid-fire succession as he moved to his wife and son.

Noble muttered apologies into the crook of his mother's shoulder, masked in sniffles and sobs.

"My love, it's alright," Jolie cooed.

Peter rubbed his hand over Noble's back in firm, reassuring circles. "It's going to be okay, Noble," he said.

Seth nodded at Peter and walked past the family to meet Sergeant Eddie Cabrera, the oldest member of the force who typically worked the graveyard shift, standing in the front doorway. Seth tipped his head, and the two men walked outside.

"How's the kid?" Eddie asked.

"He's shaken more than anything," Seth said as they walked out to the front lawn. "Might need a couple staples in his forehead, black eye, busted nose."

"Ouch. So, what's the plan?"

"We're going to set up a search," Seth explained as he walked to the corner of the house. "I want a line moving from here, just under that window, down the street. We know the perpetrator entered and likely exited through the window of Zoe Andalusian's bedroom. We need to get fingerprints off that window and the frame. There's also a fair amount of blood in the room. Get multiple samples. It may not all be from Noble's wounds."

"I'm on it," Eddie said, his eyes narrowed on the upstairs window. "We'll make sure to look for and collect hair as well."

"And I need you to get an Amber Alert out immediately. Get a photo of Zoe from the family."

Eddie turned back to Seth. "Was already the first thing on my mind."

Seth pulled out his notepad and tore out the page he dedicated to the description of the man who may or may not be Raymond LaRange. Noble was positive in his assertion, but he was also in shock. And with no one having laid eyes on this man in over three years, and even then it was in the darkened woods, Seth was keeping an open mind. It wasn't like there was even a current record of LaRange's existence. Seth handed the paper to Eddie. "We've got a solid description of the man that took her. Make sure this gets on that alert."

"Got it."

"After you get that out, call for backup to set up barricades at both exits out of town. No one drives through without their car being searched."

Eddie was taking notes on his phone.

"Ask Peter for access to a computer. Download footage from every traffic cam in town in the last hour to a flash drive. Log every vehicle that passes in and out of town, which won't be many at this hour. Call the Victorian Inn and every bed-and-breakfast. Get a list of every guest currently there and anyone staying there in the past week. If any of them ask their guests for car information for parking, get that as well."

"I'm on it," Eddie said as he finished typing.

"Good. Has Joe radioed in?"

"Nope."

"Where the hell is Bill? We need to get this search underway."

Eddie's gaze traveled down the side of the house and across the lawn. "It was raining earlier, so we may get footprints."

Another set of sirens drew up outside the house, and on cue, Chief Bill Richards jumped out of his personal vehicle, the magnetic beacon askew atop the roof.

Seth placed his hand on Eddie's shoulder. "Okay, take care of everything inside the house and keep an eye on the boy," he ordered and ran over to Bill.

Bill jogged up to meet Seth. He was carrying a heavy flashlight and had his gun holstered between his arm and chest. "How's Noble?"

"He'll be fine. We've got to arrange teams and get moving."

"I called all our volunteers. I told them to reach out to friends and neighbors. Should have a big crew here in minutes."

Seth nodded. "That's great."

"You really think it was this LaRange guy you told me about this morning?"

"It could be. Noble was firm about it, but the only pictures of this guy are from thirty years ago. If it is him, I don't know where the hell he's been living."

Bill blew into his hands and then rubbed them together. "You think Dr. Owens was lying? You think he's still there?"

"He definitely knew something. It's hard to believe his criminal sentence was lowered. There'd be a record of his release in our database.

329

He'd have a contact, registered as a sex offender. I've found none of that. If it is in fact LaRange, that's the only place I can think he's been staying. Noble gave us a solid description of the man, regardless. That'll be going out with the Amber Alert."

Running down the street came Sasha, only living a few blocks away. She hadn't even had time to get out of her uniform, her shift only ending minutes before Seth got the call from Nate. "I'm ready! Let's find Zoe!" she shouted as she made her final strides to join them.

Seth nodded at her. "I'm going to have you and Bill each lead a group. Sasha, you take a team east toward the high school. Bill, lead your group west of town toward Mourner's Beach. I'm going to head north past the cemetery and meet up with Joe at the edge of the town leading into the cursed woods."

"Cursed woods?" asked Sasha.

"Town myth," Bill explained. "Why there, Seth?"

"A hunch." Seth pulled the radio from his hip. "Joe, have you seen anything?"

Joe's voice came back over the radio. "No, sir."

"Stay planted there. We're breaking up into groups. I'll be heading your way." Seth's hand dropped to his side. People were stepping out of their homes, pulling on coats. The neighbor across the street, a large man Seth was only familiar with in passing, was already walking across the road. A small group was hurrying down the street, the same way Sasha came. Lost Grove was congregating.

"I'll start assigning teams," Bill said and strode off toward the incoming townspeople.

"What the hell is going on here lately?" Sasha asked Seth.

"The storm brought a storm."

"Clearly. You want me to—"

"Hold on," Seth said, holding up a hand and looking over his shoulder. Sasha followed his gaze to the entrance of the Andalusian home to see Peter walk out into the light of the front porch carrying a flashlight with a gun on his hip. She looked up at Seth, wondering how in the hell he knew to look over when he did.

"Follow me," Seth said to her, striding toward Peter.

Sasha followed behind, quickly registering the cold look of vengeance on Peter Andalusian's face.

"I assume you've got a permit for that?" Seth asked, placing one foot

LOST GROVE

on the step below Peter.

"We heading out?" Peter grumbled.

"I'll take that as a yes," Seth replied, locking eyes with Peter. "We're breaking into groups, and you're coming with me. We catch this son of a bitch, the goal is to take him alive. Don't make matters any worse for yourself than they already are."

"I just want my daughter back. This is solely for protection. I'll leave any shooting and cuffing to you."

"Good. We understand each other."

Peter stepped down to join Seth and Sasha. "We do."

Seth nodded and turned around, surprised to see at least twenty people gathered into three groups in the street.

Bill stepped forward onto the curb. "We're ready."

"Good job, Bill." Seth walked up to meet him.

Sasha followed behind Seth, keeping her eyes on Peter.

They came to a stop, and Peter glanced over at her. "Officer Kingsley," he said, nodding.

How and why Peter Andalusian knew Sasha's name was mildly concerning, but the look on his face had changed from fury to respect. Sasha gave a curt nod back and looked out at the people of Lost Grove.

Seth stepped forward to address the group. "Zoe Andalusian has been abducted. The culprit is a man, about five-ten, wiry, with wild ash-blond hair, wispy facial hair, and has a greenish tint to his skin."

Confused murmurs came from the crowd.

"He was wearing a dark jumpsuit at the time of the abduction, but that could have changed. We don't believe he's armed, but he should be considered very dangerous. If you don't have flashlights with you, use the lights on your phones."

Seth pointed to the first group, making his way from left to right. "Group one, you'll be led by Chief Richards. Group two, you will follow Officer Kingsley here to my left. Group three, you're with me," Seth said, making eye contact with Paddy, who he spotted in the throng of people.

"Stay with your groups! Do not go on any wild goose chases. If you see something, say something. Call out Zoe's name loudly and often. We're not trying to sneak up on this guy. We want him to know we're coming. The more voices he hears, the more liable he is to panic and make a mistake. The more voices our neighbors hear, the more volunteers we can get out into the field for the search. Circle every house. Do not worry about startling or offending your neighbors. A young girl's life is at stake. That is all that matters. Now, let's move out!"

A knock on the door threw Noble from the couch. He launched himself at the front door, pulling it open to greet a concerned-looking Anya. She flinched when she saw his face, yet instinctively reached up. The cold tips of her fingers glanced over the hot, swollen skin of Noble's cheek, and he found it comforting.

"What happened?" she asked.

Noble grabbed her hand, pulling her inside.

"Oh, hey, Anya," Nate said from the end of the hall.

"Hi, Nate," she responded.

Nate started walking toward them, saw the way Noble was slouched, the proximity of their bodies next to one another, and spun back around.

"Did he text you?" Noble asked Anya.

"Nate? No. I was over at Ryker's. I mean, I was trying to find Ryker. He hasn't answered my calls or texts. He isn't home. His mom's probably on shift. I saw the people and… What happened? Why are there police all—"

"He took Zoe," Noble interrupted.

Anya looked up into his downcast face. "Who took Zoe?"

"The Green Man!" Nate responded from the living room.

Anya's eyes opened wide. "LaRange? You're sure?"

Noble nodded. "Yeah."

"Did he look that much similar?"

He looked up and met her eyes. They were brilliant aquamarine blue, surrounded by oddly dark eyelashes. Her nose was pink from the cold outside. "Trust me. It was him."

"I believe you," she replied. "What happened? Where did you see him?"

Noble's gaze shifted back down. "I went to grab her for dinner, and he was…he was just standing there with her in his arms about to leap out the window. I could have stopped him. I swore I had him, and then… like, something in my head made me slip."

"What do you mean something in your head?" Anya whispered, leaning closer.

Noble shrugged. "Like a blip. I don't know how to describe it. Just a blip."

Anya's already creased forehead cinched further. "Like what Emory and Ember can do?"

"I don't know."

"Haven't you asked him about it? Emory?"

Noble shook his head. "I should have stopped that asshole."

Anya's brow softened. She grabbed Noble into a hug, both awkward and comforting. "So everyone is out searching?"

"Yeah. They wouldn't let me," he said as their bodies parted. He wouldn't have minded staying in the hug longer. "I had to wait for an ambulance to look at my head."

"It looks pretty gnarly."

"They put temporary sutures in. They said I needed staples, but there was no way I was going to the hospital. Plus, Officer Eddie said it's always best for someone to stay at home in these situations. If Zoe gets free or whatever, she'll likely come back here."

"That makes sense." Voices from upstairs drew Anya's attention.

"That's Eddie and a forensics team," Noble explained.

Anya felt tears welling up in her eyes. "I just can't believe it."

Noble gulped, feeling sick. The nausea churning his stomach hadn't abated since he came to and recalled the sight of Raymond LaRange holding his sister like a doll. What would he do to her? The thought caused bile to rise up his throat.

"Have they searched the caves?" Anya asked, sensing he needed a distraction from his thoughts.

"No," came the response from down the hall just as Noble was about to answer. Nate stepped out from behind the living room wall. "I swear I'm not eavesdropping. I've just been waiting."

Noble snorted, and he and Anya moved into the living room off the kitchen.

"Hey," Emory greeted her.

"Hi," she said with the appropriate dearth of cheer as she sat on the couch and pulled her legs up under her.

"They haven't searched them yet," Nate said. "But Sergeant Wolfe has one of his best guys over by Nettie's house now, monitoring the woods." Nate was typing on his phone, in constant contact with Stan, who couldn't make it over because she was on babysitting duty until her parents or an older brother got home.

Anya looked at Noble. "Well, that's good, right?"

Noble reluctantly nodded. If it was up to him, Noble would be in the caves by now, chasing the sicko down.

"They said if the search parties don't find Zoe, they'll go into the cave themselves," Emory added.

Anya offered a smile. "Well, hopefully it doesn't come to that."

Nate looked up from his phone. "Look, guys, Sergeant Wolfe knows what he's doing. I mean, fuck 'Sergeant.' He was a homicide detective for almost twenty years. Detective Wolfe once found a girl who was missing for over a year back in 2018 that everyone thought was dead. He refused to give up. That family said they're indebted to him for life."

"Is that what you're doing over there?" Noble asked. "Looking up old cases?"

Nate scoffed. "Please, I've got that shit up here," he said, pointing at his head. "Just keeping Stan up to date. All I'm saying is, Detective Wolfe will find her."

Emory looked over at Noble and Anya and nodded. "He will."

For the first time since he woke up on the floor in Zoe's room, Noble felt a glimmer of hope.

"Bill, you out front with that group?" Seth spoke into the walkie, leading his group back toward the Andalusian home. Peter brought up the rear.

"Yeah, just got back. Got a host of new volunteers here." Bill's voice came back through.

"Is Sasha or Eddie out there with you?"

"Eddie's out here."

"Put him in charge of the crowd, and tell him to keep everyone off the Andalusian property. Meet me in the front yard."

"Will do."

With all search parties coming up empty, finding no trace of Raymond LaRange or Zoe, Seth was ready to tell Bill his backup plan. He spun around to face his group, walking backward. "Everyone, thank you again for your service. You're all free to go back to your homes. If you'd like to continue volunteering your time, wait with the group in the street. Officer Cabrera will be your contact for the time being."

Seth started to turn back around when he caught a figure galloping down the adjacent street in lace-up boots and a flowing dress. He quickly changed direction, hoping to meet her before she got to the group.

"Who is it?" Story asked as they closed the distance.

Seth could see the frantic look in her eyes. "We've got a—"

"Who is it, Seth?" she demanded.

"It's Zoe Andalusian."

Story's face crumpled. "Dammit," she cursed and turned away from the group, some of them gazing in their direction. She held a hand to her mouth. "I knew it. I sensed it. I had a premonition. I should have come straight back then."

"Story, you couldn't have done anything."

Story swiped one tear from her cheek. "I felt it and I still went through with going to that silly conference when I knew in my gut I should turn around and come home. I thought maybe, at first, it was you. But there was so much innocence. What happened to her?" she asked.

"Someone took her," Seth answered. "We just finished searching the town and now—"

"Someone?" Story's eyes narrowed. "Or are you saying—"

"We believe it was Raymond LaRange who took her. Noble tried to fight him off."

"Mother, Maiden… Is he okay?"

"He's got some bruises and a nasty cut on his head, but he's going to be okay. He blames himself."

"Oh, that poor boy. I'm sure he does. He dotes on his sister. I just can't believe—"

"Story," Seth stopped her, "how long ago was it you said you saw LaRange?"

Story massaged her temples, a headache setting in. "It was a little over three years ago. I think."

"Can you tell me what he looked like?"

"It was dark," she admitted.

"Anything. Height? Build?"

"I don't know, five-nine, five-eleven. Shorter than you. Longish hair, a bit untamed. I don't know the color. He wore dark coveralls, but he had the top off, sleeves tied around his waist. It was a hot night. Scrawny, wiry sort of build. That's all I can think—"

"Ms. Palmer?" Peter had crept up on them. He looked drawn, like a ghost of himself.

Story turned to face the father of the young girl she'd recently brought under her tutelage and immediately regretted it.

His expression shifted from the kind look of a grieving father to the knowing sharpness of trained ex-military. "What is… There's something you know," he surmised in the half-believed vein of all in Lost Grove who saw that Story Palmer was more than met the eye. The only difference was that he wasn't skeptical of her like most in town. He found himself believing her words.

"Yes," Story said. She looked at Seth, then back at Peter. "I had a premonition. I felt something was wrong, something very off. I could sense the urgency of it, but my intuition told me it was Seth that was in danger. If I would have known… I'm so sorry, Mr. Andalusian."

Peter felt himself momentarily soften. He had felt nothing but rage and guilt ever since Officer Cabrera came to get him and Jolie. "It's certainly not your fault," he said, inwardly torturing himself. It was his refusal to abide by Dr. Owens's demands that caused this. Nothing more.

"There's something else we need to discuss," Seth added.

Peter's face instantly went rigid again. "What?"

"Did Noble tell you why he and his friends were at Story's last night?"

"No. I didn't…" Peter didn't have a sufficient response. His primary concern was dealing with Jolie, but he should have found the time to speak with his children more.

Seth pushed on. "I believe it's something that may help our current situation."

"Then let's get to it," Peter said and turned on a dime, heading toward his home.

Seth looked over at Story. "Go with Peter. I need to speak with Bill before we get into it."

Story nodded and followed behind Peter as Seth headed toward Bill.

Peter turned toward the group in front of his house and whistled. It drew some attention, but only the person he meant it for left the pack of volunteers. Paddy ran to catch up and followed Peter and Story into the Andalusian home.

Bill greeted Seth as he approached with a grim nod. "We've got to find this girl, Seth. I don't think this town can take another—"

"I know," Seth interrupted, "and we will."

"So, where do we go from here?"

Seth looked over to the crowd of concerned townsfolk and then back at Bill. "The caves."

Bill raised his eyebrows. "You think there's credence to that story the kids told you?"

"I initially found it difficult to believe Raymond LaRange was still somewhere in Lost Grove, somehow going unnoticed by the general populace. But Story claims to have seen him in the woods three years ago, and—"

"The woods?"

"Yeah. And apparently Mary has seen him as well."

Bill rolled his eyes. "Of course she has."

"Him showing up tonight just cements the fact that this guy has been living somewhere nearby. The way I see it, he's either been living like a nomad in the cave system, or—"

"The Orbriallis," Bill said.

"Only one way to find out." Seth hadn't mentioned the potential link between the cave and the Orbriallis. Leaving Story's house last night, he wasn't even considering Peter's plan for getting into the facility, but now there was a child's life at stake. Another child. He didn't like leaving Bill out of the loop, but Seth couldn't have him in the know. He couldn't have Bill be an accessory to something like this.

"So, what's the plan?" Bill asked.

"I need you to call Search and Rescue. Have them send as many people as they can. Have them meet you, Eddie, and Sasha at the station. You bring one group to the Rollins caves over by Mourner's and have Eddie and Sasha bring the other group to Devil's Cradle. The caves are connected, but it's dangerous. Get all these volunteers to either go home or continue searching within town limits. We don't need any other disasters on our hands."

Bill nodded. "I'm on it," he said, pulling out his phone and stepping away to call Search and Rescue.

Seth grabbed his walkie from his waist and clicked the button. "Joe, you still on Mulberry?"

"Yes, sir," his voice came through.

"I need you to head back to the station and touch base with Eddie. He set up blockades at both exits out of town and has been in contact with the Victorian Inn and all the rental houses to get their guest lists. I need you to take over all those communications."

"Heading there now."

Seth hitched the walkie back on his waist and hurried into the Andalusian home.

"I'll stay," Emory said, the group of kids all gathered together in the living room.

"No! *You* can't stay," Nate declared. "We need your magic brain shit.

Anya can stay."

"Hell no," Emory responded quickly.

"Why not?"

Emory scoffed. "She's the best chance we have of finding this place again without Stan." He didn't want to bring up the fact that it was Anya who had done most of the leading and finding of the cave in the first place. Not to mention the person who they all followed as they walked out of the cursed woods. No one seemed to notice but him, and he wasn't about to out Anya. Something told him she didn't want the entire world knowing she could not only navigate the cursed woods everyone seemed afraid of, but she also seemed at home in them.

"He has a point," Noble suggested.

Nate threw his hands up. "Okay. Well, I have to go because I'm the most level-headed. Emory has to because…" He swirled a hand around his head to indicate Emory's magical brain powers. "I think you should stay," he said to Noble.

"You must be out of your fucking mind if you think I'm going to just sit here while—"

"I don't think anyone, technically, needs to stay behind," Anya suggested.

"Okay, look," Nate said, pushing his thermal sleeves up to his elbows and crossing his arms. "We'll all go. But we have to tell Stan that we're doing this and—" Nate turned and did a double take. "Hey, Mr. Andalusian."

Noble, Anya, and Emory all spun around.

Peter had been standing with arms crossed for some time on the edge between the informal dining area and the living room. Paddy leaned against the wall behind him. Story was waiting half in and half out of the room. Peter had listened intently to his son and friends discuss some course of action, noticing the backpack, climbing gear, ropes, and oddly, an assortment of baseball bats from when Noble still played sitting propped against the wall.

"Hey, guys," Peter said in a chummy, fatherly way. "Going somewhere?"

"Yeah," Noble answered, turning to respond to his dad. "We're going to find Zoe in the cave."

"What cave?" Peter asked.

Seth entered, stepping into the discussion. "You're not going. I'm going. We already discussed this."

Peter's head swiveled to look at Seth. "Discussed what?" Then he glanced back at his son. "What cave, Noble?"

"This actually relates to exactly what I told you we needed to discuss," Seth clarified.

Paddy made his way to the other side of the room.

Anya stood up from the couch. "Mr. Andalusian, I think it would be best if I explain, since this all started with me. Well…my friend Nettie Horne, um, she has a brother, George."

"I know the Hornes."

"Of course. What you may not know is that Nettie believes that the boy living with them is not her real brother. She believes her real brother was stolen. Now, he doesn't talk, George. He mumbles and grunts, but a few days ago, he said something that sounded coherent. I asked Noble for help in deciphering it because you guys play Mad Gab a lot, and he found information pertaining to a man whose alias is Papa LaRange." Anya felt herself get tongue-tied. How was she ever supposed to explain who and what Raymond LaRange was?

"Who is Papa LaRange?" Peter asked, meeting Paddy's eyes across the room. Paddy had clearly been picking up on all the details and would run a background check on all this information when he had time.

"He was charged and tried, um…" Anya pulled her lips into her mouth, unable to say the words to the father of the missing girl.

"He was charged and tried for sexual misconduct with two minors in Ohio in 1992," Seth answered for her.

The room turned, all attention now on him.

"He and his mother were brought to trial. He was deemed unfit to serve time and was sent to a mental health facility. That facility transferred him to the Orbriallis Institute. They," Seth said and pointed around the room to the teens, "brought me this information last night before you arrived. I had a busy night. Apparently, your son and all present have been doing a little digging. They've tracked some information linking this man to the cave system behind the Horne house."

"A cave?" Peter asked, turning toward Seth. "In those woods you had your guy stationed outside of?"

Seth nodded. "I sent him there the moment I got the call from Nate telling me what happened."

Nate stepped forward and pressed his phone into Peter's hands. Peter watched as the video of the cave, the hall, the linoleum floor, the door, and the surveillance camera played.

"That door is about four hundred meters short of directly sitting under the Orbriallis Institute," Nate explained, tapping his phone and showing Peter further pictures of the cave. The little doll made Peter flinch.

"You're telling me that we have evidence of a child molester who… When was he released from the Orbriallis?" Peter asked Seth, trying to put the pieces together in his head.

"I can't find any record of there being a discharge, and Dr. Owens says he can't recall a patient of that name."

Peter looked over at Paddy. "You come across this name?"

Paddy shook his head. "I haven't come across anything with the name Raymond LaRange."

"I've been working all day to secure information about this man," Seth said. "Anything still linking him to the Orbriallis. I was hoping—"

"Wait, wait," Peter stopped the sergeant. He cocked his head, looking from his son to Seth. "Are you saying this is the guy who took Zoe? The description of the guy in the Amber Alert?"

Seth nodded.

Peter's eyebrows pitched into his hairline. "Whoa," he said and clenched his jaw. He placed his hands on his hips to keep from balling them into fists. He spoke measured and slow. "So this whole search, you've known who we're looking for."

"Your son ID'd him. I didn't know how much he told you."

Peter stepped up to Seth and roared, "You've wasted hours of time with my daughter in the hands of a sexual predator."

"The search we carried out was essential, by the books," Seth bellowed back. "We set up roadblocks on both sides of town. We spread out and covered every area of town in a strategic and methodical search with the sole purpose of finding your daughter before her abductor reached whatever destination he was intending. You don't divert all your efforts to one unverified location when your kidnapper could go anywhere."

"What the fuck do you mean 'unverified'? You just told me that Noble and his friends identified the location that—"

"The last time anyone witnessed Raymond LaRange near that cave was nine years ago!"

Noble and his friends were frozen in place, eyes wide. Story had come to the entryway of the living room and watched nervously, one arm across her chest and the other hovering over her mouth. Paddy leaned back against the wall, calm and unfazed by the heated exchange.

"And that was by an eight-year-old Antoinetta Horne," Seth continued. "The only other people we know of who have even laid eyes on this guy are Mary Germaine and Story Palmer, who both saw him in different locations. And the most recent sighting was over three years ago. Raymond LaRange has no known home. There is no vehicle registered in his name. He could be anywhere. The search we carried out was the first and best chance we had of catching him and saving your daughter. Now is the time we focus our efforts on specific locations."

Peter, his face red with rage, looked over at Paddy.

"He's right, Peter," his friend answered the silent question.

"Fuck," Peter fumed. He turned, tossing his hands through his hair and then down to his sides.

"We've got Search and Rescue on the way here now," Seth said calmly. "Bill's going to have them search the known cave entrances near Mourner's Beach and Devil's Cradle. I'm going to search the cave your son and his friends uncovered, which appears not to be connected to the rest of the caves. And I'd like it if you and Paddy accompanied me."

Peter turned back around, leaned in closer to Seth, and said in a low voice, "You know who's behind this. And I think we both know where she is."

"I'm inclined to agree with you," Seth whispered. "I didn't want to break open that can of worms in front of your son."

Peter closed his eyes. He was in the middle of telling his wife the truth about everything at dinner, but the conversation was cut short when Officer Cabrera came in to get them. Peter's biggest fear wasn't Jolie's reaction but Noble's. He knew his son idolized him and that confessing his hidden past would likely destroy that. But saving Zoe was all that mattered, and he didn't have the luxury of time.

Peter turned to face his son. "Noble, I'm sorry this is how you've got to find out, but we need to save your sister. I've been working for the Orbriallis for over twenty years. I mainly deliver highly classified documents. But over the years, things became very…complicated."

Noble's face flushed, embarrassed that his friends were in the room more than anything. His dad's confession did not surprise him, but it didn't dull the pain.

"They asked things of me I was fully against. I rebelled against them. Against Dr. Neil Owens. He threatened me and, by proxy, our family. I'm firmly of the opinion that Dr. Owens is behind your sister's kidnapping."

Anya risked slipping her hand into Noble's, and she was relieved when he accepted her gesture and squeezed her hand tight.

Noble could see the agony in his dad's eyes. There were a lot of things he wanted to say, wanted to yell. If it weren't for Anya's hand calming him, he might have. "We just need to find Zoe."

Peter nodded and turned back to Seth. "Let's get to the cave and see what's behind that door. I have a feeling I know where it comes out."

"Where?" Seth asked.

"The bottom of the parking garage. That level is only for people with special access or on special projects. There's an old metal door in the corner, burrowed into a stone wall. If it doesn't lead there, we'll go in a different way." Peter had seen the door, so oddly placed in the stone wall, just over eight years ago when he went to confront Dr. Owens for making him get rid of Kelly Fulson's body. The parking lot was empty aside from his car and Dr. Owens's tan 1968 Jaguar 420G that hadn't left the lot in all the years Peter worked there. Water dripping from a broken pipe near the door had drawn Peter's attention. If that was indeed their way in, he would be eternally grateful for the broken pipe.

Seth took in a deep breath and sighed. "Look. On the whole, we know the Institute is corrupt, but I'm looking for your daughter right now, not to take down Neil Owens. We can search that cave and see if we can get behind that door, but breaking into the Orbriallis? That's another story. Putting aside for the moment that it's illegal, you told me we had a slim, one-time chance if we went your route of getting into the Institute. If I waste that and we still don't find your daughter because she's out there in the cave systems or somewhere else, we're fucked. Am I right?" Seth finished, turning to Paddy for confirmation.

Paddy nodded, and Seth looked back at Peter.

"I told you, there's no way they'll let you in there to search the place," Peter said. "And getting a warrant based on the outlandish information we have will not happen. And even if we could, we don't have time."

Seth leaned toward him. "I may be trying to solve a larger case here, but your daughter has priority. I can't make the decision to go into the Orbriallis and not come out with her. We don't know where she'd be, and from what you told me, we wouldn't have the time to search the whole damn building. One time, limited chance, that's how you explained it. I need proof she's in there."

"What if you did have time?" Emory's soft, deep voice felt out of place in the room. "And proof."

Nate snapped his fingers. "Oh, fuck yeah!" He jumped on the balls of his feet.

"What?" Seth asked. His eyes darted around the teens in the room, all of them brightening at a shared idea, an inside scoop, that he didn't have the knowledge to grasp.

Emory stepped forward, took a deep breath, and swallowed back his hesitation. *What if you did have time?*

Seth's head snapped back. Peter and Paddy both tilted theirs like dogs hearing a high-pitched whistle. Story narrowed her eyes while her lip curled ever so slightly upward.

Seth slowly opened his mouth. "I'm sorry, what the—"

I'm talking inside your head.

"What the hell?" Peter voiced in disbelief.

Paddy stared at the kid, more intrigued than confused.

"He can talk inside people's minds," Nate added aloud, grinning from ear to ear.

"He can do more than that," Story said.

Emory felt her eyes pierce into him. He couldn't feel her, but he knew she could read him like a book. It was unsettling. It reminded him of the older woman in Dr. Bajorek's office.

Seth blinked several times and nearly laughed. "In the video, the orderlies just let you walk away. At the time, I didn't want to interrupt the flow of information, but it definitely bothered me. What did you do?"

Emory nodded slightly. "Yeah, I can kind of make people do things they don't really want to or weren't going to do in the first place."

Seth looked around to where Story stood. Her eyes flicked from Emory to him. Inside, a fire danced, one he'd come to find reassuring. Her eyes gave away everything, if you just knew how to look, and Seth felt as if he was starting to. There was nothing to suggest Emory had ill intentions, and Seth was certain Story's eyes would have told him so if such were the case.

"Well, goddamn," Paddy said.

"There's another video?" Peter asked, the question directed at his son.

"Emory is being treated at the Institute. He and his sister are in these sleep studies—well, they're being treated for PTSD because of a—it doesn't matter," Noble explained.

Seth suddenly felt like it did matter. Quite a bit, in fact, given his recent, albeit brief, look into why he knew the young man, Emory Graff.

"So, one night, when he's there, he goes walking," Nate continued. "He didn't think anything of it. He gets in the elevator and it takes him down to this sublevel and he finds these kids, like our age and younger, getting put in weird pods and hooked up to all kinds of weird shit. So he takes a video. And he showed it to us."

"Then he showed it to Nettie," Anya added.

Noble looked down at her by his side and nodded. "Yeah. Nettie saw it. And guess what?"

Peter briefly shook his head.

"She saw George. Her real brother, George."

"You got into the basement?" Paddy asked.

Emory shrugged. "I don't think I was supposed to. It was the middle of the night. Not sure why the elevator let me press the button, but it did."

"Years of looking for shit on Dr. Owens, and your son and his friends uncover more in one week than we ever could." Paddy laughed.

"Okay, let me get something ironed out here," Seth interrupted, moving toward Emory. "You can make people think, what, exactly?"

"I'll make it like you were never there. Just like I did with those orderlies. We can walk right through the front doors if we want to."

"We're not going in the front door," Peter jumped in. "It's too complicated to get back down to the sublevels. We'd have to go up, then back down. We should go through the cave."

"Good. I'll take you," Noble said, moving toward his gear.

Peter grabbed him by the arm. "You aren't going."

"I'm going, Dad."

Peter faced his son. "You are not going."

"You can't expect me to just sit here and not… I'm the one who found the cave. We are. I have to get out of this house, and I know the way. I know the cave."

Peter pointed to Noble's friends. "And so do they. Nate was down there with you—"

"Without the caving experience I have."

Peter continued. "And I'm what? A novice? Who taught you?"

"This is bullshit!"

"Hey, you've got staples in your head—"

"Sutures."

"Sutures that need to be staples, and a possible concussion. You're not going into a cave tonight," Peter said.

"At least let me come to the cave," Noble argued. "Let me out of this house, Dad. Please."

Peter sighed. "Okay. And she'll make sure you don't try anything stupid," he said, nodding toward Story.

Noble looked at Story. She smiled at him, and he was relatively certain she had a way of making sure he couldn't do anything, even if he wanted to. It made him shiver.

"Paddy, we'll need to get everything together," Peter said.

"Already assembled. I'm on my way. Give me eight minutes," Paddy said, heading for the door.

"Okay, Nate, you'll take us down."

"I think Anya should," Nate said. "I mean, me and Anya, but Emory's right. She knows where she's going. I mean, she and Noble found it first."

Peter smirked at Nate. "Yeah, you and Anya lead us in. When we get to the place where it opens up, you head back. Understand me?"

Both teens nodded at the assertive father in front of them.

Anya pulled her knit hat off and ran a hand through her hair to ease the tension. She'd started the evening with increasing anxiety over the lack of response she'd been getting from Ryker. Now her anxiety ratcheted up, but somehow the promise of heading into the woods gave her a feeling of calm. A sense of duty and confidence in her ability to guide her friends' father and police officers to rescue Zoe gave her focus.

"Alright. Now you," Peter said to Emory. "Let me hear how this works."

Emory shrugged. *I just focus.*

The men flinched.

"Can you"—Peter held out his hands—"not do that anymore, please? Not to us anyway."

"Shit, sorry," Emory replied.

Peter smiled. "How close do you need to be? How long does it take?"

"Oh, um…" Emory tipped his head from shoulder to shoulder. "It doesn't take long—a couple seconds. The closer the better. I can feel people around me, so I'll know if someone is coming up."

"Wait," Seth interrupted. "We haven't decided on this course of action."

"Haven't we?" Peter asked, the question weighted, daring Seth to argue.

Seth offered him a tight smile. "No. First, how old are you?" he asked Emory.

"Eighteen," Emory replied.

"Thank Christ for that." Peter sighed. "Paddy will come back with comms. He'll be able to gain access to the video feed within the building, but I doubt he'll be able to access the surveillance in the basements."

Seth shook his head. "Let's just slow down. Yes, he's a legal adult, but that doesn't mean he isn't a—pardon me on this—a child," Seth pointed out. "You're not letting your son—"

"My son is injured," Peter interrupted.

Seth paused, staring at Peter. "You wouldn't let your son within a hundred feet of that place."

Peter looked away.

"I can do it," Emory interjected. "Look, I want to do it. I know I'm new here, and so, maybe you're thinking, why the hell does he care? There isn't enough time for me to explain how…" Emory caught Seth's look and didn't need to be a mind reader to know the sergeant was already putting pieces together. That he knew the story of what happened to Cassidy Zimmer. "That explanation notwithstanding, maybe you can understand it from my perspective."

"Which is?" Seth asked.

"Noble explained it, right? My sister and I are being studied like lab rats, man. And that video, that shit I saw up there? You think it hasn't crossed my mind that we might be destined for something like that? We came down here to get help. My sister needs real help. She's fucked up because of what happened," Emory said, looking right at Seth.

"What happened?" Peter asked.

"Maybe we can explain that later," Nate said.

"She needs real help. Therapy. She doesn't talk anymore. And on top of that trauma, this place, the Orbriallis, has got her terrified to even leave the house. So I want to go. I want to help find Zoe. And call it selfish, but that place is fucked up, and the way I'm hearing it, you guys plan to put an end to all the weird sci-fi bullshit happening up there. So, I'm coming. I'm helping," Emory finished. He looked at Story. "Sorry for all the language."

She grinned. "I like all the language. Foul-mouthed or gilded in gold."

Emory couldn't help but laugh at that.

Seth ran a hand through his hair, tugging at the roots. "You mentioned something about proof. Do you mean proof Zoe's there?"

"I'll be able to hear her."

"How will you know it's her?" Peter asked.

Emory shrugged. "I know what you and Noble feel like. It kind of runs in the family, the vibe."

"Does it?" Story asked, curiosity getting the better of her.

"Yeah," Emory smiled.

"This plan makes sense," Peter said to Seth.

"Just give me a minute," Seth said in return, stepping away.

Story followed him partially into the hall. "Are you going to be okay?"

He nodded. "It's not ideal, but we have probable cause. I can think of enough later to justify probable cause. I hope."

She smiled. "I meant going into the cave."

Seth looked at her, and his lips curved into a smile. "It'll be therapeutic. And I've got this," he said, holding up the acorn he kept in his pocket.

"Not to mention the protection sigils on your boots," she commented.

"Those too." Seth hung his head, hands on his hips as he thought. "Is it right, though? To ask that kid to help?"

"You didn't ask. He volunteered."

Seth glanced up at her and she raised her shoulders in a shrug.

"Do you believe in coincidences, Sheriff?" Story asked.

Using his incorrect moniker made his pulse quicken and tugged at the corner of his lips. "Yes. Being a detective makes it hard not to believe in coincidences."

Story nodded. "Kind of a conundrum, coincidences. If you don't believe in them, then it means you wouldn't see how fortuitous it is that this young man recently involved in some incident brought him to Lost Grove. Not only Lost Grove but the Orbriallis Institute. And he befriended the young man whose sister was just kidnapped."

Seth raised his eyebrows. "And since I do believe in them?"

"Then you already know the answer to your question."

Peter interrupted. "Paddy just texted with an ETA. I'm doing this, Sergeant. I'd like it if I had the law on my side."

Seth nodded, joining the group back in the open-concept house. "We appreciate your help," he said to Emory. "Here's the caveat. You never leave my side. You don't go wandering off. I'll lead, and you'll always stay behind me. If things get out of hand, get down and get out of the way. Do you understand?"

"Yeah. Yes, sir," Emory responded right away. "Just…"

Peter raised his brows.

"Just what?" Seth asked.

"It's a lot of effort, what I do. So, if you see me slowing down or something, that's all it is. It's just a lot of…energy expended."

Seth's brow wrinkled. "Do you have a time limit or…"

"No, no. Like, if it's one person at a time, I can manage that. But two, three, more…that takes energy."

"I have something," Story said, mulling through her bag. "Might I use a pan?"

Peter nodded, and she walked off into the kitchen to concoct some tincture. Seth watched her float through the family kitchen with ease.

"We need to get on the same page," Seth said to Peter.

"I thought we were?"

"We're going in to find your daughter, but if this is our chance, our one chance, then we need to plan what comes next," Seth explained.

Peter nodded. "Yeah, I'd been thinking of that. Splitting up."

Seth half shook his head. "No."

"You don't trust me?"

"That's not the issue. The kid can't split himself in half. And yes"—Seth stopped Peter, raising his hand—"you know your way around, but if the alarm gets sounded, we're both screwed. We have to do this with, well, with military precision. Right?"

Peter nodded. "Yes."

"Finding your daughter comes first. Second, we get evidence. I'm assuming Paddy has a plan for that. Files? Electronic? I mean, what are we going after?"

"Electronic access. Paddy will have a loaded flash drive. It's plug and play. Once we connect it, Paddy takes over and downloads everything."

"Good. I'll leave all that to you. I'd also like to find the young man you showed me in the video. The one who looks like George Horne," he said to Emory.

Emory nodded.

Peter cocked his head to the side. "About that. I don't quite understand the whole George swap thing."

Seth couldn't help but laugh. "I'm not sure I do, either. We'll try to explain on the way."

Peter shook his head. "Whatever the case, they're probably keeping him in the same area we'll need to search." Peter reached for his son's pack and examined the contents. "Is this all set?"

"Yeah. You'll need another harness," Noble answered his father.

"I'll grab one," he said, heading for the garage.

"Here," Story said, producing a water bottle full of brown liquid.

Emory took the bottle from her and looked at its contents with skepticism. "Um…"

"It doesn't look great, but it'll give you a quick recharge. That's all I could make, given what I had at hand."

"What is it?" Emory asked, his nose wrinkled as he jostled the bottle.

"It's…like an energy drink." Story shrugged.

Peter returned. "Are we set, then? Anything else?"

Seth felt like there was a lot more to go over but knew there wasn't time. They had an opening. They had to take it. He'd seen enough of these moments, knocking on doors, expecting assailants with knives or guns waiting behind them. This was a little different. He was heading into a cave to sneak into a research facility with a kid who could manipulate minds and an ex–Special Ops Marine to illegally acquire evidence.

Seth shook his head. He had to stop thinking of it that way. He was entering a building on probable cause, having tracked the man, Raymond LaRange, to the location.

"Are we gonna wait for Paddy?" Noble asked, following his father toward the front door.

"I texted him where to meet us," Peter answered.

"Before we go," Seth said, motioning to Peter's backside, "I need you to leave your firearm here."

Peter opened his mouth to protest but stopped himself short. He was already in enough legal trouble as it was. He didn't need whatever sentence he would eventually receive to be any worse. His family needed him. Peter nodded and removed his gun. "Let me go put it back in its case," he said and raced up the stairs. When he came back down, he held out his arms so Seth could check him.

Seth patted him down and nodded. "Thank you."

"Now, let's go," Peter said.

"Let's head out, everyone," Seth ordered and headed toward the front door.

The ragtag group shouldered on their coats and headed out of the Andalusian house.

A Voice from Beyond the Grave

Peter cautiously extended a slim mirror at the end of a long metal wand around the corner, angled downward so that none of the ceiling's fluorescent lights would reflect. He slowly turned his wrist, watching as the craggy stone floor gradually morphed into gaudy checkered linoleum. He steadily bent his wrist backward until he came upon the door cut into the stone.

"The door's closed," he whispered from his perch on the ground.

"No surprise there," Seth said as he crouched over Peter, trying to get a glimpse of the mirror.

"It's steel, like we thought. Looks like a standard bolt lock above the keyed handle."

"Should be easy enough to pick."

"For me or you?" Peter asked.

"I can do it in under forty seconds."

Peter raised his eyebrows, impressed. "All you. Could be a surface bolt on the other side. Might need to bust it down."

"We're already breaking and entering," Seth grunted. A water droplet fell from his hair onto Peter's head. It was the third time it happened, and it impressed Seth that Peter had yet to flinch.

Halfway to the cursed woods, a massive thunderstorm had descended upon the group, drenching everyone from head to toe. Two blocks before they reached Mulberry Street, Paddy materialized from the sheets of rain to deliver the comms and a small bag of supplies that Seth inspected to ensure it didn't contain any weapons or explosives. Finding shelter under the massive cypress tree in Mr. and Mrs. Englen's front yard, Paddy, Peter, and Seth tested out the tactical in-ear comm system while Noble, Anya, Nate, Emory, and Story huddled together to create some semblance of warmth.

Although there was plenty of tree cover in the woods surrounding the cave entrance to shield Story and Noble from the rain, Peter allowed his son into the cave's corridor, where the temperature was noticeably higher. Noble and Story perched themselves on the top of the scree before it sloped steeply down to where climbing equipment was necessary. The plan was for them to wait for Nate and Anya to return, hopefully without Seth, Peter, and Emory, signaling they had successfully made it through the mysterious door.

"The camera looks old, Paddy," Peter said, eyeing the mirror. "From the eighties, I would guess. But there is a red light blinking, like in the video Nate took."

"No reason it wouldn't be working and feeding into their security system." Paddy's voice came clearly through the comm.

Peter pulled the mirror back and looked up at Seth. "You want to come down here and get a look yourself?"

"I saw enough from here." Seth ran a hand through his hair. The plan was far from optimal. Paddy had never tested to see if he could successfully breach Orbriallis's security camera monitoring system, fearing it could blow their one chance to get in. "So, Paddy, if you get in, how long before you'll be able to tell if this camera is, in fact, connected to the Orbriallis?"

"Hold on, guys," Paddy said.

Peter shimmied up the wall to a standing position and leaned in to Seth. "Whether it is or not, we're going to have maybe three to five minutes before someone notices we're manipulating the feed."

Seth sighed as he glanced over to Emory, who was standing next to Nate and Anya about ten feet away, waiting for the signal. "Then it's all up to a kid who can speak inside other people's heads. I wish I could say I felt confident."

"Tell me about it," Peter said. "I knew I was coming back to a heap of shit but not the fucking *Twilight Zone*."

"Ha!" Paddy's voice sounded triumphant.

"What is it, Paddy?" Peter asked.

"Tell me you've got good news," Seth said, "and you're not just laughing at Peter."

"Better than good news," Paddy said. "While you guys were working your way through the caves and scoping out that weird hallway to the door, I've been working on something else."

Seth looked at Peter with wide eyes. "Something besides getting us into the facility?"

"Yes and no. Running through that cyclone to get back home got me thinking. What's the most common occurrence when a storm like this hits?"

"Flooding?" Seth guessed.

"Okay, the second most common occurrence."

"Paddy, just get to the point. We don't have time for games."

"Oh," Peter said. "That's brilliant, Paddy."

"What's brilliant?" Seth said.

"He's going to cut their power."

The corner of Seth's mouth lifted as that thought sank in.

"It's even better than that," Paddy said. "Infiltrating anything connected to the Orbriallis is potentially dangerous. But the city of Lost Grove? It was a piece of cake. I could have gotten into here after downing a bottle of scotch."

"That's reassuring," Seth said.

"Plus, when I knock the entire city's power out, it won't look like they've been targeted. Anyone working can look out the window and see the town's lights went out."

"What about your power, Paddy?" Seth asked.

"I've already switched over to my generator. We're good."

Peter nodded. "This is great news. How long before their backup generators kick in?"

"Well, they won't fuck around with that. They've got high-risk and dangerous patients in their psych ward, so I'm guessing it will kick in right away. *But,*" Paddy emphasized, "the computers will still need time to reboot, which will give me plenty of time to get in undetected. As soon as their security system is back up, I'll be there, ready to loop camera feeds. Then, if we run into any dicey scenarios where looping footage isn't an option, meaning someone is already visibly walking in a hallway, I can execute another outage. I can do them periodically to look like power blips. This is all assuming they don't latch onto me somehow."

Seth and Peter felt a palpable sense of relief. This didn't guarantee success, but it sure upped the odds.

"Does this mean you're ready to pull the plug now?" Seth asked.

"On your command, Chief."

Seth turned and motioned for the teens to come join them.

Nate approached first. "Is the camera recording?"

"It is now," Seth said. "But it won't be in a moment."

Emory stepped up next to Nate, Anya trailing slowly behind. "We ready?"

"We've got a slight change of plans, but it's going to work to our benefit. Paddy is going to trigger a city-wide power outage to stop the cameras."

"Smart," Nate enthused.

"Orbriallis will have a backup generator, but it will still take minutes for the computers running the camera monitoring systems to reboot. By then, Paddy will get in to, hopefully, control them."

"We're goin' in dark," Emory said.

"Maybe not for long. If these lights are part of the Orbriallis and connected to the backup generator, they could be back on in seconds. But keep your cell phone lights out and on. Nate, as soon as we get that door open and I give you the signal, I want you and Anya to hustle your asses back up to meet Noble and Story."

"I'm on it, sir," Nate said.

Peter leaned his head in. "And do not let my son do anything stupid. He's going to want to come down here or go storming through the front doors of the Orbriallis. I'm entrusting you to get him back home and keep him there."

Nate smirked. "I always beat him in wrestling. I'll take him down and hold him if I have to."

Peter slapped Nate on the shoulder.

Seth looked at Emory. "You sure you—"

"Yeah, man, I'm sure. Let's go get Zoe."

Seth nodded and turned back to face Peter. He slid his flashlight into his utility belt and reached inside his jacket to get his lock pick kit. "You lead the way to the door, and keep your flashlight on the locks."

"Yep," Peter said and turned around to ready himself to go down the bizarre hallway.

Seth closed his eyes and briefly focused his energy on the protection sigils on his boots. "Okay, Paddy, we're ready."

"Good luck, boys," Paddy said. "Here we go, on—"

Seth held up three fingers so the kids could see.

"Three, two, one—light's out!"

The cave went to pure blackness with a loud click coming from the fluorescent lights, which then stopped buzzing.

It took a moment for Seth's eyes to adjust and focus on the light coming from Peter's flashlight. They crept down the hallway, wet rubber soles squeaking on the linoleum. Seth got down to one knee as Peter took a step back to make space for him to work, keeping the light fixated on the bottom lock. Peter glanced at his watch, and within seconds of looking back up, the lock on the door handle clicked open. He shifted the light up to the deadbolt.

Emory had his phone out and was aiming the light at the same lock, focusing his energy beyond the door. "No one is behind the door," he said.

"That is great news," Peter said. "And also highly disturbing."

Emory chuckled. It felt amazing to be using his powers for something good. Not just good, but hopefully to help in saving a young girl's life. There was some sort of poetic justice in the thought, and Emory just hoped he could tell Ember about it with Zoe home safe and sound.

The deadbolt clicked, and Peter looked back at his watch. "Thirty-two seconds. The door's unlocked, Paddy."

"Excellent work, Chief," Paddy said.

Seth looked back at Peter. "You were timing?"

"Didn't know if you had some sort of personal record you were hoping to break."

Seth stood up, and just as he was preparing to throw the door open, the overhead lights flickered back on.

"Backup generator has been engaged," Paddy said. "You have lights back on down there?"

"We do," Seth said. He looked back at Nate and Anya and held up his hand, signaling to hold. He then looked at Peter. "You ready?"

"Let's go."

"Stay behind me at all times, Emory."

"Yep, yep."

"Oh my God," Peter said in a shallow voice.

Seth turned around to see Peter reaching toward something on the ground. He registered it was a bracelet in just enough time to slap Peter's hand. "Don't touch it. What is it?"

"It's Zoe's," he said and looked up at Seth with desperate fear behind his eyes. "She just showed it to me last night."

"Oh, shit," Emory gasped.

"Nobody touch it," Seth stated as he reached inside his jacket for a pair of latex gloves and an evidence bag. He knelt down as he slid on the gloves.

"Can I tell Nate and Anya?" Emory asked.

"Yes. No one is going to overhear us."

"They were here," Peter said. "They really came through this goddamn cave."

Emory turned and yelled, "Yo, Nate!"

Nate and Anya both came running up.

Seth looked up at Peter as he snapped the second glove on. "I'm sorry we didn't come directly here. I had to—"

"It was the right thing to do. I reacted, which is something I rarely do."

Seth nodded as he first took a picture of the bracelet with his phone.

"It's Zoe's bracelet," Emory said.

Anya leaned in to look and covered her mouth, the sad sight of the bracelet on the disgusting tile somehow making this all feel more real than it already did. "That's the one Story made for her last week."

"Shit, you're right," Nate said. "Which also means that fucker does live down here!"

"That fucker doesn't live down here," Seth said as he placed the bracelet in the evidence bag and sealed it. He stood up and looked at everyone surrounding him. "He travels through here to get to his home."

"I knew he never left," Nate said.

Seth held up the bag to Peter. "This gives me legitimate probable cause. All bets are off. Let's go rescue your daughter."

Peter nodded.

Seth pocketed the bag and pulled off the gloves as he turned toward the kids. "Nate. Anya. As soon we're in, you get out of here."

"Yes, sir," Nate responded.

"Good luck," Anya offered.

Peter smiled at the young woman he'd rarely met but knew was in the same social circles as his son. "Thank you."

Seth clicked back on his flashlight, turned the handle, and pushed the door, which opened without impediment. He shined his flashlight in and around. No one was there. He looked over his shoulder and gave Nate the thumbs-up.

Nate returned it and then put his arm around Anya. "Lead the way out."

Seth held his flashlight by his shoulder, heading down the tight corridor of a man-made tunnel, complete with a rounded ceiling and sporadic wall lights, which had either not come back on with the generator or had been out for years. They traveled together as a tight unit, soft with their footfalls. The atmosphere in the tunnel was humid and deathly silent.

Emory could sense no one was in there with them, but that didn't stop him from imagining a creepy cave dweller from *The Descent* hanging from the ceiling, ready to attack.

"I can't believe this has been here the whole time, and we never knew about it," Peter said, speaking to Paddy. "I should have looked behind that door in the garage ages ago. It bothered me when I first saw it, and now I know why."

"There's no record of its existence anywhere I can find," Paddy said. "But it must lead to the Orbriallis, considering the lights in that hallway went out and came back on with their generator. The rest of the town is still out."

Seth looked back at Emory, who had, thankfully, stayed close behind him. "You picking up on anything yet? Or anyone, I should say."

"Nope. If there were anyone within a hundred yards, I would sense it."

As they rounded a corner, Seth shifted his flashlight from the ground upward. "There are stairs," he announced. "And another door."

Peter brought his light up to the door, which was, presumably, the end of the tunnel. As they closed in on the short metal stairway, Peter got a better view of the door. "That's got to be the door. It has the same handle and the same aged-rust color."

Seth placed a foot on the first step up and turned to face Peter and Emory. "So, tell me again about this retina scan."

"Well—"

"It—"

Peter and Paddy both replied at the same time. "Go ahead, Paddy," Peter said.

"There's no way around it. Even if I shut down the power again, that door wouldn't budge until the generator kicked back in and they reactivated the retina scan. So I need to reinstate Peter as an active employee for you guys to get in. There is no chance this won't raise a red alert, which means everyone will be looking for you guys. Now, I've got an idea that as soon as that door opens and you verify you're in, I can knock the power out immediately and we can hope that no one saw the flag, or the power cycle might mean it won't pop up again. Plus, it will get you through the millimeter wave scanner without being detected. Either way, it's going to be a breakneck speed of a maze run once you're in there."

"There's someone over there," Emory said, pointing to his right. "They're eating. I can hear them chewing. It's really annoying."

"That's the direction of the entrance," Peter said, looking at Seth. "The guard behind the door."

"Christ, I hope it's not Seamus," Seth said.

"Who's that?" Emory asked.

"One big, tough son of a bitch," Peter said.

Emory shrugged. "Doesn't matter how big they are. If I tell him he won't see us, then he won't see us."

"I hope you're right, kid."

Seth felt a tingling sensation under his scalp. It was different, the polar opposite of when Emory spoke in his head or when Apolonia had intruded into his brain. He was doing it. He was latching onto Emory's power.

Emory's head darted from Peter to Seth, eyes narrowing. This dude was tiptoeing around his senses. Emory grinned. "No shit?"

"What the hell's going on?" Peter asked, looking from Emory to Seth.

Seth broke the connection and turned to Peter. "Nothing. We ready?"

"I'm ready," Paddy replied.

Peter nodded. "Yeah. You or me?" he asked Seth.

"I'll lead us through the door to make sure there aren't any surprises. And then..." Seth turned to Emory. "When and where do you need to do what you do?"

"The closer I get, the better."

"I have eyes on the S11 garage," Paddy said. "Only one car down there—Dr. Owens's Jaguar. I am definitely not seeing a door in a wall."

"No," Peter said. "It's not in line with the camera down there."

"Okay, hold tight. I'm going to loop the footage on this camera. As soon as I say go, you'll be free to move around. Just know that I won't be able to see any movement down there."

"You have eyes on the guard, though, right?"

"I do now, but I'll have to start looping that footage before you enter."

"Understood," Seth said.

"Okay, the garage camera is looping. You're a go."

Seth nodded at Peter and looked at Emory. "We're ready to go. You good?"

"I'm good. I got that guard chomping on his food in the crosshairs."

"Crosshairs?" Peter asked.

Emory shrugged. "Video games."

"Let's go," Seth said and headed up the stairs.

From inside the garage, the handle of the rusted metal door in the far corner turned, the door slowly creaking open.

"It's not locked," Seth said and peered through the crack in the door. He carefully pushed the heavy door farther open, eyes dancing around to every corner of the garage. "There's nothing I can see besides that beige Jaguar you said belonged to Dr. Owens."

"Looked clear to me before I started the loop," Paddy said.

Seth looked over his shoulder and motioned for Peter and Emory to follow. The door hinges were rusted and cried as he put his shoulder into the door and pushed it open just enough so he could squeeze through. The metal screeched, a loose piece of the steel door catching on the concrete. Seth winced.

One by one, they stepped out from behind the door into the garage, Seth followed by Peter followed by Emory.

Just as Emory cleared the door, he stopped in his tracks. "Wait!" he whispered loudly.

Seth and Peter both froze in place. "What is it?" Seth asked over his shoulder.

Emory had his eyes closed. "It's from above. One person, but they're getting closer. Must be an elevator or—"

A tire lightly squealed and headlights hit the wall opposite them.

"Shit! A car's coming, Paddy." Seth spun around and pushed Peter and Emory back, everyone tripping over someone else's feet as they stumbled back into the cave and shut the door. The awkwardness made Seth feel like they were all goofy kids hiding from their parents.

"Christ," Peter exclaimed with a sigh. "You would never know I was ex–Special Ops, and you were a homicide detective."

"Exactly what I was thinking," Seth said.

"I'm trying to get eyes on the car from the floors above," Paddy announced.

"See if you can make out anything about the driver," Seth said.

"Hold tight. I'm looping the floor above and watching the recorded footage back. Okay, got it. Black sedan, one driver, no passengers. It looks like a woman. Long dark hair…"

Seth spun around and grabbed the door handle, slowly pushing it back open.

"What are you doing?" Peter seethed.

"Don't worry," Seth said and slid back out into the garage.

"Don't worry, he says. I swear if he blows this—"

"He won't," Emory said. "I'll handle it if necessary."

Seth crept forward as the driver's door opened. He knew who it was before she stepped into the light. "Dr. Bajorek?" he whispered loudly into the echoing parking garage.

Jane stopped and looked around, noticing a dark figure in the far corner. She recognized the voice. "Sergeant Wolfe?" she asked, approaching, his details becoming clearer.

"I know this must look strange," Seth said. "But there is a reason—"

"Emory Graff?" Jane exclaimed, looking over Seth's shoulder.

"Hey, Dr. B."

Seth turned around to see Emory quietly coming up behind him, just as Peter stepped out from behind the door. "Shit," he muttered to himself and turned back to face Jane.

Jane looked past Emory. "Mr. Andalusian? What on earth is going on here?" she asked, keeping her voice low.

"Dr. Bajorek," Seth said, grabbing her attention, "Peter Andalusian's daughter, Zoe, was kidnapped from her home approximately two and a half hours ago. We received information that led us to believe the kidnapper took her through an underground cave system leading to the Orbriallis. That's where we just came from."

"A cave system?" she asked, her eyes darting to the closed door behind the three men.

"Our suspicions were confirmed when we found this at the door on the other side of the tunnel that led us here." Seth pulled out the bag containing the bracelet.

Peter stepped forward. "That's my daughter's bracelet, and the pedophile asshole who took her is a patient here. And if you know who he is, I swear—"

"Hold on," Seth ordered, placing a hand on Peter's chest. "*Was* a patient here. We don't know if he still is, but regardless, this is clearly where he took her. Dr. Bajorek, do you know a man by the name of

Raymond LaRange?"

Jane's eyes blinked rapidly, desperately trying to process all this information. "I don't…I recall coming across his name, but I—"

"But what?" Peter said, his temper rising. "You know what's going on in this place and—"

Seth turned around and looked him in the eyes. "Stop. Now."

Peter nodded. Turning off his emotions and slowing his heart rate was something they trained him for in crisis situations, but all that seemed to disappear the moment any mention of his daughter's peril came to the fore.

Seth turned back to Dr. Bajorek. "But what?"

"His name was on a project that was started well before I got here. I have no access to it. I don't know who the man is, and I've certainly never met him."

Seth sighed. "It's imperative we get in this building to find her."

"Why don't you just—"

"I think you know why I can't just go through the front door and demand to search the premises," Seth said.

"I'm sorry," Jane said. "Of course that's not something…but why is Emory Graff here?"

Seth opened his mouth to respond.

"They need my skills," Emory said, "to navigate through this place."

Jane looked at Seth. "Sergeant Wolfe, Emory is just a boy. Bringing him in here to—"

"It wasn't their choice," Emory interrupted. "I was the one to bring up the idea. Sergeant Wolfe didn't want me to come, but I'm eighteen and have a right to speak for myself. My friend's sister just got kidnapped, and I'm gonna help. Besides, considering some of the shit I've seen you guys doing to other people my age. I'm here to stop it."

"What do you mean? What have you seen? Has someone done something inappropriate?" Jane studied the boy's eyes. He had a fierce tenacity, something she sensed upon first meeting him. There was also a protective nature in him he displayed whenever she raised his sister's name.

"You mean you don't know? That I walked around this place last weekend and ran into a bunch of your coworkers?" Emory stepped inside her thoughts and scanned for knowledge of George Horne or any other kids being hooked up to pods and wires.

Jane shook her head, black strands swishing loose around her face from the bun she'd piled on top of her head. "Listen, Mr. Graff, you are technically an adult, but…" She trailed off as her words seemed to bounce off him. He was unmoved by her concerns. "Very well," she said, looking back at Seth. "You protect him, then."

"With my life," Seth said and meant it.

"Emory," Peter said, keeping his eyes on Dr. Bajorek, "you said there was a lot of fucked up shit here and that certain people were studying you like lab rats. Can we trust her?"

Jane closed her eyes, feeling a dull jab in her guts.

Emory found no knowledge of not only his previous escapades, which he thought would definitely be shown to her, given she was their doctor, but he also didn't see she knew a single thing about pods or other children being kept in the basement. "Dr. B is okay, man. She's actually like one of the few real people in there. I've done some of my own peeking around, and she's a good person. I don't know about that weird older lady she brings in that fucks around in my head, but Dr. B is good."

Seth had to bite down on his lip not to laugh.

Jane opened her eyes and looked directly at Mr. Andalusian. "What can I do to help?"

"Open the door for us."

"You took the words right out of my mouth," Paddy chimed in their ears.

Peter pointed toward the entrance. "If we have to use my eyes to get through that door, we're going to set off alarms like fireworks."

"How will you get past the guard?" Jane asked. "I can't make up—"

"That's where I come in," Emory said. "The guard will only see you. I promise."

Jane swallowed heavily, simultaneously contemplating the ramifications of these actions and Emory Graff's powers.

"Why are you here, Dr. Bajorek?" Seth asked.

Jane batted her eyes and looked at him. "I…Lina Orbriallis called me. She…she told me I had to come because something was about to…"

Seth felt his insides glow as that slight tingling below his scalp returned. Another moment of coincidence, or fate, intervening.

"Right," Jane said, nodding as she saw her own understanding coagulate in the facial expression of the police sergeant across from her. "This must be the 'something' Lina was alluding to."

"Dr. Bajorek, we're here to save Peter's daughter, but we're also here to gather evidence."

"Hard evidence," Peter added.

"Give her the drive," Paddy implored. "She has the exact access we—"

"Already there," Seth said.

"What?" Jane asked, her brow furrowed.

Seth pointed to his ear. "Our eyes and ears. Our access to the cameras."

"How... It doesn't matter."

Peter handed Seth the flash drive.

"You need evidence," Seth said. "We need evidence. You're here for a reason. A reason you didn't remotely understand until this moment. After you let us in, if you're willing to, all we need you to do is plug this flash drive into your computer and sit back and let our man collect the evidence. Will you do that for us?"

Jane brought her trembling hand to her forehead and squeezed her temples.

Peter clenched his fists, trying to remain patient.

"Give her time," Paddy said, somehow sensing Peter's angst. "This is divine intervention if I've ever seen it."

Jane dropped her hand and nodded. "Yes. Of course I'll do it."

Emory pumped his fist. "I knew you were good."

Seth smiled at her. "Thank you."

Peter extended his hand toward Dr. Bajorek. "I'm in your debt. Truly."

Jane exchanged a quick handshake and held out her hand to Seth, who placed the flash drive in it.

Seth looked at Emory. "Are we clear to move?"

"Like glass."

Seth turned away from Jane, pulled Emory close to him, and lowered his voice. "Paddy, what about the guard not seeing her car or her walking in?"

"Nothing I can do about that unless you guys want to appear on Candid Camera."

"Emory," Seth said, "the guard won't see—"

"I'll take care of it."

"Okay." Seth looked back at Jane and nodded. "We're ready."

Jane let out a long sigh and took one step toward the entrance before a hand grabbed her arm.

"Sorry," Seth said, quickly pulling his hand away. "There's one more thing."

Jane rolled her eyes.

"It's just an answer. There is, actually, a third reason we are here. Do you know about the kids, young adults, being hooked up to machines and put in pods."

"She doesn't know about the pod people," Emory interjected.

Jane flinched away from this turn of phrase. "I'm sorry, the what?"

"What I mentioned earlier. This place hooks kids up to devices and puts them in pods," Emory said and thrust his phone toward the doctor, the video already playing.

Jane watched, feeling ill as each frame ticked past. "What in the world is this? Is this—" She looked up. "Please tell me this isn't here. This is here, isn't it?"

Seth and Emory both had their eyes locked on Dr. Bajorek. Emory was already sure but took a fresh peek in her head. He and Seth simultaneously turned to Peter and said, "She doesn't know."

Peter slowly nodded. "Okay." He didn't like whatever was going on between the two of them and cared less for the feeling niggling in the back of his mind that he understood it.

"I don't know what this is," Seth said, "but there is a boy in here by the name of George Horne. As a child, he was… actually he ended up here the same way Zoe Andalusian came to be here."

"Kidnapped," Jane said, culminating the information she'd received so far. She felt as if a day had gone by of her standing here, learning horror after horror about the hospital where she worked.

"On what floors might we find whatever the hell this is?" Seth asked.

Jane felt like her head was going to explode. Years of questions about how and where she and her fellow doctors received information, test subjects, and DNA were colliding in a frenzy of hellfire in her mind. "The only floors I don't have access to are S3 and S6. Whatever that is… it would have to be on one of those floors."

Seth nodded, hoping that Dr. Bajorek didn't get sick or pass out. She was fair-skinned to begin with, but she had turned an ivory white over the past few minutes. "Thank you."

Jane turned around and made her way toward the entrance, praying that the sergeant didn't stop her again with any more cataclysmic information.

"Paddy, is the guard a massive guy with short spiky hair and a mustache?" Seth asked.

"Seamus Owens? No, definitely not."

Jane looked over her shoulder, narrowing her eyes at Seth.

"It's all good," Seth offered.

Jane turned back around and let out a faint moan as she approached the retina scan. She stopped and looked back at the group, focusing on Emory. "Are you sure—"

"Positive," Emory said.

Peter looked at the boy. "And we what? Just walk past him?"

"Just stay behind Dr. B. Don't talk to or touch the guy."

"What happens if we bump into him?"

"I can handle it, but the less energy I have to spend out the gate, the better."

Peter nodded and looked at Seth. "Let's do it."

"Paddy, we're heading in," Seth said.

"Looping the guard's footage now."

Seth turned to Dr. Bajorek. "Okay."

Jane bent down and let the red laser scan her eye. The lock beeped and clicked. Jane took a breath, put on her professional face, and walked through the door, leaving enough space for the others to get in while the door closed.

"Dr. Bajorek?" the guard stood up, awash with confusion.

"Hello, Geoffrey."

"I didn't see you— My evening's going well. How about yours?"

Seth looked at Emory and smirked.

Jane lowered her eyebrows and tried to wipe the shocked look from her face. "Fine, Geoffrey, fine," she said and held her arms straight out to her sides.

Emory, Seth, and Peter watched as the guard quickly patted down the doctor and took her cell phone. Peter prided himself on remaining deathly calm under any kind of pressure, but his heart was racing as he witnessed Geoffrey look past them with no recognition. It was surreal.

Seth focused on watching Dr. Bajorek. The mind control of the guard was Emory's job. Seth needed to make sure everyone remained safe and calm.

"Okay, Doctor, you're good to go." Geoffrey smiled and motioned for her to go through the millimeter wave scanner.

"Fuck," Seth whispered, glancing at Peter. "My gun."

Peter pointed to the ceiling. "The lights."

"Hold tight, Chief," Paddy replied. "As soon as she leaves the scanner, I'll activate a power hit."

"Right," Seth said, shaking his head, momentarily forgetting the plan. Dr. Bajorek getting them in didn't change the need for the power hit.

"Okay," Geoffrey said. "Have a good night, Doctor."

Jane nodded and exited the scanner.

Seth turned to his team and whispered, "Emory, grab a hold of my jacket. Peter, grab hold of Emory."

Geoffrey was returning to his seat when everything went black. "Dammit! Not again."

Seth reached out his hands and felt his way toward the scanner. He found the entrance and slowly walked through. Emory bumped his knee into the machine as he stepped in.

"You okay, Doctor?" Geoffrey called out, clicking on his flashlight and shining it in her direction.

Seth froze, placing all three of them in the middle of the scanner.

"I'm fine!" Jane called out. "Just stubbed my toe."

"Here." Geoffrey walked around the scanner and handed Jane her cell phone. "Under the circumstances, I think you should hang on to this."

"Thank you so much."

"Power came back pretty quick last time, but you never know. Might want to take the stairs."

"I think I will, thank you."

Geoffrey walked back toward his station and picked up the phone. "Seamus, you dark up there, too?"

"Let's go," Seth said and led the way out.

Jane activated the flashlight on her phone. "Follow me," she whispered and led the way toward the stairwell.

"Can we use our flashlights?" Seth asked Emory.

"For sure." Emory walked shoulder to shoulder with Seth, who turned on his flashlight.

Behind them, Peter clicked his on. His body was on a constant, controlled swivel, scanning their surroundings for threats.

"Anyone else down here?" Seth asked Emory.

"There's only one other person on this floor, and I've already taken care of it."

"I cleared cameras for this floor," Paddy said. "All looping."

Jane stopped at a doorway next to the elevators. "This is the stairwell. Should we wait for the power to come back?"

"No," Peter said. "We should all stay out of the elevators. God forbid it malfunctions because of the power hits, and we're stuck in there."

"Paddy, do you have eyes inside the elevators?" Seth asked.

"That I do. Just let me know before you decide to use one."

Seth looked at Peter. "Just in case we're in a bind and have to use them."

Peter nodded and looked at Emory. "I know you've got a lot to deal with, but your primary job is to locate Zoe."

"My mind is right."

"Anything?"

Emory shook his head. His eyes focused on the space between him and the doorway.

"Paddy," Seth said, "you need to be in contact with Dr. Bajorek. I can't risk something not going as smoothly as you think it will when that flash drive gets plugged in."

"Give her my cell, and tell her to call me now. I'll guide you both."

"Can you focus—"

"No offense, Chief, but I've led many more people than this in and out of life and death situations."

"Understood. Give me your number." Seth relayed Paddy's cell to Jane, who dialed it as he spoke. She brought the phone to her ear.

"Yes, I can hear you."

"Stay in your office until I call you," Seth said. "If something happens to us, Paddy will let you know."

Jane nodded and opened the stairwell door.

"Doctor!" Peter called out to stop her.

Jane turned around, holding the door.

"You said S3 and S6 were the only floors you don't have access to."

"That's right."

"Is it safe to assume that if Raymond LaRange has been staying here, he'd be on one—"

"No question."

Peter looked at Seth. "We start on S6."

Seth shifted his light over to the elevators and spotted the S11 sign between the two sets of doors. "I'm guessing that we're counting backward on the way up."

Peter nodded.

Seth walked over to Jane. "We'll accompany you up to S6."

Jane gave him a faint smile. She was relieved to have an escort at this point and wished either Seth or Peter could stay with her the whole time. She had a feeling that, regardless of the measures they had taken for this mission, she had compromised herself.

"Hold tight," Paddy said. "I'm going to start looping both those floors. You let me know before you go anywhere else."

"10-4," Seth replied. He looked at Emory and Peter, who both nodded. He turned to Jane. "We'll follow you."

Jane let out a heavy exhale and headed up the stairs.

Peter grabbed Emory before they walked through the door. "If you sense anything on the way up—"

"I got you." Emory smacked Peter on the back and followed behind Seth. He reached inside his jacket, pulled out the bottle of the concoction Story made for him, and took a swig. He cringed at the sweet, earthy taste but felt his energy buoyed.

Seth quietly closed the door to room 12A7. The combination of letters and numbers on the plaques outside each door had no rhyme, reason, or order. It was like each plaque was a license plate from a different state. He looked over at Emory, slouched against the wall next to the door. His eyelids were heavy, his breathing raspy and labored. "You sure we don't need to take a break?"

"I'm good," Emory mumbled, shaking the bottle and lifting it to take another sip. This was the ninth room they had entered on S6 and the seventh person he had to control, the other two so deep in sleep they hadn't woken when a light shone on their face. This was besides the three guards he had to contend with on the way up and through this first floor.

Peter walked behind Seth from the other side of the door. "We don't have time to take a break. Our primary mission here is—"

"I know what the mission is," Seth said. "And Zoe could just as easily be in one of these rooms."

"I'm telling you, it's not this floor. It's gotta be S3. All these kids are suited up for experiments."

"And neither of us knows if she will even be on either floor."

"Guys," Emory called out, now standing up, forcing his eyes to be open and alert. "If she was in serious danger, like screaming for help, I'd sense it."

"And how many floors up do your senses go?" Peter said, snarling.

"Peter," Paddy cut in on the comms. "Just keep moving. You're killing time right now. The kid could hear Seamus talking on the phone from the main lobby, so I think you can back off."

"Next room," Seth said, striding down the hallway. The plaque outside the door read 2JV9. He turned to Emory. "You ready?"

"Let's do it," he said, pumping his chest out.

Seth could tell the boy was forcing his gung-ho attitude. He didn't know how Emory's powers worked, but he was clearly fading. Regardless, Seth nodded and opened the door, sweeping his flashlight across the room, the light landing on the head of the next test subject.

Emory walked in first. The first thing he noticed was the longer hair. Each of the prior inhabitants had their head shaved. "Oh, shit," he said, rounding the bed and swiftly getting down to his knees. "It's him."

Seth moved behind Emory and bent down. "Are you sure?"

Peter poked his head in from keeping watch on the outside. "You find him?"

"It's definitely him," Emory said. "He was the only one I saw that had longer hair. They called him G."

The boy with buzzed dark hair stirred, awakened by his code name. "It's not time," he said, eyes still shut.

Emory made room for Seth, who squatted down next to him. "George?"

The boy's eyes shot open. It had been years since anyone called him by his real name. He jumped back on his bed, not recognizing the man staring at him.

"It's okay. It's okay. I'm a police officer. I'm here to help you."

George gripped his bedsheets, his voice lodged in his chest. He wasn't sure if he would scream, even if he could find his voice. Was this man with the flashlight really the police? Or just another new guard?

"Hey, George. My name's Emory."

George jumped again, not having registered the boy standing next to the officer, blinded by the flashlight. He held a hand up in front of his face.

Seth pulled the light slightly off George's face so he could see.

George's eyes widened, the boy calling himself Emory coming into focus. "You. I saw you."

Emory nodded. "That's right. You did. I'm a friend of your sister's."

George's lip trembled. Could this friendly looking boy be telling him the truth? His beloved sister he thought he'd never see or hear of again? "Nettie?" he cried.

"Yeah, man."

"Nettie Horne is your sister?" Seth asked, still feeling the need for verification.

George broke down into an uncontrollable sob. "My sister," he wailed.

"We gotta go," Peter said, looking back into the room. "You need to shut him up."

Seth dared to put a hand on the boy's shoulder. "George, I know this is a lot to take in right now. Try to breathe."

Breathe. Emory instilled the thought into the boy's mind.

George opened his mouth and took in a shaking breath.

"George," Seth said. "I need you to answer me. Do you want us to take you out of here? Do you want to leave the Orbr—"

"Yes," George cried, grabbing hold of Seth's wet jacket.

Seth gripped the boy with both hands. "I'm going to take you home," he said and turned to Emory. "I need you to calm him further but not so much that he passes out."

Emory nodded. "On it." *Breathe slowly, George. Let the muscles in your hands—*

"Agh!" Emory toppled over, grabbing his head.

"Peter!" Seth shouted, unable to reach Emory while holding on to George.

Peter rushed in, dropped to his knees, and wrapped his arms around Emory. "What is it? Are you hurt? Can you—"

"It's Zoe," Emory managed, hands still pressing into the sides of his head to stop the pain.

"What? Where?" Peter yelled, giving the boy a firm shake.

"Three floors up, two doors down. Away from the elevator."

Peter jumped to his feet and flew out of the room like a bat out of hell.

"Peter!" Seth stood, trying to hold on to George, extending a hand down to Emory. "Dammit!"

"Do you want me to go live on S3?" Paddy asked.

"Emory, can you stand?" Seth asked, contemplating the question.

Emory pushed himself up, his knees giving way briefly before catching himself. "I can do it."

"We can't risk it, Paddy. We've got George. Dr. Bajorek has the flash drive—"

"I agree, but you better get your ass up there."

"I'm working on it." Seth hoisted George up to his feet, and Emory put an arm underneath his shoulder. "George, I need you to come with us, and I need you to move as fast as you can and not make any noise. Can you do that?"

"I think so," the boy said.

Emory summoned as much energy as he could, which wasn't much after the assault on his brain that Zoe caused. *Move your legs. Stay with us.*

A muffled click sounded in Seth's ear with the comm in it. Seth held up his hands to halt them from leaving the room. "What was that?"

"Shit," Paddy swore. "We lost Peter."

"What? Did he turn his comm off?"

"No, he's completely offline. He might have broken it."

"Why would he do that? He needs your eyes."

"I agree. I'll keep eyes on as many floors as I can. You gotta move, Chief."

Seth gritted his teeth. They had to find Peter quickly, or he was going to be a moving target. "Let's go," he said. The trio walked out of room Y2JV9 to find three heads sticking out of their rooms.

"Fuck," Emory said. *Go back to your rooms, and don't come out. You saw nothing!*

Seth had no chance to catch Emory as he collapsed to the ground. "Son of a bitch," he swore under his breath. "Emory's down," he relayed to Paddy.

"Shit. Can you carry him?"

Seth looked at George, who thankfully looked more cognizant than he did a minute ago. "Can you walk on your own?"

"Yes," he said, stepping in place.

Seth furrowed his brow, hoping George didn't interpret that as walking in place. He pulled his arm out from under George's other shoulder and bent to grab Emory. "Thank God this kid is skinny as a rail," he said as an answer to Paddy's question and hoisted Emory up and over his shoulder.

"The elevators are working. I suggest you use them," Paddy said.

"No argument here." Seth looked back, thankful to see that George wasn't still walking in place or, worse, had wandered off. "Follow me."

Seth fell into a sprint, and George stayed in stride next to him. Just as they reached the elevators, thankfully with no guards in sight, Seth heard what was unmistakably three gunshots.

"Christ. Tell me that wasn't gunshots," Paddy said.

Seth pressed the up button for the elevator about fifteen times. "It was."

"Shit. You better slap the magic kid awake because I cannot control what people hear."

Seth felt Story's calm wash over his body in the moment of sheer chaos. Mercifully, the ding from the elevator sounded. Seth pushed George into the opening elevator and propped Emory up against the wall inside. He pressed S3 and turned to the boy. "Emory," he said, slapping his face. He checked the boy's pockets until he found Story's elixir. He untwisted the cap and helped the boy put it to his mouth and drink. "I need you back."

The doors shut as Emory's eyes fluttered open. He finished swallowing the drink. "Did I hear gunshots?"

"You did. Which means we're going to have company."

"I don't know how much I can handle right now."

"Can I help?" George asked.

Seth spun around, almost forgetting that George Horne, the real George Horne, was with them. "Yes. You can help by holding him up."

George switched places with Seth as the ding announced their arrival on S3. The doors opened, and the next thing Seth heard was the sound of running footsteps heading their direction. He held his arm out to stop George and Emory from exiting and stuck his other hand over the door chamber. "Shit."

The footfalls suddenly stopped and then picked up again, this time heading away from them. Seth turned around to Emory.

"I got it," the boy said, giving Seth a thumbs-up.

Seth grabbed a hold of Emory's shoulder, closed his eyes, and focused his mind on sending some of his energy to the boy.

Emory's body sprung up. "Whoa! What was that?"

Seth opened his eyes to see a more alert Emory standing in front of him. He shrugged. "I don't know. Let's go."

"Whatever you say." Emory looked at George. "I think I'm good now. Just stay behind me."

Seth took two strides out and saw a guard down on the ground, bleeding from the mouth and his forehead. "Shit. There's a guard down, Paddy." He went over and checked his pulse, breathing a heavy sigh of relief when he felt one. "He's alive, injured, and, fuck, his gun is gone."

"That explains the shots. Look, you better make this quick, Chief," Paddy said. "I'm seeing guards on other levels talking on their walkies, heading your way. On multiple floors."

Seth was heading down the hallway and looked over his shoulder, slowing his stride. "We've got guards all over."

"I'll do what I can," Emory said, already sensing too much commotion to control on his own.

Seth saw the one open door from three rooms away, as well as a bullet hole in the wall opposite. He pulled his firearm for the first time since arriving in Lost Grove and slowly approached the room. No light was coming from within. He heard nothing, but that meant nothing. Someone could have a gun trained on the doorway, just waiting for anyone to pop their head in.

Seth held his hand up behind him to stop Emory and George from advancing any farther. He stood against the wall, shoulder up against the doorframe. He grabbed his small Maglite with his free hand, spun around, dropped to his knees, and extended the gun out in front of him, scanning the room with the flashlight locked to the gun. "What the hell?"

"What is it?" Paddy asked.

"The room where the gunshots came from. No one's here now, but I'm guessing this is the room Zoe was being kept in. It's decorated like… like a child's room." Seth looked over and nodded at Emory and George and then stepped into the room, looking from one side to the other.

The wallpaper was painted with a happy picture of Swiss alps and fluffy clouds. There were shelves lined with books far too young for a girl Zoe's age. On the floor was a small dollhouse, some baby dolls, and stuffed animals. A small bed nestled to one side of the room.

"Jesus Christ," Seth muttered, holstering his weapon.

"What the hell is this?" Emory asked.

"What?" Paddy's voice reverberated in Seth's ear, drawing him back to the present and out of the nightmare of the room.

"There's padded handcuffs on the bed."

"Padded?"

"Yeah, like white-and-pink frilly shit over the cuffs." Seth turned around and looked at George. "Have you seen any rooms like this?"

"It might be for younger test subjects," he replied.

"Has someone ever handcuffed you?"

George looked at the ground with a subtle nod.

"Fuck this shit," Emory said and then spotted something on the ground. "Hey, Seth—sorry, Sergeant—look at this." Emory pointed at the shattered remains of an earpiece.

"We found Peter's comm. It's broken," Seth said, picking it up and putting it in his inner jacket pocket.

"Looks like the kid stalled the guards or sent them in other directions," Paddy said. "I've got a lot of cameras to check, but you still better get the fuck off that floor."

Seth stepped out of the room, eyes checking both directions, and spoke quietly to Paddy. "At this stage, I've got to believe Peter is either looking for a way to get out of this building, hopefully with Zoe safe, or he's heading up to see—"

"That's what I was thinking," Paddy said. "He's got a score to settle, and I'm not sure anything is going to stop him."

"Son of a bitch." Seth turned to Emory and George. "Guys, we've got to get moving."

"What are you going to do with the kids?" Paddy asked.

"What the hell do you think I'm—"

"You can't take them up there with you. What if it's a full-blown standoff?" Paddy threw a litany of new imaginings into Seth's head he didn't need right now.

"I'll drop them off with Dr. Bajorek," Seth said. "Where do we stand with the drive?"

"Eighty-two percent."

"Good. I'll take them up to her. How are we looking?"

"One guard on S2 is talking on his walkie, hurrying toward the stairs," Paddy said.

"We've got to run," Seth explained to the boys and took off down the hallway.

"There's someone heading our way," Emory said, trailing behind with George in tow.

"That's why we're running." Seth got to the elevator and rapidly pressed the up button.

"I've got him stalled in the stairwell, looking for an earring," Emory said.

Seth looked over his shoulder. "You're something of a miracle."

"Thanks."

"Chief," Paddy said, "we've got multiple guards heading to the elevators on different levels."

"Dammit! Emory, we've got multiple guards looking to get on the elevator."

"Where?" he asked.

"All over."

Emory took in a deep breath and went to work.

"Come on," Seth said, cursing the elevator.

"Hey!" a voice came from down the hall.

Seth, Emory, and George turned to see a guard running toward them.

"Shit," Emory cursed and recalibrated his efforts on the immediate threat.

The guard stopped mid-stride, spun around, and began sprinting the opposite direction.

The chime of the elevator sounded, and Seth pulled out his baton. The doors opened to an empty cabin. "Let's go, boys."

George stepped in and quickly extended his arms, readying himself to catch a wobbly Emory.

Seth led Emory into the elevator. "I've got you," he said, placing his baton back in its holder.

"There's a lot of them," Emory mumbled and fell back against the side wall.

George swung around Seth and put his arm under Emory's shoulder. "I got him."

Seth nodded and pressed the button to the seventeenth floor. "We're in the elevator heading up, Paddy. If this thing stops before we get to floor seventeen, we're in a heap of shit."

"I wish there was something I could do."

"Loop the cameras on seventeen," Seth suggested.

"Already done."

"I stopped three guys," Emory said as his legs gave out. George squatted down to the floor, staying under him.

"Emory passed out," Seth told Paddy.

"Get to Dr. Bajorek's office, and stay there until we can get this under control," Paddy said.

Seth watched the floor numbers ascend, focusing his newfound powers on keeping anyone from stopping them before they got to seventeen. "I'll stash the kids with her, but I've got to get up to the penthouse. Any sign of Peter?"

"That's a negative."

Seth slowly let out a meditative breath as the digital number struck fourteen, fifteen, sixteen, seventeen. The ding precipitated the door opening. Seth helped George drag Emory out of the elevator.

"What the fuck's goin' on here now?"

The voice that came from down the hall was unmistakable, and it sent every ounce of calm and control Seth had straight out the window. Before turning around, Seth whispered to Paddy. "It's Seamus."

"He'll have orders," Paddy replied succinctly. "You're going to have to shoot him."

"I can't do that." Seth looked at George. "Stay down on the ground, and protect Emory."

George bravely nodded, his eyes filled with terror.

Seth turned around, eyes locking with Seamus, thirty feet down the hall and approaching rapidly. Seth stood to his feet, held his hands out to show he wasn't holding a weapon, and spoke with force. "There have been multiple kidnappings—"

"The doors are locked! No way in. And it looks like you're the one—"

"Seamus," Seth said, backing away from the kids into a waiting area with couches, chairs, and floor-to-ceiling windows facing downtown Lost Grove, "I don't know how much you know, but your uncle ordered the kid—"

"Me uncle gave me orders." Seamus broke into a sprint, heading directly at Seth.

Seth tensed his body, poised to move, and stumbled backward. He felt a moment of panic as he bumped into the edge of a table. Losing his balance, Seth tried to correct his movement, shifting left. Seamus lunged forward and drove his shoulder into Seth's gut with enough force to launch him through the air. His back crashed onto the wooden couch frame, flipping it over onto him with a thunderous crash.

"Just stay down, mate, and let me cuff ya," Seamus said as he grabbed the couch and heaved it off of Seth's body like it was a child's mattress. The wooden armrest of the couch hit one window, causing a stress crack that looked like a two-foot spider web.

Seth, dazed, tried to push himself up. Instead, he found Seamus's boot smashing into his chest, knocking him back to the ground.

"Stay down! I don't want to have to hurt ya."

Seth grabbed Seamus's boot and tried to push and twist it off his chest. "I think you already have," he grunted.

"Stop it with the boot, huh?" Seamus pressed down further on the sergeant's rib cage.

Seth struggled to keep his breath held in so the Irishman didn't collapse his lung. He swung his right leg over his left and in between Seamus's legs and whipped it back into his shin, causing him to fall forward, off balance. Seth rolled away from him and spun up to his feet.

"What the hell was that?" Seamus said, surprised. He turned around and caught the sergeant's fist in his hand before it could make contact with his face.

Seth countered and threw a series of left jabs into Seamus's ribs. It was like punching a bear and seemed to have about as much impact.

Seamus grabbed a hold of Seth's right elbow, still gripping his fist, and hoisted him off the ground.

Seth howled in pain. "You're assaulting an officer of the law."

"Who illegally entered the facility and abducted two children."

"I'm rescuing—"

Seamus lunged forward and pushed Seth toward the window behind him.

His skull hit the glass with force. The frail window behind Seth groaned in protest, its edges quivering beneath the strain. He slipped down the glass, his legs weakened by the pain ricocheting at the back of his head. A deep chord of fear struck Seth as he heard an ear-splitting crack. Icy air lapped at his heels, and Seth felt himself falling backward. He closed his eyes tight as visions of Sarah Elizabeth on the beach flooded into his mind, just before Seamus's callused fist grasped his shirt collar and yanked him back to safety.

"Look what you made me do, you eejit," Seamus said, lifting the sergeant up to his feet.

The flood of sweet relief Seth felt being saved by the man pummeling him was short-lived, as Seamus didn't pull him away from the window but extended his arm out.

"Now, stop trying to fight me, pal. Your life is in your own hands."

If Seth could have found the words to yell "I quit," he would have, but feeling no ground under his left heel had him in a state of paralysis. He meekly shook his head, hoping Seamus wouldn't interpret it the wrong way.

"No, you're *not* going to stop trying to fight me?" Seamus said, his eyes wide.

Seth shook his head again and squeaked out the words, "No, that's not—"

"Have it your way," Seamus said.

Seth felt the hairs on his body lift a millisecond before a ghostly, deafening female scream shattered the night. The sound pulsated around him, within him.

Seamus winced, stumbling back two steps. He looked around, seeing no one fitting the wail of anguish, just a terrified-looking boy holding onto a young man who was either passed out or dead.

Seth instinctively grabbed Seamus's shirt as he balanced his body on his right foot and kicked his left heel into Seamus's right kneecap.

Seamus bellowed in pain as he fell backward, pulling Seth down on top of him. "You broke me bloody leg!"

Seth held onto Seamus's body like a life preserver. He looked around the room but knew he wouldn't see the source of the young woman's scream. He closed his eyes, feeling Sarah's presence like it was his own, and thanked her.

"Get off of me!" Seamus grunted, throwing Seth from his body.

Seth rolled over to his feet, panting, and pulled out his handcuffs. He locked one around Seamus's right wrist and used all of his power to swing his body around and lock the other cuff onto a steel rod on the ground just outside the broken window.

Seamus gripped his quadricep, just above his busted knee, wincing. "I wouldn't a let you go," he moaned.

Seth stood to his feet and backed away from the beast masquerading as a man. "I didn't get that impression."

"I was just tryin' to scare you into giving up."

"You succeeded."

"I don't think so, mate. I'm the one in bloody handcuffs."

Seth turned away from him, still trying to capture his breath. "Paddy, I've got him subdued," he breathed.

"How the hell did you do that?"

"I'll tell you later. Any sign of Peter?"

"No, sir. He's still in the building. I've been watching all the exits."

Seamus let out a high-pitched whine. "Look what you did!"

Seth turned around to see Seamus in a sitting position, having pulled up his pant leg, staring at the grotesque angle of his kneecap, currently floating over his upper shin. The skin was already ripe and swollen. "It's not as bad as it looks," Seth offered, his stomach churning at the sight.

"Well, it looks pretty feckin' bad."

"Sergeant Wolfe?"

Seth turned to see Dr. Bajorek peeking around the corner of the hallway. "Are you okay?"

Seth nodded, heading toward George and Emory, who had just woken up. "I'll be fine."

Jane ran over to the boys and squatted down to check on Emory. "Mr. Graff, are you okay?"

Emory nodded and pointed toward the shattered window. "What happened?"

"Long story," Seth said, reaching a hand out to him.

Emory gripped Seth's hand and pulled himself up to his feet. George stood and joined them.

Jane stood up. "Where's Mr. Andalusian?"

Seth pointed up. "I'm guessing up top, which is where I need to be. Now. Paddy, where are we with the flash drive?"

"Almost done. I'm at 93 percent."

"Dr. Bajorek," Seth said, "can you watch over the boys in your office while I go find Peter?"

"Of course," Jane replied.

"Oye!"

Seth turned around to Seamus. "What is it?"

Seamus was reaching toward a table two feet away from him. "Can you grab me a water?"

Seth looked at the bottles of water on the table and walked over. "Why should I give you a bottle of water?" Seth asked, walking back toward him.

Seamus scowled at him. "Why? Because I'm thirsty, and you broke me leg."

Seth shook his head as he grabbed one bottle. He squatted down next to the table, a safe distance away. "Give me your keycard," he said.

"Huh?"

Seth pointed at his belt. "Your keycard. Slide it over, and I'll give you this water."

"You clearly already have one," Seamus said.

"It's not for me."

Seamus dropped his head. "This is complete shite. Me uncle's gonna deport me for sure."

"You don't have a green card?" Seth asked, wondering why he was engaging in a discussion under the circumstances.

"Yeah, I do. But he'll figure out somethin'." Seamus, with a pathetic look of defeat on his face, unclipped his keycard and tossed it at Seth. "I'm well fucked already."

Seth caught the card and rolled the water over.

Seamus grabbed the bottle. "Thanks, pal."

"If I kept fighting, would you have dropped me?"

Seamus glared at Seth, his lip curling up. "What you take me for? A bleedin' murderer?"

Seth nodded, satisfied with the answer, and walked back toward Jane and the boys. "You have a lock on your door?" he asked Dr. Bajorek.

"I do," she said.

Seth looked at Emory and George. "You guys okay?"

"Yeah, man," Emory said, still trying to clear the cobwebs from his mind.

"I'm scared," George answered.

Jane put her arm around the boy. "Come with me. I'd like to speak with you," she said and led him down the hallway.

"You sure you don't need me?" Emory said.

"I need you to keep both of them safe. Keep everyone away from her office and make sure that door gets locked."

"I'm on it." He turned to follow the doctor and Real George.

"Emory?" Seth called out.

Emory turned around.

"You're a hero. Thank you."

Emory smiled and nodded before turning back around and sprinting to catch up.

Seth pressed the up button on the elevator. "I'm heading up, Paddy."

The elevator door chimed open and Seth held his gun at the ready, entering the quiet, charged manor. He didn't relish pulling his firearm again, but Peter was clearly armed. If he was somewhere in this multi-floor maze of a residence, Seth had to be ready. He scanned to his right, then swiveled to his left. A set of stairs led up a dark hallway that would bring him deeper into the home. Seth moved to the stairs, looking up.

Seth dropped his gun by his side and leaned back against the hallway wall. He heard the shuffle of feet as he turned the corner and saw warm light spilling out from the room at the end onto the dark hallway floor. As he got closer, he could see Peter. His back was toward him, and his daughter clung to his neck. Thank the heavens she was all right. Just as he registered the conversation Peter was having, a figure appeared from an invisible room amidst the darkness in front of him. The warm light caught the liquid black of a handgun as it pointed toward its target.

Seth lifted his weapon. Instinct had him briefly open his mouth to call out a warning, "Police. Drop your weapon," but registered there'd be no time, nor would the warning be absorbed and obeyed. The gun had a silencer. The man wore gloves, and he moved with ease and precision.

Seth aimed for a lethal shot and pulled the trigger.

The assailant's gun went off, firing wildly up and away from Peter and his daughter. Peter dropped to the ground, covering his child. A surprised, masculine shout echoed from deeper inside the room. The assailant crumbled to the ground as blood and viscera dripped down the partially open door into the room.

Seth moved to the body, his gun covering the assailant the whole time. "Peter?" he called. "It's Sergeant Seth Wolfe. Are you injured?"

"No," Peter called back. "Owens has a gun," he warned.

Seth kicked the gun away from the assailant and checked for a pulse. A common misconception was that head wounds were always lethal. In this case, it was. Seth pressed his back to the edge of the entry. "Dr. Owens? This is Sergeant Wolfe with the Lost Grove Police Department. I'd advise you to put down your weapon."

"I…yes, I…" came the voice of the older man.

"I'm going to step into the room now," Seth advised. He looked down at the floor where Peter lay. Peter made a slight gesture with his hand to tell Seth the direction where Dr. Owens was standing.

Seth slowly poked his head around the doorframe and saw Dr. Owens, looking rather shell-shocked, standing behind a large oak desk, holding a shiny gun in his hand like it was toxic. Seth held his gun to his chest. "Are either of you injured?" he asked Peter.

"No," Peter responded. He tipped his head down to his daughter, shielded beneath him, and reassured her with fatherly whispers.

Seth entered the room and approached Dr. Owens with caution. The ceilings weren't just tall, they were vast. Art Deco sconces ran along the wall, casting warm beacons of light upward. Seth imagined the lights dimmed just like the theater models they were copying. Expensive-looking Persian rugs softened the wood floor. A seating area of leather couches sat perpendicular to a small, stately fireplace set into a wall of floor-to-ceiling bookshelves.

Seth approached the desk, noting there was only one large window running parallel to the ceiling. The wall behind Dr. Owens had a massive, absurd painting of two very young, nude women, one white, one black, with astute attention to detail and realism set on a backdrop of multicolored polka dots. They were standing on a crocodile whose mouth was open, head tossed back as if trying to eat the girls on his back. One of the young women in the painting was throwing up a peace sign.

"I need you to lower the gun. Place it on the desk, and step back," he instructed.

Neil Owens's mouth parted, his eyebrows darting into an arch. "Of course. I only had it because he stormed in here like a cowboy, guns ablaze." Owens set his small gun on the far edge of his desk and took three paces back, clutching the unbuttoned portion of his flowing silk shirt together in some showcase of modesty.

Seth moved to the desk and grabbed the gun—a miniscule weapon, polished silver with gold filigree. He checked it and placed it in his belt, dropping his own to his side. "Who is that man?" he asked, pointing over his shoulder at the dead man.

"I have no idea," Neil responded.

"You don't know who that is? He was in your house with an FNX-45 tactical handgun and a silencer." The situation felt as absurd as the painting behind Owens.

"I am sorry, but I don't know what those things are."

Seth nodded, already feeling the bullshit piling up. "Neil Owens, you are under arrest for aiding and abetting a known criminal in the abduction of Zoe Andalusian—"

"Pardon?"

"You are under caution regarding the medical mistreatment of Sarah Elizabeth Grahams. You have the right to—"

"Wait a minute," Owens said, shaking his head. His hand raised in supplication.

"An attorney. If you cannot afford—"

"Wait, wait, Sergeant!" Owens raised his voice. "Wait a moment, sir. Do you not understand this is a research facility?"

Seth took a breath to settle himself. Dr. Owens had been read enough of his rights. Seth had done his best to play this by the book. "I am aware of the Orbriallis Institute's focus."

"Then, sir, Sergeant." Owens spread a charming but empty grin. "You are aware that there is no such thing as medical mistreatment."

"I can use the word misconduct if you'd prefer," Seth responded.

"Mis-misconduct?" Owens splayed his hands upward, a look of shock layered on his face for his audience. "I dare say I am at a loss. Misconduct of whom?"

Seth ground his teeth, fighting the urge to pull the trigger again. "Sarah Elizabeth Grahams."

"Oh, no, my dear man, no." Owens shook his head. His body shifted into a casual repose. Neil took a deep breath. "Miss Grahams was a research candidate. A candidate, see. She wasn't a patient. It is true," he said, lifting a finger, "she came to us as a patient. But her long-term stay at this hospital was as a candidate."

"And do your candidates not qualify as humans?" Seth growled.

"You make it sound as if I kept her in a cage, like some chimpanzee or a lab rat. Let me, shall I show you her quarters? I assure you, Sergeant, there was no malfeasance here. Miss Grahams had all she could want at her fingertips. In exchange, and under her permission, her body became ours to test. She signed the waivers."

"The misconduct I refer to—"

"Sergeant, if I may. Because I see you don't quite understand. And why would you?" His smile hung like a mask on his face. "You're not a doctor. You're not a scientist."

"I don't need to be in order to know that your patient, or candidate, as you call her, ended up deceased and on the local beach. And she wasn't the first one."

"Sir!" Neil implored firmly. "I cannot, I just cannot stand for this talk of my life's work in such a way." Neil shook his head, clenching his eyes shut tight. "You talk about it as if I've done something terrible. Something wrong. I'm saving lives. I'm making lives better. There are risks and rewards in research science. And if you took half a minute to understand that, if the world took a moment to understand, we'd be all done and away with this nonsense about misconduct and mistreatment." Neil dramatically shivered.

"You can explain it in depth if you'd like at—" Seth started.

Neil moved away, not as if trying to elude capture but like a professor pacing across the front of an auditorium as he prepared to speak down to his students. He clutched a hand to his chest. "I am wounded, Sergeant. Do you know, when I met you… Well it was just earlier today, wasn't it? Seems like a lifetime ago. But in that moment, I felt like you saw me. Those piercing eyes, I mean, who can escape those?"

Seth's eyes widened, completely thrown off by the description of his eyes from Neil's mouth, which felt delicate and longing.

"You're a well-educated man, Sergeant, but there is so much more to you. I could tell that, straight away. You're the type of man who can collect information and see the bigger picture." He clutched his hand into a soft fist, thumb pressing into the joint of his index finger, a politician punctuating the points of his speech. "Yes, you are a person who can look down on the whole picture, like a god." Neil met Seth's eyes. "I am like that. I can see the picture, the whole picture, and know what must be done. You must see that. The whole picture? I know you do."

Seth sighed. Dr. Owens posed no physical threat to anyone, and Zoe was safe, so he allowed him to continue on with his performance, which he had to admit was impressive in its audaciousness.

"My team has had recent trouble seeing the whole picture. I try—daily, I try—to paint it for them. You know how taxing it is to step into the boardroom and lift them up. Like a general leading his army to charge the frontline? They want to go on and on about Nucleotide A337 and Catalyst FLH13 and research studies in the UK that have shown ill effects in rats. Rats! My test subjects, my candidates," he said, as if he were about to shed a tear, "are not rats. How are we to know what the lasting effects of Catalyst FLH13 on a woman are? We can't. That is the answer. We can't."

Seth glanced over at Peter, who gave him a hopeless shrug, like there was no way to avoid this dissertation.

"That is why we are conducting this research," Dr. Owens continued. "They, my board of doctors, want to say Project Eve is defunct, inoperative, they say. It should be dissolved, and we should move on. They are monstrously incorrect. Out of three test subjects, we have finally seen progress. We've had success! Who cares if Nucleotide A337 influences unnatural occurrences in the fetus that result in unforeseeable dangers to the mother? Long-term health, short-term health, they're constantly bickering over it. 'Don't use them,' they say. 'We should try testing with another covalent.' I mean, the lunacy!" Neil shook his head wildly. "This is research. This is progress. This is evolution! Do you think this comes without costs?"

Seth sighed and holstered his weapon, forgetting that he was actually still holding it. "You want me to look past the lives you've trampled in the course of your godly planning?"

Neil shut his eyes. "I must remind myself to have more patience with you," he uttered. "You can't conceptualize why I must continue. We need Nucleotide A337 and Catalyst FLH13 to support the extra chromosomes. We're building new humans, not making the same old ones. Does that result in a stronger embryo? Yes. But isn't that magnificent!"

"Sarah Elizabeth bled to death in childbirth," Seth said, his voice raised, tipped toward anger.

Neil looked flummoxed, then annoyed. "You don't understand, do you? I could never explain it to you, someone like you. No, it'll make no difference. You don't understand what I'm saying."

"I do," came a woman's voice from the hallway.

The occupants in the room turned to the unknown voice. Dr. Jane Bajorek walked through the doorway, stepping over the body and into the study.

"How did you get in here?" Neil asked.

Jane held up Seamus's keycard, coming farther into the room, and stood to the side of Peter and Zoe, both still on the ground.

Neil snorted. "Dr. Bajorek, your presence here is tedious and unwanted."

"You used Nucleotide A337 and Catalyst FLH13 through our protestations. You refused to listen to your board of physicians and scientists, who are better equipped and educated to know the repercussions," she said. "God help us. We may not have seen it in time for the first two victims, but we definitely saw it in Sarah. And you went ahead with the second pregnancy, anyway. You discounted our research and—"

"You lack the guts. The fortitude—"

"—implanted a second baby, resulting in further health deterioration. Malnutrition, mental stress, bodily transmutations, child endangerment—"

"Second baby?" Seth asked.

"You are weak, just like your mothers," Neil bellowed.

Jane's lips pursed. She set her face like stone, giving away nothing. It was some time before anyone in the room spoke. "You killed Sarah Elizabeth Grahams, knowingly. We knew how hard the first pregnancy was on her. And you gave her no time to heal. By then, we, your board, had our suspicions. You agreed we'd try other chromosomes and catalysts. But you didn't actually follow through with that, did you? You needn't answer. You've already said as much to Sergeant Wolfe."

"And look at the beautiful child it wrought," Neil sneered.

"Dr. Owens, I need to caution you," Seth stepped in. "You've been read your rights and anything you say—"

"Phooey with your rights, Sergeant Wolfe," Neil said, waving his hand in the air. "I've done no wrong. I'm not in the wrong!"

Jane sniffed, trying to stop the tears from falling. "How did she die?" she asked Neil.

"You see, this is why I don't like women on the team. They get attached, emotional."

"Oh, Christ. You killed a child!" Jane roared. "Sarah was twenty-one years old, Neil. She was a goddamn child, and you lured her in on her abilities, on her visions. You capitalized on that. You took advantage of her, not to mention the others. Kelly Fulson. How much money did you promise her? How much wealth and fame did you lure her in with? Hollywood promises. Fake promises, as if you actually knew any directors or heads of studios who would put her in a film! And poor Daisy Sutherland. She wanted something simple, didn't she? Did you even purchase the land? Were you ever going to name a park after her? A beautiful nature preserve, that's all she wanted. Instead, you tossed her out like yesterday's trash. And you'll do it again."

"Of course I'll do it again. That is what it takes!" Neil's face pressed forward, his teeth bared and vicious, the ligaments in his neck stretched taut. "Progress takes sacrifice."

"How did she die?" Jane asked again.

Seth stepped into the conversation. "Neil Owens, I'm going to place you in handcuffs."

Neil ignored him but didn't move away as Seth approached. "She died in childbirth."

"What were the complications, you asshole?" Jane said. She knew Sarah had died during birth, and he knew she knew that. His answer was a jab, but she wouldn't fall because of it.

Seth shook his head, annoyed. He'd removed the second set of handcuffs from his belt and had hold of Neil's right wrist. "She died from blood loss. Trauma."

"It was a marvel, really. You should be proud," Neil cooed as Seth placed his hands behind his back and clasped on the cuffs. "The umbilical cord was wrapped around the baby's neck. She was dying, suffocating. And within the womb, that barely formed baby knew she had to free herself. She pulled herself free. Can you fathom that? Is that not the most miraculous thing you've ever heard of?"

Seth, holding on to the cuffs, stood to the side of Neil Owens. "If the child was in danger, why not perform an emergency C-section?" He couldn't keep himself from asking, wanting to know. Maybe a part of him wanted Neil to put the final nail in his own coffin.

Neil looked at him, blinking as if he had no idea who Seth was or why and when he'd moved so close. "How would I have known the child was worth saving if I hadn't let her try to save herself?"

Seth could feel his whole body tense, clenching into the anger he wanted to let out. He took a deliberate breath in through his nose. "I'm going to check you for any weapons or items on your person," he commented.

Neil nodded absently. "You cannot comprehend the work I do here. And what are you doing to me? You've got no proof! No proof!"

Jane held up the flash drive she had been gripping in her hand. "We've got enough to put you away for the rest of your life," she said, glowering at the doctor.

"What is that? Some sort of microchip? You've got nothing. Now, uncuff me at once, Sergeant."

Seth ignored him. "Dr. Bajorek? Do you know the deceased man in the hall?"

Jane looked from Neil to Seth, swallowing forcefully. She turned, one hand raised and scratching at her forehead, flicking her hair aside. She leaned down, trying to get a glance at the man's face. "I do not."

"The baby…in the womb, you see?" Dr. Owens continued. "She had the wherewithal. Fathom that, Sergeant Wolfe. Take a moment to see what a miracle I created."

"You didn't create it," Jane said in a half-hearted protest. "Sarah created that child. Her womb molded and crafted that child. And a few scientists put together some DNA sequences. But it was Sarah who was the miracle."

Neil looked at her, the whites of his eyes shining, wild and exposed. "I know! I knew it all along!"

Seth maneuvered Neil Owens to an armchair and lowered him into it before turning to Peter and his daughter. "Is she alright?"

Peter nodded.

Seth turned on his walkie and pulled it from his belt. "Bill, it's Seth. I need you to send—"

"Seth, where the hell have you been? I've been calling for—"

"We found Zoe. She's alive and safe now."

"Who are you talking to?" Neil asked, disgusted.

Seth ignored the mad doctor. "Send every unit you have to the Orbriallis Institute. And send as many medical units as you can. We've got multiple injuries."

"I'm on it."

Seth placed the walkie back on his belt and looked at Peter. "The EMTs will have a look at her. Probably best to take her to the hospital."

"Of course," Peter nodded, understanding what Seth was leaving unsaid.

Zoe turned her face to look at Seth. He offered her a warm smile, and she accepted it before turning to bury her face once more in her father's neck.

"Do you know who that is?" Seth asked Peter, pointing to the dead man.

"If I had to guess, it's the man who killed the Grahams," Peter explained. "If you track down his ID, he'll likely be ex-military."

"Yeah, I figured," Seth sighed.

"Killed? Are you two mad?" Neil barked. "It was a suicide!"

A door shifted toward the back of the room. Seth stepped in front of Peter and his daughter, pulling his gun from its holster. The door opened, revealing a small room, and inside stood an older woman, her face concealed by a veil. On one side stood a young boy. In her arms, she held an infant that looked too young to be holding its own head up. Seth holstered his weapon.

Lina exited the secret, luxurious elevator. The little boy at her side had a birthmark on his face, an abnormally large head, a cleft lip, and vibrant green eyes. He tugged on Lina's hand, and she looked down at him.

"She wants to see him. Up close. She can't see him from this far," the little boy said.

Seth watched the infant swivel her head from looking down at the boy up to the older woman's face, concealed by the veil, then out to Seth. The baby smiled.

Seth gulped.

"You're the one behind this." Neil glared over his shoulder at Lina. "I always knew."

Lina, ignoring Dr. Owens, let go of the boy's hand and moved into the room. She approached Seth and held the little infant girl for him to take.

"She wants to see you," Lina said. When Seth made no move, she pushed the child in his direction, coming even closer.

Seth's heart was beating heavily as he reached out and took the baby girl, the same one he had encountered on his last journey into the future. He held her up, locking eyes with her. The baby, whose own eyes held a depth of clarity uncanny for a child that age, smiled again. She leaned forward, and though advanced beyond her young age, her movements still had the wobble of a newborn child.

Seth brought her closer until her forehead pressed to his. Her delicate fingers danced across his cheeks and latched onto his lips like any normal baby.

"Her name is Cleo," Lina explained.

The boy came skittering over, clinging to Lina's leg.

"I know." Seth shifted the baby to his side, still staring at her and she at him. "Hello, Cleo."

"She says, 'Hello, Seth,'" the little boy whispered.

Seth's eyes burned hot with tears. They came falling down his face, and he couldn't explain why.

"You won't take them, will you?" Lina asked.

Seth looked over at Lina and at Jane now standing beside her. The older woman moved her hands, fingers gripping the edge of her veil. She lifted it, revealing a heavily made-up face, an attempt to cover the uneven skin, the scars. Her chin was weak to the point of nonexistence, and her nose was uneven, one nostril far higher than the other. A massive scar depicting the cleft she'd been born with covered part of her top lip. One eyebrow hung lower than the other. But for all that, Lina wasn't monstrous to look at. Nothing could conceal the brilliant blue eyes, vivacious and loving.

Seth looked back at Cleo, who reached up and pulled at his nose, the other swinging enthusiastically in the air. "No," Seth answered. "I won't take them."

Resolution...of a Kind

Noble stood in line at Christopher Wolfe's pharmacy, looking at the faces of everyone in the store. He felt anything but normal. He and his friends' recent experiences were once in a lifetime events, and yet the world surrounding them kept on as if nothing terrifying was happening right under their noses. He supposed it wasn't because no one else in Lost Grove would ever know. They couldn't tell anyone that Emory had made himself and two other grown men invisible, that Sarah Elizabeth had died giving birth to a baby who was cognizant in the womb, or that the real George Horne had endured experiments in an underground lab with strange wires connected to his head.

Noble sighed and practiced breathing. He knew he couldn't expect everyone to see what he saw or understand what he understood. But the fact that they didn't made him feel rather alone. Even with his close-knit group of friends in the know, he couldn't escape the pressure of the unspoken words he'd never be allowed to utter. He wanted to scream out loud, *The Green Man Raymond LaRange is a convicted child molester who kidnapped my sister and is on the loose in Lost Grove!*

"Hey, check this out." Nate drew up beside Noble in the checkout line, holding out his phone for Noble to view.

Noble's eyes flicked to his friend's face, then to the screen. It read, *Government Cover-Up in Small Coastal Town*. "What is this?"

"It's on the conspiracy site I told you about," Nate responded. "Yo, Zo! Grab me a Coke. Please."

Noble stole a glance toward the side of the store where his sister,

Zoe, was selecting drinks for their lunch break. She shot an exasperated look at the back of Nate's head before grabbing a can of Coke. She was recovering each day, and he was doing his best to treat her normally.

"We're not talking about this," Noble said.

He actually enjoyed listening attentively as his friend expounded upon his theories, occasionally throwing in an idea of his own. However, when Zoe was around, the topic was forbidden. Not to mention, they shouldn't talk about it. For Nettie's sake. For George's.

"Yeah, I know. This is us not talking about it," Nate agreed and shoved his phone into Noble's hand. "Read."

Noble scanned the text of a post written on an obscure website filled with outlandish stories and intense paranoia. Certain details rang true, and Noble's heart pounded hard against his rib cage as he read them. He thought frantically, begging for this not to be some elaborate ploy concocted by his father and Paddy. He quickly scrolled to the poster's name, DiamondCream86. What sort of name was this?

Noble looked up suspiciously at his friend. "You better not have posted this."

Nate turned and met Noble's gaze, aghast, with one hand lifted to his collarbone like a proper Southern lady.

Noble leaned and whispered, "Seriously, was this you?"

"Fuck no," Nate whispered back. "You think I want the Feds throwing me in the back of a van and carting me off to wherever the hell they took—"

"Can I get a creme pie?" Zoe called to her older brother.

Nate and Noble both looked over at her, smiling like they were gossiping about high school frivolities. Nate actually let out a forced laugh that was about as believable as icicles in the Sahara.

"For sure," Noble answered, patting Nate on the back. "Nice laugh, dickhead," he whispered without moving his mouth.

Zoe smiled widely, her eyes twinkling in anticipation as she clutched the cookie tightly in one hand and ran up to the counter.

Noble jammed Nate's phone back into his hands between a bag of chips and a sandwich from the deli. "You shouldn't even be looking that stuff up if you don't want the Feds on you."

Nate cocked an eyebrow. "Good point."

The weather had turned sunny after weeks of torrential rain. The trees were exploding with red, orange, and yellow leaves, falling and skittering along the sidewalks and roads in a colorful cacophony of natural confetti.

The sun made a daring move to peek through the clouds, and Main Street lit up as they exited the drug store. Across the street, Anya was taking a seat at a picnic table outside the creamery. Next to her, Nettie sat huddled in her coat, sipping on a cup of soup. Noble's eyes met Anya's, and she gave him a small smile as their gazes locked.

Family preoccupations had taken over what was left of Noble's social life when he wasn't busy with cross-country. He'd won the track meet, just like everyone hoped and wished, despite his concussion and busted nose. Anger had driven him to push himself hard. He wanted to run as far as possible. He wanted to feel something other than the gut-wrenching remorse of his failure to protect his sister. The result of his pain had pushed him to not only win but break the county record.

Noble almost wished he hadn't channeled his anger so well. Now he was a town hero. Everyone thumped him on the back and yelled across the street, "Way to go!" Their encouragement made him feel lonelier than he already was.

"I got you the club. They didn't have the Italian," Stan said in greeting as she joined Nate, Noble, and Zoe.

Noble nodded, taking the sandwich. "Thanks."

"Joining them?" Stan asked with the flick of her head toward Nettie and Anya. Emory and Ember had just arrived and sat directly across from them.

"Duh," Nate huffed over his shoulder, already on his way.

Zoe walked beside her brother, his hand on her shoulder, guiding her. Her forgiveness for his inability to protect her wasn't even necessary. Zoe hadn't been conscious during the incident, so she didn't remember that he'd failed at his job as her guardian. He was working on forgiving himself. He was working on forgiving his father, too. Both seemed impossible.

Zoe hadn't gone a single night since being rescued without waking from night terrors. She hated them most when her screams would wake her family. She liked when her brother placed a hand on her shoulder and her dad's eyes constant watch. Even though it should have been bothersome, she found comfort in their protectiveness. It gave her a sense of safety. When she wasn't with her family, Story was there.

Story brought calm to her overall state of restlessness. They always listened to each other intently, Zoe opening up about her newfound fears and feelings since being kidnapped. Story told her there would be a time when her fears would go away, but only the passing of time could heal that wound. Zoe wished there was a spell to make time move faster. Then maybe she, her brother, and her parents could leap forward to a time when they were all healed and everything was right again.

"…on the East Coast somewhere. She was vague," Anya finished explaining as they approached.

Zoe liked Anya and skipped around the table to join her. She couldn't put her finger on it, but Anya radiated a power of her own. She was working up the courage to ask Anya if she was a witch. Maybe she'd ask Story first.

Nettie's face creased inward. "That's all she said. He got an opportunity to study at a school on the East Coast? That doesn't explain his inability to return our texts."

"I know," Anya half-heartedly agreed. She moved over, making room for Zoe, who sat beside her with a grin.

Noble sat across the table from his sister, not wanting her ever to be over five feet away from him at any time.

Anya looked at Noble and pointed to her nose. "Your nose is looking way better."

Noble shrugged. "Thanks?"

His nose was healing amazingly quick. He suspected this was because of the balm Story Palmer had brought by their house following The Event. That's what they called it—The Event. Capitalized. Important to the small circle of people who got caught up and twisted in the net of the Orbriallis Institute.

"You guys talking about Ryker?" Nate surmised as he climbed over the picnic table and plopped down next to Nettie.

Anya nodded.

"Yep," Nettie said.

Nate pushed his bag of chips over to her. "Here, I got a big bag. Have some."

Nettie set down her soup and opened up the bag. "Thanks, I will."

"Really? You couldn't just walk around the table like a normal person," Stan said as she grabbed the seat across from Nate.

"The fastest route between two points is a straight line," Nate said.

"I hate you." Stan rolled her eyes and bit into her sandwich.

Nettie laughed. Ask her a week ago where she thought she'd be now, and she would have guessed a padded cell in the Orbriallis Institute.

Anya amplified those feelings when she came over last week and said she had to tell her something. Nettie couldn't take another revelation. The panic truly set in when Anya tried to escort her up the stairs of Story Palmer's house.

"What are we doing here?" Nettie had asked, snapping her hand back from her friend's warm grasp.

"We need to tell you something," Anya replied as Noble opened the door.

Nettie stepped backward, nearly falling off the first porch step.

Anya grabbed a hold of her. "Nettie, I need you to trust me," she'd said and eased her into the warm house that smelled of spicy gingerbread and cocoa.

The cozy atmosphere washed over her in an unnatural calm.

Looking back, Nettie wished she could say she had trusted Anya, her best friend. But the events of her life in the days leading up to this moment hadn't put Anya in Nettie's best graces. It seemed like every time they met, Anya and Noble had new terrorizing material about her actual brother and the dreadful man who took him.

But she had her amazing friends to thank for what happened, what was still to come. Most important, the person who truly saved her from a life of insanity was the local police sergeant, Seth Wolfe.

He'd listened to them, listened to her friends, who laid out a litany of proof that the Green Man existed and so did the real George. He'd believed them enough to go looking for George. What he said next had changed her life.

"We can bring him back. He can rejoin your family. But only if you understand the terms I've just explained," he'd said.

George could come home? Nettie was right. She'd been right all along, and this man, this officer, had believed her and was bringing George home. On one major condition.

His memory of the time spent under experimentation was going to be wiped from his brain. The story would go like this—new research suggested that a small, almost unseeable lesion was blocking the executive functionalities of the brain. With removal and transcranial magnetic stimulation to coerce the nerves back into play, George would return to the normal, functioning state from before his diagnosis. The only person in her family who would remember, who would know that George was once replaced by Not-George, would be Nettie.

None of it made sense at that moment at Story Palmer's house. It made little sense now, but Nettie could live with that. She could live with the unknowns, with the secrets they weren't telling her, with the details of what led them to the moment where they sat her down and told her she'd have her real brother back.

Of course, these events with Ryker had her tiptoeing back into her old sense of paranoia. The way he was just gone one day, not answering their calls, had her set on edge. There were still spots in Lost Grove you couldn't get cell service, so she wasn't blind to that being a possibility. It was the fact that he'd said nothing before leaving. That there had been no text or call saying he got this amazing, supposed, opportunity to study at this elite school somewhere in posh upstate New York and wouldn't be as easy to reach. It set her teeth on edge.

"His mom said she'd pass the message on. He's supposed to call me tonight," Anya explained to baffled faces staring at her. No one could make heads or tails of Ryker vanishing from their lives overnight.

Anya glanced in Noble's direction and saw his downturned mouth, the brows furrowed together in concentration. He took a large bite out of his sandwich and chewed slowly. He had to know she and Ryker weren't together. Didn't he? A knot of anxiety formed in her stomach.

Zoe's small hands reached out and grabbed the other half of the sandwich, taking an enormous bite without even looking up from her book. Anya watched her for a moment, marveling at how much she had grown. She was twelve now, after all—not so little anymore.

"What are all those scribbles?" Anya asked, peering down into the book.

Zoe paused mid-chew and lifted her head to meet Anya's eyes. She swallowed. "What?"

"The scribbles." Anya smiled, lifting a hand and pointing at the notations made all over the book. "Where did you get this book?"

"You can see those?"

Noble glanced up from his meal, heart warmed by the exchange between Anya and his sister. He kept reminding himself that Nate had assured him nothing was going on between Ryker and Anya, that Ryker had a girlfriend up in Eureka, but they just seemed oddly close.

"See what?" he asked just as both of them lifted their gaze in an eerily similar fashion, gazing at something just over his head.

Noble turned to find Story Palmer walking nonchalantly past. Her long coat looked like it was made from Mary Poppins's carpet bag. It brushed along the pavement. Her sheer gauze shirt looked like something from the cover of a romance novel, revealing a black corset top underneath it and tawny leggings ended at the ankle. Fleeting glances of her soft forest-green cardigan sandwiched between her coat and shirt played peek-a-boo with passersby. Her boots clacked along the sidewalk as she strode ahead, her signature satchel swaying with each step. A knitted beret cast a shadow over her dark brows and tucked her hair away from her rosy cheeks. She gave them an enigmatic smile as she stopped on the sidewalk in front of them.

"Ms. Bury. Mr. Andalusian," she said.

Noble nodded. "Hi, Ms. Palmer." He was grateful for the care and mentorship she had been providing for his sister.

Story's gaze locked on Zoe. "Merry met, Zoe."

"Merry met, Ms. Palmer." Zoe grinned back.

Story felt a tug of laughter before she heard it snorted from Nate's nose. She turned, registering his roving look, knowing that like most young men, he'd no doubt circulated rumors of her naked dancing during the full moon. Of course, she had done such things, not that Nate had ever seen her, but it was a scintillating witchy notion that stuck in the minds of men. She gave Nate a long, measured look, her eyebrow cocked in question. Nate swallowed and looked away. She turned as a Bronco pulled into a recently vacated parking space.

Seth Wolfe exited the vehicle, wearing sunglasses, his police-issued jacket, faded jeans, and signature boots. He walked over and stood near Story, removing his glasses with a warm smile on his lips that matched hers. They locked eyes in a silent exchange before turning their attention back to the teens.

Main Street was usually full of kids during lunchtime, but this crowd seemed different to Seth from the others. Each one possessed a newfound gravity, or maybe they'd had it all along and he hadn't noticed. He couldn't help but feel an unexpected pang of nostalgia. These kids seemed far wiser and more capable than he remembered himself being at that age. How had they grown so mature? How were they seemingly prepared to face a world beyond Main Street?

His heart felt like it was being wrung out of his chest when he wondered if Sarah Elizabeth had looked as prepared as these young adults before him now. He had known she wanted to go to college, but she must have been excited about what lay beyond that. A life helping others. A future with Tommy Wilder.

"Kids," he said in greeting, tipping his head.

Nate jumped to his feet. "Afternoon, Sergeant Wolfe," he said, nodding back.

Seth contained a wide grin. Nate had called him on Tuesday to ask if officers wrote letters of recommendation to colleges. Seth kept the boy on edge by saying he'd consider it. Nate had all the drive and shockingly good instincts for a boy his age, but he needed to learn patience. Of course, he'd write the letter and make some calls to his former instructors at San Francisco State University. Nate claimed he had always planned on attending the school, despite Noble's protestations otherwise. Nate had also recently signed up for the Junior Volunteer Officer League, which was some nonsense Bill drummed up to appease the boy.

"Sit down, you bozo," Stan said. "He's not your lieutenant."

"Shut up, you don't know," Nate said, sitting back down across from her.

"Don't know what?"

"Whatever."

Nettie looked at Seth with a warm smile. "Hi!"

Seth nodded at her. "Ms. Horne."

"Whatup!" Emory said, looking over his shoulder at Seth.

Seth's tight, guilty smile quickly widened. "Hello, Emory." What he and the mind wizard of a young man had gone through was still hard to believe, thinking back. He looked at Noble, who was sitting next to Emory but facing him and Story. "Noble."

Noble stared at Seth in something of a stupor. The man who grew up in Lost Grove had returned home from a long tenure as the lead homicide detective for the San Francisco Police Department just in time to save him from getting pummeled by two drunken assholes, rescue his sister from a deranged child molester, and save his father from prison. Noble struggled all week to keep himself from sliding into an unbearable depression after his father confessed to him the many illegal atrocities he had committed. Part of Noble felt like his father deserved to go to prison for what he had done, but the overriding part of himself was thankful that Seth spared him, mainly for the sake of him and his sister.

"Sergeant," Noble strangled out, along with a grateful nod.

Seth looked past Noble to his sister, who had her head buried in a book. His chest tightened as he tried to push out the image of Peter holding Zoe in his arms, her body barely clothed. Seth turned his attention to Story. "Coffee?" he asked.

"That is precisely where I was headed." Story smirked.

"Mm-hmm." A sly smile tugged at Seth's lips. He still marveled at her uncanny ability to show up at just the right time and place. Seth waved at the group of teens. "See you guys around."

"I'll hit you up later," Nate called after him.

Stan leaned over the table and punched Nate in the arm.

"Ow!"

"I'll hit you every time you say stupid shit."

Seth laughed at the uncanny resemblance to his two deputies, Sasha and Joe. Maybe Stan would follow in her father's footsteps and enter the force, and he'd have two sets of officers always baiting each other. If he even stayed here. He wiped the thought from his mind and proceeded on with Story across the street.

"How does it feel to be looked up to as a hero?" Story asked.

Seth huffed. "I sure as hell don't feel like one."

"They all do, you know. Not just your biggest fan, Nate."

Seth chuckled as he told Story about Nate's call earlier in the week.

"Well, I think that's just adorable," Story said.

Seth opened the door to the cafe, allowing Story to enter before him. "Just the word I was thinking of."

Story grinned. One thing she most admired about Seth was his dry sarcasm.

"Afternoon, Seth. Story," Clemency Pruitt called out over the heads of the two young girls at the counter as she made their drinks.

"Hey, Clem," Seth replied.

"Afternoon, Clemency," Story said.

"Didn't see you this morning, Seth," Clemency yelled over the sound of the frothing milk. "Must be busy with all that ruckus going on at Orbriallis. Never seen so many damn police vehicles in my life, not so many for you, though, I'm sure."

Seth sighed, defeated. All the fury that had been surging through his veins all week drained away. True to Peter and Paddy's predictions, the Feds had swooped in on the Orbriallis like they were just waiting in the nearby woods for something to go down. Black sedans, vans, and armored trucks filled the parking lot, quickly ushering Seth, Joe, and Eddie off the premises. Back at the station, Special Agent Eve Hutton of the FBI walked through the doors, flashed her ID, her face rigid, her steel-green eyes penetrating, took Dr. Owens from his holding cell and left, neither being seen nor heard from since.

Story laced her fingers through Seth's and squeezed his hand. She had only exchanged sporadic texts with him since The Event, as the kids were calling it, but she gleaned enough to grasp that things were not going well with the case against the Orbriallis. "I'm sorry," she whispered.

Seth squeezed her hand in return, grateful for her calming presence. The two girls grabbed their coffees and stepped away from the counter. Seth smiled and forced a change of subject. "Looks like you're ghost-free," he said.

Clemency held her hand out, as if testing the surrounding air. "It seems so, thanks to your lovely lady friend. I knew it was just a matter of time before the two of you—"

"I'll have a triple iced Americano, Clem," Seth said, casually pulling his hand free.

"Triple? Your eyes don't betray you, dark as plums they are."

Seth turned to Story, brow knit. "Do I really look that bad?"

"You look tired. Not bad."

"Story, how about you, darling?" Clemency asked.

"Large iced green tea. Sweetened, please."

Seth looked around the cafe and was happy to see the one small table separated from the rest of the seats was clear. "You want to grab a seat?" he asked Story.

Story nodded. "I do."

"Clem, you mind bringing those over to the table?" he said, already heading away.

"Sure thing!"

Seth and Story approached the small wooden table up against the window.

"How's Zoe doing?" Seth asked. Story had texted him that the younger Andalusian had come to the library or over to her house every day this week.

Story rolled up the sleeves of her long forest-green cardigan. "She's confused, scared, but so genuinely brave."

Story was the only person Seth had told about Zoe's condition after Peter found her in that haunting room. Peter asked Seth not to say anything to Noble or Jolie about it. By the time they arrived at the hospital where Zoe was getting checked out, the outfit she was wearing had already been bagged for evidence and taken away by Sasha.

"Has she remembered anything yet?" Seth asked.

"No. And she's struggling with whether she wants to remember."

Seth pursed his lips. "That's a tough scenario. She's at such a delicate age. She may have genuinely been unconscious most of the time, but she was definitely awake when Emory heard her screaming for help. Has she talked to you about that?"

"She says that she just woke up, saw him kneeling down next to her, and then screamed. She said that he jumped back like he was terrified of her and then waved his hands in the air, trying to shush her."

"Here you guys go. You look so natural and perfect together, I have to say," Clemency rambled as she placed their drinks down on the table, along with a plate containing two small scones. "Those are on the house. Thank you for your dedicated work, Seth."

"Thanks, Clem," he called out as she jogged back behind the massive espresso machine. Seth shook his head and took a long sip of his iced Americano. "Do you believe that's all she remembers?"

Story drank some of her iced tea. "I believe she woke up when she said she did. She says she doesn't remember anything about being taken, which I'm not so sure about. And then there's the matter of what her unconscious mind might have perceived."

Seth nodded. "Well, I'm glad she's coming to see you. She'll be in good hands if she recalls something. Have you thought about…"

"No. I wouldn't interfere in that way. Not unless she specifically asked for my help in that regard."

"Does her family know she's coming to see you?"

"Yes. Noble drives her everywhere. When he picked her up from my house on Wednesday, he told me his dad said thanks."

"That's good."

"I'm concerned about Noble, though," Story said. "He's carrying an immense amount of guilt with him. It's so palpable it's like a green mist hovering around him."

"I thought green was envy," he said as his eyebrow tipped into an inquisitive arch.

"There are many shades of green and many meanings. It's tinged with deep violet, like a healing bruise."

"That makes sense."

Story swirled her cup, dispersing the sweetener. "I've been contemplating a spell to help him, but I feel as though Zoe would be upset, my interfering with him."

"Would it be overstepping?"

She smiled at him, at his genuine interest in her culture. She surmised his natural inquisitiveness was the very thing that made him such a good detective. "It's frowned upon to intercede on another witch's family."

"But she's just learning," he commented.

"You have your morals, Sheriff, and I have mine," Story said with a smirk before taking another sip of her tea.

Seth watched her pale lips, then looked away. "I'll reach out to him."

"Thank you."

"Speaking of which, I saw Tommy yesterday."

Story sat up, her eyes instantly filling with tears. "That poor boy."

"I called him first thing Monday morning. No one may ever hear what actually happened to Sarah Elizabeth or why, but I wanted to give him the option, if he wanted to hear." The looming probability that no one would ever publicly pay for what happened to Sarah or her parents was a terrible fact Seth would carry with him for the rest of his life. The district attorney informed him that the Feds had confiscated all the evidence, and he had an intolerable gut feeling that they would never hear about it again.

"And did he?" Story asked.

Seth nodded. "I met him by the stream running along the high school after his shift. I, of course, left out the grizzly details of her death, but I told him everything else. He was relieved to hear that she had recovered from her treatment for her sleep issues and had control of her visions. I could feel the relief washing over him when I informed him that her pregnancies were artificially induced. He said it was just like her to agree to the experiments, knowing that she could help so many other women and children."

Story wiped the tears from her cheeks. "It's just dreadful, thinking of what Tommy's been going through. What he'll have to live with."

"It is."

"Is he going to the funeral on Sunday?" Story asked. Lost Grove was holding a funeral for the Grahams family at the town cemetery. Story had already agreed to accompany Seth, who had offered to be a pallbearer.

Seth shook his head. "He said it would be too much for him to take and that he'd go see her on his own."

"So much talk of grief and loss."

"There have certainly been happier times in Lost Grove."

"Not all bad has come out of it, though," Story said. "Noble and his group of friends give me hope for the future. Nettie will get her real brother back, despite the stipulations. In a matter of years, Nate will be your future partner."

Seth burst out laughing. "That kid is something."

"I don't think I've ever seen someone so beaming with excitement as the night he laid out the maps for you," she said, giggling.

"And I thought I was motivated at his age to become a detective."

Story reached across the table, and Seth met her hand with his. "I'm sure you were as motivated. Just quieter. Still waters run deep."

Seth found the idiom intriguing. "I know we're meeting up for the funeral Sunday, but I was wondering…"

Story's smile widened. "Are you asking me on a date?"

Seth met her eyes, sending his heart fluttering. "I just thought we could maybe get together and cook some dinner or something."

"You know, watching you in your element, you're so confident, so in charge. Where does all that certainty go when you want to ask me on a date?"

Seth grinned. "I didn't go to college to master in dating."

Story laughed. "So, are you inviting me over to your place?"

"God, no. I've got a microwave and a fridge."

"Ah, I see. That's just yours and Mary's special place."

Seth playfully tossed her hand aside. "Please."

"She told me she kissed you."

Seth buried his head in his hands. "Jesus."

"I think it's cute."

Seth dropped his hands. "She caught me totally off guard."

Story couldn't stop grinning. "I'm happy you didn't push her away or turn your head. That would have crushed her."

"Well…I'm glad you're happy."

Story grabbed his hand again and gave it a strong squeeze. "How about dinner at my place tomorrow night?"

"Sounds like a plan. Or, sorry, a date."

"There you go!"

When they were done with their drinks, Seth and Story exited the cafe and exchanged a brief hug before parting ways. He offered to drive her back to the library, but she insisted on walking. Seth crossed the street and hopped into his Bronco. He grabbed his walkie and pressed the talk button. "Joe, Sasha, you guys ready?"

"I'm ready, boss," Joe responded.

"*I'm ready, boss,*" Sasha mocked him.

"What am I supposed to say?" Joe said.

"I'm ready, Seth. Where are we meeting?" Sasha asked. "See how professional and not childlike that sounded, Joe?"

Seth shook his head, smiling. "I'll meet you guys at the station, and then we'll head out in my Mercedes and see how close we can get to the Orbriallis."

"10-4," Joe replied.

"That's better," Sasha said.

Seth clicked off and started his Bronco. The biggest question consuming his thoughts lately flashed to the forefront of his mind. How long was he going to stay in Lost Grove? He never planned on his return home to be a permanent one. His boss at the San Francisco Police Department checked in with him every week, begging him to come back. A couple of weeks ago, Seth had almost caved in and told him he'd be back at the start of the New Year. But then The Event happened, along with everything else that surrounded it, including his eerie experience with time traveling.

Seth drove down Main Street and rolled down his window to wave at Story as he passed her. She waved back, and looking at her smile in the rearview mirror sent shivers down the back of his neck. Before turning down 6th Street to go to the station, he passed by Noble and his friends heading back to school. He gave his horn a quick tap and extended his arm out, waving at the group of kids he had to consider his friends now. A slew of hands went into the air, waving at him, and Seth had the feeling maybe the New Year was just a bit too soon.

Epilogue

The chill of November had settled, and the relentless rain had passed, giving Lost Grove a merciful reprieve from the somber transgressions of October. The soft blue moonlight passed through the leafless trees, speckling Mary's cheeks. Sparse stratocumulus clouds drifted across the aqua sky like wagons crossing an expansive river. Mary didn't notice the ferocity of the cold that most felt this time of year—her body was impervious to the discomfort from the altered blood that ran in her veins.

The woods around her were quiet in the pre-dawn stillness. The only sound came from the night creatures foraging in the undergrowth. A nearby owl let out a soft hoot. Story told her this time was known as the witching hour—that time between midnight and sunrise, when supernatural beings, like ghosts, witches, and demons were thought to be at their strongest. And it was Mary who would prove strongest this morning. She peered through the trees, feeling as if something ancient was watching her.

At a young age, Mary had been transformed in ways she could never have predicted, and as she worked her way back to accepting the supernatural parts of herself, Story listened with a kindness that made the path easier. Her friend—the town librarian and an unspoken witch—neither role diminished the other. For all that kindness and help, Mary owed Story a great deal, though she'd never ask for something in return.

As Mary cocked her head to the subtle sound of footfalls, she wondered if Story—a creature of the shadows—had an affection for this time when the veil between us and the monsters was thin. Mary was one of those creatures of the night. She knew she shouldn't think of herself in this manner, but she was. For what she craved, and what she was about to do, she knew the proper word for her affliction. Monster.

Mary felt the gentle crackling of dead leaves underfoot as she crept through the woods. She ducked behind the dwarf redwood tree and held her breath, her senses on high alert. The stillness was almost unnerving, yet Mary knew exactly where he was—she could feel it in her bones. His heightened presence seemed to fill the gaps between all things, body and soul, and with this newfound clarity, Mary could anticipate his every step. It was peculiar how easy it was to track when listening for nothing.

As she approached him, a warm wave of static electrified the air around her, and then his scent, an untraceable amalgamation of things, awoke Mary's blood. She felt every muscle in her body tingle with anticipation as he shifted closer to her.

"They'll never find him," Story had said that one afternoon in Mary's living room. It had been a welcome visit after all the turmoil happening at the Orbriallis and the return of the stolen child, George Horne.

"You don't think they will?" Mary had responded. For all else the government had taken out of the Orbriallis in a single fell swoop, they'd left one thing behind.

Story had looked at her, wrinkled her nose, and shrugged before taking a sip of the claret wine they shared.

"He should be locked away for what he did. Taking children. Taking Zoe." Story had trailed off, not wanting to speak on it. She told her how they'd found Zoe, how she had been in a state of undress, the hours with no memory. It all injected Mary with a simmering rage, waiting to be unleashed.

"And what does Seth tell you?" Mary asked.

"That there's no way to launch an official manhunt because there is no proof of his crimes, no proof that he was even—ugh. If I found him, I'd hex him myself," Story raged before taking another, longer swig of the wine.

Mary had gasped. "You wouldn't!"

"I would! A proper hex on him. I can't see the universe throwing that back on me when he's done such wrongs."

Story's voice grew quiet, and Mary's heart ached. And that had been the last of it. Story had said no more, and Mary knew better than to press her—this was still too painful a tale for all involved, especially the child taken away from her family and home.

And poor Noble. Mary dared to call him a friend. When, on occasion, they saw each other on early morning runs, Noble would break into a wide grin and fall into stride with her, matching pace. Adrenaline and competition fueled them as the bitter wind beat against their faces, pushing them further than they thought was possible. His dark hair flying behind him, Noble would look over to Mary with an expression of equal parts joy and fear as his feet pounded against the ground. The two of them would race, laughing as they pushed themselves until their chests heaved and their legs felt weak.

She knew he suffered a great deal of pain. Namely regret and remorse that he'd been unable to keep his beloved sister safe. Mary should have had an older brother like Noble, someone who could protect her and shield her from the world's hardships, affliction or not. But it was too late for that now. The closest she had was Seth, her former classmate and the town sergeant, whose genuine kindness warmed her in the coldest of mornings.

Mary tilted her head at the sound of an opossum snuffling in the distance. Her greater acceptance of who, rather what, she was afforded her the ability to ascertain any animal in earshot with her eyes closed. Mary's eyes snapped open. She felt him, her prey, take notice of the opossum as well. He was alone. Mary wondered where the not-children were, but their absence would not be missed today.

Swift and silent as an owl, Mary sprinted across the wooded terrain, footfalls dampened by long pine needles and the fleeting swiftness of her toes barely touching the ground. She felt him tense and pause. Mary had prepared for this. She came dangerously close to him without him noticing, and even closer, drawing his perception, but he was too slow to catch what was hunting him.

She found delight in the merry game of stalking a victim and knew she could never erase that thrill. This would change her forever. But for the people she cared for, it was a sacrifice she was willing to undertake.

The Green Man paused, stopped dead as a small deer sensing the predatory eyes of a wolf. Mary stepped around the edge of a cedar tree. Her body was lithe and strong. Every movement felt like breathing. There was no tension in her preparation to leap or jump. She was languid, soft, and threatening.

The pain of her bicuspids piercing through her recently healed gums felt like the most intense pleasure she had encountered in her life. She welcomed the ghostly taste of warm iron as the change in her mouth released blood, seeping under her tongue, swirling with her saliva.

Mary could see the whites of his eyes as they grew in fear. He could sense her, but Raymond LaRange couldn't gain an inch on his target. She knew he was trying, using his—what Dr. Owens had called special abilities—to suss her out and eliminate the threat. But she was like him. A monster. A demon. A supernatural being out for a walk during the witching hour. The only difference was, she was in complete control.

Mary swallowed. The audible gulp sounded like a cannon going off in her eardrum. The Green Man turned, half jumping, and fell over his own feet, a feeling he had not encountered in years. He was meant to be fleet of foot and silent as a leopard approaching his prey.

Mary snatched out a hand and, in movements she couldn't explain and had no way of recalling afterward, captured her victim and felt her mouth swell with his warm blood. She dug her teeth into the vein pulsing wildly in his neck. The relief, the blissful release, the ecstasy. As the Green Man's heart slowed and then ceased to beat, Mary felt satiation unlike any she'd known existed.

"For you, Story."

LOST GROVE

Acknowledgments

Once again, we need to thank the town of Ferndale, CA, for inspiring Charlotte's mind to conjure this wild story and its setting. We want to thank our launch team for being our early readers and staunch supporters. We dedicated our last book to our immediate family, but fuck it, thank you again, fam! And thank you to our copy editor, Lisa Gilliam, and our proofreader, Heather Preis.

I (Alex) would like to thank Joel Pike for encouraging him to read at an early age. Every birthday and Christmas, I received books. I may have wanted a Transformer (the real metal ones) or a new Atari 2600 game (boy, do both of these age me), but I got books. And I eventually read them. And most importantly, I enjoyed them.

I (Charlotte) would like to thank my mom for always dragging me out of my comfort zone, booking flights and explorations, and arranging adventures near and far. I feel grateful for all the acumen acquired from museums, the knowledge travel bestowed on me, and the memories made meeting people from all walks of life.

In our acknowledgments for Part One, we thanked some of our favorite literary influences. Super logical, right? It's a book, after all. For Part Two, we would like to take a detour to the world of film. When we first met, one of the main things we bonded over was our love of movies. We came up with this fun pastime called our 'Chalkboard Movies'. Charlotte painted our first shitty refrigerator with black chalkboard paint, and on the side we each wrote 10 movies the other person hadn't seen before. We've gone through over a dozen lists throughout the years.

We also share an unbridled passion for horror movies. We keep a detailed log of all the new horror films we see each calendar year (it's a lot), and at the end of each year we host our Horror Movie Oscars. And by "host", that means we host ourselves, have good food, and good cocktails. Anyone who would like to join next year, just let us know.

To the following filmmakers and actors who have inspired us with their visuals and vocals that help us paint our worlds and characters: Pascal Laugier, Ozgood Perkins, Ti West, Maika Monroe, Daniel Kaluuya, Stanley Kubrick, Daniel Myrick & Eduardo Sánchez, Alexandre Bustillo & Julien Maury, Alysson Paradis, Béatrice Dalle, Christian Tafdrup, John Carpenter, Kurt Russell, Alfred Hitchcock, Sam Raimi, Bruce Campbell, Wes Craven, Brad Anderson, Charles Laughton, Mia Goth, Robert Mitchum, Xavier Gens, Simon Rumley, Noah Taylor, Jordan Peele, Amanda Fuller, Stuart Gordon, Jeffrey Combs, Barbara Crampton, Adam Wingard, Sharni Vinson, Sigourney Weaver, Ridley Scott, Marcin Wrona, Marina de Van, Julia Ducournau, Christian Bale, Roman Polanski (deal with it), Frank Darabont and sweet, sweet Thomas Jane for one of the most gut-wrenching and horrific endings to a horror movie ever.

Lastly, we'd like to thank a potpourri of random people who make us laugh, smile, and cheer with delight, helping to bring positivity into our lives: Gino Vannelli, Anthony Edwards, Seth Rollins, Florence Welch, Bobby Flay, Mike Patton, Simon Miller, Michael Bolton, Chris Van Vliet, Tim Legler and Adam Mares, Rhea Ripley, Andrea Subissati, Bee Gees, Zach Lowe, Guy Fieri, and obviously Nicholas Cage.

About the Authors

Charlotte Zang

From the moment her mother started reading her bedtime stories, Charlotte has cherished literature. The first stories introduced to her were fairy tails and folklore, and these weren't the kind you'd find the princess living happily ever after. Thanks to one oddly placed door in a friend's basement, her first novel, Satan's In Your Kitchen, sprang to life in all its glorious comedy. She also wrote a fairy tale of her own, a dark retelling known as Consuming Beauty. Blooding is her third novel.

She is an author of fantasy, horror and magic, master of her garden, queen of delicious recipes and mother of basset hounds. She lives in the Pacific northwest with her three hounds and adoring husband.

You can follow her on Intagram @charlottezang and visit her website www.charlottezang.com.

Alex J. Knudsen

ALEX J. KNUDSEN was born in Minneapolis, Minnesota, and attended the University of Southern California. He first started writing in the third grade when he created the short story, Mr. Raquetball. He went on to write numerous unpublished short stories and a bevy of screenplays. Knudsen is the founder of Gantry Productions and is the writer-director of numerous films, including the Independent award nominated feature film, Autopilot and the award nominated short horror film, Consuming Beauty, which was adapted from his wife's novel of the same name. Knudsen is a self-taught mixologist and devourer of horror films. Alex currently lives in Oregon with his wife and three Basset Hounds. The Nawie is his first novel.

You can follow him on Instagram @knutzauthor and visit his website www.alexjknudsen.com.